REALM AND REIGN

REALM AND REIGN

STRANGER MAGICS,
BOOK FIFTEEN

ASH FITZSIMMONS

REALM AND REIGN. Copyright © 2022 by Ash Fitzsimmons.

Print Edition ISBN: 978-1-949861-38-9

Cover design by BespokeBookCovers.com

www.ashfitzsimmons.com

CHAPTER 1

.

The warm July morning, with its clear blue sky and soft breeze, might have been perfect were I not about ninety percent sure I'd just swallowed a mosquito.

Our state bird's annual reappearance was nature's cruel joke: during the hottest months of the year, the time at which we most wanted to be hanging around in the open air, we didn't step outside the compound without a generous spritzing of deep-woods bug spray. Even with that precaution, all of us kids had been chased home at one point or another by an aggressive swarm of the whiny little bloodsuckers. In the summer pictures of us taken when we were elementary age, we often looked like we'd been struck by a pox, spotted as we were with itchy red welts on our bare arms and legs. My favorite such photo came from when we were five—well, most of us, Gaw then still being only four and Aurie, our eternal babysitter, almost nine. We'd scrunched up on the boulder by our lake: Edie and me in the polyester princess dresses we'd worn everywhere that season, by then stained with the leavings of our outdoor excursions, our hair worn in matching tangles differentiated only by hue; Kenna with her pink plastic-framed glasses and braided brown pigtails, grinning from ear to ear despite the fresh scabs on her knees; blond Gaw in a T-shirt and shorts, nervously eyeing the water and clutching Aurie's hand; Aurie, kneeling beside him with her blue hair swept over one shoulder, the cool grownup; and Dec, identifiable only by process of elimination, as he'd insisted on dressing in full Batman costume that day, complete with stuffed pecs and a cowl.

The boulder had become our hangout over the years, but Gaw and I had sneaked off early enough in the day to snag a private moment by the lake. I'd been up for hours—as far north as we lived in Alaska, the sun barely set at midsummer, which left me wired through the bright months and sluggish all winter—but we'd packed snacks and made a second breakfast of it.

Gaw laughed as I grimaced and spat to the side. "Bonus protein?"

"*Yech*. One fewer mosquito, I guess." I took a sip of water to clear whatever bug bits might have lingered, then returned to my bagel and glanced out over the water. The lake, blue-green in the morning sun, was barely ruffled by the wind. It would be busy later, I reasoned, on a day as nice as that Monday was forecast to be, but for the moment, the canoes were still in their rack, the pebbly shore was empty, and Gaw and I had the place to ourselves but for the birds in the ringing pines.

"You know," I said with all the limited subtlety I could muster, "this would be the perfect spot for a proposal, don't you think? The lake, the mountain view, maybe with the aurora out…"

He chewed thoughtfully as I let that idea hang. "Well, you'd have to wait until winter for the aurora," he mused, "and by then, it's damn cold out here."

"But you could snuggle for warmth," I pointed out. "Far more romantic than swatting mosquitoes."

"True."

We grinned at each other and slid closer, and I sighed as I rested my head on his shoulder. "Love you, Gaw."

He leaned his head against mine, his proximity carrying with it the mingled scents of soap and insect repellant. "Love you, too, Cici."

"Want to run away with me?" I murmured, only half in jest.

"Not a bad plan. Little skimpy on details, though. Want

to sit here for a while and think about it?"

He knew the answer to that—I would have happily sat on the boulder with Gaw until twilight fell, talking of our grand plans that never seemed to come to fruition. But before I could do more than stretch out my legs on the rock, rapid footsteps crashed over the litter of branches in the woods behind us, and Gaw and I softly groaned in unison.

I turned in time to see Dec emerge from the trees, red-faced and panting, his dark hair stuck to his head with sweat. "Hide me," he begged without preamble.

Gaw and I shared a look. "Mina?" I asked.

"I think I lost her at the tree line, but *damn*, she's relentless," he groused. The lake level was low, exposing a brief stretch of pebbles on the far side of the boulder, and Dec edged around to conceal himself. "You'd think she'd take no for an answer."

"I'm sorry, when has *Mina* ever accepted no?" Gaw retorted, sliding toward Dec to keep his voice down. "What, she's after you for conditioning?"

"Yeah."

"You're gross already. Why not just give in and do a little training, eh?"

Dec slapped at a mosquito on his neck. "Because I'm not in the mood for pain."

I smiled to myself as Dec griped and skulked. Training with Mina had been a part of our lives for almost as long as I could remember, one more block in our homeschooling schedule. Sometimes, my aunt Artur would join in, especially when Mina made us fight with blades and shields. I hadn't seen the point of working toward proficiency in archaic weaponry—not with plenty of guns in the compound—until the day that Mina had been out hunting alone and was caught by a grizzly. Her rifle had jammed, and she hadn't brought a sidearm, but she'd fought it off with her backup sword and carried the pelt home as proof. The hide lived on as her furry bed throw.

While the five of us were in college down in Anchorage, we'd worked out regularly, knowing that Mina would be merciless during our school breaks. Well, all but Dec, who'd enjoyed collegiate life a little *too* much. He'd packed on his freshman twenty, eschewed the track for frat parties, and had a good time when he wasn't cramming for class. Unfortunately for Dec, we'd graduated last spring— even Gaw, who'd started with us a year early—and now, back in the wilderness full time, his sins were catching up with him.

We shouldn't have left Anchorage. We'd had an apartment there, the five of us kids, and we'd managed to keep ourselves fed and reasonably healthy. Classmates from farther afield had remarked that Anchorage was only a modest city, but it was the most bustling place I'd ever lived. Heck, it had paved roads, a major step up from home. Museums, theaters, restaurants—an embarrassment of the riches of civilization compared to the compound where I'd grown up. Sure, we'd made occasional trips to Fairbanks when I was a kid, which wasn't terribly far by plane, but those had always been quick jaunts, just long enough to run errands, stow food in the cargo hold, and head back. Our parents had pushed for us to consider the University of Alaska's Fairbanks campus, but we'd held out for Anchorage, going as far from home as our families would allow. But now, equipped with a degree apiece, we'd been recalled.

Recognizing that we were, technically, adults, our families were trying not to be smothering. They'd set us up in a house with Aurie, a bachelor pad for the compound's youngest residents, but boredom gave rise to thoughts of escape. Maybe we'd catch a ride to Fairbanks one day and just refuse to get back on the plane. We'd strike out for Canada or head south, see the world while our faces could still match our IDs. Edie would have no problem in that respect, but of the rest of us, Gaw, Kenna, and I had been cursed with the fae allergy to iron and silver, meaning that we were almost guaranteed to stop aging in a few years' time. Dec had been luckier on that front, but he also never seemed to get sick—a good sign that he, too, was sufficiently fae to avoid aging, though no one could be certain. His father was half-blooded, but his mother, my grandaunt, was a witch-blood. No one could say *what* Dec was, and without magic around, there was no way to test what sort of talent he might have inherited—or, more importantly, what sort of longevity. And then there was Aurie, whose newest fake ID made her almost twenty-six. Mostly of draconic extraction, with a splash of fae and mundane human genes thrown in for variety, Aurie was naturally blue-haired and had been fully grown at five, when the rest of us were all under two. The closest thing she'd had to a friend in the compound had been Allie Copeland, fourteen years her senior, but Allie had fallen hard for another young wizard and moved with him to Juneau to run a bed and breakfast. That left only the five of us little ones to entertain Aurie, and now that we were of age, our parents had striven to keep us from making our own escape.

Hell, we couldn't even escape training with Mina.

"You're just making the inevitable worse," said Gaw as Dec tried to shrink behind the boulder. "The longer you hide, the harder on you she's going to be."

Dec glared up at him but didn't deny it.

"What if we go back together?" Gaw offered. "I'll be your buffer this once. If she's going to make you spar, better to fight me than a master, right? And, uh, right cheek."

He slapped his face, killing the mosquito mid-meal. "Thanks," Dec muttered, and slunk back around to the woods side. "If she asks, I've been with you all morning."

"Of course." Rolling his eyes at me, Gaw slid off the boulder and landed in the gravel. "Rain check?" he asked as I started packing the breakfast leavings away.

"I'll hold you to it. Go kick his ass," I said, and shooed

them on their way.

Dec's jaw dropped with feigned hurt. "I'm your *cousin*!"

"Yeah, and Gaw's my boyfriend," I countered, grinning as he tugged Dec along. "Have fun, guys!"

"I hope you get eaten by mosquitoes!" Dec called back.

"At least I was smart enough to put on spray!"

With the food back in my bag, I made myself comfortable and watched a hawk circle over the lake. The sudden soft clearing of a throat caught my attention, and I looked to my left to find my brother standing at the water's edge. "Room for two?" he asked.

I nodded and motioned him up. He didn't climb— Publius seldom bothered to make the effort. Instead, he simply appeared at my side an instant later and took a seat, pulling his tunic over his knees as he stretched his bare legs toward the lake.

So, I asked, *do you think he got the message?*

He smirked. "If he didn't, he's an idiot."

Be nice, Publi, I warned.

"Or what?"

He had a point. The breeze that was doing its best to tangle my hair didn't affect his, and no matter how much I sometimes longed to give him a sharp elbow in the ribs, that was out of the cards. The only revenge I could take against my brother was to ignore him, and that seldom lasted long. I settled for sticking my tongue out at him and turning my attention back to the pleasant morning.

"Oh, very mature, Cecilia."

There were, I reflected as he chuckled, certain downsides to being a medium.

In a town comprised largely of refugee faeries and former wizards, I was born a certified freak of nature.

For months, my mom, Kitty, and her little sister, Beth, were locked in a joke of a race to see who would deliver first. Dr. Bee, who did everything around the compound from treat burns and scrapes to set bones and deliver babies, put her money on Beth. My aunt was the younger of the two by almost a decade, only nineteen, and seemed to have gotten pregnant slightly earlier than Mom did. But the two of them had gone into labor within hours of each other, and Dr. Bee set them up in rooms on the opposite sides of her home, which did double duty as an infirmary on the ground floor. As the hours ticked by on that cold March day, she did what she could for her patients, but there was little she could offer to dull their pain or speed their labor along. Dr. Bee knew *how* to administer medication, but getting her hands on powerful drugs was another matter, especially without American licensure. She certainly couldn't offer anyone an epidural.

Instead, as Mom and Beth tried to distract themselves with movies and ice chips, the doctor took the fathers-to-be into her office and gave them the same speech she'd given Dec's dad five months before: this was the twenty-first century, their patients had made it clear that they wanted their husbands in the delivery room, so that was bloody well where they were going to be. There would be no fainting, no weird faces, and no attempts made to find an emergency elsewhere. "You got them into this," she told Pa and Ed, "and you're going to hold their hands, mop their brows, and do whatever else they ask of you. And if you comment about *anything* that comes out of my end of the bed that's not a newborn, I *will* punch you, and I know how to make it hurt. Remember that."

I wasn't privy to that warning speech, of course, but I'd heard about it repeatedly over the years. The end result was that my poor mother had to deal with both her contractions and my nervous father, who stayed close to her head and kept glancing at her swollen belly as if it were liable to explode at any moment. I could cut him a little slack. Pa was Roman—*old* Roman, pre-empire Roman, and a city boy at that—and he'd been nowhere near his first wife when his son was born. Mom demanded full paternal participation in the blessed event, however, and though she'd shown him books and diagrams explaining what was about to happen, Pa was far out of his depth.

Ed was no better. Younger than Pa but still a product of the tenth century, he'd never planned to participate in a birth. In a previous lifetime, he'd been a father of twelve, but he'd never witnessed the moment itself. Nothing in his experience quite prepared him for my aunt, who apparently grabbed him by the shirt after a bad contraction, yanked him close to her, and threatened bodily harm should he bolt.

All through the day and into the evening, Dr. Bee checked on the patients' progress while her wife and quasi-nurse, Daisy, did her best to make everyone comfortable. Finally, a few minutes before midnight, Mom won the race. I emerged into Dr. Bee's waiting hands with all my major bits accounted for, a green-eyed baby with a fuzz of brown hair—and weirdly enough, en caul, delivered veiled within my amniotic sac.

My father would later say that I was destined for good fortune. In the moment, however, he'd watched dumbfounded as Dr. Bee freed me, wiped me off, and handed me to my mother, who'd cried with joy and relief. And then, as Mom's delivery continued, she'd smiled at Pa through her tears and asked if he wanted to hold me.

According to Mom, he'd cried harder than she had.

Once Mom's ordeal was over and I'd been cleaned, inspected, weighed, and printed—and a pair of steel scissors held near my leg to see whether I'd react with distress—my parents invited my grandfather in. He'd beamed and congratulated them, then joked that they still needed to figure out what I would call my father, as Mom had ruled that the Latin equivalent of *daddy*—unfortunately, *tata*—was off the table. My grandfather, at least, could be Avus to me without causing a scandal. Taking his turn holding me, he asked if they'd decided on my name.

They had: Cecilia Maria, a modern twist on my long-dead grandmother's name and a nod to my mom's best friend, whom Avus had raised.

And at that point, per Mom, he'd cried, too.

As the clock ticked over to the new day, the rest of the family slipped in: Maria, the deeply distant grandniece I'd always consider an aunt; Artur, my actual aunt, who wasn't at all comfortable with the notion of holding me but deemed me a fine specimen from a safe distance; and finally, my parents' old boss, Ted Girard, the honorary uncle to all of his colleagues' children. Ed was even released from his bedside duties long enough to get a report and send Beth's congratulations. Shortly after one in the morning, the party in Mom's room heard the cries of a second newborn from across the house: another girl, named Edith because her parents could agree on it and Hilda for her father's mother. Edie was declared healthy as well, a chubby baby with her mother's brown eyes and, as soon became apparent, her father's weird hair—dark but for a white forelock. Born as close as we were, barely on opposite sides of the date divide, Edie and I were soon dubbed "the twins," cousins who would grow up more like sisters. But that was still to come, after the chaos of our early days.

Beth and Ed adapted well to the sudden presence of a squalling newborn in their lives, and Ed, perhaps fearing for his safety if he didn't pitch in, took on the brunt of the duties while Beth recovered. At least no one needed to cook; Luce Stowe, who'd once been a professional chef, was happy to deliver for a couple weeks while the new parents came to terms with their upended schedules. Edie was healthy, Beth healed well, and soon, the three of them found a rhythm.

Like Ed, my father took over at first, letting my mother rest. Faeries need less sleep as they age, and while Pa had missed most of his two millennia in stasis, he'd still reaped the benefits. He could go a few days before crashing, and so the early nights usually found him sitting up with the TV and me, giving Mom space to recuperate. In his waking hours, Pa seemed like the perfect new father, a little overwhelmed but thrilled to have me.

But he had to sleep eventually. When Mom took over and Pa crashed, his sleep was punctuated by screaming nightmares, and nothing she could do made them subside. If she woke him to offer reassurance, he'd no sooner fall asleep again than he'd return to his personal hell. And so, after a few rounds of torture, he silently resolved to just stay awake, which his sleep-deprived mind must have perceived as a great solution to the problem.

Anyone who knew Pa knew what was haunting him. Ten days after the birth of his first child in 154 BC, his wife and cousin had turned him over to a gang of wizards. Pa had never hurt anyone—his talents had tended toward the healing end of the spectrum, back when magic still existed—but they'd put him to sleep and locked him away all the same, burying him alive for millennia. When Maria and Mom broke the spell on him, they'd been forced to explain that the infant son who'd quickly become the most important person in his life was long gone.

Even in a world devoid of magic, Pa's subconscious feared a repeat. He didn't sleep at all on my tenth night, nor in the three days following, even after his father offered to sit up and guard the both of us. After a week, with Pa nearing the edge of a breakdown, Dr. Bee came to the house, kit in hand, and threatened him with a sedative if he didn't go to bed. The nightmares subsided eventually, and Pa was able to sleep again by the time I was a month old, but they didn't fully stop for nearly a year.

My parents never told me any of that, nor did I bring it up. It wounded Pa's pride that his irrational fear could mess him up so badly, and I saw no need to let him know that I was aware of those sleepless nights.

All the same, my brother had filled me in. And as Publius had a big mouth and nothing but time on his hands, having died in 68 BC, I knew *plenty* of things that my parents never discussed with me.

I don't remember a time without my brother and his frequent, unpredictable visits. For most of my childhood, he seemed about a decade my senior, authoritative but still relatable. Once I was old enough to understand my own gift, he didn't hide the truth from me: he'd died in his eighties. But he could appear at any age he liked, he explained, and since Pa and Avus both seemed to be about twenty-five, he decided not to complicate matters by hanging around as an old man once he realized I could see him.

Though he'd had a large family of his own, Publius had lacked a sibling, and curiosity brought him to me, his infant half sister growing up in the middle of nowhere centuries after his time. He stopped in sporadically at first, as did our grandmother—Caecilia, but Avia to us—who even in death fretted about her family's safety in the wilderness. But when I was four months old, he leaned over my crib and instinctively made a face at me—*and I laughed*.

There are many superstitions surrounding babies born with a veil. In my case, at least, the one about having the ability to see spirits panned out.

For my brother, this changed everything. I wasn't just his baby sister—I was a baby *medium*, and I'd soon become a magnet for the dead. He couldn't prevent me from crawling toward sharp objects or bumping my head into the furniture, but he decided to do the fraternal thing and guard me against those spirits who wouldn't respect my youth or my boundaries.

But while my brother and Avia—and Granddad, my mother's adopted father, who also made frequent visits—realized pretty quickly that I was a rarity, my parents didn't catch on until I was two.

A heavy storm had rolled through one summer night, waking me when thunder rattled the windows and the wind screamed in the eaves. Terrified, I'd huddled beneath my blankets, too scared to cry or to run for help, when Publius had appeared by the door and hurried to my bed. "You're safe, Cici," he'd soothed—or so he told me later, as I have little memory of that age. "It's only noise and light. Just the rain. Go back to sleep."

I don't know if the sensations are identical for all mediums, but as for me, I've never had a problem understanding spirits. Whatever they say seems to translate itself. Unfortunately, the process only goes one way—I have to think my responses in order to be understood if I can't speak the spirit's language. As a little kid, I had yet to grasp that, but my brother had picked up enough of my burgeoning vocabulary to know what I meant when I told him I was scared.

"Would a story help?" he'd asked.

I'd been willing to be distracted, and so I'd sat up in my twin bed, back to the wall and stuffed unicorn clutched to my chest, while he took a seat on the open end past the protective bed rails and started the story. Unlike my parents, Publius never used my collection of picture books—he couldn't turn the pages—but he could rattle off an impressive selection of tales to make me laugh or calm me down, and he was *very* good at doing all the voices.

And that was how Pa had found me: sitting up in bed in the nightlight's glow, giggling at nothing, while lightning flashed around us.

"Cici?" he'd asked, peering in at me. "What's going on?"

But Publius had nearly reached the denouement by then, and I'd turned to the door, scowling. "Quiet! Story!"

Unsurprisingly, this reaction had concerned my father, and the storm outside had surely done nothing to minimize the general horror-movie vibe. "What story?"

he'd asked.

At that point, in my toddler frustration, I'd simply jabbed my unicorn toward my brother and announced, "Publi talk. *Shh*."

Pa told me later that the hair on the back of his neck had stood up, and he'd hastily scooped me out of bed, ignoring my protests that I wanted to hear the end of the story. He'd carried me downstairs, where he and Mom had been watching TV, and told her, "Either Cici has an excellent imagination or my son is in her bedroom, and there is nothing in the parenting guides about this possibility."

As he and Mom had talked over each other, Publius had appeared behind the couch and folded his arms. "Do you want to play a game, Cici?" he'd asked.

I'd nodded.

"Good. I'm going to say some things. You repeat them back to me just like I said them. Can you do that?"

"Uh-huh."

My parents, spooked though they were, had fallen silent when I began parroting my brother—or rather, offering my lisping interpretation of what I'd heard from him. "She is like Hope," I'd said slowly. "Not as strong. Scared of the storm. We keep her safe."

Pa had tightened his grip on me and followed the line of my sight to the place behind the couch, an empty spot to his eyes. "Publi?" he'd murmured.

I'd listened and repeated again. "Yes. And Avia and Orson. But only me tonight."

According to my brother, I'd soon tired of the game, snuggled down between my parents, and fallen asleep. With his mouthpiece out of commission, Publius had taken his leave soon thereafter—where he went, he was never at liberty to tell me—but not before Pa had whispered his thanks.

As I grew up, I slowly came to understand my awkward familial situation and why I could have long talks with people no one around me could sense. My parents fretted, though really, I couldn't blame them. It had to be weird for them to peek in and find me having an animated tea party with thin air, or later, once I understood the nuances of communication, to catch me staring off into space, my face twitching in response to a conversation only I could hear. They encouraged me to go outside, to play with Edie and Kenna and the boys, sometimes dragging me out of my room when all I wanted was to talk to my brother in peace.

"Be patient with them," Avia told me. "This is far beyond their experience, and they're wise to worry about you."

Avia was right that they were somewhat clueless. The most interaction anyone in their orbit had had with a medium was the few times they'd crossed paths with Hope Lozano. I wished I could have asked her for pointers, but that was impossible. Hope had lived in Conota, the so-called Gray Lands, and that realm had been destroyed along with Faerie. I'd been told that her people were born with the sight, but more impressive than that, they'd been able to empower spirits, making them briefly visible and audible again to those unable to perceive them. Hope had been a legend in that respect, a young woman who could raise an army of the dead. But no matter how much I tried, I could never manage that trick, and Avia chided me every time she caught me making an attempt. "You're not cynaeli," she often reminded me in those moments. "Don't hurt yourself, dear girl."

I wished I could figure it out. I'd caught some of Pa's wistful looks when he found me with Publius or his mother, and I'd have loved to give him a chance to talk to them. But with that option out of the cards, I did the next-best thing and passed the occasional message. Over time, my family made its peace with the reality that I was seldom alone and might offer a word from an unseen watcher at any moment—brief greetings, Avia's hint to Pa that he'd over-salted the vegetables, Granddad's warning in the middle of our family trip to Denali that our tires were low and one of the brake lights was out.

Mediums are rare, and I was a gifted little girl. Maybe I wasn't as talented as Hope had been, but my eyes and ears were open to visitors from beyond the veil, and I had no way to close myself off. Publius and my grandparents stayed near me in my most defenseless years as a barrier, keeping other curious spirits at bay while I went about my childhood in innocent ignorance. As I grew older and more secure in my talent, they gradually allowed others to approach me—and there was plenty, even in the middle of nowhere. Indigenous Alaskans, weathered trappers, explorers lost to the elements, even the occasional hiker of more recent vintage—they came to me from across the state, then from Canada and points farther south. I wasn't as attractive as Hope was, to Avia's relief, but I had my fair share of spirits stop in. Some were merely curious. Others wanted information or asked that an anonymous message be sent to a loved one. Anyone too pushy received a swift dismissal from my grandmother, who was anything but shy. I was her namesake, after all, and she looked after me.

But my most frequent visitor was Publius, my playmate, tutor, and protector. He seldom seemed bothered by my antics, he encouraged me when my parents' efforts to raise me trilingual left my head spinning, and on at least three occasions that I could recall, he checked under my bed for the monster I was *certain* was lurking, ready to eat me once the lights went out. That he had died some twenty-one centuries before I was born never really fazed me—he was my big brother, he knew how to pick at me without leaving me in tears, and I loved him fiercely.

Still, there was no one who gave me quite so much grief over Gaw as my brother did.

"You know," said Publius as a fishing duck flipped tail-up in the lake, "there's no need to rush things. It's not as if you and Gawain are running out of time."

I glanced at him and saw that he was being serious. *There's no guarantee.*

"You both have the allergies. Why wouldn't the two of you be immortal?"

There's that part about how no one has ever studied fae genetics, I countered, shrugging. *Pa's just an augmented quarter, Mom's an augmented <u>witch-blood</u>, and who really knows how that combination interacts? And Gaw—sheesh. Sam's half, but there's no telling what Ros is. His parents said they won't make any predictions about Gaw until he's forty.*

"Un-ageing and allergic," he replied, "so I would think decently fae. Gaw should be in no danger." Leaning back on his elbows, he contemplated the woods ringing the lake. "You're young yet. Take your time."

You say that, but I love him, and I'm pretty sure he feels the same way. Why not encourage him to make it official with me?

"Because none of your parents are eager for you to pursue marriage quite yet. You should listen to them."

I laughed aloud. *Right, like you're one to talk. How old was Cornelia, sixteen?*

"That was different!" he protested.

How many kids did you two have by the time she was my age, huh?

"Three," he reluctantly allowed, "but Cici—"

But what? Gaw and I are adults.

"Just listen to your elders. Please?"

I rolled my eyes and watched as a pair of ducks joined the lone fisher. Sure, the lake was beautiful on summer mornings, peaceful in its quiet tranquility, but more and more of late, the compound felt like a prison.

We should never have agreed to move home. Our families had more than enough money to support the five of us until we could find work in Anchorage or farther afield, and we should have insisted on keeping the apartment. But no, our parents had cajoled us for months, wearing down our resolve like a glacier over stone. Even Ennis, the lone mundane living among us, had nagged Kenna to come back.

Part of me understood. Unless my family and the rest of the compound had shared some grand hallucination, there had once been a place called Faerie, separate from our world but accessible if one knew the way. Magic—real magic, not the stuff with the top hats and white rabbits—had flowed from that realm across the border, giving faeries like my parents the power to enchant and wizards like Edie's the power to cast spells. The difference between the two seemed hazy to me—and without a source of magic any longer, it was all academic, really—but what I'd been taught was that enchantment was a wilder, more explosive sort of ability, while spellcraft called for precision and finesse. But none of that mattered now. Magic was gone, Faerie was dead, and many of its refugees had banded together with a handful of former wizards in the backwoods of Alaska to make lives for themselves. Dec, Edie, Gaw, and I were the only kids born in the compound in its quarter-century of existence, and Kenna had lived there long enough to count as native. We were the next generation, our families' stab at a legacy. Still, though I could rationally comprehend why our parents were clingy—traumatically losing family, friends, and a home could do that to a person—I didn't have to *like* the smothering.

Our families had tried so hard to instill in us an appreciation for our vanished heritage. They'd added to our school curriculum lessons about Faerie's history and politics, about the rise and collapse of the wizards' Arcanum, about the rudiments of the manipulation of magic. While I didn't mind learning to speak Fae—it made snide commentary all the easier when going to parties with my crew in college—I never saw the point in studying spellcraft or enchantment. Magic had been destroyed, it wasn't coming back, and all we had was the mortal realm. Why shouldn't we make the best of it?

It had been our parents' decision to hide in the frozen north. Now, while the five of us could still pass for our real ages, we and Aurie wanted to travel—to backpack across Europe, drive Route 66, maybe sail the South Pacific like Aurie's grandfather and great-grandfather had once done. But our suggestions had been uniformly shot down as too dangerous, an unnecessary risk. Graduate school had likewise been discouraged. As for my hints to my parents that Gaw was the one for me, all they would say was that I was too young for marriage.

Frankly, it was stifling.

I wanted out. I wanted control over my life, I wanted to be with Gaw, and I wanted to see the world. I was a grown woman with a bachelor's degree and a decent ability to tell pushy spirits to butt out, and I yearned to *fledge*.

Footsteps in the woods behind me pulled me from my moody reverie, and I turned to see Kenna approaching. She'd pulled her brown hair back into a high ponytail, and the lenses of her turquoise-framed glasses flashed sunlight in my face. "Hey," she called up to me. "Where's Gaw? I thought you were having couple time."

"We were until Dec showed up," I replied, and slid off the boulder. "They've gone to face Mina."

"Poor bastards." She planted her fists on her hips and heaved a dramatic sigh. "Edie's being boring again."

No surprise there—prying my cousin away from her books took skill, patience, and a fair bit of luck. Edie researched for *fun*. "So you came out here to interrupt Gaw and me?"

"I don't see Gaw, so I guess I'm not interrupting."

"I *was* talking to my brother, you know."

"Uh-huh. Salve, Publi," she said, and waved in the wrong direction as he chuckled from atop the boulder. "Come on, I'm *bored*. Let's do something."

I started to tell Kenna that this wasn't my problem, but

then I noticed the ducks on the lake again.

"Are you thinking what I think you're thinking?" Publius asked.

Maybe.

"Want to see something neat?" I asked Kenna, and started toward the edge of the water. "I think I found a nest."

"What sort of nest?" she asked.

"Dunno. Come see."

Not until she reached the shore and caught my evil grin did Kenna realize the error of her ways. "Shit!" she yelped. "Watch my glasses—"

I grabbed her around the waist, threw my weight into her, and wrestled her into the lake as we shrieked at the cold water. Kenna struggled, but soon we were both soaked, and she swore vengeance as I laughed. "That's so mean!" she protested.

"You said you wanted to do something."

"Not like this," she muttered, then cupped her hands in the lake and heaved water at my face. The ducks flew off in alarm, I splashed Kenna in turn, and within minutes, she was laughing with me, our voices ringing across the spreading ripples as they had so many times before.

CHAPTER 2

Once upon a time, for this is how such stories usually begin, there was a little prince who grew up with the world at his feet.

Technically, he wasn't a prince in the usual sense. His family had no titles, no crowns, no thrones. But they *did* have land—several hundred fertile acres in the Sonoma wine country, to be exact. When Eric Hayward married Jessica Frost, the newlyweds united their families' substantial holdings, slowly bought out less productive neighbors, and built Hayward Wines into a top competitor in the crowded market—the sort of bottles that one might find at the grocery store but bring to a party without embarrassment. What wasn't to like about them? Hayward's blends tended to be inoffensive, won their share of awards, and remained reasonably priced. Moreover, Eric and Jessica were a picture-perfect couple, him with dark hair and a rugged "Old West" charm, her with a loose blonde braid, a winning smile, and twin dimples in her freckled cheeks. The Haywards featured in much of their advertising, which made their ad team's lives so much simpler.

By the time they reached the status of Sonoman royalty, the Haywards had beautiful children. Daniel, the eldest, was every inch the heir apparent. Blond like his mother and blessed with his father's square jaw and strapping build, Daniel was bright and athletic, a natural in the classroom and on the soccer field. Three years younger was Victoria, their parents' darling princess. But where

Daniel found easy success, Tory struggled. She floundered in her studies, much preferring the company of her girlfriends to boring hours spent with her lessons. Born in Daniel's long shadow, she fought for attention, striving like a sapling beneath a mighty tree to find a place in the sun. Eventually, she discovered an outlet in the theater. With a pretty face and a decent voice, Tory made for an above-average actress. Still, she bristled at criticism, and as she grew older, her general disdain for rules morphed into outright rebellion. Instead of following Daniel to Stanford, Tory struck out for Hollywood.

Last was Ennis, the little prince, the calm after Tory's storm. Dark-haired like his father but softer in his features, Ennis was his parents' sweet baby. Beyond that label, however, he was left to find a path for himself. Daniel was the heir, Tory was the rebel...so what was left for him?

Though the Haywards' children were of different temperaments, their parents loved them all the same. No gift was too expensive, no experience too exotic. As a boy, Ennis learned to ski—downhill, cross-country, and water—and to ride horses, though he could never compete with Daniel's skiing medals or Tory's equestrian skills. Trying a different avenue, when Ennis was old enough, he convinced his parents to pay for flight lessons, and he had earned his private pilot's license and an instrument rating by the time he started college. The elder Haywards promised him that if he finished school with honors, he'd have his own plane at graduation.

The family's generosity didn't end with their children, however. Both Jessica and Eric had come from families that stressed the importance of charitable giving—that of those to whom much has been given, much will be required. Watching his parents make large bequests and more modest donations, Ennis learned the meaning of "noblesse oblige" at a tender age. As the business flourished, their giving became more substantial: a literacy foundation, a state-of-the-art oncology wing at the children's hospital, a lump sum every year when wildfires ravaged the state. They paid their workers well above the industry standard, even setting aside a portion of the annual profits to enrich a scholarship fund for the children of their employees.

"We've been very blessed," Jessica told Ennis at a company holiday party as he watched a hired Santa distribute gifts to all the children present, regardless of whether their parents were managers or vineyard workers. "Your dad and I aren't special or better than other people—your grandparents had money, and we've been lucky. But since we've been so fortunate, we have a responsibility to use what we've been given to make other people's lives a little easier. And so will you."

As he grew up, Ennis took this lesson to heart, and he observed his parents, trying to learn what would be asked of him. At charity galas, they were polite and friendly, generous with their time and their money. Daniel shone at those events—with natural charisma and easy charm, he could work a room almost from the time he was old enough to talk, socially precocious and gifted with a memory for names and faces. Once she grew out of her little-girl frocks, Tory attended only when obligated, and she was just as likely to smile and shake hands as she was to disappear into the bathroom and emerge with a freshly-spiked fauxhawk and spider lashes. As for Ennis, though he wanted to please his parents, he could imagine no fate worse than being asked to give a speech in front of a crowd, and so he often tried to blend into the buffet table. Daniel could have the spotlight, and Tory could fight for it—Ennis didn't want to compete.

Given their wealth and standing, the Haywards made provision for their children's financial security, though only to a point. Much of the family's wealth was earmarked either for the company or for their various charities. Still, not wanting to leave their children to struggle, the Haywards established a modest trust fund for each, which the children could tap once they turned twenty-one. But while the trust would have been sufficient to maintain the average person for years, it wouldn't keep a Hayward child in the lifestyle to which they'd become accustomed for long. This was by design: their parents wanted the children to strike out on their own and make something of themselves, not sit back and squander the family fortune. But if, for some reason, a child chose not to work, then the trust would provide a modest living if properly managed.

Daniel, the first to fledge, was everything the Haywards could have hoped for. At Stanford, where he pursued an economics degree, Daniel made friends and earned glowing recommendations from his professors. He started community service initiatives, tutored underprivileged children, and still found time to date a few of the more eligible ladies in his year. None of his relationships lasted more than a few months, but each ended in a more or less amicable split, and Daniel cultivated a reputation as the sort of gentleman who walked inebriated girls home—the perfect heir to the Haywards' Sonoman kingdom. He barely touched his trust fund when he came of age, using it to fund a spring break jaunt to Mexico with a few of his friends and pay for his car insurance.

When Daniel graduated, his parents took him into the family business, moving him among offices and production sites until he learned every aspect of the company. He pursued an MBA online as he worked, and by the time he was twenty-five, he was able to purchase a small vineyard of his own, a place where he could grow experimental cultivars. His parents couldn't have been prouder, and anyone with ties to the company knew it was almost a foregone conclusion that Daniel would be chairman of the board someday.

Three years behind Daniel came Tory. Whereas he had

excelled in honors classes in their private high school, Tory had eschewed upper-level calculus for the theater. Her parents tried to be supportive, paying for dance classes and voice lessons in an effort to further her chances of success, even hiring a drama coach for individual lessons. But Tory's theatrical success in the small pond of her high school didn't translate into stardom upon graduation. While she found a job in a modest theater company, she wasn't given the leading roles that she craved. Television was no better—the best work she could find was as an extra in the occasional episode, and she made more money from her brief appearances in commercials than anything else. Film was a distant dream.

Frustrated by the struggle, Tory took to spending more and more of her days with her school friends, several of whom had wealthy families that weren't quite so reluctant to support their children's party lifestyles. By the time she turned twenty-one, Tory was spending more time on her friends' yachts than in auditions. She attacked her trust fund as soon as she could, funding lavish vacations for herself and her friends. Though she told her parents the photos of her in exotic locations were for her portfolio, no one bought the lies.

More troubling for the elder Haywards were the whispers that Tory's habits were endangering her health. They'd known for years that their daughter smoked pot, but neither parent had any room to talk, and even squeaky-clean Daniel had smoked the occasional joint in school. They could even overlook Tory's alcohol consumption, which had markedly risen as soon as she was old enough to purchase it for herself. But the rumor mill suggested that Tory's tastes had shifted from booze and pot toward cocaine and amphetamines, which allowed her to keep partying for hours. Her weight, which had never been more than a pound or two above average, dropped noticeably, and even Tory's skillfully applied makeup couldn't hide her sunken look from her worried parents.

But though they offered her rehab and whatever support she needed, she rebuffed them. As far as Tory was concerned, she was living her best life.

As the Haywards fretted over their daughter's choices, Ennis quietly started toward independence. He followed in his brother's footsteps to Stanford, though he pursued a history degree and worked diligently to excel. His proud parents kept their promise, and on graduation day, they handed him a picture of his very own Cessna parked at the small hangar near his family's home, the one from which their chartered flights ran. The second part of his gift was a check to pay for his first few months' rent at a hangar in Philadelphia, as Ennis had decided to pursue a Wharton MBA. While his parents had offered him a position in the company, just as they had Daniel, Ennis had his reservations. Daniel was the obvious heir, Ennis the less adroit spare, and Ennis could well imagine the constant comparisons he'd face if he tried to copy Daniel's rise in the business. Besides, Daniel had winemaking in his blood. Ennis wasn't sure what he wanted to do with his life, but heading to the East Coast for a time to stake out a place for himself where he wouldn't be in competition with his siblings seemed like a sound bet.

Alone on his own path for the first time in his life, Ennis finally shone. He made friends, put together a modest apartment, dated the daughter of Vermont dairy farmers for a semester and let her show him around New England. He took his plane up on the weekends to keep his skills sharp, and his day-tripping passengers, all of them classmates, tipped him in scotch and beer. As for his trust fund, Ennis hired a money manager and had his assets applied to sound, largely conservative investments with generous dividends. The income was sufficient to fund his living expenses and allow him the odd indulgence beyond his recreational flying. If he wanted a bit of quick cash, his friends knew that "Air Ennis" would be a cheaper option than any other chartered jet, and his services stayed in high demand around school breaks and holidays. Quietly, Ennis began to talk with a few of his classmates about drawing up business plans for a proper charter service and seeking investors.

The elder prince was primed to inherit the kingdom, and the princess might be running toward a precipice, but the little prince was flying high and smiling at the world opening up before him.

The call came early one Saturday morning in October, a few weeks into Ennis's second year at Wharton. It was still Friday night in California, albeit barely, when he mumbled a greeting into his phone. Seeing the familiar area code, he'd expected a telemarketer or a wrong number, maybe even Daniel forgetting how late it was in Philly.

But it was the sheriff, and his message made Ennis slap himself in the face to be certain he wasn't caught in the middle of a terrible dream.

Ennis's parents and brother had been flying to a charity banquet in San Francisco early that evening when their helicopter had disappeared from radar. Frantic calls to emergency services reported witnessing a helicopter crash into the San Pablo Bay. Rescue crews were on the scene, but no one knew what had happened, nor had there yet been any sighting of the pilot or his passengers.

A quiet calm descended over Ennis as he suppressed his urge to scream and panic. Instead, he sent a brief message to his professors to explain the situation, packed a bag, and headed for the airport. Logging his flight plan and making refueling arrangements along the way, he bought the largest cup of coffee he could find at that hour and headed west.

Though fear urged him to fly straight home, exhaustion forced him to rest at the halfway point. When the local traffic control crew learned why he was on an unplanned cross-country run, they offered him a cot in a back room for a few hours. Ennis was the worse for wear when he taxied into his final destination late Saturday night, dirty and mentally running on fumes, but he had enough presence of mind to call the sheriff's department for an update once he landed.

All day, he'd hoped for a miracle. The news of the aquatic recovery effort sent him to his knees.

Sylvia, his mother's personal assistant, a grandmotherly woman who'd known Ennis since he was a baby, picked him up at the airport and drove him home. The house was still lit, the security system armed. Leftovers from Thursday night's dinner were labeled in the refrigerator. For a moment, Ennis stared numbly at the faces that smiled at him from the snapshots on the fridge, the parents and brother who'd dressed up for an evening affair they'd never see, and then he collapsed on the couch.

The maid found him the next morning and almost called the police, thinking him an intruder until she recognized Ennis beneath the grime and grief. Half an hour later, while Ennis was still curled up and silent, Sylvia returned to the house and took charge. Never mind that he was a grown man—Ennis needed direction that morning, and so he acquiesced when Sylvia ordered him into the shower and didn't make a fuss when he found that she'd unpacked his bag and asked the maid to iron his shirt. Once he was clean, dry, and partway through breakfast, he asked Sylvia if Tory knew. Sylvia's lips pursed at the question, but she nodded. Tory, who'd been on a yacht off the coast of Oahu, was on her way.

The next week passed in a blur: releasing a public statement on behalf of the family, planning the triple funeral, and then holding himself together when confronted with the identical coffins. The medical examiner concluded that the crash was a freak accident—the pilot had no water in his lungs, so he'd been dead before they hit the bay. While a cause of death couldn't be confirmed beyond all doubt, the pilot was in his mid-fifties, one of his coronary arteries appeared to be blocked, and the other was at least eighty percent of the way there. His heart attack had killed them all.

Ennis didn't ask to see his parents' and brother's autopsy reports. He didn't need fodder for his nightmares.

The Monday following the funeral, the Haywards' attorney asked Tory and Ennis to come to his office to go over the wills. Ms. Yi was sympathetic but professional, and while Ennis shifted awkwardly in his new suit and Tory picked at a scab on her arm, she pulled out the notarized documents and her own summary of the pertinent information. It came as no surprise that Eric's and Jessica's wills had made bequests to all of their surviving children, including equal shares in the family house. Daniel, who was still unmarried and childless, had named his siblings his heirs, and aside from a few charitable bequests, his sister and brother stood to inherit a considerable sum from him. But once Ms. Yi made clear to the siblings what they'd inherited, she followed it with a surprise announcement. Though both Eric and Jessica held substantial shares in Hayward Wines, they had decided to take only one seat on the company board, opting to put it in Eric's name by coin flip. In case of Eric's death, the seat went to Jessica, and both wills provided that the next heir was Daniel. If Daniel were unwilling or unable to take the seat, then the seat and the company shares were to fall to *Ennis*—not Tory.

Never mind that Ennis was halfway to his MBA and Tory had never shown the slightest interest in the family business—she yelled at Ms. Yi and screamed profanities at her dead parents before she was escorted out of the room.

Having seen his sister's condition and learned from Daniel the truth about her lifestyle, Ennis thought his parents had made the right choice about the seat on the board. Still, he felt terrible for Tory. To make it up to her, he gave her his share in the house, then returned to Philadelphia to finish his studies.

But the little prince was now a king of sorts, the majority shareholder of his parents' company, and he had a responsibility to their legacy and to the Hayward Wines employees. Over the next months, he divided his time between his coursework and company matters, appearing virtually at every board meeting and listening more than he spoke. He had long conversations with each executive and lower manager, trying to learn quickly and at a distance what Daniel had absorbed during his hands-on training. By the spring, it was clear to the other shareholders that although Ennis might not know everything about the company, he was putting in a solid effort. His only demand to that point had been that none of the generous employee benefits be abolished, which secured his popularity. The new king wasn't quite like his predecessors, but the shareholders breathed a collective sigh of relief as they realized the company was in capable hands.

Besides, they murmured to each other, it could have been *so* much worse.

No one had to say Tory's name to know the crisis they'd avoided. While Ennis became a dutiful student of the company, Tory spent her time on beaches and in clubs. Ennis made careful investments and lived frugally, despite coming into unexpected wealth. Tory's extravagant purchases were chronicled by her social media feed and the occasional gossip columnist. Ennis buckled down, dealing with his grief through work. Tory coped with her through hedonism.

Ennis cried alone in his apartment on the night Sylvia called to inform him that Tory had put the family home on the market. It sold in less than a month for half its value, and he barely made it across the country in time to salvage his own furniture and knickknacks from storage before his sister called in the movers.

He rightly assumed that the quick sale was less a fuck-you to their parents than a sign of Tory's financial distress.

His sister had no income beyond her trust fund and her inheritance, and she seemed unacquainted with the concept of frugality. Tory hadn't had a gig in at least a year by the time she moved out of the house, and as she never called her little brother, Ennis kept track of her through her public postings, a long string of exotic trips with smiling, pretty people.

Until the trips suddenly stopped.

Shortly after his graduation, as Ennis was making plans to move back to Sonoma, Sylvia asked him to help her stage an intervention. She'd managed to hold open a line of communication with Tory, and Ennis learned, to his horror, that Tory had called Sylvia from a drunk tank in Los Angeles after she'd been picked up while stoned out of her mind. He hurried to Sylvia's home with a group of family friends and a few cousins, and there, he begged his sister to go to rehab. Broke and abandoned by her friends, Tory agreed, and Ennis paid for her inpatient treatment at a place more akin to a spa resort than a hospital. When she emerged sixty days later, bright-eyed and less skeletal than she'd seemed at their last meeting, she hugged her brother and came home to his new place, where he'd prepared the guest bedroom for her arrival. During the long drive, he suggested a plan of attack for her: she could take classes at a community college, maybe transfer if she found a course of study she liked, then get a job. She wanted nothing to do with the company—a relief for Ennis, as the board wanted no part of Tory—but he promised to use his connections from Wharton to find solid employment for her once she graduated.

But Ennis was far too optimistic. Although he put a roof over her head and offered to pay Tory's tuition, he wouldn't bankroll a new wardrobe or nights on the town with her crew, who began sniffing around once word spread of her release. He refused to buy her a new Mercedes to replace the one she'd sold along the way. And when he had the temerity to suggest that Tory get a part-time job to provide her own spending money, she disappeared the next day while he was at the office—and she took the contents of his liquor cabinet with her. Though grateful that he'd left his little jewelry and important documents in a wall safe, Ennis could only sit back and wait to see where his big sister landed.

When Christmas came and went with no sign of her, Ennis hired a private investigator the following spring, who eventually trailed her to a Los Angeles flophouse. Seeing his evidence made Ennis sick to his stomach: Tory was homeless, strung out much of the time, and prostituting herself to get the drugs she craved. In desperation, he and Sylvia tracked her down, took her to a decent hotel to let her clean up, then begged her to go back to rehab. After having spent months on the street— and with the heat of the southern California summer upon them—Tory relented, and Ennis once again dropped her off for a long inpatient stint. Two weeks later, however, she checked herself out and vanished once more.

"Let her go," Sylvia counseled Ennis. "She'll reach out for help when she hits rock bottom."

That didn't sit well with Ennis, but what else could he do? He wasn't Tory's guardian, and he couldn't force her to turn her life around…but neither could he bring himself to sit in Sonoma, day after day, and wait to hear that she'd been found dead with a needle in her arm.

He needed a change, *something* to distract himself from his missing sister, the company he'd never intended to inherit, and the hole in his life where his parents and Daniel had been.

And so the young king looked north.

Ennis's "Walden period" began with a call to a real estate agent who specialized in hunting properties. A few months after Tory's disappearance, the realtor showed him aerial views of several promising tracts—a few in Montana, two in Idaho, and half a dozen in Alaska. A remote property in the Alaskan interior caught Ennis's attention: nestled around mountains, with forests, lakes, and meadows, the land was beautiful even from above, and the price was more than reasonable. Even to his novice's eye, Ennis thought the land might be perfect for a hunting lodge, a side business he could operate to distract himself from the situation in California. The company didn't need him on the premises for the day-to-day operations, and he had his own plane—why shouldn't he live out his life in a place that didn't remind him so terribly of how his family had fallen apart?

The realtor warned him that the land was far from anything he knew in Sonoma. "It's almost totally undeveloped," she cautioned him. "The nearest paved road is Route 11, and given the isolation, just getting the equipment and supplies in to improve the area will cost a fortune. There's a hunting trail over the mountain, it seems," she said, consulting her photos, "but no one's been up to check in a few years. There's no power, no water—*nothing*. You'd be starting from scratch."

"Someone's lived here," Ennis pointed out, tapping one of the pictures.

"An old cabin, abandoned maybe ten years ago," the realtor explained. "Squatter. You find all kinds up there, especially in the interior. Survivalists and other nuts. I'd go armed, if I were you."

Her warning was well taken, but Ennis had his heart set on the property. He purchased it with his first major withdrawal from his trust fund, then set about figuring out how he was going to *get* there. The nearest city was Fairbanks, a seven-hour drive, and though Alaska was pocked with small airports, he didn't see any signs of one on his new land.

Undeterred, he called some friends in the aviation business to pick their brains, then purchased an amphibious seaplane with retractable wheels. Though he was eager to explore his new property, Ennis decided that the prudent course of action would be to first master his new plane, and so he spent the winter learning the ins and outs of aquatic takeoffs and landings. The plane wasn't as fuel-efficient as his conventional Cessna, but he scoped out potential refueling options along his route. The following spring, satisfied that he could handle the plane, Ennis spent every free moment with a grizzled mechanic who could teach him basic repairs. The last thing he wanted was to be forced into an emergency landing in the wilderness and left trapped. Ennis didn't have an engineering background, but he was eager to learn, and he made rapid progress.

In June, having checked the short- and long-range forecasts for the area and feeling confident that he was ready to risk a trip into the interior, Ennis loaded his seaplane with a small duffel bag, several days' emergency rations, gallons of water and a filtration system, a solar charger for his satellite phone, a tent in case the cabin was too rotten to provide shelter, and a selection of parts and tools. He set off from his local airport before dawn one Friday morning, anticipating close to fifteen hours of flight time. A straight shot would have sent him well over the Pacific, and he had no desire to test the limits of his floats on ocean swells. Ennis refueled in Washington a few hours later, then again in British Columbia and outside of Anchorage. He made a final stop in Fairbanks, ensuring that he'd have enough fuel to get him back to civilization, and then, with butterflies in his stomach, he pressed westward, guiding himself in by GPS and grateful for the late northern daylight.

Circling, he spotted a lake that he recognized from the realtor's photos—a decent-sized body of water about two miles from the abandoned cabin, which he'd decided was his target landing site. But aerial inspection revealed something he hadn't anticipated: habitation. Not far from the lake was what appeared to be a walled town, and he thought he could make out a solar panel array nearby. Some of the pristine fields had been tilled and planted, and as he made his final pass, he picked out a barnlike structure, though whether it held crops or equipment was a mystery.

Still, he'd come too far to turn back. He made a soft landing on the lake, then taxied to the shore, tossed out an anchor, and hopped down into the shallow water. Checking to be sure his pistol was loaded and within reach, he shouldered a messenger bag containing his deed and property photographs, then struck off to visit the squatters.

The wall, he found, was perhaps ten feet high and made of stone. Ennis didn't know much about polar bears, but he wondered whether a hungry one would be able to scale that and come in for a snack. As he pondered the town and thought about the best way to approach without being shot, the heavy wooden door in the wall opened, and a pretty young woman with curly brown hair stepped out.

Ennis was pleased to see that she didn't have a rifle aimed at him, though the sword hanging at her hip gave him pause.

"Who are you?" she demanded in an accent he couldn't place.

He showed her his empty hands and kept his distance. "I'm Ennis Hayward," he said. "I bought this property last fall. I, uh…no one mentioned you," he finished lamely, conscious of how outnumbered he surely was. "Um…could I speak to whoever's in charge here? Please?"

The woman's mouth tightened, and then she offered a curt nod and motioned for him to follow her inside.

Ennis wasn't sure what to expect within the walls, but after all the dangers his mind had conjured, finding himself on a gravel road in what seemed like a modest subdivision was bizarrely reassuring. He saw no one out on the porches or front lawns—perhaps, he mused, the locals were shy of strangers—and then he recalled just how late it was despite the glow in the sky. A few blocks into the compound, the woman turned up the walkway at one of the homes and rapped thrice on the front door. When it opened, Ennis was surprised to find a man of about his age looking back at him, a dark-haired figure with striking green eyes and a bad sunburn on his face and neck. The woman murmured to him in words Ennis couldn't understand, and then she stepped aside as the man emerged onto his front porch.

"Hi, there," he said, stuffing his hands into the pockets of his jeans. "Just flew in?"

"From Sonoma," Ennis replied, suddenly feeling the hour.

The man's eyebrows rose. "What, today? Alone?"

He shrugged. "Kind of a hard sell when you suggest flying out at zero dark thirty to go primitive camping in Alaska."

"Moon and stars," he muttered, then waved Ennis closer. "Come in. You want a beer or something?"

At that moment, a beer sounded like the most wonderful idea Ennis had ever heard, and he gladly followed the man into the house. His host sat him down on a couch and returned with three open bottles of Guinness, plus a glass bowl of peanuts. "Thirsty?" Ennis quipped as he took one of the proffered beers.

The man grinned and selected his own. "Not *that* thirsty. My wife will be downstairs in a moment. Colin Leffee," he offered, extending his hand.

Ennis shook it. "Pleasure. Ennis Hayward."

Releasing him, the man settled into a recliner, though he kept the chair upright. "Mr. Hayward, I'm afraid there's been a terrible misunderstanding about this property," he began as Ennis drank. "We—this community here—purchased the place about a year ago, or we *thought* we did. We only realized in the last few weeks that our title was fraudulent, so it looks like we're trespassing on your land."

Ennis tried to square that timeline with the tidy house

and the well-built compound, then wondered how they'd managed the feat. Judging by the grim picture his realtor had painted, it would have taken roughly an act of God to erect the settlement so quickly, especially with the frozen months. "I'm so sorry," he said, putting his bottle on a ceramic coaster. "That's…wow, that's shitty luck. You've obviously spent a fortune here."

"You could say that," Colin replied. "By any chance, could we convince you to sell us part of your property? Just enough to keep the community together. We're not mining, we're not doing anything illegal—"

"Cult?" he asked, then immediately regretted it.

Fortunately, Colin chuckled. "*Absolutely* not. Look, if you just bought this bit here, we understand that you'd prefer we not stay. But if you bought some substantial acreage, would you consider selling off this portion? Better than market value—we'd make it worth your trouble."

"If you don't mind me asking," said Ennis, "what *are* you doing up here?"

His host flashed a tight smile. "Nowhere else to go. Nothing for us farther south. No one here is a wanted criminal," he assured Ennis, "that's not what I mean, but…quite a few people here have lost everything. We thought we'd start over. Clean slate, you know?"

A town didn't jive with Ennis's imagined hunting resort, but he had to admire the settlers' tenacity in establishing a community so far off the grid…and, well, noblesse oblige.

"I'd like to keep the property intact," Ennis told Colin, reaching for his bag, "and I'm happy to show you the bounds. It's a pretty big tract, though, and all things considered, it probably wouldn't be a bad thing to have neighbors up here."

Colin regarded him with a curious stare—an unsettling stare, Ennis thought, unable to shake the feeling that something was slightly *off* about the other man's eyes—then sipped his beer. "What would you want in rent, then?"

"I'm not hurting," Ennis replied, "but…I guess if you were chopping firewood or something, think of me, eh? My plan was to see if I could make the cabin habitable—"

"It's not a lost cause, but you're not sleeping there tonight. Needs a new roof, if nothing else." Hearing footsteps on the stairs, he turned and called, "Toula, honey, come meet our new landlord."

To Ennis, Toula seemed rather normal, a young woman in an oversized T-shirt and yoga pants with a dark, blue-tipped pixie cut and smiling blue eyes. She settled in with a beer, then learned exactly how far Ennis had come that day and berated her husband for offering only peanuts. Chastised, Colin retreated to the kitchen to heat up the leftovers, and Toula showed Ennis to a guest bedroom. "The hot water tank is a little on the small side," she warned, "but go ahead and get cleaned up. We'll have dinner on the table once you're finished."

Not quite believing how the day had concluded, Ennis stood under the pounding spray until it chilled to lukewarm, then toweled off, made himself presentable, and slipped downstairs to find a curried chicken casserole waiting. Almost too tired to see straight, he gratefully filled his stomach, thanked his new tenants for their hospitality, and stumbled off to bed.

Over the weekend, as Ennis met the other residents of the compound and discussed his plans to renovate the cabin, he was struck by the fact that so many of them seemed to be about his age—twenty-somethings who'd packed up their lives and moved into the wilderness. He saw only a handful of teenagers, plus a few older adults, most of whom kept their distance. As far as Ennis could tell, decision-making authority seemed to be vested in Colin and Toula, and in her brother, who'd introduced himself simply as Val. But as no one pointed a gun at him or came forward claiming to be an all-powerful priest of an ancient snake god, Ennis decided that his new tenants were harmless.

More importantly, they knew how to construct and repair. Ennis hadn't brought building supplies with him on that trip, intending to lay eyes on the cabin first and see whether it could be salvaged. The settlers gave him a lift in a battered pickup truck, and Ennis saw that Colin hadn't been wrong: the roof had sprouted natural skylights, and one wall exhibited an alarming list. As Ennis poked his head around the site, he noticed one of the other men making notes on a pad of paper and scowling at the building. "Got some ideas?" he asked.

The man, a brown-haired Brit—or so Ennis guessed, based on his accent—nodded and continued to make his scribbles. "My first suggestion would be to tear it down, but if you want to preserve the bones, it *should* be doable. If you plan to make this anything more than a basic shelter, you'll want to expand it, and trust me when I tell you that you'll need proper insulation."

He peeked over the man's shoulder to glance at his notes. "Done this before, huh?"

"Architect," he murmured, "and yes. So, now, what sort of a footprint do you want this place to have, and do you want it habitable before winter?"

"What kind of a timeframe would that give us?"

"Conservatively, two months until the snow window opens." As Ennis's eyes widened, the man laughed. "First time in the frozen north, eh?"

Ennis's new architect introduced himself as Robbie Stowe, and though Ennis wasn't sure how much he trusted a peer to redo his cabin, Robbie seemed confident and didn't ask for payment. Given Robbie's warnings about the weather and their limited building window, Ennis decided to take drastic action. He called Sylvia and asked her to see about his house, announcing that he'd be spending the summer in Alaska. Sylvia asked if he'd lost his mind, but

Ennis insisted that he needed to clear his head—and besides, he had satellite internet access, so he'd be popping in for meetings as needed.

The first problem was getting materials out to the property. The compound's barn did hold several vehicles, some tools, and a selection of odds and ends like roofing shingles and PVC pipes, but unless Ennis planned to fell his own trees and plane boards on site, he needed to make a trip to civilization. The seaplane wasn't large, but he dumped most of his repair kit in the compound for safekeeping, then flew back to Fairbanks with Robbie, Robbie's brother Adam—the local brew master, apparently, a guy whose good side Ennis intended to stay on—and a hulking giant of a man named Frank, who wore sunglasses at all times. Leaving the plane with a crew for refueling and an inspection, the foursome got a ride to a home improvement store, where Ennis got a healthy dose of far northern sticker shock. Still, he decided it was cheaper to buy and fly from Fairbanks than from home, and he tried to stay out of Robbie's way as the man made his selections in the contractors' part of the building.

By the time Ennis paid, Frank and Adam had rented a moving van to haul his supplies away. No one pretended for a moment that the plane would be sufficiently large to carry everything back, and so Robbie flew out with Ennis, leaving the others to make the long drive. "They'll be fine," Robbie assured Ennis as they banked west. "Certainly not their first trip from Fairbanks. But we'll need to offload the van at the paved road, and that might take a few hours."

While Ennis was grateful for the guidance and assistance, he never meant for his new tenants to *build* his house, but they came out en masse to pitch in, men and women alike. Following Robbie's instructions, they'd greatly expanded the cabin and made it snug against the winter by the first autumn snowfall—and they refused payment. "You're allowing us to stay here," Toula explained when he voiced his exasperation. "That's payment enough."

But renovations weren't the end of their assistance. They connected Ennis's cabin to their solar grid and helped him dig a well, and while the community brought in the last of their harvest, Colin and Toula sat down with Ennis and a checklist. The squatters had survived an Alaskan winter. If Ennis intended to do likewise, then he needed to prepare.

Ennis thought about his comfortable home back in Sonoma, where the electricity reliably flipped on at the touch of a switch and the water came pre-heated from the taps. He thought about the long silence from Tory, about the office he missed less by the day.

He asked his neighbors what he should buy.

Fairbanks wasn't an easy trip, even in good weather, and as Ennis was the only person in the area with a plane, he offered to make a few supply runs for the compound while he was stocking his own larder. After all, noblesse oblige.

They took him up on it—and shared their membership cards for the warehouse stores. Ennis refused all offers to pitch in for fuel, though he gladly accepted a passenger or two to help with the loading. He flew in pallets of canned food, boxes and bags of dried goods, gallons of pickles and supplies to make more with the compound's own produce. He spent thousands at several pharmacies in town, stocking up on first-aid supplies and all the necessities for cold and flu season, then raided a sporting goods store for extra outerwear and layering pieces. One trip was just for propane and bottled water.

His tenants had money—that much was clear to Ennis—and they seemed to keep it in individual accounts, which lessened his fear that he'd stumbled onto a cult. But having seen his land, he understood why they stayed in the wilderness. The place was beautiful, and given the size of the animals he'd observed being butchered outside the compound's walls, he could have made a small fortune with an exclusive hunting lodge. But then there were his tenants to consider, as well as the other scattered survivalists in the area, a handful of loners who kept to themselves when company could at all be avoided. Though they were technically trespassers, the young king felt an odd sense of duty to them.

His new cabin had been designed with plenty of storage, so he filled his spare rooms with extra food, fuel, medicine, and clothing. When the occasional survivalist came around that fall, he had supplies on offer, and he didn't ask for payment. He subscribed to the best satellite Internet access that money could buy and offered the password to anyone who needed it. His big-screen TV was usually on—Ennis liked having company for Saturday-night football—and he set up a makeshift bar in one corner of his den, a thoroughly unlicensed spot for a drink or two. Sure, Adam's beer was excellent, but Ennis stocked a full liquor cabinet, not to mention several cases of Hayward's better bottles. While he didn't mind being alone, Ennis was grateful that his solitude could be interrupted whenever he grew lonely.

In short order, the compound residents made his cabin a sort of social outpost, a place beyond the wall where they could congregate for a drink, a bit of television, and a change of scenery. Ennis welcomed them all, and when they went home, he noticed the things left behind in return for his hospitality: an armload of firewood, a fresh growler of beer, a jar or two of tart jam made from the summer's wild berries. When the deep snows arrived that winter, his new friends still made the trek, sometimes by snowmobile, often brandishing shovels in case the drifts had grown too high against the side of his house.

Two of Ennis's more frequent guests were Colin and Toula, who offered bits of advice whenever they saw him poised to repeat a rookie mistake they'd made the year before. Colin had a taste for single-malts and insisted that Ennis accept compensation for the scotch he drank. Toula was less picky when she drank, though her infrequent imbibing came to a screeching halt in February when she announced her pregnancy. While the others celebrated the impending birth, the first in the compound. Colin seemed to Ennis a bit like he'd been hit between the eyes with a two-by-four, and Ennis kept the whisky flowing.

His growing social circle included two other young couples in particular: Kitty and Marcus, and Beth and Ed. The women were sisters, he learned, though separated by a decade. The elder had been married for a year and a half, while the younger, not quite nineteen, simply held herself out as married to her similarly aged boyfriend, and the rest of the compound went along with it. Over the winter, Ennis gleaned information about their past: Kitty and Marcus had been researchers at a small British university, Beth had become their orphaned ward, and Ed was a school friend of Beth's. As to why they'd left a seemingly comfortable life for the Alaskan wilderness, they offered no firm answers, though Kitty hinted that they'd had personal issues and needed a fresh start. Never one to pry, Ennis let the matter go and simply enjoyed having peers around who didn't want to do business with his company or ask difficult questions about his sister.

The only true oddity he noticed about the compound folk was the tendency among many to wear gloves inside. He kept his cabin warm, but still, his guests often left their hands covered while they drank and ate with him. Otherwise, they gave him no cause for complaint. If that was the worst criticism he could muster, he decided, then he'd truly lucked out. Lying in bed as the show whipped around the cozy cabin, Ennis congratulated himself on his escape and saw nothing but potential in his wild kingdom.

Toula delivered a healthy boy the following October, and

his parents named him Declan Pavli. Why they chose Toula's surname over Colin's, Ennis couldn't say, but prudence counseled him to keep the nosiness to a minimum around the under-slept new parents. At least little Dec wouldn't be alone for long—both Kitty and Beth had conceived, and the community was placing bets as to genders.

As Ennis faced his second winter in Alaska, the calls from Sylvia grew more insistent that he come home. Yes, the company was flourishing in his physical absence, and yes, he could handle his position by phone and computer, but it wasn't *natural* to abandon sunny California for the frozen north. His reminders of wildfire season did nothing to sway her. Plus, Sylvia scolded him, his parents had been present in the community, attending balls and giving speeches as necessity dictated. His charitable giving hadn't gone unnoticed, but several of his more prominent beneficiaries wanted him to present awards at a banquet or smile for a publicity photoshoot. To that, Ennis remarked that his Alaskan exile was serving an important purpose if it kept him out of a tuxedo, and even from his cabin's office, he could imagine Sylvia's mouth tightening in disapproval.

Besides, he'd grown to appreciate the slower pace of compound life. The most exciting thing that happened was his flights in and out, and he was happy to play taxi for neighbors who needed a few hours in Fairbanks. If a meeting irritated him, he could always make an early exit by blaming a bad connection. A decent hunter, he accompanied the compound's parties in search of caribou and rabbits, and his neighbors joined him that May in clearing a proper landing strip for his plane. Ennis had plans in mind for a hangar—a matter to address with Robbie—but as he sat at his computer one June morning, scrolling through kits for inspiration, Sylvia called. Seeing no reason to endure another half-hour's nagging, he almost didn't pick up, but duty made him take the call.

Ten minutes later, duffel in hand, he called Colin to let him know that he was heading south. "My sister's in the hospital in LA," he explained, making a last check of the darkened lamps. "I don't know when I'll be back. In case of emergency—"

"Be safe," Colin interrupted. "Are you able to make the flight?"

"With enough refueling—"

"That's not what I meant. Are you able to do this alone?"

Ennis pulled the front door shut and shouldered his bag. The question was a loaded one—Toula and Colin were among the few people in whom Ennis had confided about Tory—and in truth, Ennis wouldn't have minded a copilot. But this was a family matter. "I'll make it," he replied. "Send me a shopping list for the babies, and I'll try to pick up supplies when I head north again."

Unprepared but steeling himself for the worst, Ennis flew south as quickly as the sluggish plane allowed. He didn't make it to Los Angeles until the wee hours of the morning, but Sylvia had a car waiting for him and instructions at the hospital to admit him as the next of kin.

And there, stinking with the funk of his long day of travel and bleary from the quick nap he'd sneaked in the car, Ennis found Tory at rock bottom. She looked skeletal, her eyes sunken, her hair stringy and limp. Her emaciation made her swollen abdomen all the more prominent, and Ennis briefly imagined that his sister had been starving before he recognized the swelling as a late-stage pregnancy.

Tory didn't know who had dropped her at the hospital or how long she'd been there. She had no ID on her, but one of the nurses was a high school classmate, and he'd called the company to find help. Though much of the last two years was a blur, Ennis coaxed a few broad contours from his sister: she'd been high whenever she could find the drugs, and she'd done what it took to get the money necessary to keep her there. Momentarily sober, she'd decided to detox for the baby's sake, the first bit of prenatal care she'd offered her child, but the withdrawal symptoms were agonizing, and she'd been restrained to the bed for her own safety—and at her request. Tory knew too well that she'd leave again in search of a fix if the craving hit too strongly, and she wanted help.

Ennis called his attorney, who sent an associate from a closer office. Tory signed a document giving power of attorney to her brother, and he leapt into action, having Tory moved to a more secure unit and placing calls to friends of friends in search of medical specialists. When he didn't leave her room for twenty-four hours, a pair of concerned nurses had a spare bed wheeled in, but Ennis didn't get much sleep. Between periods of lucidity, Tory sweat, shook, hallucinated, and railed at him for holding her captive.

On the fourth day of Ennis's vigil, Tory went into labor. The baby arrived that night—a girl, premature and undersized, who was rushed off to the NICU. As Tory slept, one of the specialist pediatricians gave him the bad news. The baby was showing signs of neonatal abstinence syndrome, though without a full list of what Tory had been taking, they couldn't be certain exactly of the cause of the baby's withdrawal. Ennis was no help on that front, as he knew as little of Tory's recent past as everyone else in the building. The only thing he could offer was a name: Baby Girl Hayward was legally Kenna, per Tory's wishes. She had no idea who the child's father might be, so a Hayward the baby remained.

Over the next difficult days, Ennis visited his niece whenever he was allowed. Kenna was a screaming, trembling mess who barely slept and vomited almost everything she consumed. Her skin was mottled with red patches, and when Ennis asked one of the nurses about the gauze on her limbs, the nurse shook her head and whistled softly. "Skin sensitivity like I've never seen before," she murmured. "If metal touches her, she breaks out in a horrible rash. Does her mother have any allergies like that?"

Ennis recalled Tory's ears turning green when she'd worn cheap earrings, but nothing like the nurse described.

The NICU team brought in titanium needles, finding that Kenna tolerated them better than the usual steel needles on offer, and dosed her with methadone and morphine. Ennis sat in a rocking chair, holding the swaddled baby and trying to comfort her as she whimpered in her sleep. While Tory rested, ate, and continued her own withdrawal, the nurses tried to prepare Ennis to take Kenna home. She would need frequent feedings and a high-calorie diet, she'd be prone to diaper rash, and she might exhibit any number of long-term complications from her prenatal abuse. Time alone would tell. But for the moment, the prognosis was looking up— Kenna had begun to gain weight, and her team thought that she could be weaned from her drugs within the week.

But where could she go once she was discharged? Ennis was trying to coax Tory back into rehab, but she couldn't take the baby with her. He didn't feel right trying to leave Kenna with one of their cousins for a few months, especially in light of her needs. That left him—twenty-eight, single, and in no way prepared to take on a newborn. He tried to psych himself up: he could do this, couldn't he? Colin, Marcus, and Ed seemed to be adjusting to fatherhood well enough, so surely he could manage a few sleepless weeks with Kenna. He'd do it for his sister, and once she was clean, he'd set up her in Sonoma and hire a nanny to help out. Problem solved.

The next day, Tory seemed calm and lucid enough to be released from her bed. Ennis pushed her wheelchair up to the NICU and placed Kenna in her arms, and Tory beamed at the sleeping, dark-haired girl bundled in blankets. "For her," she promised Ennis. "I'll get clean for her, and I'll make it stick this time."

That evening, as Ennis was giving Kenna a bottle, one

of Tory's sometime boyfriends visited with a grocery-store bouquet. Once he was safely in her room, he produced a pocketknife and revealed that the packet of flower food had been emptied and refilled with white heroin—a gift. Tory allowed herself just *one* more hit and smiled as the needle found her vein.

Unfortunately, her friend's dealer had been less than forthcoming. The seeming heroin was mixed with fentanyl, and as her friend escaped out an emergency exit, Tory died of a massive overdose on the floor of her hospital room.

The police put the pieces together, and the friend confessed all when he was collared, but his tearful explanation did nothing to bring Tory back.

For the second time in five years, Ennis buried a sibling. The service was private, attended only by a few family friends, and Ennis barely heard their words of condolence. He was well and truly alone now, the last of the Haywards...except for the newborn back in the NICU, who was adjusting to life without methadone. Sylvia told Ennis that he didn't have to shoulder the responsibility of dealing with Kenna—they could find a loving couple who'd welcome a baby.

He listened to Sylvia, and he thanked her for her advice.

Two months later, the young king and the little princess, now legally his daughter, flew north as if they could escape the wreckage of Tory's life.

CHAPTER 3

Ennis hadn't been expecting a homecoming party, or even a welcoming committee. He'd called Colin from Fairbanks to apologize for the long silence and ask if anyone needed supplies, as the list he'd taken south with him in June was surely outdated. Colin had told him they were fine and to be safe, and that was the end of it.

But when Ennis circled the area in the glow of the late summer evening, he found a hangar waiting for him at one end of the runway and the landing strip clean and smooth. A small crowd was waiting as he taxied in, and Colin, wearing Dec in a sling across his chest, waved as he parked the plane. "Welcome back," he called when Ennis opened the door. "How's your sister feeling…"

The rest of the question fizzled as Ennis carefully disembarked with Kenna's new car seat in hand.

Frowning, Toula hurried closer to inspect Ennis's passenger, then looked from the sleeping baby's face to his. "Oh, *hon*," she murmured, and put her arm around his hunched shoulders. "Come on, you're staying with us tonight. We'll air out the cabin tomorrow."

Too exhausted to protest, Ennis held the car seat while Toula climbed into the plane to retrieve his duffel and diaper bag, then let her escort him up the short trail to the compound and into their house. She said nothing beyond quiet encouragement to keep walking until the door was latched behind them, then directed Ennis to the couch and headed for the kitchen. "When did you last eat?" she asked over her shoulder.

"Lunch, I think," he mumbled.

She tutted and opened the refrigerator. "I've got half a potpie in here, and I'm not taking no for an answer. Want a beer? I *know* you're not breast feeding."

As the microwave whirred in the other room, Kenna began to fidget in her sleep, and Colin peered down at her as her mouth puckered. "I give that five minutes, tops," he said. "Do you have a bottle ready to go?" When Ennis shook his head and reached for the diaper bag, Colin stayed him with a hand to the shoulder. "I've got it, kid. Is milk okay, or does she have any allergies?"

"Milk's fine. Thanks."

By the time he returned with a warmed bottle, Ennis had unbuckled the baby and was holding her, hoping to stave off the screams. She took the bottle eagerly, and Colin chuckled as he settled onto the couch beside them, shifting sleeping Dec. "Hungry little thing. This one doesn't care to miss meals, either, and the twins are no better. The trick is plugging the hole before the tears start."

As soon as Toula brought out the food, she took Kenna and put a fork in Ennis's hand, and he inhaled his dinner. When he finally came up for air, she laid Kenna over her shoulder to burp her, then asked, "How's your sister?"

Ennis tried to answer, but the sudden constriction in his throat choked the words before they could form, and his vision began to blur. He barely gave thought to the idea that he was weeping in someone else's home until he felt Toula rubbing his shaking back. "It's okay," she soothed. "It's going to be okay. Do you want to talk?"

Kenna was asleep again and his second beer was almost drained by the time Ennis finished recounting Tory's troubled history. As Colin rose to bring in another round of drinks, Ennis looked down at Kenna, who was sprawled on a blanket atop the rug. "There's no telling yet what sort of problems the poor little kid's going to have," he said.

"Hell, she's already got one weird allergy to deal with."

Colin paused and turned back, grimacing. "I'm sorry, I thought you said she *didn't* have—"

"No, she has no food allergies," Ennis clarified. "Not that I know of, anyway. What did they call it…God, my brain's fuzzy," he muttered, then snapped his fingers. "Contact dermatitis, that's it. Pretty severe case. It means—"

"A skin reaction on contact with the allergen," Colin offered. "What's her trigger? Latex?"

"No." He paused to finish his beer, then wiped his mouth on the back of his hand. "Metal, actually. She gets a horrible rash…I put her in a onesie with built-in mittens and feet to protect her. Some of her blisters are still healing up, and I was going to ask Doc if she has any more gauze, I forgot to buy another roll…"

Ennis looked up, found his hosts staring at him, and blinked. "Something I said?"

"What *kind* of metal?" Toula asked.

"Steel, at least. Surgical steel. She was fine with titanium, but I don't know if anything else bothers her. Not like they gave her a full panel in the NICU. Still, I mean, you know how much steel is out there? It's *everywhere*."

"Preaching to the choir," Coilin muttered, and turned to his wife. "Would you—"

"On it," she said, and headed upstairs for a moment. When she returned, she carried a manicure kit, which she put on the coffee table by Ennis's empty plate. "We have a theory," she explained as he observed bemusedly, then knelt by Kenna. "Do you mind if I test her sensitivity? I won't hurt her, I promise."

"If you're sure…" Ennis replied.

Carefully, Toula unzipped Kenna's sleeper, then hissed at the sight of the bandages beneath. "What did they do, take a stethoscope to her?" she said, then cooed, "Oh, sweet girl, I'm so sorry," as Kenna fidgeted in her sleep.

"Good call on the plastic zipper, but there's steel in this, too," she told Ennis. "You're going to want to sew a patch along the inside, just in case. Now, let's just get this off you, little miss…"

Ennis hurt just seeing the dressings all over Kenna's limbs and torso, and he glanced up to catch Colin wincing as Toula peeled the baby's outfit away. She pulled a small metal nail file from her kit, then held Kenna's arm steady and murmured, "Watch for me."

Colin stood over them, holding Dec and studying Kenna's face. "Whenever you're ready."

Moving slowly, she eased the flat side of the file closer and closer to Kenna's arm. The baby began to whimper when the file was a full inch away. At half that distance, she was pulling back and awoke wailing in fear. Toula tucked the file in its case and picked Kenna up, holding her against her chest and blowing into her ear until she quieted.

"A learned reaction," Colin told Ennis. "There's a tingling sort of sensation whenever she gets too close. It's not steel that's the problem—it's *iron*. Anything ferrous sets off the warning feeling, and it's not pleasant. That's not just a rash under the gauze, right? Open sores?"

"Uh…yeah," said Ennis, surprised. "How'd you know?"

"Long experience. The good news is that the scars will heal—probably quickly at her age. But she *will* be scarred for a time." As Toula pushed herself from the floor, he asked, "Do you still have—"

"Of course. Just because we're together doesn't mean I threw out all my jewelry," she replied with a quick, teasing grin, then disappeared upstairs once more. On her return, she carried a mahogany box with brass handles, which she put on the floor beside Kenna. "Okay, let's try this…"

The brass produced no reaction, not even when Kenna's hand was pressed against it. Nor did Toula's gold hoop earrings cause the baby distress. Her platinum wedding ring was likewise harmless, as was an old penny fished from her purse. At last, she pulled a delicate silver necklace chain from the back of the jewelry box and let it coil in her palm. Cutting her eyes to Colin, who stood at a safe distance with their son, she shook her head and said, "It really doesn't hurt, I swear."

"I'm going to break out in hives just watching you," he protested.

"Eyes on Kenna," she replied, then waited until he edged closer before dangling a bit of the chain near the baby's arm. As with the nail file, Kenna was crying before the necklace could make contact, and Toula put it away. "Hon, I just did a load of towels. There should be a few swaddling blankets in the basket…"

Colin brought her a pale green swaddle, and she wrapped Kenna and passed her to Ennis. "Well," she said to Colin, "it's strong evidence, but I'm not going to be able to give a definitive answer without the sword."

Ennis clutched Kenna more tightly. "*What* sword?"

"It's not coming anywhere near the baby," she assured him before turning to Colin again. "Do you think…"

He gave Ennis a long, searching look, then nodded. "I don't think we have a choice. It's the responsible thing to do."

"Then I'll call Artur," she said, and slipped out of the room.

Ennis wasn't at all sure of what was going on, and as Colin left to put Dec in his crib shortly after Toula stepped away, all he could do was hold Kenna and try to force his weary brain to focus. The baby was awake but comfortable, and she'd almost slipped back to sleep when someone knocked at the front door.

Toula and Colin quickly reappeared from within the house and admitted the visitor. Ennis recognized Artur, Kitty and Beth's more taciturn sister, but the leather scabbard hanging against her leg gave him pause.

"I'll be quick," Toula assured her.

When Artur unsheathed the weapon, Ennis's eyes bulged. The handle had been interesting, a metal far closer in color to gold than to brass, but the blade seemed to have been crafted from diamond, a translucent length that glittered in the light and threw tiny rainbows on the walls and ceiling. "What…" he managed.

"That would be Caledfwlch," said Toula as Colin cleared a place for the sword on the coffee table. "The one remaining source of magic in this realm or any other. I hate to tap it, but we need the truth about Kenna."

"Magic?" Ennis echoed.

"Bear with me." Kneeling beside the couch, she placed one hand on the naked sword, then stretched out the other toward him and the baby and said, "This won't hurt."

Ennis started to protest as her lips soundlessly moved, but his words died unspoken when a ball of white mist coalesced in the air before him. A few seconds later, the mist thinned into a sphere composed of a lattice of dark blue filaments that swirled together with no apparent pattern. "Aural signature. Blue means mundane," Toula explained, then flicked a finger. The sphere split and flattened into a sheet, and she waved it to one side while Ennis watched in slack-jawed astonishment. As Toula continued her work, a second sphere manifested near Kenna—but unlike Ennis's, hers was an even mix of red and blue, and it glowed far more brightly than Ennis's did. Quickly, Toula flattened Kenna's, then split it into its component halves, dark blue and brilliant red. When she moved the blue lattices together, even Ennis could see the perfect match. With a soft sigh, she released the sword, and her creations vanished.

"So," said Toula, pushing herself back to her feet, "that answers *that*."

"Do we know whose—" Colin began, but she shook her head.

"My ring's upstairs, and checking her signature against the database would take more juice than I'd like to expend.

We have the more important answer," she told him.

Ennis shifted on the couch, uncomfortable to find himself the focal point of three pairs of eyes. "Uh," he squeaked, then cleared his throat and tried again. "Uh…is anyone going to tell me what the hell is going on?"

The others looked to Toula, who shrugged and turned her attention to Ennis. "As I mentioned, those were aural lattices, yours and Kenna's."

"What's an—"

"Living creatures produce auras—energetic fields. An aural signature tells you what sort of energetic field you're dealing with, and the spell I use color-codes for convenience. The brighter the aura, the more magically gifted."

"*Huh?*"

Toula ignored the interruption. "The other nice part about aural signatures is that everyone inherits a copy of their parents' signatures. Full siblings' lattices match. I split Kenna's to be certain—you saw how I pulled a copy of yours from hers?"

Ennis nodded warily.

"That was your sister's signature. You two share the same parents, so your lattices match. Blue means mundane—neither of you is magically gifted. But *red* is the color used for a fae signature, and from the looks of it, Kenna's father was full-blooded."

"Stop, *stop*," Ennis begged. "Fae?"

"A faerie," she said simply. "I realize this must sound insane—"

"*Yeah*," he snapped.

"—magical sword notwithstanding. That's crystalline magic, by the way," she said, nodding to the sword as Artur sheathed it. "Glittery as hell."

"Does the trick," Artur murmured.

"Oh, I'm not criticizing," Toula hastily added, then turned back to Ennis. "There's…well, there's a lot you need to understand, all at once, and we probably should have waited until you'd gotten a night's sleep before springing this on you, but..."

"Why don't I get Kuni?" Artur suggested.

The three of them traded looks, and Colin nodded. Looking down at Ennis as Artur left the house, he said softly, "We haven't been entirely...*forthright*...with you about why we're up here. We weren't trying to get off the grid and back to nature. You see, we're, uh..."

"Refugees," Toula offered.

"Yes. Homeless. When we lost everything almost three years ago, we tried to find a place on the edge of the map, somewhere that we might be able to live without attracting attention. We thought we'd chosen a location that no one would want, but...well." He shrugged. "I guess we didn't go far enough."

"I...I don't understand," said Ennis, "Refugees from *where*?"

"Why don't we wait until Artur gets back?" Toula suggested. "I think you'll have an easier time believing us with a visual aid."

The three of them sat in awkward silence until Artur knocked twice and let herself in. But to Ennis's shock, she wasn't alone. A tiny ball of golden light seemed to be perched on her shoulder, and as she wiped her shoes on the interior mat, the light left her and made a beeline toward the coffee table. As it neared, Ennis could make out a shape within the glowing orb, a source like a filament...

No. *Not* a filament. A *body*.

He stared, dumbfounded and gaping, at the little creature standing before him—a man perhaps six inches high with a blond ponytail, a tank top, and dark leggings. He was barefoot, which wasn't altogether unusual, and his dark eyes were too large for a human face, which was striking, but the feature that left Ennis speechless was the man's wings, which looked to Ennis's layman's eye like a scaled-up version of the wings of a monarch butterfly. He folded his muscular arms and considered Ennis for a moment, then squeaked in a voice like a chipmunk on helium, "Welcome back. How was civilization?"

Toula took the baby from Ennis before he could drop her.

When he was finally able to do more than flap his mouth like a dying fish, Ennis whispered, "Oh, my God. What…is that…"

He reached a fingertip toward the little man, who pressed his hand against it before he could be poked. "I am Kuni," he said.

"Is that…that's a *fairy*…"

"Well, technically," Colin interrupted, "he's native to Faerie, but he's a piq. A pixie, you might say. Do us all a favor and don't try to pet him, eh?"

Ennis hastily withdrew his finger, and Kuni nodded his thanks.

"We're some of the lucky ones who escaped Faerie before it collapsed," Colin continued. "At least some of Kuni's family got out alive, but he hasn't seen them since. The realm…look, it's a long story," he said as Ennis gnawed his lip in agitation, "and you're exhausted, but the important thing you need to understand is that Kenna's only half human. It's less of a problem than it could be— without magic, she won't be able to do much more than tantrum—but she'll have a *nasty* temper, and she'll need to learn to control that…"

He fell silent as Toula patted his arm. "Short version," she said to Ennis. "Kenna's immortal. She'll never get sick—though believe me, she *can* get a hangover," she muttered—"and unless someone goes *Highlander* on her, she'll live indefinitely. She'll stop aging in her mid-twenties. You've already seen what iron and silver can do to her, and animals will lose their shit if she gets too close, but those are the only real downsides. Well, that, and the problem of getting a driver's license when you're eighty-seven years old and look like *this*," she added, pointing to her face.

"Getting carded does lose its luster after a while."

"I…wait…you…" he stammered, then took a deep breath to produce a coherent utterance. "You're *how* old?"

"Eighty-seven last February. And other than you and the babies, I'm the youngest person in this house."

Ennis stared at the faces around him, all of which appeared to be about his age, then looked down at Kuni again. "Even him?"

Colin laughed softly. "*Especially* him. The piq system of time demarcation isn't particularly helpful for outsiders"— Kuni offered an exaggerated shrug—"but he predates my mother, and *she* predated cuneiform, so make of that what you will."

"You know, Ennis," Toula cut in before he could fully process that fact, "you've had one hell of a long day, and Kenna's going to be up again soon. Let's get you to bed. We'll answer questions once you can see straight again, okay?"

Part of Ennis wanted nothing more than to demand information—for heaven's sake, there was a *pixie* standing not two feet away from him!—but the louder part of his mind insisted that the baby-faced old lady made a good point.

"Come on, kid," said Colin, pulling him off the couch. "Bedtime."

She might have been premature, but Kenna was born with a powerful set of lungs, and her wail made Ennis bolt upright in bed. Briefly, he panicked as he tried to recall where he was, but then he saw the nightlight and the blackout curtains and the plastic laundry basket serving as a makeshift bassinette, and the previous evening came flooding back. This was Colin and Toula's house, there'd been a magic sword, an honest-to-God pixie, and Kenna…

He could dwell on Kenna's larger problems later. The

baby had a cry to wake the dead, and she was hungry.

Ennis found a wall switch and pulled the formula cannister from the diaper bag he couldn't recall bringing upstairs, then measured out powder. His bottled water was down to the dregs, however, and so he scooped up the protesting infant and hurried downstairs to finish making her meal.

As he descended, he spotted Colin sprawled on the couch, feeding Dec. "That kid of yours has a promising future as an air raid siren," he said, and cocked his head toward the kitchen. "Filtered water's in the pitcher. Help yourself."

Once he'd mixed the formula, Kenna needed almost no prodding to take the bottle, and Ennis sighed with relief as he shuffled back into the den. "Sit down," Colin offered, swinging his legs off the couch. "And good morning," he added dryly. "I hope that'll do her for at least a few hours. You should try to crash again once she does."

"That's what the nurses said," Ennis croaked. "Your turn for the overnight shift?"

"I normally take it. Don't need much sleep at my age, and as long as I get a solid night every few days, I don't start talking to myself. Well, 'night,'" he added, glancing toward the twilight sky of August. He grinned and shifted his arm under Dec's head. "This little guy's sleep schedule has vastly improved, but we're still fans of midnight snacking, aren't we?" he asked the baby, who sucked at his bottle as if he hadn't eaten in days.

Ennis hesitated, then cleared his throat. "When you say 'at my age'…"

Colin gave him a long, appraising stare, and Ennis was struck once again by his eyes, which seemed subtly *wrong* in a way that Ennis couldn't name. They were perfectly ordinary at first glance, but the longer he felt their weight on him, the more strongly blatted the warning klaxon deep in his mind.

"Eight hundred sixty-four, I think," said Colin as

nonchalantly as if he were discussing the weather. "And before you ask, yes, I'm ten times her age, our relationship sometimes has its weird moments, but age doesn't mean as much for us when looking for a partner."

"And, uh…you're…"

"Fae. Half fae, to be technical about it. I'm Kenna all grown up." He pulled the bottle from Dec's mouth, watched the last few drops slide down the inside, then held his son to his shoulder and began patting his back. "Do you believe me, or do you think I'm insane? I used to be able to tell, but with magic gone, I can't poke around in other people's heads anymore."

Ennis decided that wasn't such a bad thing, but he kept his opinion to himself. "You sound nuts, but there were those orbs that came out of nowhere, and then…what was his name?"

"Kuni. Thought he might do the trick. We've got a few people here with shifting abilities," he added, "but Kuni was the less terrifying option."

"Shifting? Like…werewolves?"

"Yes, but there's no full moon necessary, and do *not* use that term. They consider it a slur. Trust me, you don't want to piss off a lupine shifter."

"Noted."

After Dec burped, Colin said, "You have questions. We can do this now, or we can wait for daylight."

"Honestly, I don't even know where to begin," Ennis mumbled. "This…*all* of this…I mean, this never came up at Wharton, you know?"

Colin laughed. "And that's the way we like it. You're taking the news well, by the way."

"I think I'm too numb to find the energy for a full-blown freak-out right now, so…" He shifted Kenna, who'd begun to slide from the crook of his arm, and sighed. "My sister's dead, her daughter isn't quite human, and I've got an armed compound full of magical creatures in my backyard." Glancing up, he found Colin watching him again, then quickly looked away. "What do I need to know?"

Nestling Dec between a pair of pillows on the middle couch cushion as the baby yawned, Colin said, "Well, first, we're not going to hurt you. That hasn't changed. Second, you have good instincts. Trust them—you'll live longer."

"Huh?"

"You get twitchy when you look into my eyes. It's a normal reaction, don't try to deny it," he assured Ennis. "It's hard to say exactly what you're seeing, but we develop that disconcerting appearance around our centennial. Toula's well on her way there. It's like the face and the eyes don't match, right?"

"I'm sorry—"

He waved the apology aside. "Don't be. If I stare at Val too long and really think about it, I get creeped out, too. It's…" He paused, considering his words. "I'd say it's a warning from deep in the lizard part of your brain, but Frank would be *highly* offended if I said that, so let's not mention this conversation around him, eh?"

Ennis frowned—Frank was huge, yes, but Ennis had never seen him so much as miffed. "Why would that—"

"Upset Frank? Half dragon, quarter fae, and all sorts of mixed up about it. One of the aforementioned shifters. In case of bear attack, he's our best weapon."

It took Ennis a moment to process that information, and even then, his mind still refused to fully accept it. "So, uh…*dragons*?"

"Not anymore," Colin murmured. "He and Aurie were the only ones who escaped Faerie, and Conota—that was another realm kind of like Faerie—collapsed at the same time. The species is native to that realm, but we had a decent population, too. All gone."

Unsure of what else to say, Ennis managed, "I'm sorry."

"Me, too. And if Val and I hadn't been trying so hard to prevent a war with the fucking Arcanum, we might still have a realm to call home."

"You're going to need to back up a bit. And since it's not quite two a.m. and I'm not at all functioning at full capacity, use small words, will you?"

"Sure. Just a moment."

As Kenna finished her bottle, Colin returned from the kitchen with a pair of tumblers, a fifth of bourbon, and a fresh burp cloth draped over one shoulder. "Here," he said, passing the cloth to Ennis before Kenna could drool all over him. "Are you drinking?"

"I'd better not."

"Fair. If you change your mind, feel free," he replied, and poured a healthy double. Sitting back on the couch, swirling the amber liquid, he said, "So, the short version. This universe in which we currently find ourselves is known to those of us in the magical community as the mortal realm. The Conotan peoples had their own terms, but let's keep it simple. Outside of this realm were Faerie and Conota. Don't ask me for the details of the cosmic arrangement—we tend to think about the realms like soap bubbles touching each other, if that helps."

"Okay, I'm following," said Ennis as he tried to coax a burp from Kenna.

"Faerie was the source of an energy commonly known as magic. Conota was the source of another one we called dark magic. Most of us who are sensitive to these energies can manipulate one of them. Faeries enchant, wizards use spellcraft—"

"*Wizards?*"

He raised a finger as he took a sip of bourbon. "Almost everyone here who doesn't appear to be your age is a wizard. They're mortal, but they can live longer than most."

"So, like…Doc?"

He nodded. "Bee's an excellent wizard. Her wife is decently talented, too. Then you've got people like Antony Copeland—have you met him and Madison?"

"Sure," said Ennis. The Copelands had stopped by his makeshift bar for the Super Bowl, a polite, middle-aged couple with a teenage daughter.

"Madison's very gifted. Antony's a wizard if you squint, but he's a borderline witch—they're like wizards with less talent," Colin explained. "Anyway, he and Bee are of an age, and so is Ros Bolin. They were actually in school together for a year."

Ennis tried to square his mental images of Bee and Antony with Ros, who seemed young enough to be their daughter.

"Incidentally," Colin continued, "we learned after you flew out that Ros is expecting. Due in November, so that'll make five kids here. Where was I?"

"Wizards, I think…"

"*Right.*" He paused to drink again. "The main body keeping wizards from going full supervillain was called the Arcanum. Trained them and hid them away to prevent persecution and such. They had a separatist offshoot called the Minor Arcanum—I don't know what's become of them since the collapse—and there was a third group operating in this realm and in Faerie, the Fringe, for witches, lesser-blooded fae, witch-bloods…" Catching Ennis's befuddlement, he explained, "Those of us who are half fae are as talented as our full-blooded peers—same perks, same drawbacks, but we tend to be less psychopathic."

"Oh, *good.*"

He smiled. "Go lower than half, however, and you run into problems. Quarter fae may have some power, or they may have youth and longevity, or they may have almost nothing. It's a mixed bag. So the lesser bloods, if they were even aware of their heritage, usually wound up in the Fringe. Now, a witch-blood—witch-blooded fae, to be precise—is a person with fae and wizard genes, usually half and half. They're normally untalented. Toula's the great exception—she can cast with the best of them, and she can enchant far better than someone of her age has any right to do," he said with undisguised admiration—"but most are powerless. My brother was in that camp until Faerie tweaked him."

"I...what?"

"Getting there. Back to the Arcanum. It's been around since the eleventh century. Ed founded it—"

"Wait, *wait*...Ed? He's younger than I am!"

Colin made a face. "Yes and no. He lived into his eighties, built the Arcanum after a bloody fifty-year war, committed genocide, tried to kill my mother...understandably, she didn't take that well...and then he faked his death and wrapped himself in a slow-acting rejuvenation spell to repair some of the damage. He meant to sleep for a few decades, but he ended up entombed for almost a thousand years, and the spell sort of...*rewound* him, so the current iteration of Ed has his previous version's memories and a healthy case of self-loathing. But that's Eadwig for you. He was the Arcanum's first grand magus, and Toula was the last real one. The Council, in its wisdom, decided to kick her out of office in favor of a guy your age."

"Why?" asked Ennis.

"The Arcanum had a real problem with witch-bloods. Toula seized power because she's a better wizard than any of the magi on the Council, and she didn't always play nice with the assholes with pedigrees stretching back to Ed who thought they were her betters. That," he said, "and Val."

Ennis thought of the dark-haired man with the unplaceable accent who'd gone hunting with them the previous winter. Val wasn't great with a shotgun, but he could expertly butcher a carcass. "What's wrong with him?"

Colin drained his glass before answering. "So, Faerie had a three-monarch system. Everyone belonged to one of the courts, and the king or queen's rule was law. Val and

Toula's mother was one of the original queens, and he eventually inherited her throne after I killed her. The fact that Toula was a high lady and in line for that throne didn't make her popular in the Arcanum."

"You killed your *mother-in-law*?" he asked, aghast.

"She wasn't my mother-in-law then, and she was trying to convince Toula to kill me," Colin protested. "Also, Toula had just killed *my* mother, so…you know, nothing brings people together like reciprocal matricide."

"Why the hell did Toula kill your mother?"

"*Shh*," said Colin, pointing to sleeping Dec, and Ennis grimaced in apology. "Because Mother had just burned one of my brothers alive and was probably going to kill the rest of us there, so it was justified. But, uh…Mother was a queen, too, and I inherited…"

Ennis's jaw sagged. "You're…a king?"

Colin glanced at his ratty sweatpants, then nodded. "I was. Sure you're not drinking?"

A moment later, with Kenna sleeping comfortably on the rug, Ennis sipped the smooth bourbon and stared at the ceiling. "Holy shit," he muttered.

"Did I mention that Val is twenty-two hundred years old?" asked Colin, who had struck a similar pose. "He looks at me like I'm ten sometimes."

"*Shit.*"

"Keep drinking. You're doing well, kid."

Ennis tried to corral his thoughts into a semblance of order. "Okay. You've got the Arcanum here, you and Val in Faerie—"

"And there was a third," Colin interrupted. "Eleanor, for a few decades. Her sister killed her for the throne just before everything went to hell, and I have no idea where *she* ended up. Might have died in Faerie, for all I know."

"Three, then. So what happened?"

"A perfect storm. Irem—that's Eleanor's sister, Irem—freed her court to do whatever they liked in this realm, and they started kidnapping kids."

"*Why?*"

Colin glanced his way. "Ever heard of a changeling?"

"Like, in stories…"

"Glorified kidnapping. I was raised by a changeling, actually. My mother snatched her from her family and told her to keep me alive, and bless her, she did. Anyway, Val and I tried to reason with Irem, we got Toula involved, and then the Council found out what was going on. They kicked Toula out and installed the idiot child, and he basically declared war on us. But he also pardoned Kitty and Beth's mother—"

Ennis's brow puckered. "Hold on, I thought she was dead."

"We don't know. She's been in the wind for years. Ended up incarcerated with her buddy after they almost killed Maria."

"The Maria who lives here?"

"Yeah, Maria Corelli. Val raised her, and he did *not* take that kindly. So those two got out and told the new grand magus exactly what he wanted to hear, and I won't bore you with the thaumaturgical specifics, but they used some of Ed's notes and a *massive* power source to obliterate Faerie and Conota. The idiot child thought they'd just seal the border but keep magic flowing. They tricked him, fucked us all over, and went on the run…and Val and I took the people we could find, along with a few of the Arcanum's refugees, and headed north."

"I thought you said the Arcanum was in this realm."

"Oh, it was, but they had to destroy their bases of operation. Wouldn't do to have castles and such suddenly appearing, and with no magic left, what's the point of calling yourself a wizard? They're just long-lived mortals now with a better than rudimentary knowledge of medieval Latin."

Ennis finished his drink, then poured a second round. "Okay," he said with a sigh, "let me make sure I'm clear. You, Val, and Toula are fae and, like…royalty?"

"More or less," said Colin. "And my brother, Aiden…and then there's Marcus."

"He's Val's brother?"

"No, his son."

In Ennis's mind, the two men seemed to be of an age. As he mulled that over, a thought occurred to him. "Wait, how old is Marcus?"

Colin groaned. "It's complicated."

"How is *that* a complicated question?"

"Mentally, he's about Kitty's age. Physically, he was born in the late Roman Republic and spent a couple millennia in stasis. Similar story for Artur: maybe a year or two older than Kitty in her own head, but on paper, she's somewhere north of fifteen hundred. Like I said, complicated."

"Jesus," Ennis whispered, and took a sip.

"Did I mention that she's King Arthur?"

His bourbon returned in a choking spray. "What?" he gasped between coughs.

Colin thumped him between the shoulder blades. "The fancy sword from last night is Excalibur…or whatever she calls it, same difference. Biologically, she and Kitty are Myrddin's kids. Do *not* mention him—fair warning."

"Holy shit," he said again, and drank. "So, uh…they're all fae, but Ed and Beth aren't?"

"Exactly."

"Okay. And Doc isn't, but Ros is…and Sam?"

"Yeah. He's one of Eleanor's nephews, actually. And Ros was the realm before the collapse…I didn't tell you about that, did I?" he said as Ennis frowned. "Faerie and Conota each had a consciousness—incredibly powerful, omniscient within the realm, able to do all sorts of things that even Val and I couldn't touch. Faerie—the realm, we called her—was the source of the kings' and queens' power," he explained. "But it's a position that's been filled by multiple people, and Ros was the last one to have that gig. She's technically witch-blooded, raised a wizard, but she seems functionally fae these days. Her predecessor was able to give Aiden talent, and Ros worked on Maria, Marcus, Artur, and Kitty. She's the one who said Faerie's gone, and she would know better than anyone." Colin leaned back and stared at the wall. "If there were any hope that Faerie was still out there, I'd move heaven and earth to find a way back. But there isn't, so we're here now, squatting on your nice hunting property."

"You can stay," Ennis murmured.

Colin perked. "Yeah? After all that?"

"I've read my share of fairytales, man. I'm not pissing off what's left of you people."

"Then I shall refrain from throwing curses involving spinning wheels at your daughter," Colin replied with mock solemnity. "Speaking of whom, what are your plans?"

"Shit," Ennis moaned, "I have no idea. I had to get out of California, but…I mean, how do you even raise a faerie?"

"The same way you'd raise any other kid, especially now that there's no magic. She'll have a bad temper, and we can help you teach her to manage it. And she can't have a puppy, no matter how much she begs. But other than that….feed and clothe her, put a roof over her head, and love her. The basics, yeah?" He paused, studying Ennis, then murmured, "Toula and I spoke last night after you went to bed. Fatherhood was obviously nowhere in your immediate plans earlier this summer. If this is too much—I mean, if you don't want to deal with a fae child—then we'd be happy to raise her with Dec. You have an out if you want it."

He gazed at the sleeping baby on the rug for a long, silent moment. "I promised her I'd take care of her. Thanks, but I'm not giving her up."

"You're a good man, Ennis."

Laughing weakly, he asked, "Any pointers? I take it this isn't your first rodeo in eight hundred freaking years."

Colin flashed a strained smile. "Dec's the first I've raised. I fathered a daughter about seventy years ago, but I didn't know she existed until she was a teenager."

Though something cautioned him that he was treading on thin ice, Ennis asked, "Did she make it out of Faerie?"

"She died when she was forty. I...tried to fix the mess my mother made with her, and I took the easy option instead of the right one, and she never forgave me. Tried to kill me. Tried to kill her own mother, too, and I...well." He shook his head. "I don't think I'm drunk enough to go there, if it's all the same to you."

"Sure, sure, I'm sorry," Ennis hastily replied. "You just seemed *competent* with Dec, and I assumed..."

"Appreciated, but that's largely due to the Stowes. You've met Rohese and Martin?"

"Oh, yeah. He's one of the brothers, right?"

"No. They're the *parents* of that brood. Thirteen all told, but two didn't make it out of Faerie. Mal's their grandson. Anyway, those two know a few things about the care and feeding of children, and if you have any questions, they'll be happy to set you straight. Rohese is a sucker for babies, so once she hears about Kenna, she'll be all over you."

"Thirteen kids," Ennis mumbled.

"Yeah, but over five hundred years. Twelve of them boys, mind you, and all very fond of their mother." As Dec twitched in his sleep, Colin rubbed the baby's head. "Toula and I wanted one of our own. She was the Arcanum's unwanted foster kid, and like I said, I was raised by a changeling. I only met my father once before he died. We want to do right by this little one." Glancing back at Ennis, he said, "I shouldn't have to tell you you're welcome on your own land, but you're welcome here. If you want help with Kenna, you'll have it."

"I don't want to interfere—"

"You're not. Hell, half this place loves you for TV and wine, and the rest think of you as the nice boy who's not all that great at homesteading yet. No one wants to see you struggle."

"Thanks," he murmured.

The two sat on the couch in silence, nursing their drinks as their children slept.

"Are you pulling my leg, or are you actually a king?" Ennis blurted.

Colin chuckled into his glass. "Had a giant throne and everything. A palace. My own personal army. A cook. Moon and stars, I miss the ability to pull food from thin air."

"Sounds nice."

"*Booze* was even nicer. The upcharge in this state is astronomical!"

"You know, Colin, I *do* own a controlling share of a fairly successful winery."

"I had noticed."

"Suppose I could bring a few more cases back after my next trip south."

"That would be quite neighborly of you. Incidentally," he said, "it's Coileán."

"Hm?"

"My name. 'Colin' is a newer form, and I made up the surname. But I've spent a long time in this realm, so I'm not picky about it. Just thought you should know, seeing as you're in on this now."

"Coileán," Ennis repeated, trying it out. "Your Majesty."

He shook his head. "'My lord,' if you must, but please don't."

"Works for me." Ennis reached his right hand across sleeping Dec, and Coileán shook it.

That night wasn't the end of Ennis's surprises. Moving into a magical community, even one devoid of magic, isn't for the faint of heart. He had a shock to the system the first time he witnessed Mal Stowe shift into his massive lupine form during a hunt and take down a moose by himself, then an even larger one that winter when a trio of starving wolves came around and Frank had himself a snack. Though unable to breathe fire without dark magic, Frank was nearly as long as a 747 in full draconic form, and his teeth made short work of the threat. Ennis, who'd run out of his cabin with a shotgun on hearing the racket, reached the scene via snowmobile in time to watch Frank shift back. As he goggled, Frank noticed him, slipped on a bathrobe, then belched and grinned.

The accumulated weirdness of the compound would have driven a lesser man away, but Ennis decided that Alaska was the best place for Kenna to grow up. He had a doctor on hand in case of scrapes and bruises, four other children Kenna's age for her to play with, and a willing babysitter in Aurie. Luce Stowe offered him cooking lessons to expand his bachelor's repertoire, Rohese had tips for every developmental phase, and several of the compound's adults pulled together to form a makeshift school once the children came of age. As former magi, Maria and Arnold Lowe had taught during their Arcanum tenure, two of the Stowe brothers had previously taught literature and debate in the Fringe's school, and the parents all took turns either instructing their kids or maintaining order in the home classroom.

To Ennis's delight, Kenna flourished. After her first difficult months, she grew into a healthy baby, then a rambunctious little brown-haired, blue-eyed girl who kept pace with the others. Aside from her odd allergies and her hot temper—Coileán hadn't lied about that—she seemed perfectly normal, albeit terribly nearsighted. Bee had noticed Kenna's squinting early on, and Ennis had returned from an ophthalmologist in Fairbanks with a baby-sized pair of pink plastic glasses before Kenna's first birthday. Between taking his turn in the classroom and calling in to meetings, he continued to make regular flights for the compound, providing much-appreciated quick access to food and other supplies. Soon, he traded in his plane for a larger model, one better equipped to ferry passengers. After all, growing children needed clothes, and their loving parents occasionally needed a weekend at a hotel away from it all.

Sylvia continued to encourage Ennis to come south, but Sonoma had lost its luster for him. The people who had made that place home to him were gone, and he jealously guarded his new home's secrets. The refugees were the young king's people now, and he would protect them.

Noblesse oblige, after all.

CHAPTER 4

Twenty-two years later, Ennis and Kenna were still living on the property, but only Ennis remained in his cabin. Kenna had moved into our six-occupant bachelor pad after graduation, which wasn't so different from our apartment in Anchorage beyond its size and the fact that Aurie was living with us. Well, that, plus the utter lack of civilization. As much as I loved the scenery of home, I really missed fast food and our trivia nights at our favorite brewpub.

I rose early Tuesday morning and wandered from my second-floor bedroom into the kitchen, following the smell of French roast. Seeing Kenna sitting on the counter by the sink and staring out the window at the brightening sky of dawn, I mumbled, "Hey. Can I poach?"

"Made a full pot," she replied, and scratched her stomach through her well-worn T-shirt. Her glasses were smudged and sat crookedly on her face, and I gathered that making coffee was the only bit of productive action Kenna had yet taken that day.

"Did you not sleep well?" I asked as I dug the milk from the refrigerator. We'd grown up almost exclusively on shelf-stable boxed milk, and I unscrewed the cap for a whiff. Still fresh, albeit barely.

"The noise woke me," Kenna muttered.

"What noise?"

"What do you mean, what noise? Shut up and listen."

Humoring her, I closed the fridge and concentrated, trying to hear anything more exotic than the humming appliance beside me and the hiss of the air conditioner in the den window. "I don't hear anything."

She frowned as I doctored my coffee. "You don't hear that staticky noise? Like...I don't know, like someone's got a TV muted in the next room?"

"No," I replied, baffled.

A flicker of movement outside the window caught my attention, and I leaned over the sink for a better view. Odd—it looked like fog, but the sky was blue and brightening. Hoping it wasn't smoke from a distant forest fire, I left Kenna to her breakfast and slipped into the den to look for signs of life.

Unsurprisingly, I found Edie asleep in our secondhand recliner with her tablet lying on her chest, her white forelock tumbling over her eye. Nothing new there—I'd awakened many a morning in college to find that my cousin had passed out over her work the night before. Edie had always been a voracious reader, especially if she could find books in print. When Ennis flew us to town as young teenagers, he'd drop her off at the library with a few bucks and let her raid the secondhand bookshop in the back room, and she'd meet us with a tote bag full of paperbacks and a beaming smile. But her taste hadn't been limited to fiction—Edie would read anything she could get her hands on, and her tendency to fall asleep over her latest book hadn't abated with graduation.

The greatest injustice of her life, as she saw it, was that Toula had locked away the Arcanum's library and its archival holdings in the castle known as Arc 2 before shrinking the complex and storing it within a snow globe. Never mind that those books were useless without magic—we'd read some of the scanned copies of Arcanum texts saved on Toula's and Maria's computers and tried the techniques, to no avail. Edie still felt cheated.

My brother had confided to me that the former magi in the compound felt that Edie had the makings of a magus, assuming she possessed talent. Given her paternity, she would probably have made a better than average wizard, and Ed agreed that her scholar's temperament would be an asset. But there were no more magi, no more wands to be wielded, no more Arcanum in need of gifted wizards to guide its path, and so Edie had to content herself with the paltry offerings of the library that had once existed. The salvaged books were few and esoteric, and the end result of reading them for Edie was like going in search of the Library of Alexandria and returning with only a handful of charred scrolls.

Despite the lack of magic, she'd been given an education in the rudiments of thaumaturgy, just as the rest of us had. Our tutors had taught us about the Arcanum and the courts, the realms and their conflicts. Kuni had shared his memories of Faerie's long civil war, while Ed, making no excuses for his prior self's actions, has relayed the gory history of the Arcanum's Great War once he deemed us old enough to hear the details. Toula, Maria, and Kitty had taught us about wards and stacks and focusing techniques, both those designed for spellcraft and those that would boost an enchantment's power, but without magic, the lectures were purely theoretical. Though Edie took careful notes, none of the rest of us could see much point in studying something we'd never use.

The same went for our language classes. While my family had done their best to raise me as trilingual, I always favored English over Latin or Fae. I could see a point to studying Latin, if only to boost my standardized test vocabulary, but as for Fae...well, while it was good for private conversations, it was surely a dying tongue. I'd never met anyone outside of the compound who could speak it but for Bert Wold, a former grand magus who kept in touch from Glastonbury. In terms of practicality, I thought I'd have been better served learning Klingon. But Edie made it look easy. Like her father, she was a natural polyglot, and she took extra language classes in college for the fun of it. We might have hated her around exam time had she not been so willing to help her roomies study.

As I nudged Edie awake, Dec limped down the stairs, clutching the banister and squinting at the morning. "Still not over Mina?" I asked with a smirk.

"*Drugs*," he grunted.

Rolling my eyes, I took the Advil from the pill stash in the kitchen and underhanded him the bottle. "Are you too wounded to get your own water to wash that down?"

In response, he dry-swallowed a pair of capsules and tossed the bottle back to me. "Wouldn't say no to coffee," he hinted.

"Sit, you big baby," I replied, and pulled another mug from the cabinet while he slid onto a stool with a dramatic sigh. "Any sign of Gaw yet, or is he sleeping in? He didn't crash in my room last night."

While Gaw and I had been a couple for years, our parents had still pretended that we needed our own rooms when they moved us into the bachelor pad. Personally, I didn't mind the extra closet space, and Gaw and I went back and forth between our beds, depending on which of us had more recently done laundry.

"I saw a light on in the bathroom, so he's probably up," said Dec.

Glancing to my left, I caught sight of my brother. "Did you ask about Gaw?" he enquired.

His English being less than conversational, I didn't mind repeating myself. *Have you seen him?*

"Bathroom. He's been awake all night. *Vomiting.*"

That gave me pause, and a frisson of fear raced up my spine. If Gaw could get sick…

Perhaps divining the cause of my distress, Publius added, "He doesn't seem ill. He's not feverish or sweating. Mina hit hard yesterday, and I wonder if she didn't cause it."

If that's the case, he's probably bleeding internally, and we need to get him to Fairbanks, I replied, uncomforted by his analysis. *If she ruptured something important—*

"Cici? *Cici*," Kenna demanded, snapping her fingers in front of my face. "Hello? Are you with us?"

I realized how I looked—staring into space, a mug clutched in my hands—and put the cup on the counter. "I've got to check on Gaw. Dec, pour your own coffee."

Jogging up the stairs, I found Gaw curled up on the fuzzy blue bathmat, covered by a beach towel. He was frowning in his sleep, and he seemed paler than usual to me. I crouched beside him and gently shook him awake. "Gaw?" I murmured as his eyelids fluttered. "Hey, sweetie, are you okay?"

"I don't know," he mumbled, his voice gravelly. "What time…"

"About seven-thirty. You want some coffee? Or tea? Might be easier on your stomach."

"How did you…*oh*," he said as he sat up against the cabinets. "Did Publius hear me?"

I checked over my shoulder and found my brother watching from the hallway. "At least," I told Gaw. "Be honest with me—have you been throwing up blood? If you have, we need to get you out of here."

He laughed weakly. "Ennis won't be back until this afternoon, so if I'm dying, I'm out of luck. But no, no blood. Just…queasy as hell. It's weird." When I didn't immediately relax, he said, "I swear, it feels like a bad hangover. I'm not sick, Cici."

"You don't know that," I murmured. None of us but Kenna had been aurally examined, and yes, Gaw's mother had once been the freaking *realm*, but if he'd ended up a witch-blood with unfortunate allergies…

"I'll be fine," he insisted, and pushed himself to his feet. "But tea does sound nice, if you're offering."

He patted his blond cowlick flat, and I helped him down to the kitchen. As we rounded the corner, I spotted Dec marking off another day on our big wall calendar, which featured a kitschy collection of tropical beach photos that year. He'd been the keeper of the back-to-college calendar since we were admitted, and he made a point of crossing off each day with an X in black marker. Of course, we wouldn't be returning to Anchorage that August, but Dec had instead marked the traditional departure date with "Bora Bora," a sad reminder of our escape plans that never went anywhere.

Only Aurie and Kenna had ever left Alaska. Kenna didn't remember California, and Aurie seldom spoke of her year in the castle in Glastonbury or of her few days in Faerie. All six of us had talked about packing our bags and heading south, just as Allie and her husband had done, but our parents seemed pained every time the notion was floated. The truth of the matter was that for everyone but Edie, we'd have to come home eventually, back to a place where we didn't need convincing identification. As for my cousin, she was something of a homebody, happy wherever she was as long as she had a pile of books at hand.

While I put on the water for tea, Aurie came in the side door, her short arm clutching a dozen plastic packages to her chest. I saw the label on one and grinned. "Did you leave them *any* bacon?"

"Enough," she protested, and stuffed several pounds of it into our chest freezer. "I'm putting a pack or two on. Does anyone else want in?"

"Ooh, *yes*," said Dec, raising his hand.

Aurie looked him over and snorted. "Get a third pack, then. You're on draining duty."

The eldest of us by a few years and nearly an adult by the time Gaw came along, Aurie was relatively slender but had a hearty appetite. As an obligate carnivore, she would even eat potted meat in a pinch, and she and Frank had permanent dibs on the offal of anything brought back from a hunt. She'd spent years keeping us from killing ourselves as kids, and when our parents gave us the bachelor pad, Aurie got a room as well. While she adored her father and grandfather, who lived together in a tidy house near one of the walls, Aurie had long wanted space of her own, and the five of us were finally old enough to be her housemates instead of her charges.

"What time is your dad due in, Kenna?" asked Aurie as she started heating the copper skillet.

Kenna plucked her phone off the table and scrolled through her messages. "About two, he thinks. Inspection was good, so he's doing the heavy shopping with Maria this morning."

"You know it's our turn to schlepp, right?"

The rest of us groaned, particularly Dec, whose limp suddenly grew more pronounced as he hobbled around the kitchen.

Offloading was one of my least favorite chores, but everyone took a turn. Ennis's hangar was about a mile away, sandwiched between the compound and his cabin, and since most of his cargo was for us, it wasn't fair to ask him to handle the unpacking and distribution. During the summer, he made flights to Fairbanks about once every other week to stock up ahead of the winter, so the plane would be loaded down with cans and dried goods. We'd avoided offloading to that point, but Aurie was right—our time had come around.

The problem was offloading was twofold. First, I had to layer up with long sleeves, long pants, and thick gloves to protect myself from the metal plane and its cargo. Second, as gasoline was expensive and reserved for snowmobiles and trips off the property, we hauled everything on foot. The trail between the hangar and the compound was relatively flat, but still, lugging cases of food on wooden carts was never fun.

"Suck it up, buttercup," Kenna told Dec as he massaged his sore leg. "Your other option is playtime with Mina…"

"I'll haul," he muttered, and opened a pack of bacon. "Who wants to be in charge of eggs?"

Ennis and Maria arrived on schedule, none the worse for wear after a few days in the city, and as we unpacked the plane, they laughed about the progressively more ridiculous cover stories they'd employed to explain a graying fifty-year-old man and a pretty brunette who, though three years his senior, looked young enough to be his daughter. "We never got quite as far as 'mail-order bride,'" said Maria, thickening her natural Italian accent as she slipped into the role, "but…how you say…"

"We didn't want to tank the Hayward brand for my indiscretions," Ennis replied, grinning back at her. "And I'm *pretty* sure Val would kill me if we started that rumor."

I concurred with a grunt as I pushed a loaded carton out of the plane and into Dec's waiting arms. Avus seldom blew his top, the result of long work, but he was touchy where Maria was concerned. That she and Ennis were friendly caused him no heartburn, but in recent years, with Kenna off at college, their relationship had begun to slowly shift toward romance. Kenna had no objection, but she agreed with me that the situation was bittersweet at best. Maria had never found love in Faerie or within the Arcanum's ranks, and when she finally met someone, he was mortal. If Ennis saw another fifty years, he'd be lucky. But they were making the best of it, odd couple though they seemed to people on the street, and Kenna didn't begrudge her father a few days out of town with his girlfriend.

As we loaded the carts, Aurie took care to strap her cargo down with canvas and bungee cords. She was the strongest of us by a significant margin—even with only one hand, she could pull more than double what Dec or Gaw managed to push with two—but large loads had a nasty habit of toppling on the uneven ground, and Aurie had learned to compensate.

When I was younger, I'd asked my parents about Aurie and how she'd lost her arm. My imagination had suggested bears, but the reality was far less gruesome: she was born that way. A transformation bind had given her a functional second hand for her first year of life, but when magic disappeared, that spell broke, leaving Aurie with a stump below the elbow. Ennis offered for years to take her to a specialist and have a prosthetic made, but she declined. By the time he'd moved in, she'd adjusted to the loss.

With the offloading under control, Maria helped Aurie finish her strapping, then set off for the cabin with Ennis and his small stash of goods to load his pantry. Half an hour later, with the plane empty and our carts laden, the six of us started the long trek back to the compound to make deliveries. As usual on those walks, we went armed. The hike from the hangar to the walls of home wasn't particularly dangerous, but when one was plodding along with a cart full of food, one was an easy target, and prudence dictated that we take precautions. I wore a .38 on my hip, safely separated from my skin by clothing and a nylon holster, while Dec and Edie, who lacked my iron allergy, carried rifles over their shoulders.

We were nearing the halfway point, passing through a stand of trees on a trail barely half again as wide as a snowmobile, when Edie said, "What's that?"

Stopping in our tracks, we followed her finger toward a hunched shape deep within the stretch of woods separating us from the lake. I squinted through the fog, which seemed only to have thickened over the course of the day, and tried to make out the contours of the animal's form. Whatever it was, it sure as hell wasn't a moose.

"Bear?" Gaw whispered beside me.

"I don't think so."

Aurie lifted a finger for silence, then closed her eyes, opened her mouth slightly, and lifted her face. The tip of her tongue twice darted from between her lips, and her nose crinkled. "It's not a bear," she murmured. "And it smells *wrong*. We need to get out of here."

"What about the stuff?" Kenna asked.

"Maybe we can scare it," Dec suggested, pulling his

rifle into position. Edie followed suit, and the rest of us drew our pistols. "*If* it comes this way. It could wander off…"

His wishful sentiment died as the creature stood. I couldn't be precise about its size at that distance, but Gaw was six feet tall, and that thing had to be twice his height. Its chest was built like a gorilla's, broad and muscular, and as it sniffed the air, it focused on us.

"The *fuck* is that?" Edie whispered. "Is it…that can't be a yeti, can it?"

"We're not staying here to find out," said Aurie, pushing Edie back from the trees. "Go, run. If I shift, I can buy us some time—"

"Shift *where*?" she snapped. "You don't have enough space! And I'm not leaving you here on three legs."

Suddenly, the creature broke into a run, making as much of a beeline for us as the woods would allow, and the discussion ceased. "*Go!*" Aurie bellowed, and no one argued with her.

Kenna and Edie took the lead. Gaw still seemed out of sorts after his rough night, but Aurie grabbed him and yanked him along, leaving Dec and me to bring up the rear. Every few seconds, he and I turned and shot at the monster, but all we accomplished was antagonizing it. Though the creature roared when one of Dec's bullets hit true, it barely slowed.

As we ran for the meadow between the woods and the compound, I realized the mistake we were about to make. The trees had offered us a slight bit of protection, but once we hit open ground, our pursuer would be able to make up for lost time. I doubted we could outrun it, and as I sprinted from the woods, the gate in the wall had never seemed so far away. Still, I shot at the beast until I ran out of bullets, and then Dec and I tore after the others, screaming for help.

The ground behind us was shaking with the force of the creature's galloping footsteps when the gate flew open and my grandfather ran out, sword in hand and guns on his hips. "*Inside!*" he shouted, waving us on. "Aurie, get Frank! *Call for him!*"

The draconic members of our community hadn't lost their natural telepathic abilities when magic was wiped out, but what little part of my brain wasn't then devoted to gasping for breath and panicking at my imminent disembowelment wondered how much good Frank could do. Assuming Aurie was close enough for him to hear her, he'd still have to get outside and shift—and with the houses built as close as they were, I didn't think he'd have room to get to full size within the compound. Whether he could complete the shift on the wing was a purely academic diversion, as I feared I was about to feel teeth on either side of my spine.

But adrenaline pushed us on, and the creature hadn't quite managed to close the distance before we reached Avus. "What *is* that?" I panted as Edie took up her stance and started firing.

"Troll. Get inside," he barked, holding his sword at the ready.

I wasn't leaving him to fend for himself. Grabbing one of his guns from its holster, I shot at the beast's eyes, hoping to blind it, but my shaking hands sent the bullets flying wide. Some of our shots *had* hit it—I could see dark blood oozing down its gray flank as it bore down on us— but even the pain of fresh gunshot wounds didn't scare it away.

A flash to my right made me look away from the oncoming danger for an instant, and I hoped someone had arrived with a flare. Instead, to my astonishment, the burst of light was emanating from *Gaw*, who had closed his eyes and was whimpering in pain. "What the hell…" I began.

Beside me, I heard Avus incredulously mutter, "Moon and stars."

I glanced back at him as he dropped his sword and clasped his hands in front of him. "What are you doing?" I cried, fearing he was going to attempt to wrestle the troll.

Instead, the air around Avus's hands seemed to burst into brilliant streams of color, and as he bared his teeth, he tightened his arms, then ripped his hands apart in one swift motion.

The troll *split*, just as if an invisible saw had landed between its eyes and cut it in half. The pieces stumbled and fell at our feet, and as Edie screamed, Gaw toppled into the grass, unconscious. His strange light faded as quickly as it had appeared, and I called his name, begging him to hear me, while Dec retched at the stench of troll guts.

Our elders could agree that the creature was a troll, and there was no way that Avus could have sliced it in two with his bronze sword. Beyond that, no one had any clear answers.

"That's enchantment," Aiden declared, standing by the corpse as Ennis puked off to one side. "I saw Val kill a troll like that when I was a kid—he saved my life, I wouldn't forget *that* day."

"There was magic here," Avus insisted, though he stood by with his arms folded, almost as if he couldn't believe what he was seeing. "I saw it, I felt it, and what happened next was instinct."

Pa, who looked almost as green as Ennis as he examined the remains, pulled me closer. "Where did you find magic? Not Artur's sword—"

"It was Gaw," said Aurie, who leaned against Frank as he wrapped a protective arm around her. "He started glowing, and—"

"Glowing?" Pa echoed bemusedly. "What do you mean?"

She frowned as she considered the question. "Not like Ros used to—Ros was brighter. But I swear, one minute he was normal, and the next, he lit up, and Val did…*that*."

Glancing up at her father, she muttered, "Help yourself. I think I've lost my appetite."

"And another thing," said Coileán, who'd come out to inspect the damage. "Where the hell did a troll come from?"

"Maybe it's been hiding here all along," Pa offered. "This place is so wild…"

But Avus shook his head and looked at Coileán. "Are you thinking what I'm thinking?"

"Formaldehyde and gardenia," he replied. "And the smell's getting stronger. Are you seeing anything?"

He nodded. "I thought it might be smoke this morning. It's growing denser, but do you truly believe it's dark magic?"

Frank cleared his throat. "Allow me," he said, then pursed his lips and exhaled a thin jet of reddish-orange flame. "The internal combustion is back. It's the real deal, and I smell it, too."

"So do I," Aurie murmured.

Kenna, who'd been pinching her nose shut while she peered at the troll, straightened and scowled at Coileán and Avus. "What *smoke*? I don't see anything, I don't smell anything…"

"No strange sensations at all?" Coileán pressed.

She shrugged. "Just the staticky noise…what?" she asked as he cocked an eyebrow. "You hear it, too, right?"

He and Avus shook their heads. "Most of us see magic, remember," said Coileán. "I smell it. Sounds to me like you hear it instead."

That did nothing to improve her mood. "So…I'm going to have this weird noise in my ears as long as there's magic around?"

"Magic becomes part of the background after a while," he assured her. "If it lasts long enough, you'll start noticing it only in its absence. But we can work with you later. For now, the more important question is—"

"Where did it come from?" Avus finished. "And if the

concentration is rising…"

"A gate," Coileán murmured. "An outflow of dark magic. It's the only thing that makes sense." Holding Avus's stare, he said, "Maybe Conota wasn't destroyed after all. Perhaps it was merely sealed. If that seal is breaking…"

"Then dark magic will return to the mortal realm," Avus replied, "and we will be powerless to fight it. Artur's sword won't last long."

"Unless Gaw's been holding out on us." Cocking his head toward the wall, he said, "Let's go have a word with the boy. Ennis," he added as Kenna's father leaned unsteadily over a patch of soiled grass, "are you going to make it, or should we get Bee?"

Fortunately, Ennis pulled himself together, as Dr. Bee was occupied with Gaw inside her home. She'd wheeled a bed into the den for him when Dec and Avus carried him inside, but an hour after the incident, he had yet to regain consciousness. Dr. Bee couldn't find anything wrong with him other than profuse sweating, and so she kept an eye on the scene while Ros sat beside her son, sponging his face with a cold cloth.

"Ros," said Coileán as Aiden shut the front door, "we need to talk."

She barely looked up from her work, then testily muttered, "I'm a little busy."

Ignoring her, he pulled up a stool on the other side of the bed. "By all accounts, Gaw produced magic."

"You don't know that."

"Occam's Razor, kid. Everyone who was there said that he started glowing, and then Val found magic enough to rip a troll in two. Either there's a massive cache of hidden objects hemorrhaging magic somewhere beneath us that we've missed all these years, or else Gaw—"

"He's never done anything like that before," she protested.

"He's *your son*," said Coileán. "We don't even know

what you are now, Ros, but it's not illogical to think that the child of someone who was once the realm could have weird abilities."

"*I* never produced magic."

"Okay, then what's your theory?" he asked, leaning over Gaw. "What makes more sense than—"

Coileán jerked and fell silent when Aiden's hand clamped on his shoulder. "Another time, okay?" said Aiden. "Let's clear out and give Bee some space." Coileán's eyes narrowed, but Aiden held his stare and raised an eyebrow, and so he reluctantly stood and moved away from the bed. "Where's Sam, honey?" Aiden asked Ros.

"Went out hunting before dawn. If you see them return…"

"I'll send him," he promised, and ushered the others out of the house.

Dr. Bee pulled me back before I could be swept away with the flow. "Stay," she murmured. "I'm sure he'll want to see you when he wakes."

I didn't want to annoy Ros, but she seemed unbothered by my presence, and I pulled up Coileán's vacated stool to help her. After a moment, she said, "He should know better than to think I'm going to sit here and discuss thaumaturgical hypotheticals while my baby is unconscious."

"They think a gate into Conota has opened," I explained. "Can you see—"

"The dark magic? Sure. But the world can burn, for all I care, until I'm sure Gaw's all right," she said, glancing up to meet my gaze.

I nodded and continued to wipe his clammy skin, wondering what had happened to him but keeping my suppositions to myself.

Not for another hour did Gaw begin to stir, and once he

was sufficiently oriented to his surroundings to answer Dr. Bee's questions, he had no answers for us. "I don't know what happened," he confessed between sips of water. "One minute, that thing was running across the meadow, and the next..." He frowned into space. "I had this pins-and-needles sensation, and it was like something exploded behind my eyes, and then I was here." At the doctor's gentle prodding, he tried to recall the feeling and trigger it on his own, but nothing happened. If Gaw had made magic in our time of crisis, he hadn't consciously done so.

Sam arrived shortly thereafter, having returned from the woods with a pair of caribou and been hustled to his wife and son by Aiden, and I stepped out to give them privacy. As I walked down the gravel lane, I found a posse forming outside of my aunt and uncle's house. Ed stood in the scraggly yard, rifle across his back and sidearm over his jeans. Toula and Coileán were similarly equipped, though Artur and Avus had opted for swords in lieu of rifles. Rounding out their party were Frank, who appeared to be unarmed, and Nico, who had just returned from the *slightly* illegal hunting trip and was still sporting an orange vest.

"They're going in search of the gate," said a familiar voice behind me, and I turned to see Arnold Lowe watching the preparations with his hands in his trouser pockets.

Arnold was one of the least frequent of my regular visitors, but he'd made periodic appearances around the compound in the decade since his death at ninety-nine. He looked younger than I'd remembered him in life, closer to middle aged than to the unsteady senior he'd been. Arnold never had a message to pass along—for all I knew, he checked in out of sheer curiosity.

Any idea where it is? I asked.

"Certainly. It's on the southern side of the mountain," he said, pointing toward the peak rising to the west of the compound. "That little valley halfway up. At least it's not the gate of the Conclave days," he added with a grimace. "Far too close to their compound for safety, and *enormous*. This one's smaller but seems stable. I can't tell if it's natural or created—"

But Conota's on the other side?

He nodded. "Oh my, yes."

Is Faerie still out there, then? I pressed, my excitement mounting.

All Arnold could offer me was a shrug. "I can't say."

Is that an "I don't know" or an "I'm not allowed to tell you"?

"That's genuine ignorance, Cici. I've seen no sign of Faerie…but that's *definitely* Conota." As the reconnaissance party continued their rapid planning, he added, "Why don't you point them in the right direction? Don't say it's from me, just tell them where to go."

And then we need to figure out how to dispose of the troll, I added, imagining the stench of the job ahead.

But Arnold chuckled. "Nothing to worry about, my dear. Frank beat you to it."

The sun had set into the long twilight before the exploratory party returned. Despite his mother's fretting, Gaw had insisted on sleeping in his own bed that night, and he and I were sitting up at the kitchen table, playing canasta like a pair of biddies, when Frank came by.

"Aurie's in the shower," I announced when Dec let him in. "Want me to—"

"Nah," he said, wiping the dirt off his shoes. "I wouldn't say no to a glass of water, though…"

Dec headed for the sink as Frank slumped onto the couch and rubbed his shoulders. Dropping our cards, Gaw and I joined him in the den. "And?" I asked.

Frank nodded. "As predicted. Your source's information was good." The corner of his mouth twitched as he regarded me, and his red eyes crinkled. "Give Arnold my best the next time you see him, won't you?"

There was, I mused—and not for the first time—little to be gained by attempting to keep secrets around dragons. Frank's telepathy was almost too subtle for me to notice.

"How was the hike?" Dec asked, returning with Frank's drink.

"Well, they seem exhausted. I got close to the mountain and shifted to hunt from above, and I ended up making loops for a few hours. I could *smell* the damn thing, but with all the pines in the area, pinpointing it took some work…and the area was too small for me to come down safely, so I had to go overland about a quarter mile."

Gaw's brow furrowed. "Why not just partially shift back and land in the smaller space?"

"Because anything involving midair wing manipulation is a good way to fall," he replied, and drained the glass.

I tried not to think about poor Frank, forced to scramble across the mountainous terrain naked and barefoot while he waited for the rest of the party to join him with his bag. "Does it really lead to Conota?" I pressed as he leaned back against the couch. "The gate?"

"If not, then the realm on the other side is a dead ringer for it. Brown grass, black trees, thoroughly overcast…and it certainly smells right."

"Okay, what's the plan?" asked Dec as the shower cut off upstairs. "Do we go through? Try to find someone friendly?"

Frank arched an eyebrow. "There's a gate into Conota a few miles from here, we have no way to seal it, you kids were attacked by a troll, and you want to go poke around? It's been twenty-five years, Dec—we don't even know if Arik and Hope are still alive."

"So…no, then?"

"*No*," he said in a voice like rumbling thunder. "And if I hear of any of you trying to sneak out there and look for yourselves, I will be *pissed*. Got it?"

"Yes, sir," Dec mumbled, shrinking an inch or two. They might have been cousins, but when Frank gave an order, Dec usually had sense enough to obey.

Before I could pry further details from Frank, my phone chirped, and I plucked it off the mantel to find my mother calling. "What's up?" I asked.

"Is Frank over there?"

"Uh-huh. Need to talk to him?"

"Not just yet. Rally the troops and come over to Coileán and Toula's place. Compound meeting on the lawn in ten."

Aurie complained about being rushed out of the bathroom, but she threw on clothes and hurried with the rest of us to hear the news with our neighbors. Dec's family home was only a few blocks away, and when we arrived, we found a sizeable crowd already gathered—even Ennis, who had spent the day with Maria within the walls rather than go back to his cabin and risk facing another troll alone.

Once the last stragglers arrived, Toula stepped onto a chair to be seen and heard. "It's a gate," she announced. "A real one. And I'd bet my life that's Conota on the other side. It's undeniable that we've got a current of dark magic flowing around here"—she paused while Frank blew another blast of flame as proof—"so now we've got to figure out our next steps."

A short burst of incredulous laughter sounded from two yards over, and I spotted Iris Johansson standing in a knot of elderly wizards. "We leave!" she called over the heads. "We can't close it!"

The rest of the Arcanum refugees began to mumble among themselves, and Toula held up a hand for peace. "You're right, we can't close the gate. I've got at least as many bad memories of Nath's invasion as you do—"

"Then you know it's suicide to stay here," Iris replied. "You *know* what comes through those gates."

That time, some of the faeries murmured in agreement, and I even caught Frank nodding.

Suddenly, with a grunt and a barked, "*Move*," Artur

pushed her way to the front and motioned for Toula to cede the floor. She stepped down, and when Artur climbed atop the chair, her voice boomed down the streets. "Have you no shame?" she asked the crowd, focusing her attention on the Arcanum faction. "No courage? You swore to defend this realm once, did you not? Isn't that part of the magus's oath—you defend the realm against all others?"

"She's been listening," Arnold remarked beside me.

She's not stupid, I replied.

"Far from it. I just didn't realize that she had any interest in Arcanum matters...though it would make sense for her to study the power structures," he mused, rubbing his chin. "Of course, the magus oath only applies to *magi*. Iris is on the hook...Maria, Toula, *Bert*, if you can coax him out here...but most of the Arcanum faction never swore to anything."

"You have *guns*," Artur continued, her voice laced with disgust. "Explosive devices. My people had an open gate, too, and do you know what we had to defend against it? Swords and bows."

"Yeah, *that* sword," Iris countered.

"This?" Artur unsheathed the weapon at her hip, and the crystalline blade glimmered in the streetlights. "This was the only remotely magical weapon we had. Everything else was mundane, and we certainly didn't have gunpowder." Putting her sword away, she said, "If Conota still exists, if the gates are retuning, then we have an obligation as the ones who understand the risk to defend this realm. Would you run? Leave the gate untouched and allow nightmares free access to this land? More trolls? The oversized wolves? Those mounted raiders? A hunting pack of Hidden Ones? What if the gate grows large enough to give hungry dragons passage? Can you imagine two or three of them descending upon Fairbanks? No offense intended," she added, picking Frank out of the crowd.

He shrugged. "None taken. It's a valid concern...and

remember, I'm undersized."

A few of the wizards flinched.

"Given the terrain," said Artur, "the logical direction for anything coming through the gate is down and toward us. Posting a watch at the gate itself might be difficult, but we need a constant watch here, eyes on the mountain and the woods. If you don't trust your martial skill," she said, cutting her eyes to the Arcanum group, "then I'm confident that Mina, Nico, or Kiet would be more than capable of offering you a few pointers. As for me, as long as the gate remains open, I will stay and fight. What say the rest of you?"

"I'll help," came a voice from the middle of the pack, and I stood on tiptoe to see Ted hobbling toward Artur, leaning heavily on his cane—Ted, who at ninety-seven could barely manage stairs but did what stretches and calisthenics he could to keep his joints functional.

Uncle Ted was many things, including grossly unfit for combat. I suspected that he wasn't anticipating being sent to the front lines. By volunteering, he was shaming his younger Arcanum peers…and from the looks on their faces, his plan was working.

Artur jumped off the chair and gripped Ted's shoulder. "You're a good man," she said, "and we can use any help offered."

"I second the plan for a watch," Avus interjected, nodding to Artur. "But in case of attack, the compound is far from secure. Perhaps it would be wise to relocate anyone too infirm to fight." As Ted opened his mouth, Avus told him, "In case of emergency, you cannot run. I appreciate your offer, but I would rather not see you hurt or dead without cause."

"Hey, just a thought," said Ennis, waving for attention. "Why don't I airlift anyone getting benched to Fairbanks? Surely we can afford a few hotel rooms while we figure this out."

The crowd waited while Avus traded glances with

Coileán, Toula, and Artur.

"A wise suggestion," Avus finally told him. "And now, as for the watch, Mina…if you'd be so kind…"

"Consider it done, Captain," she replied with a little smile, then cracked her knuckles and surveyed the crowd. "Right," she barked, "listen up. If I call your name, do *not* make me hunt you down."

CHAPTER 5

Mina hadn't tapped any of the six of us for the first shifts, perhaps out of pity for our troll encounter earlier in the day. Still, by Wednesday afternoon, I was nearing the point of volunteering just to get out of the house.

By parental edict, we were confined to the compound. While Ennis shuttled the most aged of the wizards out of harm's way, we ineffectively tried to fight our growing tension. The dark magic concentration had risen overnight, and I watched in the den as wispy puffs drifted past. Kenna, blind to the dark magic but hearing it loud and clear, shoved noise-cancelling headphones on and played a game on her computer. Only Aurie enjoyed the experience—for the first time since she was a year old, she could breathe fire, and she sat at the kitchen table with a pair of white tapers, practicing precision. Meanwhile, Edie and Dec had retreated to his room with one of our board games. For the first time that I could remember, Edie was too distracted to read, and Dec, still nursing his wounds from Monday's practice session with Mina, was staying out of sight in case our coach came by.

And then there was Gaw, the worst of us all. By turns, he hid in his bedroom and paced the house like a caged animal, tired but unable to rest. I finally cornered him and dragged him outside to get to the bottom of his unease, but his explanation gave me pause.

"*Something's* wrong," he insisted, rubbing his elbow. "I've never felt like this."

"Like what?" I asked.

"I…" He frowned as he tried to put the sensation into words. "It's like I'm full of lightning. Not painful," he reassured me, "but…it's energetic. It wants to break free."

"What happens if it does?"

"I don't know," he admitted, and leaned into me as I hugged him. "Would you think less of me if I told you I'm scared to find out?"

I insisted that I wouldn't…and I did so again later that afternoon, once he began throwing up every few hours. As Dec knelt beside the toilet, shaking and squeezing his eyes closed, I wondered if the troll was the only thing that had come from Conota. Mom and Pa had told me that there were no diseases in Faerie, but was that true for the other realm? Gaw had never been sick like this before, so what was wreaking havoc on him?

"It's just nerves," he claimed when I found him in the bathroom at one in the morning, sweating through his pajamas, but he didn't try to stop me when I called Dr. Bee.

She could find nothing organically wrong with him, so she gave him some anti-nausea medication and a mild sedative to help him sleep. I lay in Gaw's bed with him while he drifted off, but when sleep came for him, it was fitful, and he moaned as he tossed beneath the blankets.

Thursday brought a bit of a break for me when Mina finally came calling, and Kenna and I took our turn sitting atop the wall with binoculars until lunchtime. Aurie and Dec relieved us, but when we returned home after our uneventful shift, I found Gaw still in bed, curled up and shivering even as he sweated. Edie, who'd been checking in on him all morning, reported that he wasn't feverish, but he wasn't keeping anything more than water down.

I stayed with him through the long afternoon and evening as he vacillated between periods of uncomfortable waking and restless sleep. While I tried to stay upbeat for Gaw when he was conscious, my thoughts were spiraling into an abyss.

Gaw and I had *plans*. We were going to get out of the wilderness and see the world. Start a family of our own. Be together for the rest of our lives. All indications to that point had suggested that we were both functionally fae, but if Gaw was sick…

If Gaw was sick, he wasn't immortal. He would age.

In another few decades, we would look like Maria and Ennis, me perpetually young, him going gray and developing deeper crow's feet. Even with a wizard's lifespan, he'd be dead within a century. As a medium, I had a certain advantage in this regard, but I wanted Gaw with me in the flesh…and now, maybe our time was running out.

Allowing myself to think those thoughts sent me careening dangerously close to a panic attack, and so I tried to focus on what I *could* control. I brought Gaw fresh washcloths to dry his face and kept coaxing water down him when he was awake, and when he slept, I lay beside him and held him, trying to calm his shaking body.

"You're going to be okay," I whispered when he whimpered in his sleep. "I'm here. I love you. Everything's going to be fine."

If I said it often enough, I almost started to believe it.

I woke before dawn on Friday morning, then carefully slid out of bed so as not to disturb Gaw. He seemed to be sleeping more soundly, I noticed, and his pillow wasn't soaked. I bent and kissed him on the forehead, then tucked the blankets back into place and padded downstairs. The house was quiet—mercifully so, as I didn't want to be pressed for an update as to the patient's condition. I made a pot of coffee, hoping that the caffeine would lift my mood, then decided to get a bit of fresh air.

Summer nights that far north were never truly dark, and the streetlights seemed like overkill as I made my way out the gate and started to circle the wall. My little act of rebellion felt *good*—I was an adult, and though my parents could try to order me to stay inside, they had no right to do so. True, I had nowhere to go and no way to get there, but at least I could walk through the grass beyond the compound instead of crunch down the gravel streets within.

As I tromped along, sipping my coffee, my brother appeared and joined me. "Should be a fine day," he said. "With this breeze, perhaps the mosquitoes will leave you be."

I paused to swat one on my bare arm. *Perhaps not.*

"Try to be optimistic," he chided. "And enjoy the morning. Gawain wouldn't want you upset on his behalf."

It's difficult not to think about him.

Publius's voice softened. "I know. But you won't cure him by fretting."

I sighed and drank. *What's wrong with him? Can you tell me?*

"I would, but this is beyond my knowing."

Stopping in my tracks, I gave him an incredulous look over my tumbler. *Whatever happened to "no secrets on the other side"?*

"I'm not omniscient," he protested. "And this isn't a secret. It's…an enigma, I suppose. Different matter entirely." He rolled his eyes as I snorted. "Come on, little sister, get your exercise."

We'd rounded the corner and were heading toward the mountain when I noticed motion out of the corner of my eye and glanced toward the woods. I'd assumed it would be a young moose, not at all uncommon in our backyard. But as my eyes picked the shape out of the trees, I saw that it was bipedal—and if the shadows weren't playing tricks on me, cloaked. It didn't look nearly as large as Tuesday's troll had been, but something told me that wasn't one of the local survivalists skulking just within the trees.

"Publi," I whispered.

"I see it. Wait here, I'll investigate."

I didn't mind taking him up on his offer—what was the creature in the woods going to do to someone already dead?—and so I hung back near the wall with my tumbler, watching as my brother neared the figure. He stopped a few yards away…and then, to my surprise, he laughed aloud.

"Cynaeli, hmm?" I heard him say as he closed the distance. "Where did you come from? Who are you?"

Cynaeli. The adults had told us about them, of course, one of the two most powerful civilizations in Conota, but the notion that I'd ever see one of them seemed far-fetched. They were supposedly smaller than their tennuwaya peers, with purple skin, dark hair, and blue eyes, and talented with dark magic, particularly illusions.

And notably, I remembered as Publius strolled up to the stranger, they were natural mediums.

My brother kept his voice down, and as the apparent cynaeli spoke to him with his mind, I had no idea what was being said. Occasionally, Publius would look over his shoulder at me and nod, and after a long moment of conversation, he beckoned for me to approach. "It's all right!" he called, waving me closer. "Join us."

Though hesitant, I tried to project an aura of calm as I neared the pair. The cynaeli was indeed purple—his skin was nearly the color of an eggplant—but when he smiled, his teeth were bright white and, to my relief, not fangs. He raised a hand in greeting—I counted only three fingers and a thumb—then said, "Howdy."

"*Howdy?*" I echoed.

His confidence wavered, and he looked to Publius, biting his lip.

"He thought that was the proper greeting," my brother explained. "Something his mother taught him. This is Raurit, by the way. Arik and Hope's son. They're alive, and Arik's still on the throne over there."

I felt the faintest surge of relief at the news. Conota's last known king had been roughly the same age as Maria and my mom, and both he and his wife were half human. Those in the compound who'd known the royal couple still spoke well of them.

He comes in peace? I asked.

Publius posed the question to Raurit, who nodded and pushed back his hood. His face seemed kind, if oddly hued, and I sensed no danger in his smile.

"Howdy," I told him, and stuck out my hand. "I'm Cici."

Raurit beamed and clasped my hand, and I glanced at my brother. "Be a dear and tell him that he's got a *long* morning ahead of him."

I didn't speak a word of the cynaeli tongue, and Raurit's English was limited largely to profanity, but with Publius acting as the go-between, I coaxed him into the compound. As he studied the houses with interest, I asked my brother, *Who here can understand him? Or are you and I going to be doing this all day?*

"Kitty and Pater, probably," he said, mulling it over. "Beth, I would think, and Maria. Maybe more. I know a few of the old Away Team went to his parents' wedding, but I can't say which of them with any accuracy."

My folks seemed like a good enough place to begin, and so I hurried Raurit, once again fully cloaked, through the streets toward home. I opened the front door—it was never locked—and caught my parents together in the kitchen, Mom at the stove making pancakes and Pa chopping fruit. "Hi, sweetie. Are you hungry?" Pa began, then noticed my companion—well, the living one, at least—and paused. "Uh…who's your friend, Cici?"

"Go on," Publius told Raurit.

The cynaeli dropped his hood and flashed a nervous smile. "Howdy?"

"Holy *shit!*" Mom cried, yanking the pan off the stove and grabbing one of the ceramic knives in the block.

"Who the—"

"He's Hope and Arik's son," I blurted, stepping between my quasi-armed parents and our uneasy guest. "Or so he told Publius, I don't know. Can you talk to him?"

Mom and Pa traded glances, and then she put her knife on the counter and stepped out of the kitchen. When she spoke, I couldn't understand a syllable, but Raurit's face lit up with comprehension. He answered rapidly in kind and with a wide smile, and after a moment, Pa joined in.

With the three of them ignoring me, I turned to my brother. *And?*

"Shh," he said, motioning for silence, "I'm listening."

"Et tu, Publi?" I muttered under my breath, but without a translator, I could only wait.

A few minutes later, my brother took pity on me. "He's very excited. His parents have told him stories about their time in this realm and in Faerie, and he's glad to see that some of their friends are still alive. They're comparing notes—you know about the RV trip, yes?"

Somewhat. I knew that two years before Faerie was destroyed, Hope had called Mom for help when Arik was dying and ended up in the Arcanum's old motorhome with Artur, Beth, and Frank on a frantic drive.

"Well, he's asking about your aunts and Frank, so it appears that his parents remember that trip fondly. They're healthy and whole, and Conota is unharmed. Something about a patch of sunlight?"

I racked my brain, trying to remember my lessons about that realm. *The sky's always overcast, but I think Arik was able to convince his father to leave one sunny spot over his palace. Arik's father is the realm*, I explained.

"That's right," my brother replied, folding his arms. "Anyway, that explains why Raurit is so dark—he has a tan. He's saying...*ah*," he murmured as our grandmother appeared, "Avia. I was wondering when you would come."

She considered the trio, who ignored us as their

conversation grew more animated. "He doesn't have his mother's talent," she said. "Gifted, yes, but not like Hope."

"Have you *ever* met her equal?" Publius countered. "He's called Raurit, by the way."

"Mm. A little disappointing—I wouldn't be surprised to find a comparable talent in her line. No matter. Good morning, sweet girl," she added to me. "Did you find him?"

A few minutes ago, at the edge of the woods, I replied. *If you want to interrupt…*

"They can't stop me," she said, a mischievous edge to her smile, then headed for the newcomer. "Raurit? Flora. How is your mother?"

Raurit paused mid-sentence to focus on my grandmother, and I smirked at my confused parents as he grinned at seemingly empty space. "Avia stopped by," I reported.

"Tell her hello for us, then," said Pa, hurrying into the kitchen to cut off the stove and shove the cut fruit into the fridge. "Kitty—"

But Mom had already retrieved her phone and was waking up her little sister. "Get over here, *now!*" I heard her exclaim. "You're not going to believe who just waltzed in."

There wasn't a building in the compound sufficiently large to hold the whole community, so once again, we piled into the street and onto the small lawns, staying clear of neighbors' vegetable gardens while trying to press as close as possible. While those among us old enough to have survived Nath's invasion seemed unfazed by the presence of a cynaeli—excited but unafraid—my housemates goggled. Even Gaw had forced himself out of bed when I ran home with the news, and he couldn't stop staring at Raurit. I caught sight of Maria and Ennis in the crowd, the former looking pleased, the latter gobsmacked. Standing atop a patch of potatoes, my brother and grandmother clustered with Granddad and Artur's father, Uther, and the snippets of their conversation that I overheard seemed to concern the impromptu RV tour of middle America twenty-seven years before. All of them but Publius had tagged along on various legs of the journey, Granddad and Uther out of concern for their kids, Avia to protect Hope—a young, incredibly talented medium who'd needed guidance in setting boundaries. Judging by their expressions, they were pleased to see Raurit, but I couldn't miss the undercurrent of worry.

Beth, who'd screamed and hugged Raurit on being introduced, served as his interpreter. At least he was happy to talk, as Toula, Coileán, and Avus peppered him with questions.

When Faerie was attacked, Conota—its consciousness, Raurit's grandfather—had sealed its borders in alarm. He'd felt the Arcanum's spell aimed at him and Faerie alike, but whereas the magic in Faerie had only strengthened the spell, the dark magic of Conota had made it fizzle. Still, Conota was ancient and wise enough to fear reprisals, and he took no chances on a similar attack, no matter how many times Arik asked him to open a gate. Arik's brother—by circumstance, if not blood—lived in a community of Conotan expats in Kentucky, and Arik feared for his safety. But the realm had refused, only opening a small test gate in an area he recalled as uninhabited a few days ago to see whether the dust had settled and what remained. That a troll had wandered through had been pure chance.

Two days ago, Raurit explained, his grandfather had come to him in private and asked him to investigate. Conota had sensed the other sort of magic in the mortal realm, but he didn't detect any gates into Faerie, and he was curious as to the source. Raurit had agreed to go, and Conota had sneaked him out of his parents' home—they both knew full well that Hope and Arik would have thrown a fit, had they been aware of the plan. Raurit had come through the gate, seen the settlement from the mountain, and taken the long way down to stay within the shelter of the woods, where he could observe. He'd been sloppy that morning after a long couple of nights of minimalist camping, which was how Publius and I had discovered him.

But this explanation left more questions than answers. "*What* source of magic?" Coileán asked. "Did he give you any specifics?"

Raurit listened to Beth's rapid translation, then shook his head. "No," he replied through her. "Just that he felt the other sort of magic here."

Coileán frowned. "The only source we have is a small reservoir in a sword—"

"And Gawain," Avus murmured.

Gaw slid closer to me as the crowd's attention shifted to him.

"We don't know that for sure," Ros interjected over the muttering, "and besides, other than the incident Tuesday, he's never done anything like that."

Raurit listened to Beth for a moment, then asked, "Would you be willing to accompany me back to the gate? I'm sure my grandfather has questions."

"Of course," said Toula as soon as Beth fell silent, then pointed to Gaw. "And I think you'd better come with us, bud."

Naturally, Ros and Sam objected to this plan. Gaw looked awful, and his claims that he was perfectly capable of making the hike rang hollow when considered in conjunction with his pale, sweaty face. But the other five of us kids volunteered to help him along, and Gaw's parents relented when it became obvious that they were outnumbered.

In the end, we made a substantial party: Coileán, Toula, and Avus, Ros and Sam, Mom and Pa, Beth and Ed, Artur, Frank, the three former captains of the guard—Mina, Nico, and Kiet—and then the six of us from the bachelor pad, plus Raurit. As Frank and Artur led the way up the mountain, Raurit hung back with those of us closer to his age, smiling awkwardly and even lending a hand when Gaw stumbled. To my relief, Publius soon joined our band, and I attempted to make complicated small talk through him.

With the eyes of the more senior adults focused elsewhere, Raurit didn't hold back. *My parents have no idea I'm here*, he confided via my brother. *They're going to murder me once they find out. I'm grateful to your parents for offering breakfast, but I fear that anything I ate would come back up.*

Are you afraid of your parents' reaction or of us? I asked.

Frankly, both. He shrugged as my brow furrowed. *I've certainly known Irojans, but faeries…*

"I don't know the translation of that term," Publius explained when I turned to him for help. After a quick discussion with Raurit, his face relaxed. "Iroja is their name for this realm. He's not confident as to whether 'Irojan' applies to all humans or only mundanes, but I don't think he's had sufficient sleep to debate the finer points of semantics."

Raurit chuckled and shook his head.

Tell him he has nothing to fear from us, I said to my brother. *I've never heard anyone here say a cross word about his parents, so he's not in danger.*

I appreciate that, Raurit replied, *but…you know, this realm has been severed for so long, and there's little magic…*

None for us, I pointed out. *The only people in town who can do anything with dark magic are Frank and Aurie, and I really don't think they're in a killing mood.*

He cut his eyes to Aurie, who had wrapped Gaw's arm around her shoulders and was talking to distract him from his fatigue. *Dragons, yes? My parents spoke of Frank and a blue one…*

That would have been Ione, Aurie's mother. She died before Aurie hatched, I explained. *And Frank's father is half fae, so they're, uh…complicated.*

Surprisingly, Raurit didn't seem disturbed by that news. "He says he's complicated as well," Publius reported. "His mother is half cynaeli, half human. His father is half human and half…whatever Conota is. You know, Aurie's a mind reader—perhaps she and Raurit should have a talk."

That suggestion was met with great enthusiasm, and as I took Aurie's place at Gaw's side, she and Raurit began a silent conversation, the only outward sign of which was their frequent shifts in expression. Frank sometimes had difficulty contorting his face in the proper fashion, but Aurie, who had been raised almost exclusively around wizards and faeries, had acquired the knack. If one overlooked her odd coloration, she could pass for human—and with a pair of sunglasses to hide her eyes and a sufficiently bohemian getup to excuse her blue hair, she did.

I was glad that Raurit, at least, had a distraction. It was a long hike up to the gate, and Gaw took much of my attention, stumbling as he did. Dec, Kenna, and Edie pitched in on a rotating basis, and we all clustered close, ready to help if his legs gave out. Weak though he was, however, Gaw soldiered on, stopping only for water breaks. He even risked a handful of granola, and when he kept it down after ten minutes, I counted it as a win.

We were feeling the strain when we reached the little valley where the gate had opened, but just *seeing* the thing made me momentarily forget my fatigue. The gate was a hole in the fabric of space, like someone had come along and cut a circle through the skin of reality. The rift was perhaps eight feet across—large enough for a stooping troll, though still too small for a dragon—and the edges flickered with flashes like pale lightning. It hung about a foot off the ground, motionless and unchanging. Looking through it, I saw a field of brown grass beneath a heavy gray sky, between which grew tall black trees with brown leaves. I would have thought the scene autumnal had I not spotted a few bright yellow fruits hanging from the nearest branches, each the size of a golf ball. More tellingly, the breeze blowing through the gate was warmer than the Alaskan morning. Dark magic poured out from the other realm like smoke—or dry ice, I mused, as it was odorless to me and didn't make me choke.

"Wow," whispered Dec, who had paused with Gaw and me to take it in. "That…is *something*."

"That's incredible," said Gaw.

"Incredibly terrifying," murmured Edie, who regarded the gate as one might a coiled snake. "Seeing as, you know, *we can't close it*."

Terrifying or not, the gate seemed to beckon us closer, and Gaw and I pressed on as our elders made their final approach. But as Artur came within ten feet of the hole, someone appeared on the other side.

The youthful man at the edge of the gate was about my father's size, average in height and reasonably trim and toned. His shoulder-length hair was black, and he wore it unbound, leaving it to wave in the wind. He'd opted to go shirtless, which left a wide swath of his deep green skin on display. I wasn't sure what was most striking about him: his singular hue, the third eye that opened above his nose as he watched us near him, the sharp teeth exposed when he smiled, or the radiance of the white corona that surrounded him.

"The *fuck*…" Kenna began.

"That would be Raurit's grandfather," Publius offered to me. "Conota."

"Well, well," the glowing figure said in queerly accented Fae as he noticed Artur. "The Sleeper is still awake, is she?"

"No thanks to you," my aunt replied, her hand straying

toward the hilt of her sword. "What's this about, then?"

"Factfinding."

"Or an attack on a sovereign realm," she countered. "We've had one troll already. Any more surprises you'd like to reveal?"

Spotting Ros in the crowd, he ignored her question. "*There* you are!" he called, pointing to her through the gate. "I was wondering when you would show yourself."

The rest of us parted, leaving Ros in front of the gate with her arms tightly folded. "Hello to you, too. I wasn't expecting to meet again."

He shrugged. "Biding my time. I had my reasons, as I'm sure you did."

"You don't seem surprised to see me like this," said Ros.

Conota chuckled. "I suspect you've enjoyed your vacation. So when do you plan to restore Faerie?"

"And how should I do that? It's *gone*. Destroyed. Why would I be in this form otherwise?" she said. "If Faerie existed, I wouldn't be in *this* realm."

But Conota merely smirked at Ros as she stared him down. "Come, now, we both know that's untrue," he replied. "You know what you must do to restore Faerie. You *must* have known it for years."

As a rumbling, confused murmur rolled through our group, Conota picked Avus and Coileán from the crowd and motioned them closer. "You two, the little kings—did she not tell you?"

"Tell us what?" Avus asked, looking between Conota and Ros with a worried frown.

"Why, that Faerie still exists. She never mentioned it?"

"Ros?" Avus pressed. "What does he mean?"

She avoided his eyes, instead focusing on Conota, her back as rigid as stone.

Conota waited for her to speak, and when she maintained her silence, he answered the question for her. "It's right there," he said. "At the back. The one leaning on the brown-haired girl."

His green finger jutted straight at Gaw.

The murmuring returned, crescendoing until Avus yelled for silence and stepped up to the gate. "What are you talking about?" he demanded. "The boy—"

"Is Faerie," Conota interrupted. "In a strange form, yes—magic incarnate, if you like—but I *know* what Faerie feels like, and I've sensed it here ever since I made an opening. When I felt its magic spike, I sent Raurit to investigate…ah, good, you didn't kill him," he added, noticing his grandson standing with Aurie. "His parents would have been insufferable. Anyway, I had thought that Faerie might have been destroyed, but seeing *her* here," he explained, jutting his chin toward immobile Ros, "I think I know what happened."

"Which is?" Toula prompted.

"A somewhat complex process, so I'll endeavor to simplify it for your limited minds."

Toula snorted her disdain. I couldn't tell if Conota's third eye winked at her or was merely blinking, but she held her peace, and he continued.

"In some ways, I am this realm," he said. "I know its full history, its secrets, the lives that have flared and died within its bounds. But as closely linked as we are, we are not precisely one and the same. I am its avatar, just as she was Faerie's"—he flicked his hand toward Ros—"though unlike my counterpart in Faerie, I've managed to maintain my position. How many of you have there been," he asked her, "four?"

"Five," she whispered.

He paused, squinting up at the clouds, then nodded as a look of comprehension dawned. "Ah, *yes*. I always forget one or two of you. As I was saying," he continued, turning back to Toula, "the realm and I are tightly connected but not inextricably linked. Should something happen to me, another could take my place. I am Conota, but Conota extends beyond me—do you understand?'

Toula's face remained neutral. "One does not typically become grand magus without an education in theoretical cosmology and thaumaturgy."

His pointed teeth gleamed as he grinned at her. "I *have* missed you. You were born in my realm, did you know that? Your mother was still licking her wounds here."

"I'd gathered as much."

"A pity you didn't stay—you might have been entertaining."

"We can reminisce later," said Toula. "Tell us about Faerie."

Conota smiled at her obvious impatience. "As you like, little one. You understand that the realm cannot exist without its avatar?"

"That's been our theory, yes."

"Fact, not theory. I saw what the wizards did—they attempted to destroy Faerie by destroying her," he said, pointing to Ros. "I suppose it was all too quick for her to pass her power to another and let them kill her. In any case, she was hit hard enough that Faerie began to collapse."

"We saw it disintegrate," Coileán interjected. "Earthquakes, the *sky*—"

"*Collapse*, not disintegrate. Had she remained within its borders, the realm would have continued to collapse into her, and both would have been obliterated. But she was extracted." His gaze landed on Beth, and he smiled again. "I'd say you were a clever girl, but I doubt you had the faintest idea what you were truly doing."

"And what's that?" asked Beth, hands on her hips.

"Faerie collapsed into its avatar, but the avatar lived because she was pulled into your realm. It wasn't destroyed—it was *within* her."

Glancing to my left as Gaw's breathing quickened, I saw that he had begun to glow.

Conota peered at Gaw, then looked at Ros with a knowing smirk. "Your child, isn't it? Has your look, I'd say." When Ros maintained her silence, Conota turned to Toula. "See for yourself. Whatever remains of Faerie is inside that shell."

"*Shell?*" Toula echoed.

He nodded. "You have a food, some of the Irojans here think fondly of it…" With a snap of his fingers, he said, "Popcorn, that's it. Tiny kernels, but when they explode, the interior expands and is edible. You know this food?"

"Sure…"

"Well, then," he continued, pointing to Gaw, "think of that like popcorn. What you want is inside. To get it, all you need to do is destroy the shell. Faerie will be restored, and things can return to normal," he said, his tone suggesting the satisfaction of one who's worked out a long equation. "We've always had three realms, not two. Faerie is necessary for balance. But there, it's a simple fix."

"That," said Ros with quiet intensity, "is my son. And if you try to lay a goddamn finger on him, I swear I will find a way to *destroy* you. Utterly."

Avus gripped her tight shoulder, but she didn't look at him. "Ros," he murmured, "is…is this true? All this time, the realm…"

"No one is killing my son."

"Of course no one is *killing* him," Conota protested. "He won't exist any longer—he's just the husk containing Faerie. That's all he's ever been."

"My. *Son*," she repeated, the tremor in her voice speaking not of fear, but of rage.

"Roslyn," Avus insisted, stepping between her and Conota so she was forced to face him. "Did you know?"

Her silence stretched before her like a confession until finally, she gave him a curt nod. "I've always suspected. Even before I felt him move inside me, I…I thought it might be. But that's my baby," she said, staring at Avus. "Val, he's my *baby*. You can't hurt him."

"Are you seriously contemplating a continued existence

without Faerie?" Conota interrupted, brow furrowed. "Over *him*?"

"You *did* hear the part about how that's her kid, right?" Toula snapped.

He rolled all three of his eyes. "She's not purely fae, is she? Irojan madness is such an annoyance. But you understand what must be done, yes?" he asked her, then looked to Avus and Coileán. "Surely all of you understand this."

Coileán stepped in before Ros could explode. "The people left behind when Faerie collapsed—are they still alive?"

"How should I know?" said Conota, and cocked his head toward Gaw, who trembled against me. "Ask *him*. Of course, there's probably no real way to find out until Faerie is restored...and I've told you how to do that. You could fix the problem right now—"

The crack of a racking pistol echoed around the little valley, and I saw that Edie had drawn her sidearm. She kept it pointed at the ground, but her voice didn't waiver when she said, "No one is fixing *anything* if it means hurting Gaw."

"Sweetheart," Ed began, taking a step toward her.

She raised the gun a fraction of an inch. "I don't want to do this. No closer."

Within seconds, Dec, Aurie, and Kenna had added their weapons to Edie's defensive line, leaving me to support Gaw as he shook.

None of the others seemed eager to take the offensive, and after a tense moment, Avus raised his empty hands and moved ever so slightly nearer to us. "No one is taking any action until we talk this through. Let's go home and think about our options," he said slowly. "There must be a solution that leaves Gawain unharmed."

"Unlikely," Conota muttered behind him.

Avus ignored the commentary. "Holster the guns. You have my word."

"It's okay," said Toula as she joined him. "Let's not shoot anyone, all right? Nobody's touching Gaw."

My housemates traded uncertain looks, but one by one, they put their firearms away.

Avus's shoulders slumped with evident relief, and he turned back to Conota, who'd watched the brief standoff with bemusement. "For now, while we work this out, would you please close the gate?" he asked. "Or build a fence to keep the trolls out, at least. We need time."

But Conota smiled as he shook his head. "If you want to close the gate, you know how to do it. All you need is Faerie's magic…"

At that, Raurit, who'd been listening to Aurie's translation, piped up. Unable to understand him, I glanced at Publius, who said, "He's offering to remain here for a few days in case of trolls. His talent for physical magic isn't great, but it's better than nothing."

My mother translated for the others, who nodded. As Conota vanished, we turned for home—me supporting Gaw, whose glow lessened with every step away from the gate, and my friends and Raurit forming a knot around us. Looking back, I saw Gaw's parents walking alone, Sam with his arm around Ros, holding her close. Unwilling to meet Avus's stare, I focused on the trail ahead and murmured reassurance to Gaw. "I'm here," I told him as we started the descent. "No one's going to hurt you. Not while I'm around."

"I'm scared, Cici," he whispered.

"We won't let them get you—"

"Not that." He tightened his grip on me until I looked into his worried hazel eyes. "What if he's right?"

"You are *not* just a fucking husk, and I won't let them kill you," I said, and willed his shaking to subside.

CHAPTER 6

Our parents left us alone for the rest of the day. In retrospect, I'm not sure they knew what to do with us. Perhaps they were wondering what they'd created. We'd been good kids, by and large, and we'd acquiesced when they'd brought us home the previous spring. Now, for the first time, we were saying no—and we were doing it together.

As the sun sank that Friday, we clustered in the den—well, most of us. Gaw continued to run back and forth to the bathroom, where he threw up until his stomach was empty. I didn't know if it was the open gate or fear for his life that spurred Gaw's nausea, but I tried to keep him comfortable and coax sips of water down his throat. The others took turns serving as the lookout at the front door, watching for a delegation. We assumed our elders were meeting, debating Gaw's fate, but if they wanted to get to him, they'd have to sneak past a rifle first.

With no reason to insert himself into the formal discussion, Raurit stayed with us, either speaking directly to Aurie's mind or using my brother or grandfather as go-betweens when I wasn't attending to the patient. At several points during that long evening, Granddad cornered me in the hallway while Gaw cleaned himself up. "You're doing the best you can, honey," he insisted. "He's going to have to work this out for himself, and you don't need to worry yourself sick, too."

Easy for him to say. The man I loved was a physical wreck, and nothing I tried seemed to do more than briefly lessen the symptoms. My own impotence melded with my mounting panic—I had to do *something*, or else I'd lose him. My family had brought me back to the wilderness when all I wanted was my freedom. I'd be damned if I let them take Gaw from me, too.

At least I wasn't alone in my distress. Dec's manifested as anger, and while he and Kenna threw together dinner for the group, he railed against our elders to anyone within earshot. "You saw the way they were looking at him," he said as Edie slipped into the kitchen for a beer. "Like wolves with an injured caribou."

She opened the fridge and rummaged through the bottles. "Why do you suppose I drew my gun, genius?"

The snide remark bounced off him. "Maybe the olds want Faerie back," he said, chopping potatoes with so much force that I worried for the cutting board and his fingers, "but we've done just fine without it. They like this place enough to have dragged us all back here, right? Well, they can deal with themselves, because *no one* is coming after Gaw."

The last slice of the knife took off part of his fingernail, and Edie stepped in to save Dec from amputation. "Here," she said, putting her open beer in his hand. "Drink that and sit down."

I knew what Dec was feeling, and from the look on her face, Kenna was wrestling with the fae rage as well. Our parents had taught us to control the deep well of anger that could boil forth with the slightest provocation, but all the regulatory techniques in the world didn't drain the reservoir. When my temper spiked, it was an ugly, violent thing that had left me in frightened tears as a little kid, and with my nerves as taut as they were that day, I feared that an explosion from any of us would set off the rest.

By eleven-thirty, with Gaw huddled on the couch beneath an afghan and Dec pacing at the door, I didn't have any good answers about how to solve our problems, but one idea blazed in my thoughts like a neon sign on a foggy night. "We've got to get out of here," I announced.

The others turned to me, and Publius offered Raurit a quick translation. "What do you mean?" asked Edie.

"As long as we're here, we're sitting ducks. What if they decide to come for Gaw?"

"We won't let that happen," Dec began. "We—"

"You want to guess how long this place would last under siege? There's more of them, they've got most of the weapons out there, and all they'd have to do would be turn off the water and power here and wait."

The rest of the room contemplated that possibility in uneasy silence.

"I'm getting out of here tonight," I continued. "Don't know where to go, but I'm getting out, and Gaw…"

He nodded weakly. "I'm with you, Cici."

Raurit spoke to get our attention, and after he gave Publius his message, I repeated the synopsis for the group. "He suggests we go back to the gate and hide out in Conota. It's a big place, and he knows a cave system."

"Not an option," said Edie, pausing while our translational relay reached him. "Conota would probably give us away—I think he wants Faerie back. Besides, look at Gaw. He's been feeling awful with dark magic around. How much worse would he be in that realm?"

Gaw nodded but offered Raurit a small smile. "Thanks for the offer."

Flopping into the recliner with a sigh, Kenna muttered, "Too bad we can't steal Dad's plane. He said he'd let me start learning to fly this year, but I don't think you want me anywhere near the cockpit yet."

"I like my limbs in their current configuration," Dec retorted. "And not on fire."

As they half-jokingly sniped at each other, Kenna and Dec's primary mode of communication, I thought about the plane parked a mile away. Going to Ennis and asking for an airlift was a non-starter…but what about the other vehicles parked down there? Way too warm for the old snowmobiles, and none of the trucks or SUVs would comfortably hold the six of us and our gear—seven, if Raurit decided to join us—but then I had an idea.

"The RV," I said, interrupting Kenna's latest friendly insult. "The old Arcanum RV. The one that your parents used," I said to Raurit as my brother tried to keep up. "That was big enough for the two of them, Frank, Beth, Artur, and, like, at least a handful of ghosts. We could bust out of here in that."

Aurie seemed less than convinced by my brilliance. "Is it even road-worthy?"

"Actually, yeah, it is," Kenna replied, sitting up in her chair. "Dad was teaching me to do an oil change just last month, and I asked if it still runs. He started it up to show me. The battery's strong, and the tires aren't rotted. That's the vehicle of last resort if there's an emergency here and the plane is out of commission." A slow smile crept across her face. "It runs on unleaded, not diesel. If we siphon the gas from the other cars and get out of here without being caught, we'll have a decent head start. Dad will have to fly out to get gas…"

"But where can we go?" asked Edie. "If they report it stolen—"

"They're not going to call in a BOLO on us," said Kenna, warming to the grand theft auto scheme. "Dad, Beth, and Ed are the only ones of them who actually look old enough to pass for our parents, and they don't own the RV. Let's get out of town and…I don't know, we head east. Canada's huge."

"Raurit has a suggestion," Publius told me, and I shushed Edie's admittedly legitimate complaints while I listened to him. "His father's brother lives in a community of Conotan refugees in a place called Kentucky. Raurit suggests you could go there, and he's willing to come along to make the introductions. Return the favor done for his parents, if you like."

Kentucky? Do you have any idea how far away that is?

Publius shrugged. "If you want to put distance between yourself and home, why stop at Fairbanks or Anchorage?"

"What is it?" Edie interrupted, catching me staring incredulously at empty space.

"Raurit suggests we go visit his family in Kentucky," I replied. "He'll go with us. Or—hold on," I said as an idea struck. Turning to Publius, I asked, *Can he make gates?*

On hearing the question, Raurit shook his head. "They're as yet too complicated for him," Publius reported. "He's sorry, but no."

"I can get you there by road," Granddad offered from the edge of the kitchen. "The last bit, I mean. They're off the beaten track. If you can get across the continent, I can help you find the compound."

Kentucky. The idea seemed insane. I remembered my parents mentioning the Conotan compound, but they'd lost contact years before. The only number they'd had to anyone living there had been stored in Beth's enchantment-made phone, which had died shortly before magic fizzled entirely.

But Gaw's face had brightened as the plan took form, and I'd go to the ends of the earth if that's what it took to save him.

"Get your passports," I told the others. "We leave in an hour."

The passports had been our parents' idea, just in case something came up while we were down south in school. Canada wasn't that far, relatively speaking, and our families didn't want us to be hampered in case we had need of crossing the border. Just as useful, though, were our driver's licenses. The five of us had taken lessons and received our licenses while in college, while Aurie had learned the basics from Frank, then let Ennis shuttle her to Fairbanks every so often for proper instruction once her face and her age matched. A five-year-old dragon might have been an adult, but no one in Alaska was going to knowingly allow someone so young behind the wheel.

The precious license lived in my purse, and I added my passport and all the cash I'd squirreled away in my savings jar. I stuffed clothing enough for a week into a backpack, plus a bath towel, my favorite pistol, and a couple boxes of ammunition. While I doubted I'd need any sort of jacket in Kentucky in July, I pulled a dark raincoat on that night to help me blend into the twilight. I tucked one pair of gloves into my jacket pockets and added a spare set to my bag—in case of strange metal, the last thing I wanted was to be caught barehanded.

I rendezvoused with the others in the kitchen, where I found Dec dumping nonperishables into a duffel bag. "The more we carry, the less we have to buy," he said as I tightened my bag's chest strap.

"We have to get it to the RV first," I pointed out.

"Raurit offered to help," said Aurie, coming in behind me with two twelve-packs of Coke. "Dec, did you pack the coffee?"

He pointed to the can poking from the top of the bag. "I don't have a death wish."

"Clever boy."

We threw spare toiletries and T-shirts into a bag for Raurit, who had carried almost nothing but a knife into our realm, then gathered in the den for final preparations. The lights remained on behind the closed shutters, a little something to give the appearance that the house was still inhabited. We double-checked our chargers and flashlights, triple-checked our IDs, and tightened our shoelaces. It was go time.

Leaving through the main gate was out of the question. Fortunately, most of the guards on duty would be scanning the western side of the compound, watching for curious escapees from Conota to come lumbering down the mountain. Our house was near the northern wall, and since most of our neighbors were among the elderly wizards hiding out in Fairbanks, there was no one out at one in the morning to catch us as we made our escape. True, scaling a ten-foot wall was never fun, especially with gear to consider, but Mina and Artur had made us climb during our training sessions since we were little kids. The fact that Uncle Ted just happened to have a wooden ladder in his unlocked storage shed was gravy. We helped Gaw over the wall almost in a sort of relay, and then Dec, sitting atop it as a lookout, pulled Aurie up and over by her good arm.

Loaded down but barely feeling it with my surging adrenaline, I headed for the tree line and ran close to the woods, making the mile-long trek in good time. When we reached the hangar, Aurie pulled the keys from the peg and unlocked the doors, and I hustled Gaw and Raurit inside with the supplies. By the time I had them situated, Kenna had located the hand siphons and a trio of gas cans, and we worked to drain the other vehicles as quickly as we could. By two, the rest of the fleet was dry, the RV was full, and we'd stashed the leftover gas in the vehicle's bedroom in case of emergency.

As I climbed aboard and latched the door, I began to allow myself to feel hopeful. We had wheels now—they'd never catch up to us. Gaw would be safe.

And I was finally taking control of my life.

"Cross all available digits," said Aurie from the driver's seat, "and sit down. This is going to be *bumpy*."

Given her seniority, Aurie had volunteered to drive the RV to the paved road, and no one fought her for the privilege. I released the breath I'd been holding as soon as the engine rumbled to life, and then she carefully backed out of the hangar. "No lights behind us yet," she reported. "Maybe luck's on our side."

I didn't want to stick around and find out, and neither did Aurie. With a grunt, she guided the RV into the grass, then headed for the dirt trail toward civilization.

Not until we were at least a mile from the hangar,

bumping along the rutted road, did we start to take stock of our escape vehicle. The very front had seats for the driver and a navigator, but the rest of the RV resembled an apartment that had been run through a trash compactor. A sitting area was situated immediately behind the cockpit, equipped with a couch and a pair of captain's chairs. Against the opposite wall sat the tiny kitchenette and a built-in dinette that might have held four skinny people if they squished. Moving toward the rear, one ran into the closet-like bathroom—I could only imagine how foul that might smell after a few days on the road—and then the bedroom, which was almost entirely filled by the low bed.

"The RV was larger the last time I saw it," said Granddad as I shoved our bags into the bedroom's tight storage nooks.

"How so?"

"Had a second bedroom, for one. Of course, I suppose that was held together by magic."

Raurit, who'd joined me in the inspection, must have spoken to Granddad, as Granddad addressed us both. "I was telling Cici that this place was larger when it was still an Arcanum vehicle." He paused while Raurit followed up, then shook his head. "Bad idea, son. If you're not great with physical magic, you don't want to mess with spaces whose insides are bigger than their outsides...and you're going to be without magic at all before long."

Raurit frowned, and then his eyes opened wide as the realization hit. We were driving away from the gate. The dark magic concentration was already dropping, and soon, Raurit would be in the same boat as the rest of us.

"Can you pick up languages by magic?" Granddad asked him. "We don't mind translating, but if you want to improve your fluency, now's the time."

After Raurit answered him, Granddad turned to me. "He says he *thinks* he can learn the local lingo from you, but he's worried that he'll give you a headache if he tries. What do you say?"

I'd heard my parents' stories about how much easier it had been to acquire new languages with enchantment—all one needed to do was pull one from another's mind or push one in. They made it sound like a painless process...but then again, they were trained and grown, whereas Raurit was only a couple years my senior. Still, I was game to let him make the attempt.

"What do I need to do?" I asked, just as Publius poked his head into the bedroom.

"Wait, now, what's going on?" he demanded. "I heard the boy say something about experimentation—"

"Relax," Granddad told him, and swept one hand toward me in invitation. "Go ahead, kid. Better make it quick."

My brother tried to protest, but he could no more grab Raurit than we could grab him. Raurit rested his fingers on my temples and closed his eyes, and when I closed mine in turn, a soundless flash went off across my brain. A bolt of pain like an ice cream headache followed, but even as I muttered, "Ow," it was dissipating.

When Raurit released me, he sank onto the bed and rubbed his face for a moment, and I patted his shoulder. "Are you okay?"

He raised his head and smiled at the sound of my voice. "I...think I am," he replied, his accent strange but not unintelligibly so. "Yes. You are not hurt?"

"It's gone. And hi," I replied, grinning back at him.

"Howdy."

I looked up to find my brother glaring down at Raurit. *Give it a rest*, I told him. *I'm perfectly fine.*

"This time," he snapped. "You shouldn't let him practice on you."

In an hour, none of us will have access to magic. Really, I'm okay, I insisted, and rose. "Come on," I told Raurit, "let's get the food unpacked."

We made our shaky return to the den, and as Raurit tried out his new English, Dec helped me unload our stash of snacks into the kitchenette's cabinets. He located a coffeemaker, to great applause from our driver, and as he put on a pot, I took a seat by Gaw on the couch. I couldn't do much to help him besides squeeze his hand, but his emergency garbage bag remained unsoiled, for which I was grateful.

While Raurit and Kenna made themselves comfortable in the captain's chairs, Edie took over the dinette with her computer and an old road atlas she'd snagged from a storage pocket. "Cici?" she asked as the coffee finished its brew cycle.

"Hmm?"

"Is Granddad here?"

"Sitting beside you."

"Oh. Hi," she said to the patch of seemingly empty space on the bench. "I need specifics about where we're going so that I can route this. Can you show me the way?"

Reluctantly, I left Gaw and joined them at the dinette to do my duty as a mouthpiece for Granddad. Edie worked quickly, comparing the atlas's pages to the maps she found online, then typed up directions.

After about ten minutes, she had news, and it wasn't great. "By the fastest route, assuming no traffic jams and minimal pit stops, we're looking at seventy hours or so on the road at posted speed."

"Good luck getting this clunker above sixty," called Aurie. "We should make better time once we hit asphalt, but this ain't a sportscar." She held on as the RV crossed a deep rut in the trail, then sighed. "Seventy hours is the best we can do?"

"Longer at sixty."

"Shit. Well, get up here and help me program this antique," she said, patting the GPS unit on the dashboard.

Edie did as instructed, then stood and braced herself against Aurie's chair as she consulted her computer. "Right, then. Once we hit the Dalton, we take Route 2 to Fairbanks, and that's going to be at least seven hours at this point. Assuming we can pick up speed eventually, I think we're looking at an arrival around ten or eleven. Shift changes then."

"I'll take it," said Dec, and flopped onto the couch with Gaw. "Someone wake me when we've reached civilization, okay?"

While Edie made herself comfortable in the shotgun seat and Kenna slipped off to the bedroom, Granddad told me, "The last time I rode along, Frank did all the driving. Every bit of it."

I relayed that to Aurie, who snorted her disapproval. "You may have noticed that I'm not my father, Orson," she replied through gritted teeth, fighting to keep the wheel steady. "And after this leg, I'll be *happy* to share."

"Everyone but Raurit can drive," Edie pointed out. "The fewer stops we need to make, the better our head start. Besides, even if we parked, what would we do with Raurit? He's stuck on the bus." She gave her phone one last glance, then powered it down. "Cici, do me a favor and be sure all the phones are off, please. No sense in making this easy for them."

With the route mapped and the phones dark, all we could do was stay out of Aurie's hair. Edie kept the coffee coming, but I returned to the couch to find that it was actually a futon, and Dec had done the honors. As he dozed on one edge, I curled up with Gaw beneath a musty-smelling blanket, grateful that his nausea seemed to have subsided even with the jolting of the RV.

"Cici? Babe?"

I woke to Gaw's voice and an odd stillness, then realized the vehicle had stopped. Someone had thought to pull the shades in the last hours, and the interior was pleasantly dark. As my eyes adjusted, I took a good look at Gaw…and to my surprise, he seemed better. His sweating had ended, his eyes had lost their feverish glassiness, and the smile he gave me was the one I knew and loved.

"Hey," I croaked. "How're you feeling?"

"Not terrible, for the first time all week. I'm actually hungry. Come on, we've got to get up."

I let him help me off the futon and hunted for my shoes. "Where are we?"

"Aurie found a truck stop outside of Fairbanks. We coasted in on fumes—this thing *guzzles* gas. The others are inside getting cash."

My sleep fog remained patchy as I fumbled with my laces. "Cash?"

"There are a couple of ATMs in there," Gaw explained. "Edie thinks the best plan is for us to withdraw as much as we can now, then use the backup accounts for expenses."

The five of us who'd been down south had left home with bank accounts from our parents, a way for us to pay our bills and have a little fun. Our parents had joined the accounts as emergency contacts, giving them limited access in case of a problem. In our second year, slightly peeved to have parental controls on our funds, we'd all opened secondary bank accounts on the sly and slowly transferred money. In a prescient twist, Dec had dubbed it our escape fund.

By making withdrawals from our parent-accessible accounts in Fairbanks, we'd give away our current location, but we still had a massive lead on whatever search party the compound sent after us. They would probably assume that we'd stick to familiar turf, either hiding out in Fairbanks or pushing south for Anchorage. Instead, Edie's route took us east into the Yukon Territory...and since only Ennis among all of our parents had a current passport, he'd have to trail us alone.

We withdrew as much as we could at the truck stop, leaving us with about a grand each. It wasn't a fortune, but we decided it would suffice to keep our gas tank full for a while. When we rejoined Raurit with our drinks and snacks, I noticed how steeply the dark magic concentration had declined—and from the way he kept rubbing his arm and staring out the window, I supposed that Raurit was anxious at the loss of potential. While I tried to distract him with candy, Dec took the wheel, and Edie jumped up front to guide him on his way.

There was little for the rest of us to do beyond doze or look out the windows. With our phones turned off for security's sake, we had no access to movies or shows, and the RV's AM/FM radio found little of note as we pushed along Route 2. Raurit, at least, was content to chat for hours—understandably, he had questions, as did we—but I caught myself napping during the long afternoon. When I was awake, I kept checking on Gaw, looking for signs of a relapse, but he seemed to improve as the miles passed. By the time we hit Alcan Border that evening, he was his old self, joking, laughing, and chowing through a family-size bag of Doritos. Yes, we were still on the run—and yes, I'd seen the hungry looks our elders had shot Gaw before our standoff—but the trip was beginning to seem more like an adventure.

"Inspection station is in Beaver Creek," Edie called from the front. "We've got about three miles. Raurit, make yourself scarce."

His brow knit. "I'm sorry?"

"Hide. We've got to cross the border."

He scrambled into the bathroom and locked himself in the shower, and the rest of us played it cool and opened the shades as Dec rumbled up to the inspection point and rolled down the window. A female agent peeked out of her booth and smiled at him. "Evening. Where are you heading?" she asked as Dec handed over our stack of passports for review.

"Vancouver," he lied with practiced ease. "We're taking a road trip before school starts back."

"Did your parents go road tripping in that old clunker, too?" she replied. "It's in good repair?"

"She's a workhorse. Want to see?"

Edie opened the side door, and the agent poked her head inside. "Now, *that* is retro," she remarked. "My brother has a dealership—this old girl's practically an antique." She gave the kitchen counter a loving pat and took in the futon and half-empty coffee carafe. "You kids be safe out there, eh? Find an RV park before you fall asleep on the road. And let me give these back…" She began flipping through the passports and handing them out, though she paused when she found Aurie's. I suspected that not many people had striking blue hair in their government photos, but if the agent had thoughts about Aurie's looks, she kept them to herself. With a cheery wish for safe travels, she disembarked, and we were on our way with a sigh of relief.

A few miles down the road, Raurit poked his head out of the bathroom. "Safe?"

"Congratulations," said Kenna, raising her root beer in salute. "You've been officially smuggled into Canada. Now, who wants ramen?"

Dec limped into Whitehorse around midnight, and Kenna took the first Sunday shift, making it as far as an RV park in Watson Lake before we decided to give the old vehicle a rest. While Kenna napped on the futon, Dec snored in the bedroom, and Raurit kept watch, the rest of us figured out how to dump the chemical toilet and refill the water tank, then bought more gas and provisions. By ten that morning, Kenna was good to go, and she pushed hard for Fort Nelson over the border in British Columbia.

With Kenna spent, I slid behind the wheel around seven for the overnight drive. Gaw took shotgun to attend to my snack needs, leaving the rest of our crew to make the most of the limited summer darkness. I'd wanted Gaw to sleep, too, but he insisted he was feeling up to keeping me company—and truth be told, he looked like himself.

By the cusp of Monday, Gaw and I were the only ones

still conscious. Even my brother was nowhere to be found, which, since I was trying to focus on the road, wasn't a terrible thing. As Gaw played with the radio, looking for something besides oldies, country, or conspiracy theorists, I sneaked glances at him and smiled to myself. Maybe we could make this our way of life for a few years, I mused—we could take the RV down the long network of roads to the southern tip of Argentina, exploring the Americas by highway and dirt lane. If we couldn't convince our parents to finance the trip—God knew they had the cash—then we could do odd jobs along the way to make money for food and fuel. We'd all get tanned and buy kitschy souvenirs and take hundreds of pictures atop Machu Picchu, our arms around each other like old times. We'd go canoeing on the Amazon and spend the night on Mexican beaches, but before that, we'd explore our own country, replacing online photos with actual memories. We'd camp at Yellowstone, shop in New York, visit the Smithsonian museums, stay out all night in New Orleans.

We would live on our own terms.

We would *live*.

The rustling of Gaw's chip bag pulled me from my pleasant planning, and he offered me a handful before helping himself. "I've been thinking," he murmured.

"Me, too." I beamed at him and stole a few more chips. "What would you say to not going back to Alaska? Not for a while, at least. How about a year on the road?"

Gaw smiled, but it seemed strained. "Sounds like fun."

"But?"

"But." He crunched on his snack for a moment, staring out at the lonely road as a trucker drove past in the opposite direction. "Cici…I think Conota was telling the truth."

My heart felt like a fist was clenching around it. I didn't want to have this discussion, not that night, not *ever*, but Gaw didn't seem to get the memo.

"I'm not supposed to exist," he said as he brushed the

salty crumbs off his fingers.

"*Gawain—*"

"It sort of struck a chord with me when he said it," he continued before I could interrupt, "and the longer I've been out here, thinking clearly…he's right. Don't ask me how I know, but I *know*, Cici, I know this." He paused, then softly said, "Maybe it would be for the best if I fixed the mistake."

I jerked the wheel so hard that I almost ran us off the road, and though I corrected course with a muttered apology, I stared at Gaw as though I could pin him to the seat with my eyes alone. "Don't say that," I replied, aghast. "Don't you *ever* say that. Whether or not you were meant to exist, you *do*, and you can't just throw that away."

"Conota's not going to close that gate," said Gaw. "This realm is defenseless right now, and I—"

"*I love you,*" I said, reaching for his hand, and squeezed as his fingers wrapped around mine.

"I love you, too," he whispered, then kissed my knuckles. "But what do we do when more gates open? What if this realm is invaded? That's billions of people—"

"And you're the one I care about."

"You think I don't care about you?" he asked. "You're in those billions. When the gates open, we'll all be in danger. I…you know, if there's something I can do to protect the fucking *world*…"

I tightened my grip on his hand. "You're not going to kill yourself, Gawain Rockwell. Don't you even *think* about that."

We sat in strained silence for a time, holding hands and listening to the staticky strains of a banjo on an AM station.

"How many people were still in Faerie when it collapsed, do you think?" said Gaw.

"I don't know. Don't think anyone took a headcount."

"What if they're still alive? What if they're trapped in some sort of hellscape?"

"And what if there's no one left?" I countered. "*If* Faerie still exists, maybe it's nothing but a wasteland. If you"—I couldn't say *kill yourself*—"do something stupid and there's nothing in Faerie, then you'll have done it all for nothing." Risking another glance away from the road, I met Gaw's eyes and held his hand as tightly as I could. "I want to spend the rest of my life with you, okay?" I blurted. "Whatever that looks like, wherever we go…I want to be with you."

"And I want you to have a life to live," he murmured, then pointed to the windshield. "*Deer!*"

"Shit!" I released Gaw and yanked the wheel to the left, narrowly missing the doe wandering onto the road. Catching my breath, I muttered, "Maybe we should talk about something else while I'm driving, eh?"

"Not a bad idea," he said, then turned and slid out of his seat. "I'm going to put the coffee on. Please don't swerve until I get back."

Left alone, I let my mind wander once again—this time, not to an imagined future, but rather to the summer when I was fifteen. We'd played in the cold lake that day, and while the others had splashed and swam, I'd climbed atop the boulder, ostensibly to sun myself. In truth, I was painfully conscious of my gawky, changing body in the previous summer's wash-faded one-piece, and with the rest of my friends down in the lake, I could hide out of direct sight. It had been Gaw, not quite fifteen himself but equally awkward, who'd climbed up to join me. He'd distracted me until I forgot to feel like such an ogre, and after a time, as we'd laughed at each other's bad jokes and swatted mosquitoes, something had clicked within me.

Gaw wasn't just my friend.

He made me feel smart and pretty. He didn't bat an eye when I stared into space, deep in conversation with people only I could see and hear. I felt less like a freak of nature and more like someone with a gift when he asked gently probing questions about my weird talent. He wasn't as strong as Dec, but he was quicker on his feet, and in our classes, Gaw easily kept up with lessons a year ahead of where he should have been. I enjoyed his company, and not just because my peer options were limited.

That day, for the first time in my life, I imagined a future that made sense: Gaw and me against the world, somewhere far away from the compound. We would escape someday and…well, what came after that remained hazy, but we'd be together.

We were making progress toward that future. An item as teenagers and a couple all through college, Gaw and I were as solid as we'd ever been. Dec joked about Bora Bora, but with every day that passed, the idea's appeal grew. Maybe the six of us wouldn't run off together, but surely I could build a life out in the wider world with the man I loved.

And nothing, not even the hope of finding long-lost Faerie, would snatch him away from me. The world could go to hell as long as we had each other.

CHAPTER 7

I'm sure I would have appreciated Alberta more had I not been driving through it sustained by caffeine and M&Ms. When I pulled over for gas in Edmonton around six Monday morning, I gladly ceded my seat to Edie, who'd awakened after a restful night with bright eyes and a distinct funk. After two full days on the road without bathing, no one on the RV was exactly *fresh*, but we didn't trust the old shower, nor did we know how much water remained in our tank, considering our coffee consumption. Kenna bought baby wipes at the truck stop, and I did my best to remove the grime before collapsing on the bed for a few hours of rest.

I briefly emerged from my sleeping cave for lunch, then retreated again until Edie finished her shift in Moose Jaw, deep in southern Saskatchewan. As she slid into the dinette with a book and her headphones, Gaw took the wheel for the afternoon, and I joined him up front for snack duty.

Around dinnertime, we reached the town of Portal, North Dakota, and crossed back into the U.S. The agent was more perfunctory than his Canadian colleague had been on Saturday, and he waved us through after seeing the stamp from a few days prior, commenting only, "You kids are a long way from home."

"First time down south!" Gaw quipped, which made the agent chuckle.

With an admonition to drive safely, we were off, pushing southeast on U.S. 52 as the GPS dictated. Seeing signs for an RV park as we approached I-94 and

Jamestown, I put the matter to a vote, and the unanimous decision was to stop for a much-needed rest. Gaw guided us in, and as he stretched his legs, Aurie and Dec quickly hooked up the vehicle for power and water. Leaving Raurit to brave the RV shower, the rest of us took advantage of the campground's twenty-four-hour facilities, and I might have fallen asleep beneath the blessedly hot water had Edie not dragged me out. Clean but weary, we all slept well that night as the RV took a deserved break.

I awoke Tuesday morning to the boom of thunder and the staccato of rain pounding against the windows. Squinting at the gray light, I sat up and took stock of my surroundings—the thin futon, the smell of canned coffee, Edie at the dinette with her computer, Publius lounging in an empty swivel chair.

"Welcome back," he said, grinning as I rubbed the dried spit off my chin. "Most of the pack has gone for breakfast—there's a restaurant in this complex. Seems questionable but smells decent."

Contemplating the pounding storm, I replied, *Should I bother trying to catch up?*

"I asked Raurit to tell Dec to bring you food, so blame the boy if you're not fed in short order." Cocking his head toward Edie, he added, "She's checking the maps to avoid the messages from home. This place has wireless access," he explained before I could worry that Edie had turned her phone back on. "Edie has shared her machine, and according to Orson, the letters from your families have been, shall we say, of a theme."

"You're grounded for life"?

"Along with, 'Come home now,' 'What are you doing?' and the classic, 'Where the hell are you?' And great use of full names. *That* much I don't need translated." He raised a hand in greeting toward the back of the RV as Granddad appeared. "Help me—so far, we've had Aurora, Declan

Joseph, Kenna Victoria…"

"And a hearty, all-caps Edith Hilda," Granddad finished, leaning over Edie's shoulder to look at the screen. "Her mom is *not* a happy camper."

I could well imagine. Though she lacked a fae temper, Beth was the first to jump our cases whenever we did something stupidly dangerous. *How mad is she?*

"Hang on, Edie's got the message up…okay, red text, italicized, and bold. 'I've played this game before. Call me.' The last bit's underlined, too."

Grimacing, I wondered what notes my own parents might have sent my way.

As I stood, Edie noticed I was awake and muttered, "Morning. Did the deluge wake you?"

"Time to get up, anyway. I heard we have mail."

"And how. You want to check?"

"Not particularly, but I probably should," I replied, and slid into the booth beside her. Bracing myself, I logged in to discover eight messages from Mom and five from Pa— even one from Avus, subject line *Call home now.*

As I scanned my family's increasingly frantic one-sided correspondence, Publius said, "That's five for five—I see a Cecilia Maria."

"Bolded and all caps," Granddad murmured. "Nice touch, Kitty."

I pointedly glanced over my shoulder at the peanut gallery. "If you think for one minute that I'm answering these, you're nuts."

"Care to translate?" my brother asked Granddad.

He patted Publius on the shoulder. "Patience. And you don't have to answer, hon—Gaw already did."

"*What?*" I yelped. "Why?"

"Why what?" asked Edie, unperturbed as usual to find me yelling at nothing.

"Why did Gaw write back?"

"Oh. Because his parents are least likely to start a manhunt, and we figured that minimal reassurance was a sound strategy. Here, do you want to read the message from Ros?" she offered, pulling her computer closer.

I waited while she retrieved it, then scanned Gaw's mail and muttered, "Six for six."

Gawain Bolin Rockwell,

> *Your dad and I are worried sick about you. We don't know how you slipped out last night, and we don't know where you're headed. We can only assume you're with the rest of the kids. While the fact that you're probably not wandering the woods alone does give us a measure of comfort, we'd much prefer knowing you were safe and sound.*
>
> *Wherever you are, I hope you're feeling loads better. Baby, I'm so sorry for everything. I should have told you my suspicions, but I didn't want to worry you, and…well, that was a terrible idea. I'm many things, but infallible has never been one of them.*
>
> *If you need to disappear for a while—even a <u>long</u> while—Dad and I understand. Just know that we love you with all our hearts, and we're not angry. If you could let us know you're okay, we'd really appreciate it.*
>
> *All my love,*
> *Mom*

"That's sweet of her," I said, passing the computer back to Edie.

"Yeah, but that's not the last message she sent," Edie replied, tapping at the screen. "Here, this came in overnight."

Hi, sweetie,

> *Just so you know, Hope and Arik are here. They arrived around dinnertime—it took them a while to convince Conota to tell them where Raurit went. Obviously, they're worried*

about their son. Please, if you could just tell us that he's safe, that would help.

"What did Gaw tell them?" I asked.

"That we're all fine, Raurit came of his own volition, and we need our space." She shut down the computer and flashed a strained smile. "And since it's Gaw's head they're after, I thought it only fair to leave the question of how much we reveal up to him." Looking up at the sound of running footsteps, she smiled as the door was flung open and our drenched companions hustled into the RV. "Any good?" she asked them.

Gaw ripped a paper towel from the kitchenette's roll and dried his face. "Greasy but filling. And we deliver," he said, holding a plastic bag toward me. "Yours is on top, Raurit's is underneath. Eggs, bacon, potatoes, toast, extra butter and grape jelly."

"Have I mentioned lately that I love you?" I replied, fishing my breakfast from the bag.

He kissed the top of my head, dripping rainwater onto my shoulder, then stole a broken piece of bacon from the carton before I could protest.

The morning rain held steady, but Aurie took us out around eight, once she was decently dry and caffeinated. Between the weather and Chicago up ahead, we wanted someone well experienced at the wheel, and Gaw kept her company up front while Edie read and I stared out the window, periodically butting into their conversation.

Around four in the afternoon, as we cut across Wisconsin on I-94 beneath clearing skies, I heard Gaw quietly ask Aurie, "What do you remember about Faerie?"

"Not much, honestly," she replied, holding the wheel with her stubby left arm while she grabbed a sip of her drink. "I was only there twice, and once was the night I hatched, which is *super* fuzzy. I mean, I've got impressions from that night, but they're mostly related to Dad."

"And the other time?"

"I was one, and Dad took me to my grandfather's house to keep me safe about a week before everything was destroyed. I remember going through augmentation—wouldn't wish that on my worst enemy," she muttered—"and Granddad's place was gorgeous. I had a big room there, and the grounds were lovely, and he played with me and read me stories until the Arcanum attacked and we evacuated. That's really all I remember of—no, one other thing. The smell of magic. It was so strong, and there wasn't enough dark magic for me to breathe fire, which I'm sure didn't upset Dad and Granddad in the slightest. But that's all I know of the realm," she said. "I didn't exactly get the tour."

Gaw munched a handful of peanuts in quiet contemplation, then asked, "How many people were left behind?"

"Couldn't tell you. I bet that not all of the courts evacuated, and I know that most of the Fringe stayed behind. Ros says some of the piq got out, but I've never seen any but Kuni. And then there's the rest of Dad's family, his mother and siblings and my cousins. They didn't make it."

"A whole world wiped off the map in a matter of moments," he said softly. "It's hard to imagine."

"It was chaos. Ed pulled me out of there as the ground around Granddad's house started breaking up, and I relived some of that day in nightmares for a few years. Dad *still* gets the panic dreams from time to time," she confided. "We were the lucky ones who made it, and if Ed weren't so good with gates, I might not be here."

I thought Gaw had dropped the matter until he murmured, "When you weigh one life against all of that…"

"Stop," Aurie ordered, releasing the wheel to grip his arm. "What happened back then wasn't *your* fault, and even if Faerie still exists, there could be nothing left but a wasteland. The last minutes were awful."

"Or," he countered, "everyone who didn't make it out could still be there. Trapped." He sighed and rummaged through the peanut can. "No way to find out unless Faerie is restored."

"Yeah, well, don't do it on my account," said Aurie as she grabbed the wheel again to straighten our course. "Dad's siblings tried to kill me. For all I care, they can rot."

The trip would have been faster had we picked up the beltway northwest of Chicago and avoided the city, but we were too close to the metropolis to miss the view.

The sun had already set when we zoomed down the Kennedy Expressway, but the lights of the skyscrapers rising ahead of us kept our crew glued to the windows. Even Raurit, who'd been trying to stay out of the view of passing motorists, pressed his nose against the glass to take in the sight. "Incredible," he declared as cars swerved around us, the thousands of headlights and taillights adding to the glow of summer twilight. "This is a city? A human city?"

"Biggest one I've ever seen," said Gaw, kneeling on the futon beside him to watch the world whizz past. "I thought Anchorage was decently large, but...*wow.*"

"The mountains have been lovely, but we have such at home," said Raurit. "Nothing like this, though. Not even the towers of High Vale can compare to such as...what did you call it, again?"

"Chicago."

He repeated the word, feeling it in his mouth. "Fascinating. Are we close to Oklahoma, by chance?"

Granddad chuckled behind him. "Closer than you were in Alaska, kid, but it's all relative."

"Not really," said Gaw. "Why? What's in Oklahoma?"

"My grandmother was born there," he replied. "Speaks of it sometimes. I didn't know if we would pass it on this trip."

"We're not going through it," said Edie, turning around in the shotgun seat. "Once we get through Chicago, it's I-94 into Indiana, then we pick up I-65 south of Gary and head for Indianapolis, then on to Kentucky and Louisville. We'll turn east on I-64 and follow that into the Cumberland Plateau—that's the edge of the Appalachian Mountains, nothing too extreme," she explained—"and then we'll follow Granddad's route to your uncle's place."

"But we could stay on the road," I hastily suggested. "Once we find this other compound, we could take the RV for a long trip down here. Head west, find Route 66, and all that jazz."

"Could be fun," said Kenna, and Dec nodded from his spot in the dinette. But Gaw didn't look away from the window, and when I joined him and Raurit, his expression was inscrutable.

Though the traffic was unlike anything we'd ever experienced, Aurie had nerves of steel on the road, and she made it safely through Chicago. Exhausted, she relinquished the wheel to Dec near Gary that night, then retreated to the bedroom to crash after her long shift.

Dec was well rested and adequately caffeinated, and Kenna kept him company as the semis rumbled past us in the darkness. Those of us wrestling with insomnia caught glimpses of the cities on the way—none of them as impressive as Chicago had been, but the sheer proximity of so many urban areas was mind-blowing to me after my childhood in the middle of nowhere. Finally, around four Wednesday morning, Edie traded places with Kenna to guide Dec along the increasingly smaller roads as we drove deep into the country.

At Granddad's strong suggestion, we stopped at a

lonely McDonald's in a tiny town for breakfast around dawn. While Dec regained his land legs and Raurit and Edie tidied the RV to clear a space to eat, the rest of us wandered into the restaurant to order and use a real bathroom. Soon, with faces washed in the sink and arms laden with breakfast sandwiches, we emerged to share the bounty. But as I neared the vehicle, my grandmother appeared by the side door, her face somber.

What's wrong? I asked, not wanting to unnecessarily worry the others.

She sighed, a feat that should have been impossible for a being without lungs, then pointed to the RV. "Inside, dear girl. I have news."

I jogged up the steps and dropped my bags on the dinette table. Noticing me, Granddad and Publius glanced up from their conversation on the remade futon, then stiffened when Avia followed me in. "If you and Uther want to relive old times, you're late to the party," Granddad told her. "We're almost to the compound."

"This isn't a social visit," she replied. "I've come with a warning." Turning to Raurit, she said, "Your parents made a gate. They're waiting for you with your uncle's family…and all of your parents," she added, cutting her eyes to me.

Publius stood, his fists balling. "You didn't tell them—"

"Of course I didn't tell them. There was no need—Hope and Arik are far from stupid. The collective wisdom suggested that the lot of you might aim for Kentucky."

"What's up?" Edie asked, frowning as she passed me with the coffee carafe.

I realized my jaw was sagging and snapped my mouth closed. "They beat us there. My grandmother came to warn us."

A chorus of incredulous groans sounded around the RV. "*How?*" Kenna demanded.

Avia waited while I relayed the question, then

explained. "Conota would not help them or allow them to make a second gate from that realm, but eventually, there was sufficient dark magic flowing near the gate for Arik to open his own within this world."

Raurit's eyes widened. *Is my uncle's family*—

"Safe," she assured him. "They've had a difficult time without glamour, but the ones among them who pass most readily for human have tended to the others. And now that they have a way out, quite a few of them seem interested in repatriation. Your father and Fikwed spoke for half the night last night…and his daughter is most interested in meeting you," she added with a sly smile.

He perked at the news. *Lilian?*

"Exactly. She's twenty-seven, so close to your age. Don't ask me for her precise bloodline—seven-sixteenths cynaeli, I believe," she said, squinting at the roof as she made her calculations—"and she looks the part. Her father claims that her aging has ceased, and several of the other children appear to have inherited the longevity and youth as well. I think you'll find her pleasing."

His cousin, right? I asked, arching an eyebrow.

In name only, thought Raurit. *My father and Fikwed were raised as half brothers, but they don't share any blood.*

Recalling that the rest of the RV was waiting for an answer, I passed on what Avia had told us. "What do we do?" I asked the group.

"If you point me in the right direction," said Raurit, "I could walk to them. I'm sensing a little magic here, so if I follow it to the source—"

"We're not turning a purple guy loose to go wander the backroads of Kentucky alone," Kenna interrupted. "Daylight's coming. Okay, idea: what if we push on and hide out in a city? We could go back to Chicago, find a motel or something…yeah?"

"No," said Edie, folding her arms.

"It doesn't have to be a terrible motel—"

"It's not the motel that's the problem. Think about it:

dark magic is back, right? That means more gates."

"They got a lucky guess that we were heading to Kentucky," Dec protested. "If we backtrack, they won't know to follow us. I like Kenna's plan."

Edie rolled her eyes. "Did no one but me bother paying attention when we learned about blood traces?"

The guilty looks on Dec's and Kenna's faces spoke volumes.

"Edie's right, unfortunately," said Raurit. "With sufficient magic, my parents can track me. Sure, it'll take time for enough magic to diffuse in this realm to make the trace work, but if they grow worried and start opening more gates to speed along the process…"

The thought of trolls rampaging through a city center made me squirm, but I didn't want to surrender. "They won't do that, not if you keep telling them you're okay. We could head for California, or maybe we could shoot for Mexico…"

But Gaw shook his head. "It's no use, Cici," he said gently. "I can sense Conota here, so I'm sure he can sense me."

"If we drive away from the new gate—"

"It has nothing to do with the gate. I've felt him ever since we left home, and that's only been growing stronger." He drummed his fingers on the kitchen counter, then sighed and set his jaw. "I'm ready to talk to them."

"*Gawain*," I began, squeezing his arm.

"Wherever we ran, we'd just be prolonging the inevitable. There's no harm in talking, is there?"

I heard the lie in his voice, and his carefully blank expression told me he knew it.

"Let's go meet Raurit's uncle," said Gaw, unwrapping a sausage biscuit. "Not like we have a better option."

The final hour of our journey was quiet. Most of the conversation came from the front as Edie navigated for

Dec. Granddad watched over her shoulder, but Publius and Avia had disappeared, leaving me to stew as the RV bumped along the rutted roads.

As the sky lightened toward sunrise, we turned onto a narrow strip of asphalt barely wide enough for our vehicle and fenced in by tangled trees on both sides. Glancing out the window, I could just discern wisps of dark magic floating by, and I looked at Aurie in time to see her tongue flick from between her lips. "You smell it?" I murmured.

She nodded. "Faint but growing stronger. I suppose they must have made the intra-realm gate near the inter-realm one to take advantage of the outflow."

I turned to Gaw, who'd taken a seat on the futon with me. "Still feeling Conota?"

"Yeah."

He stared straight ahead, and I squeezed his arm to reassure him. "We're with you, okay? We won't let them ambush you—"

"I'm not worried about that. Raurit, would you…uh…"

Raurit, who was sitting at the dinette with the last of the fast food, frowned in query. "Would I what?"

"Bag. Under the sink."

"*Oh.*" Jumping out of the booth, he pulled a garbage bag free and thrust it into Gaw's hands. "Are you—"

Gaw snapped the bag open, then took a deep breath and buried his head inside it. I rubbed his back as he threw up his breakfast, and Kenna pulled a can of ginger ale from the tiny fridge for him when he came up for air. "Thanks," he muttered, popping the tab, and took a sip. "Oh, that's *gross*. I'm sorry."

"We're almost there," Edie called back. "Do you want to ride up front? It's better for motion sickness."

"I'm queasy from the dark magic, but this road isn't helping," he said. "Damn it, Dec, are you trying to hit every pothole?"

"It's a skill," our driver retorted. "Just keep the puke in

the bag, eh?"

We passed a wide patch—a turnaround spot, I thought—then crawled along the deeply rutted road for another few minutes until we crested a little hill. Dec stopped at the top and called, "Come see."

The rest of us pressed toward the front of the vehicle to look out the windshield. Ahead, tucked into a little valley, was a compound of brick and wooden buildings, maybe three dozen houses and storage barns. Unlike our community, they hadn't bothered to put up a wall, but the ring of thick woods around the clearing served as a natural barrier. Within, the houses sat along dirt tracks on plots of summer-green land, some with lawns, most with gardens. A few large trees between the houses offered shade. To my surprise, the windows in every house glowed. Either the locals were early risers or something major had occurred.

Approaching us at the edge of the settlement, where the asphalt finally surrendered to patchy gravel, was a figure in a wash-faded green T-shirt and jeans. In the glow of our headlights, he looked human: decently tall and muscular with black skin and handsome features, his long hair worn in a thick ponytail comprised of tiny braids. As he closed the distance, I noticed his eyes—a curious blue-green shade, striking with the rest of his coloration.

"Is that your dad?" Kenna asked Raurit.

"No," he replied, but he sounded excited. "Let me out here, I'll talk with him."

As Dec put the RV in park, Raurit jumped from the side door and ran to meet the man, who flashed an ear-to-ear grin and threw his arms wide to embrace the newcomer. I couldn't hear their conversation—and even if I'd been able to, I'm sure I wouldn't have understood a word—but their faces spoke volumes.

"That must be Fikwed," said Aurie. "And…yeah, looks like he's coming aboard…"

Raurit found us in an uneasy clump near Dec and Edie when he hopped up the steps. "This is my uncle!" he announced, stepping aside to let him board. "Fik, this is, uh—"

"Your posse," he finished with a grin, his English accented by a curious mix of cynaeli inflection and a drawl. "Goodness, I haven't seen this hunk of junk in twenty-seven years," he said, patting the wall. "You kids drove down from freaking *Alaska*?"

We nodded.

"Damn. Well, you certainly made good time, and welcome. I'm afraid we don't have a breakfast spread for you—quite a few of us are prepping to go home while we've got magic and a gate," he explained. "But your parents are all waiting down below."

"Scale of one to ten, just how filicidal are they feeling?" Aurie asked.

He wiggled one hand below his waist. "Probably a solid two. They've been worried, and I don't blame them, but I think they want you alive. Want me to show you where to park?"

Fik guided Dec down the hill and behind one of the barns to a patch of scrubby grass, where several old trucks and vans were lined up in two neat rows. A small crowd ran up to greet us, and we let Fik disembark first. As soon as Raurit was out, a man a hair shorter than Fik and with a far more violet complexion grabbed Raurit by the shoulders, tried to produce words for a few seconds, then gave up and hugged him. The purple-skinned woman who threw her arms around them both was a head shorter but held on just as tightly, and it didn't take a genius to deduce that Raurit's parents were happy to see him in one piece. By the time they released him, Fik was leading a young woman toward their huddle. Svelte, with a cynaeli skin tone and Fik's distinctive eyes but brown hair too light to be anything but human, she smiled at Raurit, spoke briefly, then hugged him around the neck. He stumbled, unprepared for the contact, but I could see his excitement when he pivoted toward the RV—understandable, as the woman I assumed to be Lilian was stunning.

Before the rest of us could exit the vehicle, Kenna retreated to the bedroom, then quickly returned with her pistol at her side. Dec noticed and followed suit, and I trailed after him to pull my gun from my bag. Soon, even Gaw was armed—everyone but Aurie, who snorted when Kenna asked if she wanted a gun. "Breath weapon, babe," she said, and sent twin tendrils of smoke out her nostrils as proof. "Don't need a .38 when I'm packing a flamethrower, right?"

"Just try not to crisp me," Kenna retorted, and led the way out.

I watched from behind as she hit the ground and drew her gun, and then I picked Toula, Coileán, and Avus out of the nearing crowd and knew why she was tense. "No closer," she snapped, though she aimed the barrel at the ground. "Hands where I can see them."

The locals kept a healthy distance, and Toula, the nearest of our parents, stopped and showed Kenna her palms. "No one's going to attack you," she said, her voice remarkably level for someone that close to a loaded weapon.

"I'm not worried about *me*."

"No one's going to attack Gaw, either. I swear it."

But Kenna didn't move. "Cici?"

"Right behind you," I said, descending with my hand at my hip.

"Do we have any assurance that they're not lying through their teeth?"

I glanced around the crowd until I spotted Arnold loitering at the edge. *Is this a trap?*

"Heavens, no," he said with a scowl, stepping around a knot of worried cynaeli before they could back through him. "Be reasonable, Cecilia. They've been scared to death that something would happen to you kids—no one's going to pounce on you."

Overhearing our conversation, Raurit's mother nodded

fervently. "He's right. This isn't an ambush," she said, putting herself between her son and our guns. She paused briefly, considering me, then murmured, "You're Cici, then?"

"Yeah."

"I'm Hope." She cut her eyes to her husband before glancing back at me. "Believe me, honey, I know what it is to jump in that thing and drive like hell because someone you love needs a miracle. I *get* it. And if I thought for one second that your families were going to hurt that boy, I'd never have brought them to you. Okay? Please put your weapons away. There are small children here, and I'd hate for something to happen to them."

"You trust her?" Kenna muttered, not taking her eyes off of Toula.

At that moment, I didn't know *what* to think, but logic warned me that we were surrounded by people who could use dark magic, the air was growing thicker with it by the minute, and if we tried to jump in the RV and drive out, we'd never make it to the road.

"Close enough," I told Kenna, and moved my hand away from my pistol. As she holstered her gun in turn, I spotted my parents standing a few yards away, Pa watching anxiously, Mom wringing her hands in agitation. "Hi," I said to them.

"Hi, sweetie," said Mom, who looked like she wanted nothing more than to dart across the distance and grab me. "Are you okay?"

"Fine." I stared at Avus until he raised his hands in surrender and stepped back into the crowd, then turned and called into the RV, "Come on out."

Slowly, the others emerged. Gaw came last, clinging to his sick bag, and I wrapped my arm around his back in case he felt woozy. We lingered close to the door, while our elders made no sudden moves.

Finally, a thin, bespectacled, white-haired man, stooped and leaning on a carved wooden cane, hobbled between our factions. "Welcome," he told us in a voice wobbly with age. "From what I've heard, you must have been hauling ass all week. When did you last stop?"

"There was a McDonald's up the road," said Edie.

"No, no—when did you *stop*? Get a good night's sleep?"

We looked at each other, trying to separate the days and nights that had run together. "Uh…there was an RV park in North Dakota…" Edie began. "We pulled out Tuesday morning…"

"And you must have driven straight through to here, then," the old man finished. "Come on, you can stay with me until the ground stops moving," he said, and began to walk away. When we didn't immediately follow, he turned back and frowned. "I raised six kids. Beds aren't a problem."

"Not to be rude," said Dec, "but who are—"

"*Oh*. Sorry," he muttered. "Steve Brownfield. Quasi-patriarch around here." He peered more closely at Dec. "You're Coileán's boy?"

"I, uh…yes?"

Steve sighed and shook his head, then pointed his cane toward Coileán. "No visitors until they sleep it off. I mean it."

Coileán folded his arms. "Whatever you say, Drago," he replied, but as we walked away, I caught him watching Dec with an inscrutable expression on his face.

"**T**his is the second time now that one of Coileán's children has exhibited patricidal tendencies," said Publius, who sat at the foot of the musty twin bed into which I'd crashed. "Of course he's upset."

As a child, I'd come to understand that I wasn't the only one of us with a deceased half sibling. But whereas my brother had been a part of my life from the start and was remembered fondly, if wistfully, by our father, Dec's sister was mentioned only enough for us to be warned not to bring her up. Of course, curiosity is a powerful motivator, and Publius had filled in what gaps he could. I learned at first that Coileán's daughter had been called Moyna and that she had died twenty-seven years before Dec was born. Not until I was a teenager did Publius give me a fuller picture: she'd died because she was trying to kill Coileán, and Avus had been the one to strike the blow. Moyna had loathed her father for binding her and messing with her memory, and Coileán knew he'd screwed up with her. I had to hope that seeing his son with a drawn gun was making Coileán worry that he was in the wrong once again, though I could understand why the situation would leave him uneasy.

If it makes him keep his hands off Gaw, then I don't care if he gets his feelings hurt, I replied, fidgeting under the light blankets. The air conditioner in the window was doing its best, but late July in Kentucky was unpleasantly warm. *How does he know this Steve guy?*

Publius chuckled. "Arnold says they crossed paths when Steve was a young wizard, calling himself—let me see if I remember this correctly—'Drago, Dark Lord of the Storm.'"

I winced. *Ooh.*

"Come, now, we all have embarrassing phases," he said with a smirk. "Anyway, I think Coileán beat him in a fight or two, but that was years ago. They seem to be on decent terms now, from what I've witnessed."

So you got here before we did? Is that where you went after breakfast?

"Only for reconnaissance purposes. And to have a *frank* discussion with Avia," he muttered. "She truly didn't betray you, I guarantee that. Once Hope arrived, Avia was able to speak to the compound...well, at least to our family. Few among the fae have better than a minimal understanding of Latin," he said, rolling his eyes.

She spoke to them? I asked.

He nodded. "I've told you what Hope can do. She gave Avia a few moments of full visibility and audibility so that Avia could tell the rest to be gentle with you runaways."

I frowned. *Oh?*

"She says she reminded them that Gaw is petrified and trying to come to terms with himself, and the rest of you are trying to protect your friend from what appears to be a threat against his life. Apparently, Avus protested that there was no danger—"

I grunted at that, and Publius nodded. We'd both seen the hopeful, hungry look on Avus's face that day by the gate.

"She raised her voice with him. Reminded him that this problem isn't merely some difficulty in the great plan to restore Faerie—this is Gaw's life up for discussion, and you're barely more than children." He leaned back on his elbow and stared at the smooth plaster ceiling. "At least Pater seems to understand why you would be inclined to run. He's not angry, incidentally, and neither is your mother. You scared them, but they're more relieved than irked."

What do we do now? I asked him. *If we make a run for the RV, they'll probably try to stop us...*

"Don't run."

Then what?

"The person here whose opinion is most important is Gaw, and he wants to negotiate," said Publius. "He's correct—if more gates open, the dark magic will only make him sicker. That, plus invading trolls and whatnot. What happens next must be his decision, Cici. Let him lead for now."

You say that, but I'm worried he's leaning toward suicidal.

My brother continued to study the ceiling, and in that moment, I saw the weight of his true age on him, the impressions left by experience.

"There are worse things than death for a greater cause," he finally replied. "And if the problem is within him…you can run as far as you like, but he'll never escape himself."

But—

"Sleep," he said, going to his feet. "I'll wake you if Coileán tries to break in."

Wait, I began, but Publius had already vanished.

Stymied and frustrated, I flopped onto my side, sure that sleep would evade me. The last week had been exhausting, however, and soon, lulled by the white noise of the window unit, I drifted off.

CHAPTER 8

I woke around two that afternoon, disoriented and parched, and stumbled to the window to reorient myself. Yes—this was Kentucky, and most of the houses I could see had stuffed bags and stacks of fresh cardboard boxes on the porches. People milled around, most of them sweating but calling and waving to each other in seeming good humor. For a moment, I just watched, curious at the mix below. A few were obviously cynaeli, but some skewed human in their features…and then there was the odd blue person. Either they were naturally bald or kept their hair shorn, and I couldn't imagine that they ever left the property—their ears were small and pointed, they had heavy brow ridges, their faces seemed to lack noses in favor of a pair of slits, and if I was counting correctly, they had six eyes, a main pair with four smaller eyes extending toward the temples, all of them solid black.

"Tennuwaya," said a quiet voice behind me, and I jumped and spun to find Gaw looking over my shoulder. "Sorry, didn't mean to startle you," he said as I caught my breath. "Steve said the blue ones are called tennuwaya. I figured that was what you were staring at."

Gaw looked like he hadn't slept in days. Pale, with dark circles like bruises beneath his eyes and a wan smile, he clutched a fresh trash bag in one hand and took a step back as I leaned against the wall. "How'd you sleep?" he asked.

"Pretty well. How are you feeling?"

"Like shit." He rattled the bag as proof. "At least this

one's still empty. I don't know if I'm going to be able to look at McDonald's ever again."

"You should rest," I told him. "Go back to bed."

"Nah. It's a lost cause. And seeing as you're up…"

He followed me into the kitchen, where I downed two glasses of water from the filter pitcher in the fridge. As I refilled it, I asked, "Where are our parents?"

"I don't know," said Gaw, "but whatever Steve told them seems to have done the trick. They haven't come snooping, as far as I can tell. Why," he asked with a grin that might have seemed lascivious, had he not looked so ill, "did you have something in mind?"

I grabbed a dishtowel off the stove handle and thwacked him in the arm. "Not if you're going to go five minutes and then puke all over me." He laughed, and my heart broke a little to hear how weak that sounded. "It's not too late," I told him, tossing the towel aside. "We could still get out of here."

But Gaw shook his head. "There's a TV in the next room. Want to watch while we wait for everyone else to emerge?"

No, I didn't want that—I wanted to grab Gaw, jump in the RV, and make tracks for the ends of the earth. Instead, I said, "Sure," and we found an old movie to watch with the volume low. After ten minutes or so, he leaned his head against me, and soon, he was asleep on my shoulder.

Our elders didn't bother us until nightfall, after Steve had seen to it that we'd had a chance to sleep, shower, and eat dinner. When I'd asked after Raurit, he'd flashed a sly smile, exposing a missing premolar. "Last I saw of him, he was helping Lily pack. Something tells me that isn't *entirely* altruistic. The first wave's leaving tonight, incidentally, so you'll have plenty of space to spread out here while you work on your, uh…problem."

After we cleared the plates and got Gaw another ginger

ale, someone knocked at the front door. As the six of us traded glances, Steve shuffled toward the foyer, calling, "Hold your horses, I'm coming." I couldn't see who was on the porch when he opened the door, but Steve said, "No one in here is armed, and I hope the same goes for you."

I would have known Avus's voice anywhere. "Likewise," he replied. "May we…"

Steve stepped aside and motioned toward the den with his cane, and they filed in: Avus, Coileán, Toula, Ed, Ros, and Sam. As they took their seats on the couch and padded window benches, Kenna stepped out of the kitchen and asked, "Everyone else went home?"

"No," said Coileán, "they're here. We just thought you'd rather not feel ambushed, all things considered."

She grunted, then gave her head a sharp toss, motioning for us to join her. We filed out, Gaw leaning on me and Aurie keeping close in case he should trip, and I took momentary comfort in the knowledge that the only person in the room capable of weaponizing dark magic was on our side. I deposited Gaw in a leather recliner and perched on the arm, and the rest of our posse pulled up seats around us, minding the clear line of demarcation in the den.

Ros broke the tense silence. "How're you feeling, sweetie?" she asked Gaw.

He offered a weak shrug. "Been better."

"Nauseated?"

"Very. Thanks, Edie," he added as she hurried back to the kitchen to retrieve his forgotten emergency trash bag. "To tell you the truth, this is pretty fucking miserable, and I'd prefer not to be close to a massive source of dark magic any longer than absolutely necessary, so…what's the plan?"

Our elders looked at each other as if hoping someone else might have a surprise answer.

After a moment, Toula scooted forward on the couch

and clasped her hands atop her knees. "We don't have one."

"Seriously?" Kenna retorted. "Aren't you supposed to be, like, the best magical experts in the world or something?"

"I might not go that far, but we're not stupid," Ed dryly replied. "That said, we're facing a situation so far beyond the bounds of conventional thaumaturgy that we're playing exclusively with hypotheticals and probabilities."

"But there's no rush," Ros interjected. "None at all. Arik has offered to put guards on the existing gates for now, and that'll buy us time to figure this out without having to worry about a monster invasion. And we *will* figure this out," she insisted, holding her son's gaze. "I swear, baby. Your dad and I aren't going to let anyone hurt you, okay? Please trust us."

"We can go back to Alaska tomorrow and work on it," Sam offered. "Let the brain trust stew for a while. Or if Alaska's miserable right now"—Gaw nodded vehemently—"we could go somewhere else. Is Fairbanks far enough? We can get a long-stay hotel, okay, buddy? You, Mom, and me. We're not going to let anything happen to you," he added, and shot a quick warning glare at the rest of his party.

"That sounds nice," Gaw told his dad, but then he turned to Coileán and Avus. "Be honest with me."

"Of course," said Avus.

"How many were left behind when Faerie collapsed?"

The two of them shared a long look, and then Avus said, "I don't know. Your mother would be the authority on that, but…"

"But everything was chaos at the end," Ros said when his voice faded. "Personally, I was in too much pain to pay attention, and I've been severed from the group mind ever since—"

Gaw lifted a hand to pause her explanation. "What

group mind?"

"It's…useful but odd," she replied. "I was the fifth person to serve as the consciousness of the realm, but it wasn't just *me* at the controls. And thank whatever gods you like for that," she muttered. "I wasn't quite twenty-one when I took over. But part of each of my predecessors remained there, a group mind that I constantly tapped into. Memories, raw impressions, wisdom—a record of everything that had come before and how problems had been resolved. That mind might know how many didn't make it out, but I don't."

"Grandma and Grandpa," he murmured.

Ros nodded. "Yeah. Most of the Fringe didn't leave, either. A lot of them couldn't. I don't know who in the courts stayed, but…" She spread her hands. "I can't tell you how many, and I can't begin to speculate whether they're alive somehow or dead. I honestly thought Faerie had been destroyed until you came along, and…I knew then," she said softly. "I felt it in you, Gaw. But that's the only thing I can tell you for certain. No one in this room has the answers you're looking for." She stood and came around the table, and he squeezed her hand. "We'll make this right. *Together.* And I promise you, baby, as long as I draw breath, no one's going to hurt you."

"So, with that said," Ed interrupted, looking at our half of the room, "how about a cease-fire?"

We mumbled our tentative assent, and with that, they stood to leave. "Why don't you stay here tonight?" Coileán suggested. "Steve says he doesn't mind."

With our plans finalized, they headed out, but Coileán stopped in the foyer and looked back toward the den. "Declan, a word?"

Someone had left a window in the dining room cracked, and with the lights off, no one outside saw me sneak in there to eavesdrop as Dec and his father stepped onto the porch. I couldn't risk watching, but as I leaned close to the window, I heard Coileán quietly say, "I'm proud of you, son. Please know that."

"I'm sorry about the gun—" Dec began, but Coileán spoke over him.

"Forget it. You thought Gaw was in danger and came to his defense. I can't condemn you for that—moon and stars, I've done so much worse. But..." He paused, then said, "If I've done something to give you the impression that I was ready to kill that boy for a chance at restoring Faerie..."

"You guys looked a little too excited for my taste."

"Excited, sure, but not homicidal. I was deeply fond of Ros's father, and I know Aiden would love to have his sister back, but I'm not suggesting we stab Gaw in his sleep and hope they're still alive."

"I hear you," Dec began, "but I just..."

"Look at me, Declan. We watched you kids grow up together. Taught you, played with you, bandaged you up. Gaw's in no danger tonight." Coileán hesitated, then said, "I love you. I'm not going to lie to you."

"I love you, too, Dad," he said, and the sound of backslaps told me the two were hugging.

"Just tell me one thing, eh?" said Coileán.

"What's that?"

"How the hell did you drive that RV four thousand miles in *four days*?"

Dec chuckled. "Teamwork and short gas breaks."

"And you crossed an international border with an unglamoured cynaeli on board?"

"Twice," he said proudly.

Coileán hissed through his teeth. "Yeah, I'm going to chalk that one up to your mother's influence. See you in the morning," he said, and I hurried out of the room before Dec could catch me.

I felt better that night than I had in a week. True, we hadn't solved the problem yet, but at least I had reassurances that we were all on the same team. Still, I couldn't quite convince myself to sleep again, my rhythms having been thrown for a loop, and I rose a little after midnight Thursday morning, intending to retrieve my phone from the RV and play solitaire until daylight. Instead, I found a set of French doors halfway down the hall cracked open, and when I investigated, I caught Gaw sitting on the second-floor balcony in a rocking chair, hugging his trash bag and staring at the muggy night and the waning crescent moon. Noticing me, he flicked on a pocket flashlight as a guide.

"Can't sleep either, huh?" I asked as I let myself out.

He smiled and gestured to the empty rocker beside him. "I've been watching the evacuees settle in. That house down the road is still active," he said, pointing to the yellow-lit windows of a modest brick home several plots away, "but almost everyone else has called it a night. Guess packing is easier when you have magic."

We rocked in silence for a time, and I watched the tendrils of smoke-like dark magic drift through the air.

"How do you feel?" I asked.

"I'm okay."

"Liar." I slid my chair closer to his and took his free hand. "It's going to be all right, you'll see. Toula and Ed will figure something out."

Gaw smiled, but I saw sadness in his eyes by the flashlight's glow. "There's nothing they can do."

"Sure, there is! They know tons about magic—they'll make this better."

He shook his head. "If they know as much as I think they do, then they know my situation is hopeless. And Conota…he's been speaking to me all evening. In here," he added, tapping his temple before I could ask. "The gate between this place and home is close enough to the main gate that he can find me. He knows we're just wasting time."

"He can't *know* that," I protested. "And I bet he

doesn't have your best interest at heart."

"He doesn't, but that's neither here nor there." Gaw's rocker creaked, and he sighed softly. "I told you before that it feels like I'm full of lightning, yeah?"

"Yeah, you did."

"That's only getting stronger. Maybe it was dormant before, but with all the dark magic suddenly around…I guess it woke up. It wants out."

"Gaw," I whispered, and gripped his hand until my fingers hurt.

"We're talking about one person against everyone left behind in Faerie—"

"Who could all be *dead.*"

"Or alive. Trapped. Who knows? And no matter how many troops Raurit's parents send to the gates, Conota *will* make more openings. He's forcing my hand."

"Maybe he won't—"

"Oh, no, he told me that's exactly what he has in mind. He wants the third realm back. Balance and all that. So if I do nothing, this realm is going discover magic and monsters it doesn't know how to fight, and people will die," he said simply. "That's the bottom line, Cici. If I do nothing, people die."

I couldn't find the words in that moment, the magical words that would change his mind and make everything okay. Instead, I settled for the only ones I could manage: "But I love you."

"And I love you," he murmured. "I want you to be safe and happy and…and not stuck up in the compound, hiding from trolls for the rest of your life."

"I don't mind, as long as we're together."

Gaw freed his hand from mine and cupped it against my cheek. "If I was never supposed to exist in the first place, then everything to this point has been a bonus, and you have been the very best part of it. I'm so grateful to have had you…"

His voice broke, and I didn't care if he felt the tears

that had begun to escape my eyes. "Don't do this," I said, covering his hand with my own. "Please, Gaw. *Please.* I need you with me, okay? You and me, just like we planned. We're going to make a run for it. Let's take the RV tonight, we'll hit the road, Publius and Granddad will help cover our tracks," I babbled. "I'm awake, I can drive. We'll be so far away from that damn gate by morning…"

I paused, desperately hoping that he'd jump up and run away with me if I just gave him an opening.

But Gaw rubbed my tears away with his thumb instead. "I've made my peace. It's going to be okay."

"No, it's not."

"It *will* be."

"Let me go get your parents," I tried. "Ros can help—"

"There's nothing Mom can do. If Conota's right, she should have restored Faerie as soon as I was born. She just delayed it. I mean, I can't really blame her—guess it would be tough to do away with your own baby—but now it's on me. It's time."

My heart was breaking, but I had to keep trying. "Tell me what I can do to change your mind," I begged. "Anything, Gaw. I'll do whatever it takes."

He sat silently for a moment, then asked in a small voice, "Would you stay with me tonight? Please? I'm really fucking scared, and I don't want to be alone."

"I'm not going anywhere," I promised, and rose from my chair to kiss him. His back arched as he leaned into me, and I thought of all the nights we'd passed together—the times we'd sneaked into each other's house, the evenings in the Anchorage apartment when the others had gone out to give us privacy, those warm June mornings in the bachelor pad when I'd awakened in Gaw's bed, tangled in his arms, his breath tickling the hairs at the nape of my neck.

Those nights were meant to go on forever.

"We'd better stop before I get sick," he muttered, then kissed the corner of my mouth and held my hand as I sat beside him. "I'm sorry, Cici."

I didn't say anything, but I tightened my fingers in his and watched the moon make its slow ascent against the starry night.

Around six, as the birds chirped in the trees around us and the sky lightened toward dawn, I helped Gaw inside, down the stairs through the quiet house, and out into the yard. We stepped off the porch together, both of us barefoot in the grass, and wrapped our arms around each other. When we separated enough to kiss, I saw the glint of tears on his face, and I knew I had to be a splotchy mess, but that didn't matter. Nothing mattered but our embrace, and if I could, I'd have stood locked with him until the end of time.

But he wanted to go, and I couldn't keep him.

Slowly, fighting the urge to grab him and run, I released Gaw and tried to smile. He kissed me one last time, then said, "Stay there. I'm not entirely sure what happens next, but it'd be best if you weren't in the blast radius."

So I stood on Steve's nice lawn, quietly crying as Gaw stepped into the dirt road beneath the brightening sky. He turned back to face me, then gave me a sad smile.

His lips moved in a familiar pattern: *I love you, Cici.*

And then, in a brilliant burst of white fire, Gaw vanished.

I couldn't take it anymore. Screaming, I fell to my knees, my heart shattering beneath the pressure of the vise wrapped around my chest.

A moment later, I distantly heard the door behind me open and someone call my name—Edie, I realized, though I couldn't lift my face from my hands, I *wouldn't*, I didn't want to see what was left behind.

But she was persistent, my almost-twin, and she shook me until I was forced to look up at her. "What's going on?" she demanded. "Where's Gaw?"

I pointed past her, and she turned. "Shit," she said, "what *is* that?"

Where Gaw had last stood, there was a new gate—a lightning-rimmed hole in the fabric of space. I could see full daylight and a green meadow on the other side, and pouring through the hole was what appeared to be the colorful twin of the dark magic swirling around us.

Of Gaw, there was no sign.

I was still on my knees a few minutes later, surrounded by my friends, when our families sprinted up the lane to investigate the commotion. I glanced up in time to catch Ros as she glimpsed the gate and a look of horror twisted her face. "*Gawain!*" she cried, and ran through the hole with Sam on her heels. "Where are you?" came her voice, growing fainter but no less desperate as she headed into the unknown land. "Gaw, answer me! *Gaw!*"

Numb with shock and grief, I stayed in the grass, convinced that if I didn't get up, none of this would be real. Suddenly, my brother was kneeling with me, calling my name. I lifted my face, barely comprehending what I was seeing—reality seemed to have broken into its component elements, flashes of light and sound and smell and pain without coherent form—and slowly focused on him.

"*Cecilia*," he was insisting, trying to snap me from my daze without the benefit of being able to give me a brisk shake. "Can you hear me? Speak to me."

Something clicked in my mind as I listened to him. Gaw might be dead, yes, but he wasn't gone…

Where is he? I asked, looking over Publius's shoulder as if I might find Gaw lurking in the trees. *Is he…okay? Is he here?*

My brother's dark eyes softened. "Cici—"

Where is he? I begged as the world blurred with fresh tears.

He glanced up, and when I blinked the film away, I found our grandmother standing by, shaking her head. "I don't sense him," he murmured. "Neither does Avia."

But he's dead...

I let that thought go as a horrifying possibility presented itself.

As a medium, I'd always had one foot in a world most people couldn't see. Death wasn't *ideal*, sure, but it wasn't a true end. My family was proof of that, and even Arnold stopped by. If Gaw had killed himself to restore Faerie, then at least I would still have his spirit by my side.

Unless he hadn't just killed himself. What if whatever power had forced its way out of him had *destroyed* him in the process?

"No," I whispered, and staggered to my feet. I had to know, I had to *find* him, he couldn't have been obliterated...

Hands grabbed for me from the sides—Edie and Aurie, I learned later, though I swatted them off in the moment. I started toward the gate, that hateful thing that had swallowed Gaw whole, and found our families clustered around it. Ros and Sam were still somewhere on the other side, and Mom was staring at the opening with her hand over her mouth, shaking her head as Pa held her. Ed looked like he wanted to be sick. But as my eyes swept over them, I noticed Avus standing alone with Coileán, and his expression...

Maybe grief blinded me. Maybe he was as shocked as the others, and I just wasn't seeing it properly. But I could have sworn I saw awe on his face—awe, yes, and relief.

Rage swelled within me like a geyser shooting for the surface. That was nothing new—I'd been taught to control my anger ever since I was a little girl—but that time, I didn't tamp it down. I was too broken to fight it, and it found a focus.

How did Avus *dare* to take pleasure in my pain?

When I clenched my fists, I didn't just feel the bite of my nails against my flesh. The air itself seemed laden with potential, practically sparking, a conduit for my fury. With an enraged scream, I shot one fist in his direction as if I could punch him from yards away.

Something moved toward him, an impulse like a ripple through water. Avus barely had time to stiffen before the air in front of him shimmered into a hazy shield-like form. The blast of oncoming energy hit it and was deflected into the woods, where it slammed into a young pine and sent it crashing into the dead leaves.

I froze, my rage replaced in an instant by confusion and terror.

Avus's shield vanished, and he ran to hold me, murmuring comfort while I sobbed with fear. "You're safe," he said as I shuddered. "It happens. It's over. *Breathe*, Cecilia."

I didn't want to. I didn't want any of this awful new world where Gaw didn't exist and I could lash out at my grandfather with enough force to down a fucking *tree*.

But I drew breath all the same, over and over, until Avus and my parents coaxed me back into the empty house.

Ros and Sam returned empty-handed after an hour's search. Sam looked shell-shocked, but Ros could barely bring herself to speak, and so he provided the answers to which she couldn't give voice. There was no sign of their son. He never responded, and Ros couldn't feel him anywhere.

"What about you two?" he asked Coileán and Avus, who sat with them in Steve's den for the debriefing. "Can you hear him?"

Coileán shook his head. "No, not like I used to hear Ros near a gate. It's…I don't know how to properly describe it, but it feels like *static*…"

"As close a description as any," Avus concurred. "If there's an intelligence, I can't sense it. And the boost hasn't returned."

"Right," said Coileán. "Faerie's open, but no one seems to be home—and if you're not at the controls," he asked Ros, "then who is?"

She shrugged, and Sam said, "She doesn't know. I thought she might get her power back once she was over the border, but…well, see for yourself." He pulled Ros more tightly against him, and she closed her puffy eyes.

Avus hesitated and glanced toward the kitchen, where I stood by the counter, nursing a double of Steve's best bourbon, then asked them, "How did it look?"

"Good as new," Sam replied dully, stroking his wife's hair. "The sky seemed to be in one piece, anyway. Air's breathable. Magic is abundant."

Coileán opened his hand, and a blue fireball flared to life in his palm. He contemplated it briefly, and it vanished without so much as a curl of smoke.

I should have been floored. Learning about magic as an intellectual exercise was one thing—*seeing* it was another matter entirely, as Kenna's sharp gasp made clear. But I was hollow, my senses dull with fatigue and loss and alcohol, and I accepted it without question. Dec's dad could conjure fire. Sure. I didn't care.

Magic wasn't going to bring Gaw back.

The Kentucky settlement was clearing out, and our hosts' patience would surely wear thin in short order. Mom called Dr. Bee, who offered to give me a sedative if I wanted to go home and sleep until I felt less like either staring into space or screaming and punching a wall, but I declined. The others were going across to explore what was left of Faerie, and I was determined to accompany them to see whether Gaw gave his life for nothing.

Stepping between realms didn't hurt—it didn't even tingle. One moment, I was in Kentucky, breathing hot summer air almost thick enough to eat. The next, I was standing in an open meadow beneath a sky spotted with puffy clouds, a solid ten degrees cooler and quite a bit later in the day. The sun was declining already, and a pair of birds called back and forth from a nearby grove. And then there was the magic—*so* much magic, currents of potential that flowed around me like colorful foam on the surface of a bath.

It was beautiful, and I hated every inch of it.

I wanted my brother, but Publius had explained that he couldn't cross. In Faerie, I'd be on my own.

Judging by the look on Ros's face, she wasn't seeing much, but her lips moved every so often in a silent call to her vanished son. Sam kept his arm around her shoulders, though whether he was trying to give her emotional support or keep her off the ground was anyone's guess.

As Coileán and Avus held a quiet conversation a few feet away from the gate, I plopped into the grass and sighed. Kenna joined me a moment later, and the others quickly followed.

Five, now. We'd become five.

I leaned against Edie's shoulder, and she wrapped her arms around me. Kenna joined in our awkward hug, and even Aurie and Dec piled on. No one spoke until we disentangled ourselves, and when Dec broke the silence, I heard the warning hitch in his voice. "Why'd he do it? Why didn't he say goodbye?"

I saw the hurt in my friends' eyes, the flashes of wounded betrayal, but I had no good answers for them.

"He didn't think he had a choice," I said, plucking a blade of grass and twisting it between my finger and thumb. "Maybe he didn't want an argument—I tried to talk him out of it, but his mind was made up."

"He could have at least said goodbye," Kenna protested.

How, I wondered, did you say goodbye to the friends you'd known all your life? To people who were as close as blood?

"He didn't want to hurt anyone," I replied, which was

as true an answer as any I could have invented.

As we sat together, taking comfort in our shared mourning, Ed sidled closer and crouched outside our little circle. "He did a brave thing," he said when we looked his way. "A *noble* thing. Restoring this realm—"

"Please shut up, Dad," Edie interrupted.

Ed's mouth clamped closed, and without another word, he rose and left.

While our elders discussed the next steps among themselves, from time to time, one or two of them would break off from the main groups and wander toward us like spaceships sent to explore a strange, possibly hostile world. Sometimes, our glares were enough to make them depart. Other times, a firm request to stop with the fucking platitudes and give us room to grieve proved necessary. The only others we'd have accepted into our huddle were Sam and Ros, but they kept their own company, bound together as they were by the sudden, senseless loss of a child.

My numbness began to wear off, replaced by a raw feeling, as though I'd been hollowed out and filled with broken glass. The half-baked plans I'd concocted in which we struck out on our own and drove until we reached the end of the land seemed as pointless and ephemeral as soap bubbles in a blizzard. Gaw was gone, and nothing would ever be the same.

But as the shadows lengthened, Toula finally approached. "We're going to see if anything's left of the Fringe settlement," she announced. "Stay here if you want, but you're welcome."

Dec's brow furrowed. "How far away is it?"

"No clue," she replied with a shrug. "Your dad suggested a gate. Coming?"

Slowly, we got to our feet—Kenna helped pull me off the ground—and joined our families. They seemed anxious, and I wondered if they were waiting for us to bite their heads off for a moment before Coileán rubbed his hands together and stepped away from the group. "Here goes nothing," he said, then raised one hand and flicked his fingers in a shooing sort of motion.

Another gate ripped open, widening until it was large enough for me to step through without stooping. I saw more grass on the other side, but as the hole expanded, I noticed fountains and buildings…a wooden park bench…a streetcar running along…

Coileán stepped through the gate first, and a cry went up on the other side.

By the time I made it through with the rest of my housemates, a crowd had gathered around Coileán and Avus, strangers babbling in Fae and talking over each other. I joined Pa and Mom, who stood by a wooden trash can in the middle of an apparent park, observing it all in stunned silence. "This is where the Fringe lives?" I asked.

"Yeah," Mom murmured. "But there should have been earthquake damage, based on what Ros said…"

"*Slim*!" Coileán cried, and I glanced his way as a thin, bald man ran across the street into the park. Coileán pushed through the throng, and the two hugged on impact. The man seemed pleased, but Coileán was giddy, actually *laughing*, and my temper began to rise until Pa squeezed my shoulder.

"Who the hell is that?" I muttered.

"*That*," said Toula, who'd apparently overheard me, "is Slim Matherson. The crafter who saved the Fringe during their captivity."

The name did ring a bell. I remembered Arnold's lessons about the Mulligan years—the few Fringers and their allies who'd tried to spirit their comrades to safety in Faerie, the long standoff with the Arcanum, and the helpless witches locked in the darkness for more than a decade. Slim, he'd recounted, had made wands to keep the usurper grand magus from killing his captives, but his torture had left him emaciated and broken. He'd given up crafting upon his release in favor of running a bar.

And contrary to what I'd been told about Faerie's collapse, Slim seemed very much alive.

"Come on," said Toula, "we'd better head that way—"

"*Toula!*"

I wheeled around at the shout to find a youthful woman with a black ponytail and thick-framed glasses jogging toward us across the park. On her heels ran a man a full head taller than she was, a burly redhead in a straining gray T-shirt and jeans.

"What the hell is going on?" the woman demanded. "One minute, the sky is practically falling, and Ros is sounding the alarm, and the windows are smashing, and there's a *canyon* forming across the park…and now…" She flopped an arm at the pristine landscaping in exasperated bemusement. "What's happ—*oof*," she grunted as Toula wrapped her in a tight hug. "Uh…hello to you, too?"

Toula stepped back, grinning like a fool, then hugged the man in turn. "We thought you were *dead*!" she said as the man patted her back. "Holy shit, you guys…" Releasing him, she gave them their space but continued to beam. "How long did the rebuilding take?"

They frowned. "There was no rebuilding," the woman replied. "Like I said, everything was chaos, and in the next minute, it was mid-afternoon, and the town looked as good as ever. What gives?" Glancing past us, she paused and did a double-take. "Wait, is that *Ros*? Why isn't she glowing?"

As Toula gaped, unable to answer the woman's questions, Mom stepped in. "Hey, Vivi," she said, and waved when the woman looked our way. "It's Kitty. Remember me?"

Vivi's face crinkled. "Of course. Why wouldn't I?"

"Uh…well," Mom said slowly, "this is going to sound insane, but we've all been locked out of Faerie for twenty-five years. We thought it was destroyed."

"I'm sorry, *what*?" she asked, staring at Mom over her glasses.

"Long story. A bunch of us who fled ended up in Alaska, and we just saw Arik and Hope for the first time in ages, and, um…" She gripped my shoulder and nudged me forward. "This is our daughter, Cici."

Goggling, Vivi looked at Pa. "Is this some sort of joke, Marcus?"

He shook his head. "The mortal realm has been cut off all this time. No magic. We thought you…all of you…"

"Are her brothers okay?" Hal asked as Vivi reeled. "What about Rohese and Martin? Mal?"

"They're all just fine," Toula assured them. "Here, let me prove it."

Without further ado, she whispered and flicked two fingers, and a new gate opened a few feet away from her. In the early morning light, I saw the familiar houses of the compound on the other side, and Mom hugged me from behind as Toula marched through. Another quick gesture seemed to do something to her throat, as I heard her voice as clearly as if she'd found a microphone in transit. "Faerie's back!" she called to our town, her voice almost breaking with her joy. "Get out here, let's go! They're *alive*!"

CHAPTER 9

I recall moments of that afternoon, bright spots through the fog.

Mal crying out to his mom and dad and slamming into them so hard that he knocked both to the ground in a tangle of limbs.

Poor Vivi, who was not a large woman, getting practically dogpiled by her brothers in the middle of the park. Their mother ordered them to stop crushing their sister, but as soon as Vivi was free, Rohese swept her into her arms and gave her an anaconda-strength squeeze.

Coileán hugging a gray-haired old man in clerical garb, who'd been sheltering in the town's somewhat ecumenical church with a group of Fringers while the world ended.

Adam and Slim, talking a mile a minute about Adam's recent brewing experiments.

And then, about half an hour after Toula called the settlement across, a small gate popped open by the fountain and disgorged a confused couple: a muscular, blond man with a short, neat beard and a pretty brunette whose dark eyes scanned the crowd for answers. The first of our faction to recognize them was Aiden, Dec and Ros's uncle, who shouted, "*Hey!*" and barreled toward them.

A moment later, as they ran with him to find Ros and Sam, Mom murmured, "Helen and Joey. Ros's parents. That's Aiden's sister, and I know Joey's his cousin somehow, but don't ask me the details."

As night fell, Toula stood atop a bench to address the

assembled, which had swelled to a massive crowd of Fringers and most of our compound. In broad strokes, she explained what had happened: as far as they knew, Faerie had been in total stasis since its apparent destruction. The instant repairs that afternoon must have occurred at the moment of its restoration.

"Question," said a woman near the front of the crowd. I couldn't see much of her beyond her hair—a dark bob with a white streak—but her Fae bore a strong English accent. "Why the hell isn't Ros glowing? That can't be right."

"Badger Parsons," Pa whispered by way of explanation. "Arnold's cousin."

"Cop," Mom offered.

"Yeah, we, uh…noticed," said Toula, who seemed irked by the interrogation. "It seems like the realm's rebooting itself. We're going to take it easy for a few days, okay?"

Her explanation was weak, even to my ears, but the town seemed to murmur its accord.

As Mom and Pa said their hellos, I headed for the edge of the throng, where my friends had gathered in a tight clump. Nearing, I caught a flash of light, and as Kenna and Aurie parted to admit me, I found the source: Dec, who was cupping a little blue fireball in his hands. "What are you *doing*?" I asked.

He stared at the fire, which didn't seem to hurt him. "I…I don't know, I saw Dad do it, and I thought I'd try, and…it *happened*," he said, his tone somewhere between shocked and apologetic.

"My grandfather showed me how to do that the last time I was here, but it's been a while," said Aurie as Dec awkwardly held his flame. "Let me see if I remember…" She stretched out her lone hand and squinted, and in a few seconds, a baseball-sized white flame burst to life. "Yeah, that's it. It's not going to hurt you, Dec," she added, tossing the flame like a terrifying stress ball. "Just will it away." Catching hers, she closed her fist, and the fire instantly died.

It took him slightly longer, but he breathed a sigh of relief as his fireball winked out. "What…how did I…"

"Magic," she replied, thumping him on the back.

"Holy shit," he whispered. "I…I mean…*huh*." He looked as though he'd been struck between the eyes, which wasn't too far from the truth. We'd grown up hearing about magic, studying the histories of its practitioners, discussing techniques we'd never be able to use. Magic was something that had, once upon a time, happened to other people. That our theretofore theoretical lessons had suddenly become practical was a bizarre concept on its own, but finding that sort of power at our literal fingertips—pulling flame from the void, downing a tree with an angry gesture—was enough to send anyone reeling.

Power to change the world to our liking. To fight back against the things that crept through from Conota.

Gaw had died for *this*.

By then, Kenna had turned to experimentation, and she laughed incredulously as an orange fireball bloomed from her palm. "*Shit*, it works!" she said as the light glinted off her smudged glasses, then glanced at Edie and me. "Go on, try it. It's easy."

I didn't want to—not after what I'd done to the tree, not after Gaw—but tired as I was, I acquiesced. Holding my hand as Aurie had demonstrated, I thought about those alien sparks…and then I felt my will go out into the world, igniting the untapped magic around me. The fire appeared at my call, a violet flame that flickered and danced like a living creature. I passed my other hand over it, and it curled into a ball, a perfect, impossible sphere.

But Edie wasn't having any luck. She tried moving her hand into different positions, flexing her fingers, and even muttering exhortations at the stubborn fire, but it refused to light. As she scowled and switched hands, her father noticed us and swept in. Seeing me standing there bemusedly, holding an odd-colored fireball, and Edie softly swearing at nothing, he realized the problem and put his arm around her shoulders. "That's a faerie thing," he told her. "You'll be able to make fire with practice and focus, but not in quite the same fashion. We'll wand-test you soon enough, dear. And as for the rest of you," he continued, glancing around our ring, "unsupervised experimentation would be a *terrible* idea right now. You don't know your own strength. In the interest of not losing anyone else today, how about giving it a rest?"

I snuffed my fireball, and the others mumbled agreement.

As Ed moved off to rejoin Beth, Edie folded her arms and regarded us with a frustrated glare. "Well, that's just *dandy*."

I couldn't help feeling a slight twinge of satisfaction. All our lives, Edie had been the best student, the quickest on the draw in the classroom, and even a solid opponent when Mina made us spar. For the first time, the rest of us were intuiting something that she could not, and her annoyance was evident. But the feeling passed almost as quickly as it came. I didn't want weird powers or fire at my command. The one thing I wanted was beyond my grasp, and none of this strange magic was going to return Gaw to me.

Our parents sent us to Kentucky just long enough to grab our things from Steve's house, where we found the old man relaxing in his den while his children and grandchildren packed for him. Aurie drove the RV through the gate into the Fringe settlement, and a group of children ran up to stare as she cut the ignition. It was, I later learned, the first such vehicle that any of them had seen in person—there were no cars in town, nothing but the streetcars and bicycles, and the old gas-guzzling motorhome was an exotic wonder.

I didn't want to go back to our house in Alaska. The idea of walking past Gaw's empty bedroom on the way to mine was unbearable, and I thought I might just camp in the RV instead. Our families, however, had other plans. Apparently, Avus had a house large enough for company, so Pa, Mom, and I would be staying over, along with my aunts, Maria, Ed, Edie, Ennis, and Kenna. Dec would go investigate his father's old place with Toula. As for Aurie, her grandfather had already popped over to check on the state of his house, and finding it as solid as ever, he'd insisted that his son and granddaughter come home with him. The massive Stowe clan had accommodations in Faerie, as did the rest of the fae refugees. But when I looked around for Ros and Sam, I realized they were missing and asked my mother if they were set for the night. "They have a house near her parents' place," she told me. "Out by the dragon barn. Probably wouldn't be a good idea to disturb them right now."

Had I been in a better frame of mind, I might have been more appreciative of Avus's massive villa, a beautiful, sprawling complex tucked into a high valley ringed with peaks but for the bit he'd blasted away to make an ocean view. It was a far cry from the modest houses we'd had in the compound, a palatial structure of fountain-dotted courtyards, manicured gardens, and complex mosaics that seemed to move on their own. Lanterns lit as we entered—I had no idea whether that was automatic or an effect of Avus's doing—and my parents showed me to a well-appointed bedroom with an attached bath. "Get some sleep, baby," Mom told me as she opened the garden door to catch the breeze. "We're just down the hall if you need us." She hugged me tightly, rubbing my back as I stood like a mannequin in her arms, and murmured, "I'm so sorry, angel. Do you want to talk about it?" I shook my head, and she squeezed harder. "Whenever you're ready. I know a very nice counselor in town who might be able to

help. Dr. Wanda has worked with me…your dad…
Maria…hell, at least half the family. I could make an
appointment, if you'd like."

"Not yet," I mumbled.

"Okay, then. You just tell us what you need, baby.
Now, try to sleep, huh? For me?"

I kicked off my shoes and stretched out on the
unfamiliar bed, and Mom smoothed my hair from my face.
"We love you so much," she murmured. "And I am *so*
grateful to have you here with us. I know it doesn't feel
like it right now, but it's going to be okay."

I held my breath until Mom slipped out, biting back the
scream that tried to tear loose from my throat. I hated her
and Pa and Avus and all the rest of them for daring to
smile that day—to fucking *celebrate*—when Gaw hadn't left
me so much as a corpse to mourn. I, the girl who'd seen
ghosts all her life, couldn't sense a trace of him. My
boyfriend, my *best* friend, had been erased from existence,
and now I was stuck in a strange world, afflicted with
magical power I couldn't begin to control, and I didn't
even know how to turn off the goddamn lights in my
bedroom. Was there a switch I was overlooking? Some
sort of magical Clapper? Was this some sick practical
lesson Avus had concocted to acquaint me with my talent?

As my thoughts spiraled, I heard a knock. Before I
could tell the visitor to go away, Artur let herself in, then
locked the door behind her. She stood on the other side of
the room, regarding me with her arms folded, and I braced
myself for the rebuke to come: *Get up. Brush your teeth. Turn
down the bed. Stop wallowing.* That Artur loved me, I never
doubted, but she wasn't the aunt I went to for comfort
and reassurance. Beth used to kiss my boo-boos. Artur was
more likely to tell me that pain was a part of life and I still
had all my limbs, so stop sniffling.

That night, however, she sat at the foot of my bed and
joined me in staring at the wall. Neither of us spoke for a
long moment, and then she sighed softly and said, "I

know, Cecilia. Your mother means well, and she knows what it is to lose someone, but…I *know*."

I didn't reply.

"For instance, I know that when you allow yourself to stop and dwell on the morning's events right now, it feels as if someone has ripped away a chunk of your soul, and nothing in the universe will ever make you whole again," she said. "You want to weep, but if you permit yourself to begin, the pain is unbearable, so you hold back your tears and *hate* yourself because you should be weeping. He was worth your tears. You can't think of him without remembering every dream you ever had in which he played a role, all of which are now ruined forever." She turned my way, and I met her blue eyes. "I know, dear girl. And the tears you shed now aren't weakness—that's your humanity on display. There's no shame in it."

I forced myself to sit up before the dam burst, and my aunt held me as I bawled on her shoulder.

After a time, when my sobs had quieted to hiccups, she asked, "Have I ever told you about Kei?"

As kids, we'd been cautioned not to ask Artur too much about her past. She brought it up on occasion, but many of her memories seemed painful, and I had a fair idea as to why. She'd lost her mother at five and the man she considered her father at ten, leaving her with a throne but very little family support. In early adolescence, she'd learned from her biological father—my grandfather, though I knew damn well to *never* discuss him—that she'd been born female and locked into a male body for political reasons. While this should have helped explain her burgeoning attraction to her comrades-in-arms, instead, it left her horrified and committed to keeping her terrible secret buried. After all, if she was a woman, then her life was a lie—no one was going to follow a warrior *queen* into battle, and she would have become a marriable pawn. By fifteen, as a martial prodigy with minimal skill at enchantment and a sword created of crystalline magic, she was made high king among her people, their leader against threats from the east and from beyond the mortal realm. It was the latter that had ended her reign a decade later, when deadly creatures like living smoke had come through the gate that her father declined to close and slaughtered her men. Had she not been shipped off to Conota in stasis, she'd have died on the battlefield, too.

It was Beth who'd told Edie and me about Artur's men—Beth, who'd been a quiet Arthuriana nut in middle school and had ended up learning swordsmanship from the real deal. Beth knew *all* the legends, but she'd given us Artur's far less romanticized version as well. There had been no Round Table, but she'd taken four of her men into her close confidence, among them a guy her age named Kei. All had died in that final, desperate battle. Beth had hinted that there was something between Artur and Kei, but she warned us to leave that subject untouched with our reticent aunt.

"You haven't mentioned him," I told Artur, pulling away to wipe my face.

"He was one of my men," she said with a brief, strained smile. "One of my dearest friends. I could ask him for anything, and"—she snapped her fingers—"done. Intelligent, brave, kind…"

"Handsome?" I guessed.

She whistled. "You have no idea. Tall, dark, *beautiful* green eyes…" She sighed. "I loved him. And I never breathed a word of it. I *couldn't*," she hastened to explain. "Such a confession, from one man to another…this wasn't done, not that I ever heard. Perhaps in secret, but…well." She cleared her throat, then said, "I sent him into battle, and he went willingly. He died under my command. I would have done anything to save him, Cici, but there was nothing I could do, and…" After a brief pause, she took my hand and gripped it tightly. "I understand, my dear."

"At least Kei's still out there," I said. "Gaw's *gone*."

Her brow furrowed. "What do you mean, he's out

there?"

Too late, I realized that I'd revealed too much, but I decided that honesty wouldn't make the situation any worse. "Kei...stops by. On occasion."

Artur's eyes flew open wide. "You've *seen* him?"

"Sure. I've spoken to him. He's a nice guy," I added. "He, um...well..."

"*Out with it.*"

I took a deep breath while I gathered my thoughts, conscious of the weight of her stare, the hint of desperation and fear in her voice. "He loves you. Very much, in fact. But he doesn't like to make a fuss—"

"That was never his way," she said, nodding. "But still...why haven't you told me?"

"Because he asked me not to let on. He knew you'd want to talk, and since everything would have to go through me...he thought it would be awkward. Nothing like hearing sweet nothings from your ten-year-old niece, right?"

She regarded me, briefly flabbergasted, then started to laugh. Relieved to not be on the receiving end of her anger, I found myself laughing, too, and Artur hugged me again. But thinking of Kei and his sweet, awkward appearances around the compound led me back to Gaw and to the visits I'd never receive.

I don't know exactly when my laughter gave way to tears again, but my aunt continued to hold me through the fresh wave of grief. "I'm sorry," I finally managed, "I didn't mean to—"

"You've done nothing wrong." As I tried to calm my breathing, she said, "I'm not going to feed you useless sentiments about what a fine boy Gawain was or how he did an honorable thing. He's gone, and it doesn't matter why. You have every right to be heartbroken, Cici, and nothing I tell you tonight will lessen that pain." She pressed me against her shoulder, and I closed my wet eyes. "What I *will* tell you is that the pain will grow duller in time. It never fully fades, but it will lessen. And then there will come a day when he's not in the forefront of your thoughts, and you'll notice something—a familiar note in a voice, a flash of color, a smell—and he'll return to you, and all the pain with him, only sharper now because you've acclimated to its absence. That happens to me," she admitted. "Happens to Val, too, which doesn't bode well for its stoppage within the next millennium. But you'll learn to cope. You won't always feel as you do tonight."

"Everything hurts inside," I mumbled.

"I know." Rubbing my back, she said, "When I went through this—the day I woke here with my life gone to hell—your father barged in and refused to leave, and we got *roaring* drunk. Not my proudest moment, but it did make me feel slightly better. Do you want a drink?"

"No, thanks."

"Wise girl." She gave me a final pat, and I extricated myself from her arms. "Listen to me, dear: he loved you, and he wouldn't want you to mourn him for the rest of your life. Allow yourself to grieve, but when the day comes that you wake without the pain and catch yourself smiling, don't tell yourself that you're dishonoring his memory. Has your mother mentioned Wanda?"

"Counselor, right?"

"Yes. Speak with her." She rose and smoothed out the blankets, then offered me an odd little smile. "And if you should see Kei again…give him my regards, won't you?"

I promised to do so, but as Artur let herself out and closed the door, I recalled that I still didn't know how to cut the lights. Resigning myself to a miserable night, I flopped onto my side and tried to will myself to sleep.

Not two minutes later, I heard quiet footsteps in the garden outside my door and sat up to see who was skulking around.

"Hey," said Edie, raising a hand as Kenna joined her on the threshold. "Can we come in?"

"Sure," I said, and they joined me on the bed, all of us

still clothed but for our shoes. "What's going on?" I asked.

"Can't sleep," said Kenna. "Gaw's gone. I can make fucking *fire*. Take your pick."

"Amen," I muttered, covering my eyes with my arm. "Does anyone know how to turn off the damn lights?"

The bed creaked as Edie climbed down, and a moment later, blessed darkness descended over the room. "There's a dial on the wall," she explained as she rejoined us. "Can I have some blankets?"

The three of us rearranged ourselves as we'd done so many times before, squeezing together in bed to whisper.

"I'm scared," said Edie once she was sandwiched between Kenna and me.

"You'll figure out your power," Kenna reassured her. "Your dad said—"

"Not *that*. What does this mean for all of us?"

"You're going to have to be more specific," I replied.

Edie snorted. "If Faerie's back, then what's going to happen to the compound? Your family will stay here, right? But Mom and Dad and I aren't fae, and Dad's got a *history*, so…what, we're going to end up in Alaska by ourselves? All the Arcanum folks?"

"We probably shouldn't worry about that tonight," Kenna began.

But Edie wasn't having it. "Our hometown is about to blow up. More than half the people I've known all my life are going to leave the realm, and I…" Her voice began to hitch. "I *cannot* lose anyone else, okay? I can't."

"Edie—"

"We drove all that way, and we still lost Gaw. Now we're going to lose our home. If you two and Dec and Aurie stay here, and I lose you…"

Kenna and I hugged her until her crying calmed, and we remained tangled in each other's arms until I fell asleep.

To my surprise, I slept deeply and almost without dreams. I recalled waking once in the pitch-black room, certain that I'd heard Ros calling my name, but the house was quiet, the room silent but for Edie's and Kenna's soft breathing. Putting the matter from my mind, I snuggled back into my pillow and knew nothing more until dawn.

When I woke, it took me a moment to recall where I was and why I was sharing a bed with Edie and Kenna, and then the previous day came rushing over me like a black tsunami. I didn't want to get out of bed, and I tried with all my might to slip back to sleep, but before I had any luck, Bonnie rapped at the door and let herself in.

Bonnie, a short, pretty brunette with a pronounced Texas twang, had been like a surrogate grandmother to Sam. In the compound, she'd run after all of us kids at one point or another, doctoring scrapes, offering snacks, and refereeing arguments. If word got back to our parents that Bonnie had been forced to correct us, there'd be trouble. I knew that she'd done a stint as Avus's chief of staff, but like everything else pertaining to Faerie, that had seemed meaningless when I was a kid. Now that we were here, Bonnie had apparently slid back into her former role, even though I could make out the shadows beneath her eyes. Sam had been one of her babies, after all, and she'd loved Gaw like her own.

"You know," she said as we squinted at the sunlight coming through the open door, "there are plenty of rooms here. You girls don't have to share."

"Misery loves company," Kenna grumped.

"Mm. Fair. Well, I stopped by to say that breakfast is in the small dining room, and you're expected within the hour."

I quirked a brow. "Expected by *whom*?"

"By Lord Valerius, and this is one of those times to choose your battles *carefully*, Cecilia Maria."

I mumbled in acquiescence and climbed out of bed, and the others followed suit. I could argue with Avus, but Bonnie was another matter.

Fortunately, the bathroom functioned as expected. Bonnie almost broke my sleep-fogged brain when she carelessly waived a basket of toiletries into existence on the counter, and then I remembered where I was. If fire from midair was possible, then surely dental floss couldn't be that much more challenging.

"Did anyone remember that it's Aurie's birthday?" asked Edie as she toweled off her wet hair. "Because *I* didn't, and I don't even have a card for her—"

"You know," I interrupted, poking at the puffiness in my face, "I think this is a belated celebration sort of year." My reflection was a mess: brown hair turned black with moisture, green eyes sunken above dark circles, a trio of pimples from the stress and poor hygiene of the road trip erupting on my forehead and chin. Though I wanted to scream at the audacity of the sun for rising, I held it together and forced myself to brush my teeth.

The only thing we couldn't locate in the well-stocked bathroom was a hairdryer, and so the three of us set off in search of food with damp ponytails and rumpled clothes that gave off a slight travel funk. I had no idea where any dining room might be, let alone the small one—it wasn't as if I'd been left a map of the villa the night before. Edie, however, sniffed the air and pointed, and since she was a bloodhound for coffee, she found the place in no time.

Avus was waiting, the leavings of his breakfast pushed off to the side and a shot of espresso in his hand. He looked up from a stack of papers when we entered, then smiled and gestured toward the spread on the table. "Bonnie said she'd roused you. I'm sorry. Coffee?"

That was peace offering enough for my cousin, who plopped into an empty chair and grabbed the carafe. Kenna joined her in short order, but I lingered at the end of the table as Avus regarded me bemusedly. For a moment, all I could see was the tree I'd felled, knocked out of the ground by the force of my deflected anger—a blast I'd aimed at him.

"I, uh...I'm sorry about yesterday," I mumbled. "When I—"

"*Cici*," he said, cutting me short, and rose to hug me. "It's all right."

"No, it's not. I tried to shoot—"

"You're grieving, you let down your guard, and the rage...it doesn't go away." Pulling back to look me in the eye, he said, "You are not the first to lose control, and you will not be the last. No one was hurt. Breathe."

I nodded.

"And know that even if it was lost in the shuffle of...*everything* yesterday," he continued, leading me to a chair, "Gaw's loss hasn't been forgotten. But as Bee would say, this is a triage situation, and mourning can't be the first priority."

Kenna frowned as she raided the bacon platter. "You've got this realm back. What's the problem?"

"The realm exists, yes, and it's open," said Avus, taking his seat, "but it's out of control."

"What do you mean? I didn't see rioting in town yesterday."

"That's an entity unto itself. The problem," he explained, retrieving his coffee, "is that there no longer seems to be an intelligence to the realm—the counterpart to Conota, yes? I'd thought that Ros might take up the role once more, but from what her parents have told Coileán, she remains unchanged. Corporeal."

"What about Gaw?" asked Edie. "Maybe, you know, he wasn't *destroyed*..."

"If that's the case, then he's been remarkably quiet. Before the closure, with the court system, the three of us were in constant contact with the realm. She was the source of our extra power, that boost necessary to maintain order."

Mom had told me enough about *that* to give me the general picture. Apparently, it was useless to negotiate with full-blooded faeries or appeal to their absent sense of altruism. The best way to keep the peace in Faerie was through the threat of force, and so the realm had given the three people in charge of the courts enough strength to pummel any challenger. But that power came from the realm, and she could withhold it—Ros's predecessor had refused to give it to Avus for years because she was peeved with his late mother. Now, if there was no longer a consciousness controlling the realm, then Coileán and Avus would have nothing more than their own talent to rely on. Maybe that wouldn't be a problem at first, but once the fully fae escapees discovered the way back into Faerie, would the momentary peace dissolve into skirmishes?

"I tried to call to the realm all night," Avus continued between sips. "I reached Ros in that way when she first took over. But I could feel her, even when she wasn't fully in control of herself. Now?" He shook his head and lifted the tiny cup again. "Nothing."

That crushed my spirits all over again, extinguishing the tiny flame Edie had ignited. If Gaw were alive, he wouldn't ignore Avus. The realm's continued silence only hammered home the fact that he was gone.

"Anyway," said Avus as his cup refilled on its own, "that's not your concern today. All of you are dangers to yourselves, and so you're going into training this morning. I would eat well, were I you. Mina and Kiet won't be gentle," he said, cutting his eyes between Kenna and me, "and as for you, Edie, you'll be working with Toula once you've been wand-tested—"

"Wait, wait, *whoa*," Kenna interrupted, waving her hands over her breakfast as she cut him off. "*No*. Getting thrown around is *not* in the cards today. We've had one hell of a week, and the last thing any of us needs right now is a black eye. Training's going to have to wait."

Slowly, Avus pushed his cup aside and folded his hands on the table. "I don't recall opening this for discussion."

"And I don't recall you being the boss of me," she

retorted. "We're not kids. You don't get to just order us around."

"Hey, Kenna," Edie murmured, "this might not be a bad idea—"

"*Stop*," she snapped. "Are you in the mood to fight Mina?"

"Well, no…"

"Exactly. So we're going to take it easy today, Val. Breathe a little, get our heads on straight. *Mourn*, for crying out loud. Got a problem with that?"

I held my breath. Avus seldom even came close to losing his temper, but when he did, it scared me.

This time, however, he seemed unperturbed by Kenna's rebellion. He said nothing, but he cocked his head and flashed the faintest of smiles…

…and an invisible force plucked Kenna from her chair and tossed her against the ceiling.

She cried out with the shock, then struggled against her unseen bonds as Avus sat there, calmly drinking his espresso and watching her wriggle. After a moment, as Kenna flushed crimson from her efforts, she screamed her frustration—and a bit of the active magic around her winked out. The rest quickly followed suit, and I noted the simultaneous looks of triumph on Kenna's face and dawning horror on Edie's. Kenna might have been able to free herself, but the ceiling was a good twelve feet high, and she still had to contend with gravity.

Avus's eyebrow twitched as Kenna plummeted toward the stone floor. Another wave of force caught her inches away from a broken nose, then gently lowered her the rest of the way. As Kenna lay on her stomach, panting, Avus said, "Not bad. And since you've demonstrated to us that you have talent and that said talent is not at all within your control, you're going into training today."

Kenna picked herself up off the floor, glowering. "You're still not the boss of me."

"Would you like to try that again?"

Muttering profanities under her breath, she plopped into her chair and reached for the eggs.

CHAPTER 10

We had tried for a compromise position—why couldn't our parents teach us instead of Mina and Kiet? Mina had been running us into the ground for most of our lives, and while Kiet hadn't had much of a direct hand in our education, I knew he was old and tough. Surely, we reasoned, the same people who'd taught us magic in theory could help us with the practical aspect.

That suggestion was vehemently shot down by Avus and Coileán alike. Training, especially the sort of crash-course training we needed, could be painful, and it did the trainees no favors for the trainer to go easy on them. Besides, Kiet and Mina had been—and were once more—the captains of Avus's and Coileán's guards, respectively, and were thus somewhat accustomed to working with novices. In particular, Mina had trained my parents and Artur, so she understood the risks of dealing with people who've suddenly acquired magical talent but have no idea how to handle it. Kenna, Dec, Aurie, and I would be consigned to their less than tender care until they deemed us relatively safe, and no amount of entreaties to our parents that morning made the slightest difference to the plan.

"Look," Coileán had told Dec when he pushed back at breakfast, "do you *want* to set your friends on fire? Because right now, I'm looking at the lot of you and seeing angry toddlers running around with flamethrowers."

While we enjoyed a fun day from hell, Edie was scheduled to work with Toula, which the rest of us deemed wholly unfair. Sure, Toula was tough, but she'd never left us bruised. But when we voiced this sentiment, Avus just smirked. "If you think Edie will have it easy," he said to me, "ask Ros and Bee the next time you see them." For backup, Toula had Maria; while she could no longer cast, she had an Arcanum education behind her, and she'd be switch-hitting as needed.

I was still grumbling about my tutor assignment as I headed out of the dining room, and Avus pulled me aside once Edie and Kenna were gone. "I don't enjoy this, dear girl," he murmured. "I know you are exhausted. But those of us with a *little* more experience know what a risk it is to leave you untrained."

"But why *Mina?*" I griped. "She's brutal!"

He squeezed my shoulder. "Because I trust her to do this well. Because *I* trained *her*. And I was training guards long before she was born, so…just remember that there are nastier options."

I glared at him, and he smiled.

At least our wheedling resulted in one small concession: we could accompany Edie while she was wand-tested, giving us a delayed start to our boot camp. True, Edie wasn't wild about the idea of having an audience, especially as none of us knew what the testing would entail. As we gathered in the courtyard to go to Coileán's place, Edie sat scrunched between Kenna and me on the lip of a bubbling fountain and muttered, "What if I fail at this?"

"You've never failed a test in your life," Kenna retorted.

"I *studied* for those," she said primly. "I don't even know what's about to happen!" Hugging herself, she glowered at the gardens. "What if I can't do it?"

"Don't be silly," I said, nudging her in the side. "Your dad's supposed to be a great wizard, right?"

"Yeah, but Mom says she doesn't have a massive talent. So what if I'm terrible at this? What if…I mean…what if

I'm a dud?"

Kenna rolled her eyes. "Oh, my *God*, Edith."

"What? It's possible! Duds happen," she protested. "Twelve wizards in a row ahead of me. Maybe I'm unlucky thirteen."

Unlike my brother, Edie's half siblings didn't come around often. She couldn't sense them, of course, but more than that, her father's condition confused his elder children. The man who had given them life had lost decades of his own and started over, leaving them in a weird no man's land. Their father was Simon Magus, and Edie's was Eadwig—were the two one and the same, or was Eadwig a mere imposter wearing Simon's face? But while he perplexed them, they bore Edie no ill will, and a few of them quietly checked in on their little sister from time to time.

"Twelve in a row is a pretty good indicator that you're going to be a wizard, too," Kenna replied. "We're not talking about dice, here."

"Everyone else managed to do something vaguely magical yesterday. What does that say about me, huh?"

"That you should try again once you're equipped," said Mom, overhearing us as she joined our huddle. "And speaking as someone who barely earned a wand, I've got a decent feeling about you, kiddo."

Edie's weak smile convinced no one, and I held her hand until it was time to take our leave.

Whereas Avus had opted for a massive single-floor residence, Coileán's house turned out to be a freaking palace, an opulent, faux-Gothic stone structure with a perfect, verdant lawn rolling out from the main gate and manicured formal gardens around the back. Comparing it to the two-story house in which I'd played with Dec, I was hard-pressed to imagine the dwellings sharing an owner. As I stared at towers and turrets, it hit me that all the stories we'd been told as children that had sounded ludicrous as we grew up—how Toula had once headed an ancient order of wizards, how Avus and Coileán had been kings in a faraway land, how Ed had embarked on a bloody fifty-year world conquest—might just be true.

This was an honest-to-God *palace*. Coileán was a king. Which meant…

I tried to cover my brief burst of laughter with a cough, but Kenna glanced at me with concern. "What's so funny?" she asked, sliding closer to me. "Are you okay? Want to go sit for a while?"

I recalled then that hysterical laughter was a real phenomenon, and after my breakdown the day before, Kenna surely had to think I was having an episode. "I'm fine," I assured her, slinging my arm around her neck. "But…you know what *this* means, right?" I continued, flapping my hand toward the palace.

"That Coileán probably has a massive cobweb problem? Sheesh, can you imagine trying to keep that place clean?"

"Not that. If Coileán's an actual king," I said, lowering my voice, "then what does that make *Dec*?"

It didn't take a mind reader to know that the same sort of images were flashing in Kenna's head as had been running through mine. Dec, my occasionally goofy cousin, the guy who'd mastered the collegiate keg stand and played on a losing intramural innertube water polo team for four years running, who I'd found snoring in our apartment common room in ratty sweats more times than I could count…

Kenna snorted as she grinned. "Faerie prince."

"Friggin' faerie prince," I echoed.

We hadn't been as quiet as we thought we were, as Edie gave us her patented *someone didn't do the reading* look as she joined our huddle. "I'm pretty sure the preferred term is 'high lord,'" she murmured, "and Cici, you have no room to talk."

"Oh, come on—" I began.

"Your dad is next in line to your grandfather, right? So what does that make *you*?"

Edie and Kenna traded wicked looks, and Kenna smirked as my mental tumblers fell. "When this is all said and done," she whispered, "*someone* is getting a pink plastic tiara with sparkles."

"Guys," I groaned.

"What? You can embrace the faerie princess ethos now," she teased. "Just, like…ballgowns. Nothing but ballgowns."

"I hate you both so much," I muttered.

At least my discomfort provided a moment's distraction for Edie. Too soon, we headed inside, then upstairs to a spacious—and surprisingly contemporary—apartment, where Coileán, Toula, and Dec were waiting. "Hi!" said Toula as we trooped in. "Hey, Val, look, my books made it through the closure!"

Avus paused inside her den, considering the laden bookshelves, then the floor-to-ceiling windows on the far wall, along which had been stacked a pile of cardboard boxes. "You're moving?" he asked.

"No, that's the stuff I brought over from Glastonbury for safekeeping. Never thought I'd see my library again," she added, nudging the nearest box with her toe. "Folks, coffee's in the kitchen, help yourselves. Amy and Kip are on their way."

As nice as the apartment seemed, I had to wonder why the eleven of us had crammed in there for the occasion when there was a whole palace at our disposal. When Dec joined Edie, Kenna, and me in the kitchen, I asked, "What *is* this place?"

"Mom's old suite," he said, pulling a clean mug from the cabinet. "Apparently. I knew she used to sleep over at Dad's when they were dating, but, you know…"

"Little bigger than a futon?" Edie offered.

"*Shit.*" He poured his coffee and sipped it black. "This

is fucking nuts. Is it like this at Val's, too?"

"Similar principle," Edie replied, taking the carafe in turn. "Are you okay?"

"I mean, for not knowing what *planet* I'm on…"

"Same." She clinked her mug against his, then reached for the sugar cannister.

While she doctored her drink, Dec gave me a one-armed hug. "Hanging in there, Cici?"

"I've had better days," I told him. "Has anyone heard from Ros and Sam?"

He nodded. "Dad called Ros's dad early this morning. Her parents are staying with them, but that's got to be awkward. 'Hi, folks,'" he said, lifting his voice toward falsetto, "'it's been twenty-five years on our end, and we just lost the son you never knew we had…'" With a shake of his head, he drank, wincing at the hot coffee. "I swear, I woke up this morning, and I thought we might still be on the RV. And then it all came crashing back."

I peeked around the wall into the den, where the mood seemed far less grim. A phone began to ring, and Toula pulled hers from her pocket. "Hey, there!" she said brightly. "Are you…okay, great, I'll have the gate open momentarily." She'd barely ended the call before she made a complex gesture and whispered, and a fresh gate, a perfect circle about six feet in diameter, ripped through the fabric of space in the middle of the den.

Two people hurried through, a petite blonde and a tall, redheaded man with a curiously deep tan, who carried a pair of wide, flat boxes. Growing up as I had among so many faeries, I was a poor judge of actual age, but the newcomers seemed perhaps ten or fifteen years older than me—a little more youthful than Edie's parents, but not much.

Beaming, Toula hugged them both as Coileán cleared a place for the boxes on the coffee table. "It's so good to see you two," she said. "I know this must be weird on your end, but I thought you were dead for decades, and—"

"It's nice to be missed," the woman replied. She spoke with a noticeable drawl, easily as heavy as my mother's when Mom got worked up. "We only got bits and pieces of the news yesterday—y'all are going to give us a full explanation eventually, right?"

"Once we have one for you," said Avus. "Things are…unsettled."

"Well, obviously." She glanced around the room, then asked, "Any sign of Irem? Her army seems to have left us."

"None," Coileán replied. "Should any of them return and try to start a fight, give us a call, but as far as I know, Irem's people scattered with the rest of us. They haven't been in Alaska, so the odds are decent that they don't even know the realm's open again. And I promise," he added, looking up at the redheaded man, "we're not going to harm Amy."

"Appreciated," he said, his accent unplaceable to my ear. "Actually, I'm here for Aiden. He said he was bringing more computer equipment over today and wanted a hand with his setup."

"Kind of you."

He waved it off. "Better for me to squeeze in with the metal bits than for him to try to do it in gloves. Besides, I want to see his new gear," he said, grinning.

"And I'll expect a full report," Amy told him.

He bent and kissed the top of her head—not a difficult feat, as he had to be at least a foot taller than she was. "Nothing less. So, uh, if someone could point me toward Aiden…"

"Ahead of you," Toula interrupted, lifting her phone as proof. "He'll be right over. By the way, Kip, Arik and Hope send their regards. We left them in Kentucky yesterday."

He nodded in acknowledgement. "Well, should you see them, please return the sentiment. That realm is unharmed?"

"So they tell me," she replied. "Conota sealed it off all this time to protect it. Arik didn't say anything specifically about your people, but I know that realm still stands."

"Good. Once you're resettled and things calm down, would you mind giving them a call for me? Just to be sure…"

"Of course, hon," said Toula, then turned to Amy. "So we have a prospective wizard…in the kitchen?" she asked, raising her voice.

Edie slunk out and offered a weak wave. "Um…hi?"

"This is Amy Levey," Toula explained as Edie hung close to the wall. "The finest living crafter. Her wands are top-notch." Amy flushed at the praise, and Toula gestured to her companion. "And this is—"

"Mr. Amy Levey, who just carries the wand cases," he joked, earning a quick smile from Edie. "Kip. Hi." He peered briefly at Edie, then cut his eyes to Ed and said, "Well, I think it's pretty obvious who *you* belong to. That hair's a dead giveaway. Are you any relation to Badger?"

After an awkward pause, Ed cleared his throat. "Distant."

"Parsons cousin?" Kip asked.

While Ed rubbed the back of his neck, Toula came to his rescue. "This is Ed," she explained to Kip and Amy. "Uh…*Eadwig*, that is."

Both stiffened and took a reflexive step back.

"See you've heard of me," Ed muttered.

"I mean, word's gotten around," Amy replied as Kip not-so-subtly slid in front of her. "But I thought you were supposed to be a kid."

"Sure, twenty-five years ago. My body thinks it's somewhere in its forties now," he said, gesturing to the faint lines on his face. "I can tell you from experience that this isn't going to get any prettier."

"He's lived with us all this time," Coileán quietly told Kip and Amy, "and he hasn't shown any outright signs of genocidal urges."

"And I wouldn't have stayed with him if he had," Beth added, then paused as the apartment door opened and Aiden let himself in, sporting a flannel shirt, leather work gloves, and plastic goggles perched atop his head. "Really, it's okay. No one's getting attacked."

"You say that," Kip murmured, "but you understand why I'm not keen on leaving my wife here with Simon Magus."

"Simon 2.0," said Aiden. "Ish."

Amy patted Kip's arm and stepped out from behind him. "I'll be fine, babe. Go play with Aiden's toys."

"But—"

"Full report, remember."

I smiled to myself at the silent conversation that passed between the two of them, a discussion made with tiny facial shifts—the self-created language of a longtime couple. Gaw and I hadn't quite reached that point, but I'd almost been able to read his mind from across a room, judging by his expression alone. The fresh reminder that I was no longer part of a couple hit me like an ice pick to the chest and blurred my vision, but I tried not to let on.

After a moment, Kip surrendered and left with Aiden, though not without a last uneasy look at Ed. When the door closed behind them, Amy broke the tense silence by unsnapping the latches on her top case. "How do we want to do this?" she asked. "Our presumed wizard has never been tested, right?" She glanced at Edie, who was still lurking against the wall as if she might go unnoticed, and nodded reassurance. "This won't hurt, honey. What was your name, again?"

"Edie," she mumbled.

"Edie," Amy repeated with a smile. "You have nothing to worry about. All we're going to do is put different wands in your hand and see which is the best fit...and before we do that," she said, glancing over her shoulder at Toula, "do we want to move the breakables?"

Toula pointed to the door across the den from the

kitchen. "Practice room."

"*Nice*. So, Edie," she continued, "some of these wands might feel like regular sticks to you. Some might give you a tingly feeling in your hand. I can't speak from experience, now, but that's what I've been told. I don't use them, I just make them," she said with a shrug.

"There's no right or wrong wand," Toula added. "All we need is to know where you stand, Edie. It's like going to the ophthalmologist and seeing how strong your glasses need to be. That'll help me tailor your training, too." As Amy moved the top case onto the couch and began unsnapping the second, Toula asked, "You brought extra wands?"

"The standard five are fine," said Amy, "but I like to offer in-between options. Shall we?"

Toula led the way into the room across the den, and the rest of our families followed suit with Amy in their midst. I hung back to give Edie a last squeeze of reassurance, and with Dec and Kenna on hand for support, we proceeded to the testing site.

By rights, Toula's practice room shouldn't have existed in that palace. It was far too large for the expected space, perhaps thirty feet tall, and our Anchorage apartment could have easily nestled within its padded walls. The floor was covered in a thick gray mat of the sort one might find at a gymnastics event, while the recessed lights in the ceiling above us, encased in plastic, offered a diffuse glow.

I recalled something my mom had once said about the laws of physics being more of a suggestion when one was dealing with sufficient magic, but actually *seeing* such blatant disregard for them in real time left me unsettled.

While Coileán pulled a table from thin air for Amy's case, Toula went to work in the main part of the practice room. A flick of her fingers and a whisper produced a set of off-white cubes halfway across the space, some the size of a brick, others larger than a refrigerator. At her direction, they scattered themselves, and she made a show of brushing off her palms as she rejoined the pack. "Okay, Edie, let's see what you've got," she said, beckoning for her to approach the box of wands. "Let's see, what should we start with?"

"Suggestion," said Amy. "Let Edie choose."

Toula nodded in acquiescence, and while the spectators backed away from the testing area, Toula positioned Edie in front of the case. "There's no rush," she said, "and you're not married to whatever you pick first. Choose the one that feels right to you."

I could see Edie's rising panic, the look of a straight-A student faced with a pop test on material she hadn't studied. "But…but I don't know—"

"It's *okay*," Toula insisted, and patted Edie's back. "Take your time."

While the rest of us watched, Edie passed her hand over the box, then paused, frowned, and moved her hand the other way. She pulled a wand free, held it for a moment, then replaced it in its foam padding. One by one, she lifted each wand and gripped it in her fist, but only when she reached the last of the bunch did she give it a little test flick as well. "How about this wand?" she asked.

Toula's face remained a careful neutral as she steered Edie toward the cubes. "All right, sweetie, here's the fun part. I want you to move one of the cubes."

"Wait…now?" Edie protested. "I don't know what I'm doing!"

"Yes, you do. You'll intuit quite a bit once you begin. The power is in *you*," she murmured, "not in the wand. It's just there as a focusing tool. So breathe, clear your mind, and remember all that meditation I made you do as a kid, yeah? Remember your theory. There's magic all around you," she added, sweeping her hand through a purplish mist. "Activate it. Impose your will upon it." With that, she stepped behind Edie, leaving my poor cousin alone with the cubes and the stick in her hand.

Edie stood there, her shoulders stiff, and made no

move to begin. Trading glances with Kenna, I joined Edie at the edge of the pack and saw the fear in her dark eyes. "You've got this," I whispered.

"I can't," she whispered back.

"Yes, you can. I'm right here."

She still seemed like she wanted to throw up, but after a few seconds, Edie closed her eyes and released a slow breath. Extending the wand toward a cube the size of our old recliner, she muttered, "Up."

I saw the magic spark around her, brightening as it activated, then looked across the room in time to watch the cube rise from the mats and begin a slow rotation. "Open your eyes," I told her.

Her face had scrunched with worry. "Why?"

"Because it worked, genius."

That got her attention, and she gasped as she witnessed the result of her first attempt. She watched the cube turn for a brief moment, then pointed the wand at another cube and willed it into the air. For the third, she used a finger in lieu of the wand. Within thirty seconds, every cube in the room was levitating, perhaps two dozen altogether, and then they began to move. The cubes fell into a neat line, which curled into an infinity shape, and then they floated along the pattern, dodging each other at the nexus point. A quick, frantic giggle escaped Edie before she squinted at the flying cubes and muttered, "Braid, braid, *braid*," under her breath.

A beam of light shot from the end of her wand—a bolt of active magic, I realized—and hooked through one of the loops of the cubes' path. Edie flicked the wand to the left, and the beam flew off the wand and anchored itself on the wall. A second one began to form and received the same treatment, then a third. As they attached to the padding, the filaments wove together, glowing brighter in their proximity, and the cubes traveling along that part of the path moved more quickly. Edie repeated the process on the other side, then stepped back to watch her creation run by itself, supported by the reinforcing braids.

Stacks, I mused. *That* was what Toula and Maria had told us about—a spellcraft technique in which channels of magic strengthened each other and reinforced the overall effect. Maria had described how the channels could be braided together for added oomph, and while I'd paid little attention to the theory, Edie—as usual—must have been listening.

With the cubes moving on their own, Edie shifted the focus of her experimentation. Pointing the wand at one, she whispered a command, and it turned a startling shade of orange. She laughed aloud, then aimed at another, which flared pink. As she continued her alterations, she made some cubes striped, some polka-dotted, and even splashed one with a tie-dye pattern. Around the time that she began setting the cubes on fire, she lost her grip on the wand, but she didn't seem to notice. Two or three pointing fingers worked just as well on multiple targets.

I couldn't decide what was more satisfying in the moment, the insanity of what Edie was doing with her targets or the look of giddy delight on her face.

Finally, Toula cleared her throat behind us. "That's good, Edie. You can put the cubes down now."

Edie jumped at the sound of her voice, perhaps remembering that she wasn't alone in the practice room, then quickly pulled the cubes from their weird orbit and dropped into a neat pile on the floor.

"Dismantle the stacks, too," Toula directed. "You can either make each one disintegrate or overload them, your call."

She opted for the first method, and within seconds, the cubes were still once more—oddly colored and a little charred around the edges, but freed from their wild ride.

As Edie and I turned around, the triumph in her eyes crumbled toward uncertainty. The others were staring at her mutely...all but Kenna, who flashed a double thumbs-up and broke the silence with a shouted, "That was *awesome!*"

Still, Edie shrank as she waited for a verdict. "Um…sorry," she mumbled, "I guess I…I got carried away. Was that…I mean, did I…was it okay?"

As she stammered, Toula moved closer, then bent to retrieve the wand Edie had dropped. "Pine," she said, putting it back in Edie's hand. "Obviously, you don't *need* it, but every wizard should have one as a formality. You'll probably want to hold one in your magus portrait someday."

Edie's eyebrows rose. "You still think I could have been a magus?"

"Oh, honey," said Toula, patting Edie's flushed cheek, "no. *Grand.*"

"Huh?"

Toula chuckled. "Your stacks were a little sloppy, but that's just a matter of practice, and for a first-timer, that's remarkable. When we used to test kids, the goal was for them to move *a* cube, not put on a show. You pulled that off with nothing but a theoretical education…" She whistled softly, then turned to the others. "Helen was no stronger at her age, and Helen was highly trained."

"I can't speak to that," said Amy, "but Badger's crazy strong, and she started on a composite in her forties."

"Exactly. I've never seen those two go head to head, but I'd wager that Badger is the stronger of the pair. Now, with that in mind, Edie's twenty-two, she's never had practical training, and if she's beyond needing a wand…" Turning to Ed, Toula asked, "Were her siblings like this?"

He shook his head, then murmured, "No. Many of them were gifted wizards, but none were ever, ehm…ever my equal."

"Hm," she replied, and smiled at Edie. "Don't worry, this won't hurt."

Before Edie could even ask what was about to happen, Toula whispered and extended her hand. A globe of white mist coalesced in front of Edie, then flared a brilliant green as it formed into a complex lattice in the shape of a hollow ball. "Your aural signature," Toula explained. "Or a representation of it, at least. This is a common Arcanum rendering. With this spell, the brighter the lattice glows, the stronger the inborn magical talent. Ed, may I—"

"Go ahead."

She repeated the process, and soon, two green spheres were floating near her, one from each of her subjects. If Ed's was brighter than Edie's, it wasn't by much.

"So, uh…what does this mean?" Edie asked.

"It means that you're going into training *now*," said Toula as the spheres winked out of existence.

"*Immediately*," Ed concurred, and Beth nodded beside him. "To be your age, with *that* talent, untutored…"

"Tell you what, Edie," said Amy, snapping her case closed. "You just keep that wand. I don't think there's any need to look at my composites, and since there's *really* no call for pine wands in town, I'll make another for the kit."

"Are you sure?" Edie asked. "I don't want to mess up your gear—"

She stopped Edie with a raised palm. "I appreciate that, but the sooner you get a wand, the sooner you get trained, and the better I sleep at night. And I really don't mean to be cruel," she added, turning to Avus and Coileán, "but could we keep Baby Magus here out of town until she's got a handle on herself, please?"

Coileán winced. "It's not just Baby Magus we have to worry about. That one's Kitty and Marcus's," he said, pointing to me, "Kenna there is half fae, and the miscreant with her belongs to Toula and me."

Amy looked around the room at the four of us with the same sort of calm nonchalance with which one might regard four unstable nuclear bombs. "Well, *shit*," she muttered.

"Speaking of training," Coileán continued, "Mina and Kiet are waiting out in the practice yard. I trust you remember the way, Declan?" he asked, the edge in his voice suggesting that dalliance was not an option.

"Yes, sir," Dec mumbled.

"Good. Why don't you escort the girls, hmm? Aurie should be along soon. And Amy, I know it's early, but could I offer you a drink while we catch up?"

As the three of us slunk off toward our painful fate, Coileán called, "Try not to make craters in my rose garden!"

The one positive I found in Mina and Kiet's School of Hard Knocks and Broken Bones was that the pain momentarily distracted me from Gaw's absence. At least he didn't have to suffer with the rest of us.

Their first lesson was shielding, and while Kiet offered pointers as to form, Mina went *hard*. Having spent two decades whipping us into shape, she knew our physical limits, and she accepted no whining. If our shields weren't quick enough or strong enough or large enough to deflect the bolts of energy she effortlessly lobbed at us, then we'd get hit—simple as that. After the first few bruises, we began to pay attention. After a bolt cracked Kenna's rib, our focus improved. Pain and the avoidance thereof proved to be an excellent motivator, and I quickly figured out how to produce a decent shield.

The only person on whom our tutors had anything resembling pity was Aurie, who was weakly talented and had barely scratched the surface of enchantment before Faerie disappeared. They didn't coddle her—Aurie yelped with the rest of us when she was too slow on the draw— but I noticed that Mina lobbed slow softballs at her, giving her time to build her defense. If Dec and Kenna perceived the discrepancy as well, they were smart enough to sit on it. Knowing Mina, any complaint that she was treating us too harshly would only make the bolts faster and harder.

We'd been going for about an hour when Kiet called a halt and plucked water bottles from the ether. "You'll make your own next time," he told us, then swigged from his as Toula, Coileán, and Amy approached. Curiously, both of Amy's cases were floating along behind her.

"They're progressing," Mina reported, and wiped her mouth on the back of her hand. "Amy, did you want to take a swing or some such?"

"Nah. I'm better with a gun, anyway," she replied, then told Coileán, "You can put those down, thanks." The cases landed at her feet, and she knelt to open the first, now missing one of its wands.

Mina's brow furrowed. "Dare I ask?"

"Since we've got Amy here," said Toula, "I thought we might as well go ahead and test Dec."

"*Dec?*"

"Yeah. *My* son, remember? And since I'm not too shabby a wand jockey myself…"

"Granted," said Mina, "but Dec is enchanting well, so there's no need—"

"Of course there is. If he can cast, then he needs to learn to do so—and it's definitely the more complex of the two," Toula replied. "Since he doesn't have the metal allergy, I think there's a decent chance that he could learn how to handle a wand."

"And I don't deny that, but *should* he?" Turning to Coileán, she said, "I don't mean to overstep my bounds, Uncle, but think of the optics if the *heir* is walking around, casting."

A grimace briefly flashed across his face. "Believe me, I have, but Toula's right. If we don't at least test him, we'll be doing him a disservice…and I don't want him picking up Edie's, giving it a flick, and discovering the talent by accident. Yeah?"

"Moon and stars," she muttered, but stood down.

Toula waved a fresh set of cubes into existence a few yards away, then studied the wands on offer. "Let's start with ash," she said, and Amy handed her the wand from the middle of the case. "Here, Dec, give this a try."

Trading uncertain looks with Kenna and me, Dec took the wand and aimed it at the cubes. "Uh…how does this work, again?"

"You're going to will a change upon them," his mother calmly replied, a tone of voice I knew far too well from our school days. "Use the wand as a focusing tool. It will feel different than enchantment—you're working with a scalpel, not a sledgehammer. We're not looking for fireworks, hon. Simple levitation will be just fine."

Dec squared his shoulders, then took up a stance much like Edie's and muttered, "Up, okay?"

The magic around him activated a millisecond before the target cube exploded in a blast of fire.

"Good try, good effort," said Toula as Coileán smothered the smoldering patches in the yard around the practice area. "A *little* too much wand, I think." She pried it from Dec's clenched fist, returned it to Amy, and gave him another. "It's okay, baby, this happens," she soothed. "Go talk to Maria about her wand ceremony sometime. Right, now, try again."

That time, though Dec cringed in anticipation of another violent misfire, the cube cooperated with his instruction. Once he had it off the ground and gently spinning, Toula patted him on the shoulder and smiled. "That'll do. Put it down."

"Got an idea," said Amy, opening the second case and extracting a light-stained wand. "Here, give this one a go."

With the third wand, the cube rose more quickly, and soon, Dec had it bobbing around the practice yard like a swooping bat. "Thought so," said the crafter as Dec returned the cube to the pile. "That's one of my birches. Nice compromise between ash and maple without having to resort to anything involving merrow skin."

"What's in it, then?" Coileán asked.

"It's a composite core," she explained. "Fine layers of ground, dried clover give a bit more power to the hematite."

One dark eyebrow rose. "*Hematite?*"

"You'd be surprised how well iron-based minerals work as wand cores."

"You're giving *my* son an iron-based wand?"

Amy shrugged. "I'm giving him the one that seems to fit best. Is that a problem?"

Coileán took a long, careful look at Dec, then sighed. "He comes by it honestly, doesn't he?"

"Oh, I should say so," Toula replied, wrapping her arm around his waist. "The Ironhand rides again."

Perplexed, Dec asked, "This is okay, then?"

"Sure," said his mother. "You may graduate to a weaker one as you get older, but there's nothing wrong with that wand. And now that we know you *can* use one, you're going to be dividing your time between Mina and Kiet out here and Maria and me in the practice room."

He perked at the news. "Please tell me that it's less painful inside."

Toula favored him with a smile that wasn't at all reassuring. "For the moment, maybe, but we'll be working on shields after lunch…"

Dec groaned, and Kiet flicked him off his feet from five yards away.

CHAPTER 11

"Cici? *Cici—*"

"I'm here!" I yelled, waking myself from a sound sleep. Disoriented, I kicked at the blankets until the body ache reminded me where I was, and I flopped back against my pillow.

Again with the dreams. My subconscious had produced Ros's voice for a second night in a row, a mimicry so good I halfway expected her to walk out of the bathroom at any moment.

I didn't want to be awake. Gaw was still gone, the healing construction that had mended the leg Kiet broke before dinner left me stiff and sore, and frankly, I didn't see the point of getting out of bed. Besides, if my calculations were correct, this was Saturday, and I was entitled to sleep in, damn it. It was my prerogative to hide my head under the sheet, curl into an achy ball, and cry myself back to unconsciousness in private.

Or so I told myself ten minutes later, once Bonnie came by with the wakeup call and ordered me into the shower. Another long day of getting the crap beaten out of me at Coileán's place wasn't in *my* cards, but with Mom, Pa, and Avus insisting, my odds of successful resistance were slim. Sure, I could escape Faerie and try to hide, but that would mean finding a gate home, and I had no idea where to look. Even if one remained open in the Fringe settlement, I didn't know how to get back there, nor could I count on anyone around me to help me make my sneaky exit. This was Faerie, after all, and my neighbors in Alaska, who'd never fully shaken off the notion that Coileán and Avus were their leaders, had quickly started peppering their conversations with "my lord." If Avus was meant to be a virtually absolute monarch in his domain, then what chance did I have at telling him no? Mom and Pa certainly weren't putting up a fuss.

Breakfast was a quiet affair for Edie, Kenna, and me. Kenna and I were still nursing mended bones, while Edie had drilled focusing techniques with Toula the previous afternoon until her eyes crossed and dreamed about them all through the miserable night. My parents had left early to continue moving their belongings from our house in the compound into Avus's storage rooms, so I sought Avus for a lift to Coileán's once we ran out of excuses to linger with the coffee. I found him in his office, and though he smiled at me, he looked exhausted. "I haven't slept," he admitted. "Spent the night trying to contact the realm, but no one's there."

As Dec and Edie were slated to pass the morning indoors, Mina and Kiet had only three victims to work with, but they made the best of the situation. Kiet took on Aurie solo, feeling out her limits so that he could push against them. Though Aurie was no great talent, she wanted to learn, and our tutors respected that drive. Meanwhile, perhaps noticing the state of our bruises even after a night wrapped in healing enchantment, Mina switched her focus away from defense, instead showing us the basics of gates. Every time she opened a fresh one, I imagined the flash when Gaw had disappeared, but I did my best to keep the tears locked down. Mina wasn't the sort of person who had much use for crying jags.

By our midmorning water break—Kenna's tasted musty, while mine seemed slightly acidic, but at least we *could* pull water from the ether—I'd learned the knack of opening a hole between the realms or between two places within the same realm. True, my gates weren't large, beautiful, or particularly stable, but Mina grunted her satisfaction as she left us for a quick meeting with Coileán's guards. Kiet also gave us a few minutes' reprieve to return to Avus's place; with a sufficient number of former guards having returned from Alaska, the captains had decided to establish a schedule.

"What's the rush?" I asked Kiet before he departed. "I don't think the people in town pose a major threat…"

"They don't," he explained. "It's Irem's people we fear. Once they begin to return—or come out from wherever they may be hiding in this realm—they may try something foolish. A good defense is *never* to be overlooked. Remember that." He paused, and the corner of his mouth twitched. "My lady."

Once his gate closed behind him, Kenna clapped a sweaty hand on my shoulder. "Faerie princess, babe."

"Shove it," I muttered, pushing her off, and she laughed as I grabbed my water bottle. I took a swig and grimaced at the taste. "What are the odds that if I try to make my own Kool-Aid powder, it'll end up being, like, salt?"

"Probably decent, I'd think," said Aurie, joining us with her own water bottle—one that Kiet had made for her, I noticed with envy. "Try making more water instead of risking the supply you have."

I concentrated, then opened my hand and waited until a second bottle appeared. Unfortunately, the contents looked like they'd come from the bottom of a murky pond, and I tossed it aside in disgust. "There's got to be some trick I'm missing," I muttered, returning to the moderately better bottle. "This *can't* be rocket science."

"*Magical* rocket science," Kenna amended.

"Isn't that an oxymoron?" I began, but glanced up as a massive shadow passed above us. "What is…*whoa*, get back!"

But before the three of us could run, the enormous dragon that had been circling overhead came in for a landing.

At least it wasn't my first dragon. I'd witnessed Frank fully shift a few times as a kid, normally when a hungry bear came too close to the compound, and I knew the general body plan: long body, four legs, massive wings, ample claws, and far too many teeth. Frank was almost pretty, in a weird reptilian way, covered as he was in opalescent white scales. But *this* dragon was bigger than Frank and deep red, and I suspected that my beginner's shield would be useless if the dragon decided to have a light snack.

While I froze, Kenna kept her wits about her and opened a gate back to Avus's. "Come on, let's go!" she shouted, tugging on my wrist. "Cici, move your ass!"

Wait! came the urgent, foreign thought. *Please, a moment.*

Oddly, the dragon seemed to be thinking in Fae, but I was sufficiently fluent for its words to register. "We're armed," I lied.

I'm not here to cause trouble, it replied. *I'm searching for my brother. Our mother heard about what happened outside the realm, and she's worried for his safety—he was probably out there. Have you seen him?* the dragon asked. *White, a little smaller than me, answers to Frank—*

That was as far as he got before Aurie stepped up beside me and held out her hand. A bright white fireball bloomed to life in her palm—one *considerably* larger than she'd managed two days before, nearly the size of a basketball, with tendrils licking up her arm. Fury blazed in her red eyes, and as she extended her stubby left arm, a small shield burst forth from the elbow.

"You've got a *lot* of nerve," she said in perfect Fae, her voice descending toward a decidedly inhuman growl. "Get the fuck out of here."

The dragon backed off a pace and cocked its head. *Really, I mean you no harm. I'm Horus—Coileán knows me. I'm not going to eat anyone, I just want to find—*

"*Go!*" she bellowed.

It might have been my imagination, but I thought her

teeth had sharpened in those few seconds.

As Horus continued to try to reassure us and Aurie yelled at him, I heard a door slam in the distance, followed by a shout. It wasn't someone on the other side of Kenna's gate—*that* had collapsed in quick order—but rather Frank, who was sprinting out of the palace, heading for the ornamental rose garden maze.

I'd seen him briefly on our arrival that morning, when Aurie's grandfather, Owain, dropped them both off. Frank had been meeting with Aiden, Vivi, and Antony Copeland, who'd come in from the compound to talk about getting the former Away Team's computers back on the Fringe network. From what we could gather, Alaska was about twelve hours behind us—or ahead of us, we couldn't be sure—and so a breakfast meeting for Aiden and Frank was just the beginning of a long evening on Antony's end. I learned later that they'd taken a quick break so that Frank could step out and check on his daughter's progress…and instead, he found her squaring off against a dragon with nothing but a hand flame and a weak shield to defend herself.

Before Frank hit the edge of the roses, he shifted in a blast of shredded clothing and took wing, and Horus looked skyward in surprise. When Frank landed, the ground shook, and Kenna had the presence of mind to pull Aurie and me out of the way. Frank moved between us and Horus, teeth bared, muscles bunching, and emitting a growl that made my arms erupt in gooseflesh.

Horus backed away, lowering his head. I was no expert in draconic body language, and I could barely make sense of the communication that passed between them—it takes a certain kind of brain to process pure, wordless telepathy—but even the little I picked up of their conversation told me that Frank was absolutely enraged, while Horus was confused. Finally, Frank returned to words for his conclusion: *Go back to the barn and tell Mom that I said you can all go to hell.*

Runt—

Frank roared, and Horus wisely retreated. After a moment, when Horus disappeared over the trees, Frank turned around to find us standing there, Aurie still primed to toss her fireball. *Did he hurt you?*

She shook her head. "No. I...I tried to scare him—"

The crack of an opening gate interrupted her, and Aiden ran through with Antony and Vivi right behind him. "*Whoa*, is everything okay?" Aiden asked. "We looked out the window, and—"

It's fine. Frank's wings, stiff and tense, began to relax. *A little wardrobe assistance?*

"Sure, bud." Aiden waited while Frank shifted back, then enchanted a fresh T-shirt and jeans into place. "Sorry, what shoes were you wearing?"

"Later," said Frank, heading for Aurie. Her shield and fire fell away, and she ran into his arms, trembling. "You're safe, hatchling," I heard him murmur as he held her. "He's gone. You're safe now."

Frank led Aurie through the gate back into the palace while Kenna and I stood by, perplexed. Once they were out of earshot, Aiden beckoned us closer, then quietly said, "That was one of Frank's brothers. I could be wrong, but something tells me that after twenty-five years, he still hasn't forgiven his siblings for trying to kill Aurie."

"Would *you?*" Kenna muttered.

"No. But shit," he said, glancing off in the way that Horus had flown, "she has every right to be shaken."

Mina and Kiet didn't bat an eye when they returned to find their pupils down to two. "Aiden said that Aurie is taking the rest of the morning off," Mina announced, and cracked her knuckles. "So, who's ready for personal attention?"

After a miserable, bloody few hours, they allowed Kenna and me to slink back to the palace and pick up

Edie, who had acquired her own set of bruises from Maria's practice bolts. Toula and Maria had already left, claiming they had a lunchtime meeting, and we found Coileán patching up Edie and Dec in Toula's apartment. He offered us lunch there, but we opted to limp back to Avus's instead, where at least we could shower before the afternoon torture session.

I made a gate into the main courtyard and managed to hold it open long enough for the three of us to cross, and then, feeling relatively proud of myself, I led the way toward the villa's expansive kitchen. But as we shuffled down a breezeway, wincing with our injuries, I heard familiar, yet somewhat agitated, voices coming from the small dining room ahead. Looking back at Kenna and Edie, I put my finger to my lips, and we flattened ourselves against the wall to listen.

"I realize that the situation with the realm is complicated," said Ed, "but that's not my main concern. Dark magic is returning to the mortal realm, and magic is right behind it. We're about to be faced with an entire generation of untrained wizards—"

"They're not all going to be Edie," Toula interrupted.

"I'm not Edie, and I fucking *killed a man* at five when I didn't know how to handle my own power," Maria snapped. "This is a disaster waiting to happen."

To my surprise, I heard an aged male voice with a strong British accent chime in—Bert Wold. "For now, we could reach out to the Minor Arcanum, warn them of what's to come, try to coordinate a response—"

"But that won't help with the remedial education," Maria countered. "The Minors don't have any structured classes. We're going to need teachers as soon as there's enough magic in that realm to allow prolonged spellwork, and I don't think we're going to find anything like that established among the Minors. They don't research, their training is piecemeal…"

"So we do the sensible thing and restore the

Arcanum," said Ed. "Now, before the chaos."

"We'd need a grand magus," Maria replied. "Someone to get us through the transition, at least."

"And a base of operations."

Bert chuckled sadly. "If you were hoping to return to Glastonbury, I have bad news. The old Arc 2 site is a business park these days. It pains me to drive past, but I live so close…"

"How are your parents, anyway?" Toula asked.

"Eh. Upright and reasonably sharp for centenarians, and they refuse to leave the cottage, business park or no."

"I'd ask you to give them my regards, but they're probably still peeved that I took your job." After a brief pause, Toula said, "I do still have Arc 2, you know. It's been in that snow globe all along."

"Right," said Bert, "but where do you want to put it? *And* ward it, of course. Just assembling a camouflage ward from scratch…bloody hell," he muttered.

"I can do it," she protested. "And we've got a remote site. Let's put the damn castle where the compound is now—"

"What, in *Alaska*? And you thought Montana was remote and unappealing?"

"Precisely," said Ed. "It's largely uninhabited, undeveloped land. With a gate or two open at the site, we could build the necessary wards in a matter of days, or at least wards strong enough to temporarily hide the castle. What do you prefer, Bert, untrained wizards descending upon a major city or being housed where they can't hurt mundanes?"

"That could work," Bert mused. "But if we're going the isolation route, I've an idea."

"Better than Alaska?" asked Toula.

"Alaska-plus. Two words: pocket dimension."

"Ooh!" said Maria, and clapped. "*Yes*. Put it in a pocket with a controlled nexus point, maybe somewhere on Ennis's land—"

"And if magic were to fail again, the pocket would burst, dropping the castle in the middle of nowhere," Toula finished. I could hear her warming to the notion. "Say we build this on the compound site and leave a guard. One way in and out if we ward the pocket against gates—"

"I vote for that to be a ward system, not something integral to the pocket," Maria interrupted. "Just in case."

"Seconded," said Bert. "And I've given this some thought in the last two days. The theory is solid—half of the buildings in this realm seem to include pockets. I think we could do it with pure spellcraft, but it'll take time to assemble."

After a pause, Toula said, "Ed, you're awfully quiet."

"Just thinking through the moving parts," he replied. "I concur—it's doable, and I think it's safer than dropping the castle back in an inhabited area and hoping the wards hold. What are your thoughts on timing?"

The room fell silent for a few seconds, and then Bert said, "A week, at least, to plan and build. The casting will be complex—"

"Understatement of the year," Maria chimed in with a snort. "I'd be happy to help you plan it, Bert, but you don't want me trying to cast it."

"*God*, no, though I'd certainly appreciate the assistance on the planning end. Toula?"

"I'm in," she said. "Let's build the pocket, and then we can work through the details of where we're putting it. Ennis might not want his property to become the Arcanum's new backyard."

"Come on," Maria scoffed, "this is *Ennis*. He's dealt with us for this long—what's one more little pocket dimension among friends?"

"Oh, *friends*, is it?" Toula asked archly.

"If it means not facing a repeat of the installation demolition from the closure, then I'm perfectly willing to play the girlfriend card," she replied.

"Wait—girlfriend?" asked Bert, a playful note creeping

into his voice. "When did this—"

"Officially, it's been two years."

"You never told me!"

"You never asked," she retorted. "Anyway, he's perfectly mundane, so no one needs to worry that I'm polluting the Arcanum gene pool."

I heard levity in her response, but it sounded forced. Before Bert could comment, however, Toula took the reins again. "That's you and me, then, Bert, and—Ed?"

"Of course," Ed replied. "And Beth could help."

"Does she have the strength?" Bert asked.

"She's not on our level," he said plainly, "but she's well trained. For a project this complex, more hands can't hurt. What about the rest of the Arcanum refugees at the compound? Iris, certainly."

Bert chuckled. "Iris *Johansson*? Absolutely. Talented magus. What about Madison Copeland, is she still there?"

"Madison and Antony, yes. Allie moved south," said Maria.

"Madison would be helpful," Toula agreed. "Antony…" She sucked her teeth.

"His talents lie elsewhere?" Ed offered.

"We'll call him in once it's time to update the castle's tech. We've got Ted Girard, too, and the rest of the seniors hanging out in Fairbanks. Not many strong wizards in that group, but I'll take whatever we can get."

"I could ring Daphne Hopkins," Bert offered. "She's down in London these days, living near the Featherstonhaugh–Gupta clan. That's another maple wand on the pile."

"Is Lakshmi still up and about?" asked Toula.

"She was when we spoke two weeks ago," said Maria. "Ash wand, if I recall, but no one does logistics quite like Lakshmi. It sounds like we're heading for a cat herding situation—couldn't hurt to have someone on hand to bark orders."

"And Rodney?" Bert replied.

"Another ash, but he'll do anything Lakshmi tells him to do. That's the wizard half of the Away Team, then."

"I wish we still had Bob and Sylvester," Bert murmured.

"As do I. And look at you," Maria added with a weak laugh, "getting sentimental over the *Team*. Didn't know you cared, Bert."

"Of the lot of them," he said stiffly, "Bob was the least likely to call me at two in the morning, and Sylvester…I mean, the man was gifted with a pastry bag. I never had a quarrel with him."

"*Focus*," Toula interjected. "Bee and Daisy, maple and ash. They'll pitch in, and that should be more than sufficient to get this off the ground…which leads us to the next problem. If we're restoring the Arcanum, what are we doing for a grand magus?"

"You were the last legitimate one," Bert began. "It would make sense for you—"

"Me? I got kicked out of office, then kicked out of the Arcanum, and I've been *frequently* sleeping with the enemy for the last sixty-five years."

"We could keep that quiet—"

"I'm done with hiding Coileán and I *will not* hide our son," she shot back. "No, thank you, I put in my time with that chain. It's someone else's turn. What about you?"

"Be reasonable," he scoffed. "No one wants the second coming of Grand Magus Wold. Maria, I don't suppose you—"

She laughed incredulously at the suggestion. "My chain was taken, too, and I look half my age, so no reasonable wizard is going to allow me anywhere near the Council, much less the grand magus's office. But…I *do* have an idea. What about Edie?"

It was Ed's turn to laugh. "*No*. Someday, but not yet. She needs further training."

"She's doing well," said Toula.

"For someone wand-tested yesterday, I'm sure she's

doing a phenomenal job, but you can't seriously think it's a good idea to put Edie in charge of the Arcanum right now."

"Yeah, I have to agree with Ed on that," Toula told the table. "And there's more to running that shitshow than just casting ability."

"Hear, hear," Bert muttered.

"Frankly," she continued, "I don't think anyone on the former Council is both sufficiently untainted and equipped to do the job. Certainly no one who jumped on the Leander Kirby bandwagon," she said to a chorus of mumbled agreement. "We need a strong personality who has experience dealing with pushback. The Arcanum's been gone for twenty-five years, and it'll take work to bring everyone back into the fold, as well as convince the new crop of wizards that it's something worth listening to. We need someone that the Arcanum can rally behind."

Silence fell in the dining room.

"Oh, don't look at me like that," said Ed. "Leaving aside the *tiny* matter of my oath to the Minor Arcanum, you do recall what happened the last time I held that position, yes?"

"I'm not suggesting we need another Great War—" Bert began.

"There was nothing great about it! And that's the problem—the Arcanum has been idolizing Simon's insanity for the last thousand years. You can't seriously be suggesting that the best solution here is for me to lead another blood-soaked campaign across three continents. Or would you prefer that I knock off in his sleep anyone who doesn't toe the line? I've not walked about in the dream space in *this* lifetime, but I assure you, I remember the way in."

"And I don't doubt that," said Toula. "But Ed, you're not doomed to repeat his mistakes."

"Taking a wrong turn is a mistake," he shot back. "*Genocide* is an atrocity."

I glanced behind me at Edie, but her face remained carefully composed. We knew what the previous version of her father had done, though seldom did he speak of it so openly.

"And you recognize that," she said gently. "Did he?"

Ed paused. "By the end, yes. Titania and Oberon gave him ample time to think about his sins."

"Then you're one up on him already. Now, here's the deal: Simon forged the Arcanum, he realized he'd screwed up, he walked away, and then he faked his death. He became you for a reason."

"To find that bloody grail," Ed replied. "And speaking of which, has anyone checked Coileán's library for—"

"It's there, it's secure, and he thought you'd want the satisfaction of destroying it yourself."

"Courteous of him," Ed muttered.

"I thought so. And okay, yes, Simon had a singular purpose in mind when he went into regenerative hibernation," Toula continued. "But fate's a funny thing, isn't it? I don't think Simon could ever have imagined the Arcanum falling apart like it did. Magic's back now, and someone needs to lead wizardkind. This is your chance to fix his mistakes, Ed. Simon set the Arcanum on one course. You could change that."

"Your confidence is appreciated," he said, "but I don't trust myself."

"We all have the potential within us for great and terrible things. Magnify that with a talent like yours, and *yeah*, when shit happens, it's awful. But look at it like this. There was no one in Simon's life to tell him no, right? He bulldozed or assimilated any arcana in his way, there wasn't a wizard alive anywhere close to his equal, and I'm guessing that none of his advisors tried to dissuade him very often."

"Grivam had more of a spine than the lot of them," Ed replied, "and he had his own kingdom to run."

"All right, so the only real voice of reason in Simon's

life was from the occasional visiting merrow. *You've* got
support. Guardrails. I'll tell you to your face if you're going
in the wrong direction, and I *know* Beth will shake sense
into you. Come on, Ed, we need you. Even if it's just for a
few years. There's no one the Arcanum will rally around
more than you."

"I don't know," he mumbled.

But Toula was persistent. "You've got a second chance,
here. Finish what Arnold and I tried to do and make the
Arcanum part of the community—one among equals, not
this conquering entity to be feared. Now's your chance to
try to put things right with the Minors, yeah?"

"And just how do you propose I put Simon's murder
spree to rights?" he retorted.

"I'm not saying you do something now to completely
make up for it. What I'm suggesting is that you can reach
out to them as an ally, not an enemy. Stop trying to
subjugate them and show them respect instead. Simon
never did, Leander didn't get the message, and…uh…."

"Just say it," Bert muttered. "I had my moments."

"You've come a long way," Maria offered.

"You're kind," he replied. "And Ed, for what it
matters, I'm with Toula on this. We could use a little
Simon to get back on our feet."

Ed sighed. "I *did* mention the oath I swore to the
Minors, yes?"

"Terms can be renegotiated," said Maria. "It wouldn't
hurt you to ask."

"Why don't we get Badger or Seamus over here?"
Toula suggested. "They're as plugged into the Minor
Arcanum as anyone in this realm. Or we could call Amy
and Kip again…"

"I make them nervous," said Ed. "May as well try your
nephew."

As it turned out, Seamus was busy that morning doing
an anti-bullying presentation at the settlement's school, but
Badger agreed to come. Edie, Kenna, and I ducked around

a corner until we heard the clap of the open gate and Badger's clipped voice, then sneaked back into listening position.

Arnold Lowe had been one of Ed's distant great-grandchildren, though the two looked nothing alike. Badger, Arnold's cousin, had acquired the familial hair. Her apparent youth, I later learned, was Avus's doing, a glamour to make up for the years she'd spent in the mortal realm. With that piece of magic in place, she seemed barely older than Edie, though she sounded far brusquer than Edie ever dared with Ed.

"You want to do *what?*" she demanded. "Are you mad?"

"Just until we get the Arcanum up and running," said Toula. "We don't have a better option—"

"Than giving Simon Magus a bloody chain? Were you concussed on your way back into Faerie?"

"They're not doing anything of the sort until I talk to whoever's in charge of the Minor Arcanum," Ed interjected. "We thought you might be able to contact that person."

"There's no one person," said Badger. "And they like it that way. I've got friends among them…or I *had*," she amended. "If it's been twenty-five years out there…"

"What about Dr. Jones?" asked Maria.

"Well, Carey would be…about one hundred thirteen," she calculated, "which would put Zeb around one hundred sixteen. It's not impossible that they're still alive."

"But the odds aren't great," said Bert.

"Not for the Joneses. Jim Wheeler, now…he's Carey's baby brother, so…ninety-six, maybe? Better odds. They're all wizards, after all."

"Could you call them?" Toula asked. "Pretty please?"

Though she muttered that they were out of their minds, Badger obliged. The Joneses' phones, however, were out of service, while Jim's old number went to a confused teenage girl pulled out of a deep sleep. "What time is it over there, anyway?" Badger asked.

The rest of the room had to think for a moment. "Probably around two in the morning," Toula finally reported.

"If you want to make friends, I'd think about trying them later," said Badger. "They're early risers, but not that early. Come find me when it's closer to dawn, and I'll get you to the ranch. But I swear on *all* that is holy, you little bastard, if you harm a hair on their heads—"

"I won't, I promise," Ed replied in a rush. "Civil conversation, yes? Nothing more."

I felt a tug on my shirt and turned around to find Kenna close behind me. "If we were planning to eat before the afternoon session, we need to go," she whispered. Edie nodded vehemently, and with reluctance, I ended surveillance in favor of a sandwich.

"So," said Kenna once we were stuffing our faces at the long kitchen counter, "sounds like Badger and your dad have a *teensy* bit of bad blood."

"Sounds more like Dad has bad blood with himself," Edie replied, picking crumbs off the granite with her fingertip. She brushed the crumbs onto her plate, then took a bite of her sandwich and glared at the wall. "You heard them, right? They want to plop the castle on top of the compound."

"Or beside it, more likely," said Kenna.

"Why would it matter? Our hometown's going to be deserted soon enough, anyway." She contemplated her lunch, then put it aside. "Shit, this is all happening too fast. I was thinking, you know, maybe grad school, maybe a month in Australia, not...*this*." When she looked at me again, I saw the sheen in her eyes. "I don't want to lose you guys, okay? And if you're in Faerie with Dec and Aurie, and Dad's talking about a frigging *pocket dimension*, then where the hell does that leave me?"

"Right here," I said, and hugged her. Kenna dropped her food to join in, and the three of us stood clasping each other in the quiet kitchen, sweaty and bruised and not at all certain about what the future held.

"When did I lose control over my own life?" Edie mumbled against my shoulder.

"When did we have control to begin with?" Kenna retorted.

I thought then of Gaw, who had nothing left to control, and hugged them more tightly.

CHAPTER 12

Having overheard the lunchtime summit, I was surprised when Ed interrupted our training that afternoon. "If you're looking for Edie," I said as he crossed the lawn toward the practice yard, "she's inside."

"Yeah," said Dec, wiping his dripping face with his T-shirt. "And probably not being quite so tortured—*ow!*" he cried as Mina remotely shoved him to his knees and grinned. "Jeez, enough with the cheap shots!"

Ed shook his head as Dec pushed himself back to his feet. "Actually, Cici, I need your help. You've been excused from your lessons early."

Kiet folded his arms. "Is that so?"

"You're welcome to ask Val if you don't believe me."

The captain grunted but released me to my uncle's custody, and I limped after him toward the palace. "What's going on?" I asked.

"I need to speak with representatives of the Minor Arcanum," he replied, "and the last time we met, we required the services of a medium. Hope presumably has her hands full at the moment, so I thought you might be willing to assist me."

"I'm not as talented as she is," I reminded him. "Or so everyone keeps telling me…"

He smiled over his shoulder. "You'll do, little girl. Are you in pain?"

"Uh…*yeah.*"

"Sit," he ordered, pointing to a stone bench outside the rose hedges, and I plopped onto the cool slate. "Let's see," he murmured, then flicked a finger at me as his lips moved soundlessly. The magic around me flashed, and I found myself clean and sweat-free, though still achy from the day's lessons. He sat beside me and made a series of complex gestures, and as the spell knit around me, the pain began to lessen.

"Not bad," I said.

Ed paused in his work and grinned. "You can do much with enchantment, but you can do quite a bit with spellcraft as well."

"Where's your wand?"

"I don't require one. Neither does Toula," he said, seeing my bemusement. "And neither will Edie someday. She can cast without one now, but while she's learning, it's a useful crutch. Stand, put weight on your legs."

I tested his work, then nodded. "Better."

"Good." He casually waved open a gate to Avus's house and motioned me through. "After you, dear. Our escort is waiting for us."

Said escort was, as I'd suspected, Badger, who gave me a careful once-over when Ed and I arrived in the courtyard where she was sitting. "And this is…" she hinted.

"Cici, my niece," Ed replied. "Well, my wife's niece, if you'd prefer to be particular about it."

Badger's brown eyes narrowed. "So…Kitty's daughter?"

"Yes, ma'am," I said.

"And I'm guessing Val's granddaughter, then?"

I nodded.

She snorted as she cut her eyes to Ed. "Try leading with *that*, eh? No sense in roping the little lamb into this sordid family." She winced as she pushed herself to her feet—despite her glamour, she had more than a few decades behind her—then whispered a gate open. The world beyond the hole in space was lightening with the recent dawn, revealing the silhouette of a two-story brick house with sun-weathered shutters and scraggly bushes at the end of a small gravel parking lot. A pair of vehicles sat nearby—a newish sedan and a pickup truck at least as old as I was—and behind the house, I could just make out a cluster of large barns. Even in the early morning, a warm wind blew through the gate, carrying the twin smells of hay and manure.

"Where *is* that?" I asked.

"That," said Badger, "is Second Chance Ranch. It's a bit northeast of Albuquerque, and it's the last address I have for the Joneses, so good luck."

Ed arched a brow. "You're not staying?"

"I'm not getting involved. If you want to work something out with the Minor Arcanum, then that's on you."

She disappeared through another gate, and Ed rolled his eyes. "Stay close," he told me. "And I'm keeping this gate open. If it closed, I doubt there would enough magic in the area to allow us an easy exit."

"That's reassuring," I muttered, but followed him through.

As our shoes crunched across the gravel, I heard something whinny from one of the outbuildings—a horse, I supposed, though I'd certainly never been near enough to one to make a study of it. It's an undisputed truth in the magical community that animals native to the mortal realm lose their shit in the presence of outsiders. Anyone with sufficient fae or Conotan ancestry, even disguised, sets off their alarms. As a safety measure, I stayed away from anything likely to bite or kick me.

Ed patted my shoulder, then climbed up the short staircase to the front door and rapped twice.

When the door opened, a middle-aged woman with a deep chestnut complexion, silver-streaked black hair, and suspicious dark eyes squinted at us from the other side of the threshold. She wore a blue flannel shirt rolled to the elbows and a pair of wash-faded men's jeans with holes at the knees over dingy tennis shoes, and I gathered that chores started early at the ranch. "Yes?" she asked, peering at Ed.

"Good morning," he began, "and I apologize for the early visit. I'm looking for Carey and Zeb Jones."

"Well, then," she said, folding her sinewy arms, "I hope you brought a Ouija board. Carey was my aunt, and she died fifteen years ago. Zeb followed her that winter. What's your business with them?"

"I'm sorry for your loss, then. What about Jim Wheeler? Does he live nearby?"

"My dad? He's in Albuquerque, in a nursing home. Been in dementia care for the last three years. Who are you, again? And, uh…" Her voice petered out as she noticed the afternoon sunlight streaming through the gate on the other side of the parking lot. "What the hell is *that* thing?"

"That," said Ed, following her stare over his shoulder, "would be a gate. Faerie's been reopened, and magic is returning to this realm. You're Minor Arcanum, I trust."

"Yeah, but are you shitting me? *Magic?*"

"The outflow doesn't seem to have reached this part of the world yet, but trust me, it's coming. Now, look, the Minor Arcanum can do as it pleases, but there are Arcanum families scattered around the world, and by now, we're facing twenty-five years' worth of untrained young wizards. The Arcanum needs to return."

She grunted dismissively. "It's the Arcanum that got us into this mess, isn't it?"

"No. It was a faction following an idiot boy and two homicidal magi with a grudge. Those of us left are going to fix the problem. Make the culprits pay."

The warning note in Ed's voice caught my attention. I knew that my grandmother and her co-conspirator were the brains behind Faerie's apparent destruction, but in the chaos of the last days, I'd yet to hear anyone suggest hunting them down.

"The Arcanum needs a leader now so that someone as

unqualified as that idiot boy doesn't take the helm," Ed continued. "I'd like to discuss the possibility of assuming that role with your people."

The woman cocked her head. "Since when has the Arcanum run anything by *us*? Why do you care about our approval?"

"Because I swore an oath to never again take office," he replied. "In light of the novel circumstances, however, I'd like to see whether we might be able to revisit that arrangement."

"I'm sorry, *who* are you?"

He paused for the space of a long exhalation. "My name is Eadwig, son of Oswald. In a former lifetime, I was known as Simon Magus."

The woman's eyes flew open wide, and with a strangled sound, she slammed and locked the door.

"Of course," Ed muttered from the stoop.

Before I could dwell on her reaction, I heard an unfamiliar woman's voice behind me: "Hey, kid."

Turning, I found a spirit standing a few feet away, observing us with her arms crossed and a little smirk playing on her lips. She seemed middle-aged, roughly on par with the frightened homeowner, and like her, she sported a worn flannel shirt and jeans—clean and intact, but clearly work clothes. She was several inches shorter than me but had an athletic build, and I suspected that in life, she would have been able to hold her own in a dark alley. Even on cursory inspection, I could see the familial resemblance between her and the other woman: same deep tan, dark eyes, and smile lines, though whereas the homeowner wore her hair long, the spirit's was chopped in a sleek bob.

Hi, I thought as I approached her. *Are you…Dr. Jones?* I guessed.

She nodded. "Carey. And you would be…"

Cici Connolly.

To my relief, her face brightened. "Connolly? You're

Kitty's girl?" When I nodded in turn, she peered at me more closely. "Got your daddy's coloring, though, didn't you?"

You know my parents?

"I had a few dealings with the Away Team," she explained, "and besides, the Minor Arcanum does its homework, especially when there are unsupervised, undertrained faerie lords running around this realm. Though really, I'd take Marcus any day over *that* one," she said, dipping her head toward Ed as he descended the few steps. "Now, what's he proposing?"

"Ed," I called, waving him over. "Come here, would you?"

He frowned but joined me, and I thought for the millionth time that my gift would be so much simpler if it didn't make me look like I was emoting at empty space. "See something?" he asked.

I paused, listening to Carey, then relayed, "Dr. Jones is here. She's got questions."

I wasn't sure what crossed his face in the seconds following that revelation—fear? relief?—but Ed shoved his hands in his pockets and held his ground. "If you wouldn't mind…"

"I'm here, aren't I?" I replied, and considered Carey, who was giving Ed a once-over. *I can't make you visible to him*, I told her. *I'm sorry, but I'm not cynaeli*—

"A mouthpiece would be just fine," she replied, rubbing her chin. "Boy's grown up since last I saw him. I mean, it *has* been a quarter-century, but he was this skinny, scared little thing last we met. A teenager, zits and peach fuzz and all."

He thinks he's about forty-two now, I replied, comparing her assessment to the version of Ed before me. He was short for a man but well built, a little pasty and with startling blue eyes. His hair was slightly shaggy and dark but for the telltale white streak, and he'd grown a full beard—a rarity in a community mostly composed of residents too fae to produce facial hair. Beth made him keep it close-cropped and tidy, but when she complained of whiskers, he insisted it was protection against the Alaskan winter.

"Tell me about him," said Carey. "What's your impression?"

That took me aback, but I tried not to show my surprise. *Well…I mean, he's my uncle. Married my mom's sister.*

"Beth, right?"

I nodded. *We've lived in a remote part of Alaska all my life. Ed…* I paused, trying to find the information she sought. *He's always been good to us kids. Taught us magical theory, even when we thought magic was gone forever. Helps out on hunting trips and stuff. Uh…he's got a daughter my age, she's really talented—*

"Has he killed anyone lately?" she interrupted.

Not unless you count caribou.

"Hm." Carey gave him another long, appraising stare. "Do you know what sleepwalking is, Cici?"

The magical variety? I've heard of it, but Ed was kind of vague on how it works.

"Probably because he fumbled his way through it until he figured out the mechanics. It's one of the four great magics for any wizard to master: wandless casting, gate creation, transformation, and sleepwalking. Unfortunately, Simon figured it out, and thousands died as a result." Studying Ed, she murmured, "Sleepwalking became impossible once Faerie was cut off, of course, but I never caught him in the dream space during the year between the time he woke and the time everything went to hell. Suppose he'll want to use it now to recover the flock, huh?"

I don't know, I replied. *He hasn't said anything about it to me.*

"Well, then, let's go to the source. How should we do this?"

Just talk. I'll repeat it as close to verbatim as I can.

She relayed her message, and I turned to Ed. "This is from Carey. What do you have in mind, kid?"

"Where is she standing?"

I stepped aside and swept one arm toward her, and Ed oriented himself appropriately. "I don't think mere words will suffice to tell you how much I do *not* want to be grand magus," he began, blind to his audience. "After the atrocities of last time, I don't fully trust myself. But Toula, Bert, and Maria seem to think it would be best for the Arcanum if I led for a short while—just long enough to put the organization back together. They think I might have the clout—"

"Do you plan to use the dream space?" I interrupted.

He paused, cut his eyes to me, then looked back toward Carey. "Only to find the remnants of the Arcanum. I have no interest in antagonizing your people."

"That's a first," said Carey. "You plan to rebuild?"

"Toula managed to save Arc 2—she put it in a snow globe, of all things. The thought at the moment is to restore it within a pocket dimension we'll build in remote Alaska."

"Glutton for punishment?"

He grimaced. "The winters are miserable, I'll give you that, but once we have the pocket constructed, we should be able to work on the climate within it. And once we reestablish basic governance and operations in the castle, the plan is to open the school to any wizard who needs it. Witches, too."

Carey's eyebrows rose. "Seriously?"

"A generation needs to be trained, and that includes the witches among them. They'll all need wands and guidance to avoid killing each other."

"Granted, but since when have *you* given a damn about witches?"

Ed rubbed his neck "I've, uh…come to know several people with lesser talents in the last years. My understanding is that they can make worthwhile contributions to the larger community, particularly if they're trained."

"A revelation the Minor Arcanum received quite some

time ago," she said dryly.

"I never said I was perfect." Ed hesitated, collecting his thoughts, then told her, "Look, I loathe Simon. I hate what he stands for, I hate how he's been glorified in the Arcanum's collective memory, and I *cannot* tell you how sorry I am for what he did. What I did," he murmured. "But sometimes, perhaps, there comes a moment in which the world needs a Simon. And right now, Simon has *scores* to settle."

Carey mulled that over, then asked, "How many people do you plan to kill?"

As I repeated the question, I saw the uncertainty in Ed's eyes. Was that fear of what he hoped to unleash, I wondered, or fear of how I would react to his answer?

"Two," he said after a moment's pause. "Francine Leighton and Eva Stanhope. They were the masterminds of the closure."

"Not that little grand magus, what's his face—"

"Leander Kirby? No. He went along with them, but he was a foolish child. Those two, however…they tried to destroy Faerie and Conota, and because of them," he continued, a tremor creeping into his voice, "a young man whom I watched grow up alongside my own daughter is dead. You know of Ros and Sam, I assume."

"Sure," said Carey.

"Their boy. He was like a nephew to me, and he and Cici would have been married someday…probably sooner than their parents would have preferred," he added, glancing my way, "and he sacrificed himself to reopen Faerie." Turning to me, he quietly said, "I know you think that no one beyond the five of you and his parents cares that he's gone, Cici. That's absolutely not true. We're managing too many fires to grieve properly, but please don't convince yourself that no one else misses Gaw."

Looking at him straight on, I knew I wasn't imagining the tears in the corners of his eyes, and I struggled to keep myself from crying in turn. With my throat clenching, I settled for a nod, and he returned his focus to Carey.

"Those two should have been executed for treason years ago for that Conclave nonsense, let alone for trying to kill Maria and frame Bert. Toula was merciful once, but it's time for them to pay."

"Take a deep breath, honey," Carey coaxed as I wrestled down the sob that was trying to rise. "There's no rush." Once I'd composed myself, she asked Ed, "What are your plans as far as the Minor Arcanum is concerned?"

"Aside from education? Nothing," he said. "I've had more than enough conquest for one lifetime."

"And what if some of the would-be Arcanum defected to us?"

"It's their business. Of course, since the only real wands are coming from the crafters in Faerie, I tend to imagine that most of the Arcanum will return to the fold."

She absently ran her hand over her elbow as she thought. "You want to be released from your oath, then? For how long?"

"I ask for five years," he replied. "Let me set the wheels in motion once more and see to my daughter's education. Once she has completed her training and understands the Arcanum's politics, I believe she could take my place."

"Wait—you want to give the Arcanum to *Edie*?" I interrupted. "Already?"

"In a few years, yes. She's bright, tenacious…highly talented. I think she'd make a fine grand magus. And if you would kindly keep that between us for now," he added, holding my stare, "I'd appreciate it."

"Sure, but…"

"But what?"

After a brief struggle, I managed, "You guys wouldn't even let us stay in Anchorage after graduation, and now you want to hand over a whole magical organization to Edie? Have you even asked her if she'd be interested?"

"I see her potential here," he said with a shrug. "Once she's comfortable with more than the rudiments of spellcraft, and after she spends sufficient time as a magus to familiarize herself with the Arcanum…why not?"

"How old is this Edie, anyway?" Carey asked.

Ed waited while I relayed the question. "Cici's age. They're twenty-two."

"They're babies."

"Edie would be young for a grand magus," he said, ignoring me as I bristled at Carey's assessment, "but she has the temperament for it. Just give me long enough to set it up again and prepare her, and I'll gladly step aside." When Carey didn't immediately reply, he insisted, "I'll do nothing to harm your people, and the school will be open to anyone who needs it, no conditions. But magic is returning as we speak, and if the Arcanum isn't functional, we'll be faced with a pack of squabbling, untrained wizards on the loose. I have done *terrible* things, and I don't deny it," he added, "but I think the others are right. We need leadership quickly, and for good or ill, Simon's name carries weight."

Carey's eyes narrowed in thought, and she turned to me. "Tell him I'll ask the others—the ones whose opinions matter. I'll be back in a few…oh, damn it," she muttered as the house's front door opened again and the woman stepped out cradling a shotgun. "Cici, say *exactly* what I tell you."

Before the woman could fire a warning shot or worse, I called, "Peanut, what the *hell* do you think you're doing?"

She froze and stared at me as if she'd seen a ghost— which, to be fair, was close.

"That is Simon fucking Magus with a gate behind him," I continued, trying to match Carey's inflection, "and you waltz out here with a lousy gun? I thought I taught you better than that, girl."

The shotgun fell from her arms—fortunately, not discharging—and she took a hesitant step toward the short staircase. "Au…Aunt Carey?" she stuttered.

"She's with us over here," I hastily explained. "I'm a

medium. She and my uncle are dealing with something, and we'll be out of here soon, so if you could, you know…not shoot us, please?"

The erstwhile Peanut continued to stare at me, and after getting an earful from Carey, I told her, "Your aunt wants to remind you that it's a bad idea to punch above your weight class when you're not even carrying a wand, you *should* start carrying a wand again, and…uh…you have a new stallion?"

She nodded in stunned silence.

"Carey says he's not interested in the mares, and he never will be. Might want to consider rehoming him if you're planning to breed. Jackson Sullivan's looking to sell one, and he's got a good bloodline. Also, she's rolling her eyes right now and suggests you go back inside until she and Ed are finished."

"Sorry, Aunt Carey," Peanut mumbled, then retrieved her shotgun with trembling hands and retreated into the house.

"Jim's littlest one always was a skittish thing," Carey told me, then vanished with a shake of her head.

"She's gone," I said, turning to Ed, who continued to watch the front door as if anticipating a sneak attack. "I think she wants us to wait."

He muttered, and two wooden stools popped into existence behind us. Pulling up a seat, my uncle quietly said, "Nice work. I didn't want to hurt her, but when someone comes at you with a gun like that…"

"Carey did all the work. I'm a glorified parrot."

His hand landed on my shoulder as I sat, then squeezed. "I know it's hard, Cici. Losing someone you love, it…well, it doesn't get easier with practice. But sometimes, even when all you want to do is lock yourself in a dark room and weep, you have no choice but to keep going. Put on the mask, put out the fires, and then, once you're free to breathe again…then you mourn your dead."

"If he were just dead, it would be easier," I mumbled,

studying the gravel. "He's been wiped out of existence."

"Perhaps he just hasn't come to you yet."

I shook my head. "My grandmother and brother couldn't sense him. If he were still around, he'd find me. Everyone else does, whether I want them to or not."

His brow furrowed with concern. "Has your control—"

"My control's fine. People still visit me, though. I can make them leave me alone, but they keep stopping by." I hesitated, then said, "Cuthbert checks on you."

Given the way Ed jumped at that, I thought he might fall off his stool. "I'm sorry, *what* did you say?"

"Cuthbert. Simon's boyfriend. He visits on occasion, maybe once or twice a year."

Ed's eyes practically bulged from his head. "You never told me—"

"Because I respected his wishes."

His lips moved for a few seconds as he tried to formulate words, and then he managed, "Is he...all right?"

"Perfectly fine," I replied. "They never tell me the details—I don't think they *can*—but he seems relatively happy. He misses you," I added, cutting my eyes to Ed. "The former version, at least."

Ed was silent for a time, then sighed. "I recall Simon's life in vivid detail, but it's...strange. I remember people I've never met." He raked his teeth over his bottom lip as he stared into the distance. "Will you do me a favor?"

"Sure."

"Should you see him again, tell him...tell him I miss him, too, please."

I had no idea what was going through his thoughts, so I hoped I wasn't about to make matters worse when I said, "He's happy for you...with Beth, I mean. He's glad you found someone."

"Kind of him," he murmured.

"He likes this version of you. Told me a couple times that it's closer to the man he knew when that guy wasn't so busy being Simon."

Ed chuckled wistfully. "There are few second chances in life, my girl. I'd be a fool if I didn't try to improve upon the first attempt. Of course, in my case, the bar was *low*." Looking back at me, he said, "All of this—the closure, twenty-five years in the wilderness, Gaw—could have been avoided if I hadn't been so desperate to conquer. If I hadn't asked Cuthbert to build a device capable of storing magic sufficient to destroy an army…if I hadn't lost the damn thing…if I'd insisted that the Team destroy it when they found it…none of this would have happened. I'm sorry, Cici. I'm so very sorry."

I took my uncle's hand and held it while we waited, listening to the distant birds chirp in the morning light and the horses call to each other in the barn. Every so often, a twitch in the blinds of one of the house's front rooms reminded me that Peanut was still watching.

Finally, after a wait of only a few minutes that felt like hours, Carey reappeared. "Hi," I said aloud—mental communication was unnecessary, given our mutual fluency in English. "Any decision?"

Ed stiffened on his stool, waiting while I listened to Carey. "I have a verdict for you," she said to him. "If you swear to work into the Arcanum's laws that the Minor Arcanum is to be left undisturbed, and if you swear that anyone born during the closure can have a free Arcanum education and a crafter-made wand, then Simon's victims will agree to release you from your prior oath."

"For how long?" Ed asked.

"Indefinitely."

"Indefinitely?" he echoed, taken aback. "I…yes, I agree to those terms, and I swear to uphold them. Let Cici bear witness."

"That's acceptable."

Ed and I stood, and he waved the stools back into atoms. "May I ask what changed their minds?"

"It's been better than a quarter-century, you're grown,

and you've shown no sign of homicidal conquest yet," Carey explained, tucking one hand into her pocket. "That, and Arnold vouched for you."

"Wait, Arnold? He wasn't…but he…"

"Oh, he was Arcanum to the core," she said as he sputtered, "but I've known Arnold for a *long* time. He was the only magus who ran away from James Mulligan to take care of this realm, and he helped rescue Fringers during that regime. We don't always see eye to eye, but I respect his judgment. And he says you're a good kid, Ed."

My uncle listened as I repeated that, then smiled when he realized she'd used his preferred name. "Thank you, Dr. Jones. I mean that."

"I know you do," said Carey. "So go on, go fix this mess, Grand Magus," she told him, making a shooing motion that only I could see. "Just don't fuck it up again."

"Understood," he replied, and waited until I told him she'd departed. His shoulders sagged as he exhaled, and then he glanced back at the house in time to see the blinds part once more. "We're leaving!" he called, cupping his hands around his mouth. "Thanks for not shooting at us!"

Peanut didn't venture outside to see us go, but really, I couldn't blame her.

I followed Ed back to Faerie, where my body was slammed with a wall of pain. As I cried out, Ed swore, and I felt the ache begin to subside seconds later. "Sorry, I should have warned you," he said as I clutched my sore ribs. "Spells and enchantments on living things break when you enter Faerie. There's some sort of protection at the border. Let me finish putting that spell back together…"

Whatever else could be said for him, Ed was a rapid caster, and soon, I could breathe without the stabbing pain from Mina's tutelage. Once I was stable, he opened another gate and motioned for me to join him. Curious, I followed and found myself in a large, stone-walled room decorated with bookshelves and tapestries. On one side was a sitting area, where a pair of blue leather couches faced each other across a coffee table beside a low-burning fire. On the other side, past a *generously* stocked bar, sat a wide wooden desk littered with papers. Half a dozen glass paperweights held the piles in place—necessary, I guessed, as the bay windows were open for the late afternoon breeze.

Coileán looked up from the old laptop on the blotter in front of him, thoroughly unfazed by the hole in space that had appeared in the middle of his office. "Back from New Mexico?" he asked, reaching for the tumbler of amber liquid squatting on a coaster between two stacks of paper.

"Just now," said Ed. "You're busy, I see."

He sighed, then sipped. "These petitions have been waiting for twenty-five years. I suppose I'd better deal with them before the petitioners return to the realm. And how is Carey, then?"

"Deceased."

"Ooh," Coileán muttered, wincing. "Seeking the next of kin?"

"No need," Ed replied. "Cici's quite talented, and apparently, Arnold doesn't think that giving me my old job back is a terrible idea, so…" He spread his hands. "Time for Simon to go to work. Where's Ennis, still with Val?"

One of Coileán's eyebrows arched. "Last I saw. You're recruiting mundanes now?"

"No, but I do need to see the man about a dimensional nexus eventually. Toula explained the plan?"

"The contours, at least. I don't envy you the construction project." Glancing my way, he said, "Training is probably about over for the day, dear. Rest up." When I groaned, he chuckled into his tumbler. "You sound like your father. Really, Mina's not trying to be sadistic."

"Couldn't prove it by me," I said, and opened a small gate back to Avus's. Coileán offered a little golf clap, but before we could take our leave, he said, "Ed? One moment, if you will."

My uncle folded his arms. "Yes?"

"Just a friendly warning. Should you decide to attack Faerie again…"

He huffed and shook his head. "Simon learned *that* lesson the hard way. Besides," he continued, "we've been neighbors for years, and Beth's brother-in-law is heir to a court. Waging war on Faerie would be a poor choice all around."

"Beth would kill you," Coileán replied, not unkindly.

"Absolutely, and if I upset her, Artur would be on my ass before I knew what hit me."

With that, Coileán lifted his nearly empty glass in a tiny salute. "Nice to know that you understand the way the world works, kid."

Ed smirked back at him. "Who are you calling 'kid'? Add Simon in, and I'm two hundred fifteen years your senior."

"Yeah, but you slept through most of it."

"It *counts*."

"Keep telling yourself that," he said, and cocked his head toward my unstable gate. "And do try not to start any major wars this time around, won't you?"

CHAPTER 13

Night still held sway over the garden beyond my bedroom when I bolted awake in bed.

That *was* Ros. Either I was having surreally vivid dreams or she was hiding in my closet...or, I mused, rubbing my face, I was experiencing auditory hallucinations.

I fumbled on the nightstand for my phone, which Aiden had taken the liberty of tweaking the day before. It no longer needed to charge, and somehow, it had full reception, even in the middle of Faerie. I squinted at the screen and noted the time, which was still configured for Kentucky. As best as I could tell, Faerie was about eight hours ahead...which meant I'd awakened around two in the morning.

Great.

The phone's flashlight didn't reveal Ros lurking in the corners of the room, but after three nights of the weird dreams, I needed to reassure myself that the voice was a product of my frazzled mind. Adding my tennis shoes to my summer pajamas—which desperately needed a wash, I noted, catching a whiff of my tank top—I thought about our lessons from the previous morning. The key to a successful gate was to clearly envision the destination. I didn't know what Ros and Sam's house in Faerie looked like, but Kiet had said that when a location was unknown, the backup option was to focus on a person. *That*, at least, I could manage. And so, hoping that Ros would forgive me for showing up in her bedroom in the middle of the night, I imagined her as strongly as I could, then ripped open a small gate.

But the gate didn't lead into a house, as I'd expected. Rather, it deposited me outside in the cool darkness beside what appeared to be a massive stone building. It wasn't like Peanut's outbuildings—this structure could have housed jumbo jets, and given the size of the doors and the low rumbling emanating from within, my first thought was that I'd stumbled across a hangar like Ennis's. Then, hearing bleating, I noticed the large fenced pasture nearby. As my sleep-deprived brain tried to reason why someone would park a sheep pen beside a hangar, I looked toward the far right end of the building and spotted the lights of a house. This wasn't a shack—it looked vaguely like a colonial with a wraparound porch in the darkness—but affixed to the hangar as it was, it seemed as insignificant as a wart. I thought I could make out another house on the other end of the hangar, though the night obscured the details.

Well, *this* wasn't what I'd had in mind.

Cursing my ineptitude, I crept toward the hangar, as I could see a few lights shining outside its wide doors. As I neared, I realized that the lights weren't attached to anything—rather, they were perfect white spheres floating about ten feet off the ground, and in their glow, I could just make out Sam and Ros. They stood with another couple, and it took me a moment to put names with the faces I saw in profile: Ros's parents, Helen and Joey.

And then, as the light glinted off a huge red eye, the shadows behind them resolved into the hulking head of a black dragon.

That was no hangar. That was a *barn*.

As I neared, I began to overhear the dragon's thoughts—which, conveniently enough, it was broadcasting in words for the sake of its companions. Pure thought, however, would still have revealed the dragon's evident distress.

Why is he so angry? I gave him space for a year, and now you tell me another twenty-five years have passed outside this realm. Surely he should have calmed by now…

"It's not that simple," said Joey.

His clutchmates miss him. I miss my son. Why does he stay away?

Listening, I realized that the dragon had to be Georgie, Frank's mother. Frank never spoke of her, at least not around me, but Ros had. Her father had found Georgie as an abandoned hatchling, alone in the wilds of Faerie, and had raised her from the time she was the size of a Shetland pony. Joey had learned to ride her, and he'd made a home adjacent to the dragon barn, staying close to his now *significantly* larger hatchling. When Georgie had mated, she'd laid six eggs. Five hatched on time and grew up together under her watchful eye, but Frank, the lonely sixth, had bonded to Ros instead of his mother.

I wondered if any of them had yet broken the news to Georgie that Frank didn't share a father with the rest of his siblings. It was Publius who'd given me the more sordid details once I was old enough to wonder how Frank had come about: Georgie, transformed by the realm into human guise and still very much in season, had initiated a one-off romp with Frank's half-fae father out of curiosity. That Frank existed at all was due to the realm's experimentation—Kura, Ros's predecessor as Faerie's consciousness, had wondered what a draconid lesser faerie would be like. The result was a runty hatchling, bright and curious in ways his clutchmates were not, who had fit in nowhere but among the other weirdos of the Away Team.

"He's pissed," Ros told Georgie, hugging her bathrobe around her, "and he has every right to be."

I don't understand.

"You and his siblings threatened Aurie. They wanted to kill her. Hell, *you're* the one who told him to take her away." Even from my hiding spot in the shadows, I could hear her anger. "Why would Frank want anything to do with you? Aurie means the world to him, and if I know him at all, he's going to do whatever it takes to keep her safe."

I didn't tell him to leave because I don't want him here, Georgie protested. *It was for his own good.*

"You drove away your own *son*."

Because his siblings' reaction to the hatchling was perfectly normal. She shouldn't have survived—

"Do not presume to tell me whether Aurie should have lived or died," Ros interrupted in a warning tone I knew far too well. "I did everything in my power to save those eggs. *Everything.* She's perfectly healthy now but for the missing limbs, and she's just as smart as her father. And your other kids wanted to *kill* her?"

Georgie's thoughts betrayed her unease. *Frank shouldn't have nested for Ione.*

"But he did, and those were his kids."

It's not right.

"He's always been a little weird, okay?" she snapped. "Aurie's still your granddaughter."

And getting her out of the barn was the kindest thing I could do for her, Georgie retorted. *Frank wasn't thinking clearly, and so I resorted to tough love. That doesn't mean I never want to see him again.*

"Keep telling yourself that," said Ros, "but that's not how your actions were perceived. And friendly advice: if you ever want a relationship with Frank, then you'd better darn well accept Aurie."

The dragon huffed what sounded suspiciously like a sigh. *Horus was surprised to see that Frank still had her with him. His siblings didn't think she would live long.*

"She was twenty-six this week," said Sam. "I think she's doing okay."

I suppose…but how was she able to summon fire? Horus said her arm was aflame. Whoever bound her and Frank couldn't have made that part of the bind, could they?

After a brief pause, Ros replied, "That's something

you'll have to ask Aurie, assuming you're allowed close enough to pose the question."

You could help smooth this over—

"Forget it. I was there, I saw everything, and I watched that girl grow up. She used to babysit my son. And if *I'm* still upset that Frank's siblings wanted to kill her, I can only imagine how he must feel. So if you want to make amends—"

Sliding closer, I stepped on a twig, snapping it with a noticeable crack.

Georgie raised her head. *Hold that thought,* she interrupted, and I could feel her mind reaching for mine. *You there, by the sheep—who are you?*

I hurried toward the barn, and when Ros saw me, her face crumpled. "Sweetie," she murmured, and hugged me tightly. "It's good to see you."

"What're you doing out this late?" Sam asked.

Helen cleared her throat, and Ros released me. "This is Cici," she told her parents and Georgie. "Gaw's girlfriend."

Girlfriend was a poor word to describe what we'd been, but it had the desired effect. As Helen's and Joey's expressions shifted from bemusement to pity, Ros squeezed my hand. "Sam's right. Why aren't you in bed?"

"I, uh…" I paused, hearing in my head how odd my problem sounded, then asked, "Could I talk to you for a minute, please? In private?"

"Of course. Come on, I'll make tea," she replied, and led me off toward the house on the far side of the barn.

Ros and Sam's home was only about as large as their house in Alaska had been, though the kitchen was spacious and tidy. As Ros pulled a cannister of tea from the cabinet, she caught me examining the room. "Little different than our last place, huh?"

"Honestly, and I don't mean this the wrong way, it's the smallest house I've seen thus far in Faerie."

She softly laughed as she opened a box of tea filters.

"That's because it was mostly a bachelor pad. When Sam built it, I was incorporeal most of the time. I didn't sleep, didn't need a place to crash. Now..." She gestured toward the copper kettle on the stove, which immediately began to whistle, and pulled it off the cold eye. "If we stay here, we'll need to expand. More closets, at least."

"Where else would you go?" I asked.

"Somewhere away from the barn. Right now, we have almost a dozen dragons next door. Sam did a good job soundproofing the house, but the adjoining wall vibrates when their snoring really kicks up. I'd forgotten how *loud* they can be." She grimaced, then asked, "Sugar?"

"Please."

I considered Ros as she made our drinks—the dark circles beneath her eyes, the too-tight lines around her mouth, the unfamiliar slump of her shoulders—and forced myself to smile as she passed me a mug. "Couldn't sleep, either, huh?"

"No," she replied, steering me toward the den. "I don't sleep much on a good night—being the realm screwed with me in several ways—but of late..."

"I get it."

Sitting beside me on the couch, she patted my arm and leaned closer to hug me again. "Now, what's on your mind that couldn't wait for morning?"

I sipped, stalling for time, then wrapped my hands around the warm ceramic and stared at the rug. "So, um...this is going to sound insane..."

"Probably not as insane as you think."

Risking a glance back at Ros, I found her dark, weary eyes—Gaw's eyes in shape, if not in color—watching me. Ros was only seventy, too young to have acquired the unsettling fae tell of age in her stare, but something in her eyes' depths still spoke of the weight of eons.

"I've been hearing you calling me at night," I forced myself to tell her. "Three nights in a row, now. Am I hallucinating, or have you been trying to reach me?"

Ros frowned. "I haven't been calling you," she began, then paused, mug frozen halfway to her mouth. "Or have I?"

"Huh?"

She put her tea aside, then leaned closer as if preparing to convey a great secret. "Gaw is still alive," she murmured. "I'm sure of it."

Though I wondered if Ros's grief and insomnia were messing with her mind, I resisted the urge to pull away. "What do you mean?"

"He's out there, but he's at sea. Can't focus, can't find himself. It's a horrible feeling…" She must have noticed my expression shift, as she sat back and explained. "When Kura died and Faerie was thrust on me, it *shattered* me for a few days. One minute, you're you; the next, you're spread across the realm and drowning in information. Everything that's happening, everything that's ever happened within the borders, is suddenly *there* in your head, and just learning to tread water takes time. Val threw me a lifeline," she said with a little smile. "He worked with me until I learned to focus again, and then I was able to fully integrate with my predecessors and control the realm. But here's the problem," she continued, picking up speed. "Beth pulled me out of here during the collapse. She may have saved my life, may have saved the realm—honestly, the thaumaturgical implications of what happened back then are going to be the subject of a brilliant theoretician wizard's thesis someday."

I winced. Theoretical thaumaturgy was Edie's forte, not mine.

"Anyway," said Ros, "I'm back here now, but I'm obviously no longer the realm. Whatever your aunt did, she severed that connection. So who's running the show?"

"Maybe no one," I suggested.

"Nope. That's not the way Faerie works, which is why I think it's Gaw. But he's probably still trying to find the surface."

Though I didn't want to lessen Ros's hope, I had to tell her what I knew. "Avus has been trying to locate Gaw, but it's not working. He said he can't feel the realm."

"That doesn't mean Gaw's not out there," she replied, retrieving her mug. "It just might take a different approach to find him. And if I've been calling you in your sleep, that's proof positive that the realm still exists as a conscious entity."

"I'm sorry," I said, willing my tea's caffeine to kick in— Ros was talking at a good clip, whereas my brain felt like it was only firing on half its cylinders. "*What?*"

"There's a group mind, you see. Whenever a previous version of the realm dies, part of her remains in that group consciousness, and her successor can draw upon her memories and knowledge. It's how the long history of Faerie is maintained," she said, and paused to sip her tea. "I was the fifth. Kura came before me—she's the one who set up the court arrangement. Before her was Inkil, the first half faerie to hold the position, then Tenola before her, who was born in the realm. And before Tenola came someone the rest of us think of as Faerie—she was the realm at its beginning, though even she doesn't know where she came from or what preceded her. She was basically Conota's twin."

"Uh…okay…"

"I 'know' all of my predecessors because part of them remains in that group mind. Now, clearly, I'm not dead, but I'm not the realm any longer. Maybe part of me is still in the group. *She* could be calling out to you."

Though it was far too early to be discussing the dynamics of collective consciousnesses, hope fluttered within me as Ros spoke. Still, I didn't allow myself to surrender completely to her optimism. "If Avus and Coileán can't even sense the realm, then how could it be talking to me?"

"Because you've always been attuned to energies that the rest of us don't sense," she replied. "Maybe you're the easiest target, the lighthouse in the night." Ros considered me briefly, then asked, "Would you be willing to try meditation?"

My mind flicked back to our long, miserable hours of meditative practice with Toula, when my attempts to clear my mind and focus were persistently derailed by the tickle of a hair in my face or the temptation of daydreaming to counteract the boredom. "If you want," I reluctantly offered. "Honestly, Edie's better at that than I am."

"I'm not talking about focus meditation. Something deeper, more akin to hypnosis. I can guide you down, and once you're relaxed, your mental barriers might drop. Could make things easier for the realm to reach you."

I nodded but gave her a weird look. "When did you study hypnosis?"

"I didn't. *Ellie* did, and I picked up the basics from her after she took the throne. The realm has a constant connection to the Three," she explained, "and with full access to her memories…I was curious. I'm also a better swordswoman than I have any right to be because I cribbed from Val," she added with a sly grin. "So…I've got a spare bed and nothing but time, if you're willing."

To hell with the early morning torture session on my calendar, I decided. It didn't matter if Ros was on to something or mad with grief—if there was any chance that Gaw still existed, I'd do whatever it took to find him, and Kiet and Mina could deal with themselves in my absence. When my options were "search for Gaw" or "obey Avus"…well, that was easy.

"Comfortable?" Ros asked as I stretched out on her guest bed. "Too hot, too cold? Do you want a blanket?"

"I'm fine," I said, and watched as she dimmed the lights to near-blackness. "How does this work?"

"It's a lot like falling asleep—probably not too difficult, considering the hour," she replied. "I'm going to guide you through an induction session, and then—"

"You're not going to make me act like a chicken, are you?"

"Of course not. It's difficult to make a hypnotized person do anything that she doesn't want to do, and anyway, I'm not going to be implanting suggestions. I may do a little visualization with you once you're down, see if we can't make contact with your mysterious voice in the night. Sound good?"

"Kind of freaky, not going to lie," I admitted.

Ros smiled as the overstuffed chair across the room floated up to the bedside for her use. "There's nothing to worry about, and this won't hurt a bit," she reassured me. "I'll be right here. Now, focus on the sound of my voice…"

Though I knew little about hypnosis, I decided that Ros had a great voice for it. Calm, soothing, and even, it stayed low but still seemed loud in the room. Before I knew it, she'd begun a slow countdown from ten…and then, as she hit two, the world around me *popped*.

It wasn't an audible pop so much as it was a physical sensation, as if reality were an exploding bubble and I'd been expelled into the void. Feeling for the comforter, I realized the bed was no longer beneath me, then stood and strained to pick out shapes in the darkness, but the world seemed formless and empty. "Hello?" I called. "Ros, can you hear me?"

No one answered.

"Ros," I called more insistently, "where are you? This is weird, I need help…*Ros*! Where are—oh, thank God," I said, my heartbeat slowing as she appeared and began to walk toward me. "Sorry, I thought you'd left me, there."

Though I was still in my pajamas, Ros appeared to have changed clothes, switching her bathrobe for a slouchy charcoal-colored sweater over black leggings. As she neared, I asked, "Is this still part of the induction? It feels oddly real."

"It's real, I assure you," Ros replied, then paused a few feet away to give me an appraising stare. "And it's about time you answered. I was beginning to think you were ignoring me."

I considered my companion, who, upon closer inspection, seemed like a better-rested version of the Ros I had just left. "Uh...you're Ros?"

"Yes," she replied, "though you have me at a disadvantage." She sounded terribly irked by this development. "Cici, correct?"

"That's me."

"Good. Who the hell are you, anyway?"

That I was being posed the question by the doppelganger of someone who'd known me since I was in diapers was disconcerting at best. "Uh...well...I'm Cici Connolly, and I—"

"Hold on," she interrupted. "Connolly? Are you any relation to Kitty Connolly?"

"Yeah, that's my mom."

Ros's jaw dropped. "Your *mom*? How old are you?"

"Twenty-two last March."

She crossed her arms tightly and scowled into the distance as if searching for answers in the void somewhere off to my left. "Okay," she finally said, "*okay*, let's...let's back this up. What happened to me?"

"That's a really good question," I replied, hopeful to avoid predawn theoretical postulation, "but as far as we can tell, it's like Faerie's been frozen for twenty-five years. What do you last remember before about three days ago?"

"The realm was falling apart. An attack from the outside, I couldn't fight it..." Her scowl deepened as she worked through her memories. "*Beth.* She tried to pull me out as everything collapsed."

"She did," I said, and Ros looked at me in alarm. "And then Faerie disappeared, or so everyone says. I certainly wasn't there for it. A bunch of the refugees moved up to remote Alaska—"

"Like the Conclave?"

"Same land, apparently. Threw together a compound before the last of the magic was gone, and you settled down with Sam." I hesitated, then said, "You two had a son."

Ros stood before me in silence as she contemplated that information, then muttered, "Well, damn. Sounds nice."

"You don't remember any of that?"

"No, because they're not my memories. When Beth dragged me out, she must have severed my connection to the realm. When Kura was pulled out," she continued, talking to herself, "the connection wasn't fully broken, but with the realm under attack, and the trauma…" She glanced back at me, as if recalling my presence. "I must not be the realm anymore. If there's a version of me that exists in Alaska—"

"She's here," I said. "She hypnotized me to make it easier for us to find each other."

"But I can't feel her! I can't feel *anything*," Ros protested. "The group mind has fractured, no one knows what's happening in Faerie, I can't even reach the Three…wait, are they here, too?"

"Coileán and my grandfather are. No one's heard from Irem since Faerie collapsed."

"Your grand…" Ros paused, then flashed a quick smile. "I see that Kitty and Marcus stuck together, then."

"So far, so good."

"Glad to hear it. I'm happy for those crazy kids," she replied, but quickly sobered. "So I can't reach the Three, the group mind has splintered into its component personalities, and you're saying it's been like this for twenty-five years?"

I grimaced. "More like stasis, I think. Faerie wasn't reopened until Thursday, and when we got over, everyone was asking why the sky wasn't falling anymore. I guess no time passed here from the moment you left until the moment Gaw made that gate, and—"

"Stop. Gaw?"

"Gawain. Your son."

A look of comprehension dawned on Ros's face. "Oh. *Oh*, wait, that would…" She rubbed her temples as she thought. "This Gaw, he's about six feet tall? Maybe your age?"

"Blond like you," I offered. "Hazel eyes—"

"Like his dad," she murmured. "I'll be damned."

"Have you seen him?" I pressed. "Is he alive?"

"I…maybe? I've never seen anything quite like it—"

"Like *what*?" I demanded, resisting the urge to give her a good shake.

As if sensing my impulse, she raised her palms to keep space between us. "Back up with me. You said that Gaw made a gate, but if this was twenty-five years after magic drained in the mortal realm, then how did he do it?"

"Conota said that he *was* Faerie. That it had somehow been pulled into you when the closure happened, then passed to him. He said…" I winced at the recollection. "He said that Gaw was like a kernel of popcorn, and the important part would only be released if he destroyed the shell. I was *really* damn fond of that shell, you know?" I said, willing myself not to cry. "And a bunch of us ran off with him, trying to keep him safe, but he decided to kill himself anyway, and…"

"Tell me what happened," Ros murmured as my chest constricted.

"He and I sat up all night," I said as the horrible memory replayed itself in my mind's eye, "and then he walked away from me, and he…he told me he loved me, and he fucking *exploded*, and there was a gate where he had been."

"His last words were to you?"

I nodded. "He said, 'I love you, Cici.' And then he was gone…"

Ros waited while I pulled myself under control. When I

was once again able to draw a breath without risking a sob, she asked, "Do you know why I've been calling for you?"

"Because I'm a medium?" I guessed. "Ros—*my* Ros—thought that it might be easier for you to reach me."

"It certainly doesn't hurt," she concurred, "but that wasn't why I tried to find you. Several days ago, when the group mind fell apart and I lost contact with the realm, this figure appeared. He doesn't seem to sense us, and he doesn't move—nothing but his lips. They keep repeating your name."

I covered my mouth as my eyes filled. "Where is he? Take me to him!"

"I will, but, uh…prepare yourself, eh?"

Before I could protest, she took my hand, and the world seemed to pop once again. When I regained my bearings, I found that we were no longer alone: four other women stood with us, none of them familiar to me. The first was a petite blonde in a diaphanous pink dress, the second a taller, dark-skinned woman with a complex braided updo and a simple purple robe, the third a blue-eyed brunette in a form-fitting orange gown who glared sullenly at the others, and as for the fourth, the green-skinned woman with the third eye above her nose was clearly inhuman and might have passed as Conota's sister. She'd opted for a cream-colored robe, though hers left much of her flat chest bared to the place where her navel would have been.

"Found Cici," Ros announced to the others. "*And answers.*"

"A solution?" asked the short blonde.

"Maybe. Cici, this is Kura, Inkil, Tenola, and…uh…"

Ros paused when she reached the green woman, who dipped her head toward me. "The original," she said, flashing a smile of pointed teeth. "Why does he mouth your name?"

"Because I'm his girlfriend," I replied, unsettled by the five pairs of eyes—and the bonus eye—on me. "We'd been talking about getting married…"

Inkil, the woman in the purple robe, offered me a genuine smile. "Love. Of course."

"Spare me," muttered Tenola, the ill-tempered brunette.

"Just because *you* don't comprehend it doesn't mean it holds no power," Inkil chided her. "Were you half-blooded, you might better understand."

"It's weakness, that's all," she retorted.

As the two of them bickered, the blonde—Kura—leaned closer to me. "Tenola was the first of us after Faerie. Full-blooded and born here. She tried to make herself an absolute ruler, and the people rose against her, so she killed herself and passed the realm to Inkil, thinking that a half-fae alternative could be controlled by the group mind. What she did not *quite* anticipate was that Inkil had a spine and common sense."

"The occasional sniping in the group mind is the price of doing business," Ros added, then raised her voice to be heard over her predecessors. "If you two could wrap this up?"

Inkil mumbled an apology, while Tenola rolled her eyes but fell silent.

"I think I've pieced together the problem," Ros continued. "*I* am no longer the realm. I'm one of you now. The rest of me is still alive, but she's been severed. When she was extracted during the collapse, Faerie fell *into* her. It passed to her son…and three guesses as who *he* might be."

The eldest of them began to nod as the rest considered that information. "A purer vessel than any of you," she murmured. "More like me, but…still tainted, I suppose."

"Faerie has been within him all his life," said Ros. "He released it a few days ago. That's why he's here."

"But why are we like this, then?" Kura asked. "The group mind has never before fallen apart at a transition."

"I don't know, but maybe because this *wasn't* a clean transition."

"Has he any experience with magic?" asked Inkil, turning to me.

I shook my head. "There was none in the mortal realm. We've studied theory and history, but nothing practical."

She made a face. "That may explain it. The boy has no familiarity with magic, and to be suddenly possessed of such power…"

"He's overwhelmed," Ros concluded. "Lost in himself. And until he can pull himself together…"

Kura picked up the thread. "We will remain broken, blind, and powerless. Do you suppose the girl can help him?"

Eleven eyes focused on me again, and I spread my hands. "I'll do whatever I can, but…I mean, I just started learning the practical stuff. I can kind of make gates, but nothing more complicated than that."

"Not impressive," the original declared, "but at this point, it's worth a try."

I barely had time to think before the world popped. "Give me a little warning before you do that, okay?" I mumbled, closing my eyes against the vertigo, and wondered if it was possible to throw up in the void.

But when I opened my eyes again, my complaints died unspoken.

Gaw.

It was Gaw, but…

"Moon and stars," I whispered. "What *happened* to him?"

"That's how he appeared," Ros told me, then gently nudged me from behind. "Want to see if you can get his attention?"

Gaw stood before me, just as I'd last seen him, his lips forming my name in silent repetition. But he was no longer made of flesh—skin and bone and muscle had been replaced by iridescent flames in the shape of his body, and his open, unseeing eyes seemed to glow like stars.

Before I could draw closer, Faerie gripped my shoulder.

"Do *not* touch him," she warned. "What you are seeing is raw magic, the very heart of this realm. Making contact with that would probably be fatal to you, so keep your distance if you want to live."

Duly cautioned, I crept closer, hoping to catch a sign of life in his burning face. "Gaw?" I murmured, then licked my lips and tried again. "Gaw. *Gawain*, it's me. It's Cici. Say something."

I paused, crossing my fingers, but he remained frozen in place.

"Gaw," I said more loudly, coming a few inches closer. "Can you hear me? You have to wake up. Please hear me. Come on, babe, I'm begging you," I said, daring another step in his direction. The flames didn't seem to give off heat, but a strengthening prickle over my skin suggested the danger in their proximity. "It's Cici, Gaw. Wake up. I need you to come back to me, okay? Your mom and dad are waiting, and I'm here."

Another pause—and nothing. Gaw might as well have been a statue for all he seemed to notice me.

"Perhaps there is someone else who might reach him," said Kura from behind me. "Ros, could you bring your other self in here?"

"Maybe," she replied. "Or maybe Val—he was great with me when I went through this."

"If we send the girl back," said Inkil, "then she can relay the problem, and perhaps someone wiser will find a solution."

I stiffened. *Send me back?*

No. Not without Gaw.

In that moment, desperation overrode sense. I ran toward the living flames and threw my arms around Gaw's neck, and as my body screamed in pain, I whispered, "I love you, too."

The others cried out, but it was too late. I locked my mouth onto his and closed my eyes, willing him to come back to me. Though I felt like I was burning alive, I clung to him in my agony, fighting to hold on until he woke.

Just as I feared I'd be reduced to ashes, his lips stopped moving.

One whispered word in my mind—*Cici*—was the last thing I heard before oblivion took me.

CHAPTER 14

Sunlight played across my closed eyes, a minor morning irritant, and I twitched beneath my covers as the ceiling fan softly whirred overhead. The pillow was warm and flattened under my cheek, my summer pajamas had wrinkled in the night, and I drew my knees closer to my chest, willing the alarm to stay silent. Still, even with the long days of the Alaskan summer, I sensed that the sun was too high, and I forced myself to reach for my phone on the old wooden nightstand.

Nine a.m.

Wow, *someone* had let me sleep in.

I rolled onto my back and stared up at the ceiling, watching the fan blades spin. I'd bought a little can of glow-in-the-dark paint before leaving Anchorage, and I'd painted constellations above my bed in my new room: the Dippers, Orion with Canis Major on his heels, the full Zodiac. The dots faintly glowed green in the gloom of the blackout curtains, and I cut my eyes back to the sliver of daylight that broke through the gap between them like a laser.

I *really* needed to get some Velcro for the curtains, I mused, and slid out of bed.

That proved to be a mistake. My head spun as I went vertical, while my body, conservatively speaking, throbbed as though I'd been hit by a train. I couldn't remember what I'd done the night before that would have left me so achy, but as the vertigo waned, I chalked it up to Mina and staggered toward the bathroom.

While I brushed my teeth, it hit me that the house seemed far too quiet. If Mina had given us the day off from her painful calisthenics, then I'd have expected to find my housemates lounging around. The TV should be on, at least, and I should have heard voices from downstairs…unless everyone had slept in. Still brushing, I checked the other bedrooms on the second floor, but all were empty, the beds neat.

Weird.

Wincing as my sore muscles shifted, I made my way downstairs to the kitchen. A cup of tea sounded like a good way to start the late morning, and with the house to myself, I could enjoy it in peace. I filled the kettle, turned on the stove, and began fixing my mug.

Something picked at the back of my mind—tea, sugar, a hot drink on a dark night—but I dismissed it as a fragment of a dream.

While I waited for the water to boil, I glanced across the kitchen to our tropical wall calendar. To my surprise, the beach picture had changed, revealing the August page with "Bora Bora" circled midway through the month.

August? It was still July—we hadn't even celebrated Aurie's birthday…

Had we?

The kettle whistled, and I poured boiling water over my teabag, growing surer by the second that something was amiss. I'd forgotten some crucial fact, some event, and the house was so quiet. Where were they? If we had a morning off, then Edie would probably be reading, but where could she have gone? Had they flown off to Fairbanks without me? Walked to the lake? Why had no one awakened me? If they'd gone to do something fun, then surely Gaw, of all people, would have checked on me—

Gaw.

Rushing memories flooded the gap in my mind, and I gripped the counter as my knees buckled. Alaska—someone had sent me back to Alaska. Why had I been tossed out of Faerie? And if I was here, then Gaw…

"No, *no*," I pleaded, and limped to the front door. Throwing it open, I found the compound unchanged, though eerily quiet. I could hear my rapid breathing and the birds calling in the woods around us, but there was no sign of life on the streets, no neighbors out enjoying the warm morning. "Hello?" I called to the empty neighborhood. "Is anyone here?"

"It's okay, Cici," said a gentle voice behind me—a voice I'd have known anywhere.

When I whirled around, Gaw was standing in the den, dressed in the same road-grungy clothes he'd worn on our last night together. His hair was mussed, but he'd lost the nauseated look…and he wasn't on fire anymore, which I counted as a positive step. But he *was* glowing, surrounded by a golden radiance that seemed to emanate from within him.

"Gaw?" I whispered.

He nodded, then smiled. "It's me. Don't be scared, I—"

His thought ended in a breathless grunt as I ran and threw myself against him, and he held me as tightly as I did him. "It's all right," he murmured into my hair. "You're going to be okay, Cici, you're safe."

When we finally pulled apart—I didn't know about him, but personally, I needed oxygen—I smiled to keep from sobbing. "You're, uh…bright," I managed.

"Yeah. Sorry about that," he said, making a face. "I'd tamp it down if I could, but this is as good as it gets."

"What happened? How did we go home?"

"I'll explain everything," he promised, and guided me onto the couch. "Sit down, I'll get your tea."

When he returned, he was carrying both my mug and a package of Oreos, which he placed on the coffee table within arm's reach of me. He sat beside me and waited while I drank with shaky hands, then pulled a coaster closer and draped an afghan around my shoulders as I put the mug aside. "How are you feeling?" he asked.

"I don't even know," I replied, and let slip a slightly hysterical giggle. "How are you?"

"Better."

"Not dead anymore?"

"Never was." Taking my hands, he laced his luminous fingers through mine and squeezed. "What you did, Cici...I can never repay you. I hope you know that."

"You'd have done the same for me," I said, brushing it off. "Your mom told me you might still be out there, so of course I went looking—"

"I *heard* you," he said, holding my stare. "I heard so much, but it was all meaningless noise until I heard you...and then I came to my senses in time to find you dying in my arms."

I realized then that I could see fear in his eyes, and I tried to make a joke of it. "*I'm* not dead, am I?" I asked with a weak laugh.

Gaw didn't so much as smile. "No. I pulled myself together and merged with the group mind in time to find a way to keep you alive. By all rights, you should be dead right now."

That sobered me. "Faerie warned me, but you weren't coming around. I had to do *something* to reach you."

"And you did, but...shit, Cici, I almost destroyed you. I couldn't live with myself if I'd...if I hadn't focused in time..."

"I'm here, okay? I'm fine," I said, tightening my grip on our linked hands.

"Well...yes and no."

"Huh?"

Gaw glanced around the quiet den. "You're alive, but you were badly hurt. I've been keeping you unconscious to give you time to heal. You've progressed nicely, and I've been getting my head on straight, so I was able to bring you back up a little."

I frowned. "So...is this a dream?"

"A projection made from our memories. We're partly in your head, partly outside it. I thought this might be more pleasant than making you hang out in the void." Nodding toward the TV on the wall, he added, "Unfortunately, I can't give you anything but reruns, but the fridge is stocked."

"Just how long were you planning to keep me here?"

"Hopefully, no more than a week."

"A *week*?" I echoed.

"If I let you wake right now, you'd be in absolute agony," he replied, "and the last thing I want to do is hurt you. Take it easy here for a few days, rest, watch old movies, eat ice cream from the carton. Give yourself a chance to rebuild your strength." Extricating himself from my grip, he pulled the afghan more snugly around my bare shoulders, and I noticed that I was shivering. "Napping is highly encouraged."

With my basic needs met, I thought of all that Gaw had missed over the last days. "Avus has been trying to reach you," I told him. "He hasn't had any luck yet—"

"I'm aware," Gaw soothed, brushing my hair from my face. "And I'm not in a position yet to talk to him and Coileán. I'll get there, but my priority right now is keeping you alive and comfortable."

"I'm *fine*. There are bigger fires to put out."

"Not to me, there aren't. And Val can wait until I'm ready."

"But if they don't get this boost or whatever back, the realm's going to fall into anarchy."

Gaw snorted. "Those two have three thousand years' combined experience—they can hold their courts together on their own for a little longer. Bluff, if they need to. *You* are my priority," he said, cupping one hand against my cheek, "and you are absolutely not fine right now. Faerie can wait."

I began to tear up, and Gaw pulled me against his shoulder, the better to rub my back until I calmed down.

"Are you hurting?" he asked.

"No, not really. I just…I thought I'd never see you again," I said, my throat in a vise, "and now you're here…wherever this is…and you're, uh…glowing…" I sat up and dried my face with the corner of my blanket. "Are you okay? *Really* okay?"

He nodded. "I feel more…*complete*…than I ever have. Conota was partly right about me—I do feel so much better with the physical husk cast off."

"I was kind of partial to that husk," I mumbled.

"Oh, no, I didn't mean…I'm still me, Cici," he insisted. "It's me, it's Gaw, that hasn't changed. It's just that what was trapped inside is out now, and I'm…" He paused, struggling to find the words. "I'm who I was meant to be. Once I came into existence, this was the only right path."

"I thought Conota said—"

"That the husk part of me wasn't meant to exist?" he finished, then caught himself. "Oh…sorry, the group mind warned me about that."

"About what?"

He grimaced as he cut his eyes to the ceiling. "Part of this gig is that I'm aware of everything that happens or has happened in the realm. *Everything.* When people come in, their minds are open to me, and I can't block it out. If I'm not careful, I'm going to be completing quite a few sentences, and that's annoying. So, uh…sorry about that."

I sat up, the better to look him in the face. "You knew what I was going to say?"

"Yes," he replied, nodding. "And I know you're feeling a lot worse than you're trying to let on. You're overwhelmed, you're scared that I've trapped you in some sort of weird no man's land, and you're a little freaked out by the light show," he added, lifting one glowing arm and letting it flop back into his lap. "Really, I'm not trying to pry, but I *can't* be unaware, especially since I'm focused on you right now."

Unsure of what to say, I kept my silence. If Gaw was in

my head, then there was no point in denying his admittedly accurate assessment.

"I'm making you uncomfortable," he said sadly, "and that's not my intention at all, but I don't know what to do to make this any easier. I'm a lot to take in, I get that…and if it's too much, I'll understand. But please know that I love you. And I know what you went through after I, uh… went *poof*…and I'm so sorry. You're the very last person I'd want to hurt."

It didn't take a mind reader to hear his sincerity, and I closed my eyes and hugged him. That *was* Gaw in my embrace—I knew the feel of him, the scent of him, and if I ignored the red glow through my eyelids, I could pretend that nothing had changed.

"If I could turn the light show off, I swear I would," he mumbled.

"I'll get used to it."

"Cici—"

"You're alive. That's all that matters." I held on for another moment, grateful for his presence in my arms again, then sat back too quickly and hissed at a sudden flare of pain.

"Take it easy," Gaw cautioned, tucking my afghan around me. "And I didn't answer your question, did I? About Conota's thoughts as to my 'husk' status?"

Settling back against the cushions, I shook my head.

"He was partly right. Mom knew while she was pregnant that I was…you know, Faerie," he said with a touch of awkwardness. "She tried to deny it to herself, but she knew the truth, and she sensed how to release me. The minute I was born, she should have done just that, thus restoring the realm. And as Faerie's last sentience, she would have had her old job back. But for understandable reasons, she was reluctant to destroy her newborn, and with every passing month, I started to gain a sense of self. The process was somewhat similar with Conota and the original Faerie—they're each the sentience born of their realms, but they didn't spring forth fully formed. They sensed their surroundings, they developed, they made connections and grew personalities. In that respect, I'm very much like the first Faerie…well, the tempered version," he added, chuckling. "Putting aside the question of *what* Mom is now, Dad's half human, and I got a healthy dose of that. Anyway, I grew up, developed sentience of my own, and so Mom's unemployed now, but *I* exist. Does that make sense?" he asked, cocking his head. "You're frowning."

"Aren't you supposed to know the answer to that?" I teased.

"Sure, but I'm trying not to be an omniscient jackass."

"It's…a lot," I admitted, "and my brain feels foggy right now, but bear with me." Turning from him, I considered the house around us, a perfect duplicate of our bachelor pad down to the colors of the bricks in the fireplace and the crack in the plaster by the door. "Once I'm out of Fauxlaska, will we be back to a strict no-touching policy?"

He laughed. "Moon and stars, I hope not."

I cocked an eyebrow. "You don't know whether you're still on fire?"

"Oh, that's been contained. The problem is that I haven't quite figured out the trick to producing a physical form…but I'm working on it," he assured me as my eyes widened. "Triage, yeah? And don't worry, my parents were able to physically interact just fine while Mom was the realm."

A sudden, uncomfortable thought crossed my mind, and Gaw nodded miserably. "Yeah. *That*, too. Like I said, I'm aware of everything that has happened here, even, uh…"—he winced—"Mom and Dad doing some things I'd rather never think about."

"Yikes."

"I've seen yours, too—"

"Gawain, if you say one more word, I will *slug* you." He

grinned, and I rubbed my temples. "Brain bleach, please. Concentrated."

"Believe me, I wish it existed," he replied, and shuddered. "And while we're on the subject of downsides to my new state, you should know that I can't leave the realm. All of that traveling that we wanted to do, the trips you were talking about in the RV...I'm afraid I can't go with you. But don't let that stop you," he hastily added. "Go have an amazing time out there, and I'll get the highlights whenever you come back."

"So...that's it for Bora Bora?" I asked, glancing past him at the kitchen calendar.

"Yep. But if you ever wanted to explore Faerie, now, I've got a pretty good idea of the contours of the realm, and I *might* have some destinations in mind..."

I snuggled against him again, cutting his pitch short. "Right now, I really don't care about the tropics. You're alive. We can work from there."

As we sat together on the plush couch, listening to a pair of birds call to each other from atop a neighboring roof, I asked, "If I'm here with you right now, am I still in a trance at your parents' place? Because Ros is going to freak out if I don't wake up."

Gaw sighed softly. "She did."

"Did?"

"Five days ago."

"*What?*" I demanded, stiffening under his arm.

"You have no idea how injured you were," he protested. "You're only now strong enough to come to this halfway point, and—"

"Where's the rest of me?"

"Back at Val's. My mom brought in your mom, and, uh...*words* were exchanged, and so you're sleeping it off in your room. Your family's keeping an eye on you."

I thought of my parents, who were probably panicking to find me unresponsive. "Can you at least tell them I'm not dead?"

"It's obvious you're not dead," said Gaw. "You're breathing on your own."

"Fine, but do me a favor and set their minds at ease, okay? Please?"

"I would if I could, Cici."

"What's that supposed to mean?"

"I told you that I haven't figured out a body yet, right? Well, I haven't figured out a voice yet, either," he muttered. "Once you're up and about, I'm going to need to have a few chats, and I'd rather not waste time. So, uh…this is embarrassing, but would you mind being my mouthpiece for a little while? Only once you're healed, of course."

"I don't mind," I replied, "but how am I supposed to hear you?"

"I'm banking on the theory that because you've always been attuned to voices no one else can hear, you'll be able to sense me even if I can't fully manifest. And, uh…" He hesitated, then said, "There may be some unintended consequences from what you did to wake me. I'm not sure yet, but we may have a connection."

With that, he kissed my cheek, then rose from the couch. "I'm sorry to leave you here, but I need to go for a bit."

"Go where?" I tried to stand, but wooziness urged me back onto the couch.

"It's a big realm out there, and I should at least check in on my obligations. I'll be back," he assured me. "Vegetate for now—it's good for you. If you're up to taking a walk, this place goes on at least as far as the lake. It's all illusion, but if it makes you feel any better, help yourself." He blew me another kiss, then vanished.

Drained, sore, and alone in the suddenly darker room, I stretched out on the couch and reached for the remote. I turned on the television, flipped to a marathon of an old sitcom I'd seen a million times before, then fell asleep to the predictability of scripted jokes and canned laughter.

When I awoke, disoriented to find myself on the couch, I noticed how the light had shifted and shuffled into the kitchen. A few minutes after seven p.m.—I'd been asleep for hours, assuming that days and nights in this liminal place worked at all like they did back home. I wasn't actually hungry, but dinner seemed like a reasonable idea, and so I opened the fridge. The shelves practically sagged beneath the weight of the food crammed inside: a huge bowl of summer berries, a plate of steaks ready for grilling, bags of the fancy refrigerated ravioli we seldom brought back from Fairbanks. Unable to muster the willpower to cook, I settled for a takeout box from my favorite Japanese place in Anchorage—chicken and shrimp teriyaki, extra vegetables—and popped it into the microwave. It reheated better than takeout had any right to do, and armed with wooden chopsticks, I returned to the den to eat with the mind-numbing television as a soundtrack.

Was this what it was like to have a true sick day? Fae as I was, I'd never been sick, only injured—the sort of thing treated with a wrap, a few painkillers, and an admonition to walk it off. Sitting on the couch, stuffing my face, I felt as energetic as the throw pillows scattered around me, and even after my long nap, I was ready for more sleep. I forced myself to finish eating and cleaned up, then climbed the stairs and crashed as the fan spun below the glowing dots of the painted sky.

I woke to a knock on my bedroom door. Untangling myself enough from the sheets to roll over, I mumbled, "Come in?"

The door swung open, and Gaw waved from the threshold. "Hello, Sleeping Beauty. Think you can drag yourself downstairs? Something you might want to see."

Curious, I followed him to the den, then ran a hand through my hair and frowned. It was tangled, yes, but not greasy…

"Because it's not your physical body," said Gaw, answering my unasked question as he switched on the TV. "I assure you, you're going to want a shower once you fully wake."

"How gross am I?" I asked as I plopped down beside him.

A fresh mug of tea appeared on the previous day's coaster, and Gaw pressed it into my hands. "It's been six days, babe. Do the math."

"Ew." I sipped—chocolate mint, perfectly sweetened and slightly milky. Curse him, he *knew* my weaknesses. "What are we watching, anyway?"

"Owain's heading for the dragon barn," he replied, and turned up the volume. "And arriving...*now*."

The TV, which had showed the sheep pen outside of the massive barn, suddenly flashed with an opening gate. Briefly, I envied Owain's skill—he made that look easy—then reminded myself that he'd been playing with magic for centuries longer than I had. Aurie's half-fae grandfather was well past five hundred years old, even if he didn't look a day over twenty-five. He wasn't a large man, a blond just a hair shorter than I was, which made for a comical contrast when he and six-foot-seven Frank stood close together. I had no quarrel with him—like Ted, Owain had been pseudo-family to us kids, and he'd always been up for reading us stories on rainy days when we were little and bored out of our minds.

"Are we *spying*, here?" I asked.

"I can't help it. If you have something better to do—"

"No, this is fine," I hastily replied. "Live TV tops reruns. And is there some reason why Owain is out for a walk by the dragons?"

"Just watch," he said, and patted my knee. A large bowl of popcorn manifested on the coffee table, and as I snorted, Gaw grinned.

As Owain strolled around the fenced pasture toward the open doors, a pair of dragons emerged and stared at him. The red one I recognized as Horus, but the black one was a mystery.

"Rego," said Gaw. "Those are Frank's brothers."

If Owain was at all flustered to find himself the focal point of two fully grown male dragons, he remained outwardly cool. "Good morning," he said in Fae once he was within comfortable hailing range. "Is Georgie around?"

The dragons bristled. *What do you want with her?* Horus asked.

"Hang on," I said, nudging Gaw, "how are we hearing telepathy through the TV?"

"Not a real TV, is it?"

She's upset, Rego added to Owain. *Who are you?*

He showed them his empty hands and stopped a fair distance from the doors. "A friend. I'd like to talk to her about Frank, if she's willing. Would one of you fellows mind asking her?"

The dragons shared a look, and Rego lumbered into the barn. Horus remained on guard, while Owain retreated to the fence and leaned against the top rail, waiting.

After a moment, I heard Rego's ground-shaking steps returning, but he slid out of the way to make room for Georgie, who seemed to my untrained eye like the smaller version of her son. Owain waved from the fence to grab her attention, and she froze.

"Hello, there," he said, tugging down his shirt as he straightened. "Might we speak somewhere in private?"

Her head bobbed. *Yes.* As her sons started to follow, she turned and growled, and they slunk back into the shadows.

The picture on the TV followed Georgie and Owain as they set off beyond the sheep pen, heading for the woods. Neither spoke until they'd reached the edge of the trees, and then Owain looked up at her and nodded. "It's good to see you again."

I…don't know what to say.

I didn't think a dragon could blush, but based on the emotional shading of Georgie's thought, had she been human, she'd have been scarlet in the face.

I'm sorry, Georgie continued, stretching out in the grass beside Owain, which put them closer to eye level. *What I did was wrong. I was young and curious and stupid, and my judgment was clouded by hormones…but that doesn't excuse it. I see that now, and I owe you an apology—*

"Dear girl," Owain softly interjected, "don't kick yourself. I was an eager participant."

But under false pretenses. You didn't know I'd been transformed.

"You're right, I didn't have the full story," he said with a shrug, "but I don't regret it."

Her red eyes narrowed. *You don't?*

"Not at all, though I wish you'd told me the truth before now." He slid his hands into his pockets and offered her a faint smile. "I've come to talk to you about Frank. Our son."

Georgie's head shot off the ground, and her wings stiffened as if preparing for flight. *What are you saying—*

"I'm Frank's father. Ask Ros—she knows the truth. The realm sees all, yes?"

The best response Georgie could manage for a few long seconds was a blink, followed by a flabbergasted, *How…*

"Apparently, Ros's predecessor saw us together and wondered what the outcome might be with a little nudge toward viability. Or rather, a large nudge, but in any case, he's ours. Your other children aren't mine," Owain added. "They're perfectly normal. Just Frank."

Her eyes whirled as she tried to process that information. *Does he know?*

"Yes. He got depressed around Aurie's first birthday and asked Ros about his father. Got a far bit more than he bargained for, I'd say," he added, chuckling, "but once she broke the news to him, he asked her to inform me, and I met him a few minutes later. He's a good lad, you know? I see a lot of my own father in him."

Georgie's head slowly returned to the ground. *That...explains so much. Why he was late to hatch, why he's smaller...*

"Why his thinking skews human," said Owain. "I'm half. He's got a touch of my temper, but I think he favors my human side. Can barely enchant, poor boy."

He can enchant?

"Ros worked on him and Aurie just before the closure, mostly to allow them to shift at will. They're not bound any longer. Both picked up a bit of talent, but nothing extraordinary. Aurie's in training now to see what she can make of herself. Frank probably should be, but I'm not pushing him. He's carrying a lot of baggage about this place."

Is he okay? she asked hesitantly. *Safe? Healthy?*

Owain nodded. "Physically, he's fine. He and I have shared a place in Alaska all this time. Aurie finally moved out, but it was the three of us for years. He adores that girl," he continued, holding Georgie's stare, "and I'm right there with him. Frank's been a wonderful father. He's my pride and joy. Brilliant."

He was always so curious.

"His Arcanum colleagues certainly think the world of him. Anyway, he and Aurie are staying at my place here for now. I wanted to put your mind at ease."

Will you ask him to visit? Or should I come to you?

He hesitated, sucking his teeth. "I...don't think it would be wise for you to visit right now. As for him coming here, I can suggest it, but I'm not dragging him out. He doesn't know I'm here," he explained, "and he probably wouldn't appreciate it. Where you two are concerned, there's a veritable flood under the bridge, and I don't know how to repair that relationship."

Though she was already on her belly, Georgie seemed to sink lower into the tall grass. *I just wanted what was best for him. That's why I told him to take her back to Glastonbury—she'd be in danger here, and he would never be happy in the barn. I know him well enough to say that with confidence.*

"Seconded," said Owain.

And yes, perhaps I could have handled the situation with Ione's clutch more delicately, but…it was wrong, you know? The whole thing. Frank nesting for her, a deformed hatchling being allowed to live… She paused as if waiting for affirmation from Owain, but when none came, she thought, *I did what I felt was right. Did I mess up that badly?*

Watching Owain's face work, I could tell he was trying to be judicious with his response. "Remember that I said his thinking skews human. His isn't a perfectly human mind, to be sure, but it's close enough in many respects. Look at this from his perspective," he offered. "Everyone abandoned him during his last week in ovo except Ros, he bonded with her instead of you, and he was always behind the rest of his siblings. They've never understood him, nor has anyone made a genuine effort to do so. He's just weird little Runt, right?"

Georgie winced. *His siblings call him that, not me.*

"Be that as it may, he feels like he's been rejected all his life, and that leaves deep scars. Then Ione comes along. I certainly never knew her, but from the way Frank talks about her, I think it's a safe bet that he was in love."

We don't pair-bond, she protested.

"Maybe you don't, but this is Frank we're talking about. And Ione, for whatever reason, was fond enough of him to accept his weirdness." Owain spread his hands. "So there's Frank, on the cusp of having a family, having found acceptance from another dragon, and then he loses Ione out of nowhere. While he's in shock and mourning, instead of supporting him, the lot of you suggest killing his children."

We were trying to help—

"I know, and I hear you, but…you're close to Joey, yes? Ros's father?"

Sure, I bonded with him.

"Okay. Imagine how Joey would feel if he lost Helen—that's his wife, correct? Helen?"

She nodded. *He went through that during the Mulligan years. The Arcanum kidnapped her.*

"Ooh…*right*," Owain muttered. "So you know how he reacted, then."

It was awful. I barely recognized him on his worst days. And once he met Ros and she had to continue going back to keep up appearances…

"Look," he murmured when Georgie's thought faded unfinished, "I'm no expert, but from what I've gathered, Frank needed his family to accept Aurie and help him raise her. Instead, his family threatened her life and drove them out. He's had twenty-six years to dwell on this."

It's only been a year for us.

"I know, and that's not your fault." He sighed. "Frank was distraught when we thought Faerie had been destroyed. He believed that all of you were dead. But now, seeing that you're alive and well, yet no one seems eager to apologize…it's an old wound, and it's festering. I got his version of what happened the other day when Horus went to the palace in search of him. Seeing Horus that close to Aurie, and her standing there with nothing but a weak little shield to defend herself…he panicked. Aurie is his world."

Georgie considered his assessment for a time, and Owain stood by in silence, waiting while she digested it. Finally, she thought, *I wasn't a good mother.*

Considering how much sadness was wrapped around that thought, I wasn't surprised when Owain tried to console her. "You have five other children who obviously care about you, so you can't have been a *bad* mother. Perhaps you just didn't know how to be the sort of mother Frank needed. But look at it this way, now. My mother was horrible, but I had my father to guide me. Frank had you, and I'd say he's turned out well.

Frank had Ros. His hatchling bond was with her, not me. She'd do anything for him, and we all know it. Pausing, Georgie lifted her head and looked back toward the barn and its pair of flanking houses. *If Helen had been killed and I'd suggested that Joey let Ros die, too, he would have been appalled. That's the basic human reaction, isn't it?*

"Most of the time, yes."

She sank back to the ground and faced Owain again. *Does he hate me? If that's the way he thinks, does he hate me?*

"I think 'hate' is too strong a word," Owain replied. "But there's great hurt." Stepping closer to Georgie's head, he continued, "I want to see you reconciled, but I don't know how to make that happen. I can almost guarantee that Frank won't make the first move, though, so if you want him back in your life, you'll need to meet him more than halfway."

Thank you, she replied, and rose to her feet. *I'll think about it. In the meantime, whatever else happens…I'm glad he has his father.*

"He loves his mother, too. Wouldn't hurt him so badly if he didn't."

As Georgie walked away, Gaw cut the feed, and I whistled low. "Damn."

"My thoughts exactly," said Gaw, and headed for the kitchen. "Can I get you some breakfast? Eggs? Pancakes? French toast?"

"You're going to *cook*?"

"Why not? This place doesn't really exist, and I *like* cooking, so I may as well while I have the chance. Any preference?"

"French toast?"

"Done." A thick loaf of brioche appeared on the cutting board, and he pulled a knife from the block as I wandered to the table. "Sit down, take it easy. Drink your tea."

I didn't mind pulling out a chair, but the conversation I'd just observed left me uneasy. "I feel kind of guilty for snooping on them," I told Gaw, wrapping my fingers around the mug. "That was supposed to be a private chat."

"True," he replied with a shrug, "but as I said, I have no choice but to overhear. And since I still can't manifest a body, if Aurie is approached by another dragon, I'd like someone with a decent talent to be aware of what's going on. She's one of us, and I'd prefer that she not be eaten."

"I'd prefer that, too," I deadpanned.

Gaw turned from the counter and grinned. "Here's to us, then, and to not becoming lizard food. Maple syrup and whipped cream?"

CHAPTER 15

On Wednesday morning, my sixth day in Gaw's version of the compound, he found me sitting atop our boulder by the lake and manifested beside me. The weather was a little too perfect to be believable, and the dearth of mosquitoes reminded me that I was living in a fantasy world, but as I watched the ducks paddle in the breeze-ruffled shallows beneath a perfect blue sky, I wasn't complaining.

"Hey, you," I said, leaning in to kiss him when he appeared. "Something you want me to see?"

"Not right now." His hand sought mine, and I curled my fingers around his. "I came to tell you that you can wake up, if you want."

Given what he'd said about my condition, *that* surprised me. "Already?"

"You're healing well. You're not whole yet," he explained, "but it's close enough that you could tolerate the pain." He squeezed my hand, and when I searched his face, I saw a flash of guilt in his eyes. "I'd keep you here longer, but with everything afoot…"

"You need a voice," I finished.

"If you're willing."

In truth, I didn't want to go anywhere until Gaw could guarantee that my return wouldn't require narcotics. More than that, I *liked* Fauxlaska—it was beautiful and quiet, and all that was asked of me was to lounge around the house, eating imaginary ice cream and turning into a couch potato. I was in no hurry to return to reality, to Mina and Kiet's bone-breaking lessons, to the anxiety and uncertainty of two political systems struggling to rebuild themselves in record time, to the knowledge that my home would soon cease to exist in any recognizable form, to my gnawing panic that my life had spun out of my control. I didn't want to return to a life in which despite his hopes, Gaw might be invisible to me. Fauxlaska felt a bit like Neverland, and something inside me knew that once I left, I'd never find my way back—not in Gaw's imagination or in the real world.

But life had moved on while I lay in unbreakable sleep at Avus's. When Gaw was with me, he'd show me clips of what was happening outside, and when he left, channel 1 on the den TV offered a livestream that shifted with Gaw's focus. This could be slightly aggravating, as Gaw was liable to glance away as soon as I was invested in a given conversation, but still, I'd never had such access to the machinations outside my sphere—and when Gaw was with me, he generally obliged if I wanted to see something in particular.

My convalescence had been a busy time. On Saturday, after Gaw left me stuffed with French toast, I'd watched Ed sit down with Ennis in one of Avus's parlors to discuss the Arcanum's future. Ed had presented him with the plan that he, Toula, Maria, and Bert had been drawing up when last I'd eavesdropped on them: they could place the former Arc 2 inside a pocket dimension and anchor it to his property. "If we were to lose magic again," Ed explained, "the castle would reappear in the mortal realm wherever that nexus lies—"

"And remote Alaska would be safer than, like, LA," Ennis finished.

"Precisely. I know that some of the remaining magi would like nothing more than to return the castle to Glastonbury, but England has grown *considerably* since our first strongholds there, and I'd rather not take the risk of anchoring in a highly inhabited area." He leaned forward in his chair, resting his forearms on his knees. "I've got a proposition for you, Ennis. Would you be willing to sell us a portion of your land? With magic back, you can name your price."

Ennis rubbed his chin as he pondered Ed's offer. "The problem," he said after a moment, "is that either we would need to set up a shell corporation to manage the property or else test the integrity of your fake IDs, and neither sounds ideal to me. It would be simpler for me to hang on to the property and deed it as necessary to someone who actually exists on paper. What about Edie? I could just change her bequest."

"What bequest?" Ed asked, brow knitting.

"Well, uh...that is...I've watched those kids grow up, you know, and they're like family," said Ennis, whose face had begun to flush. "Obviously, I'm not going to live forever, and not to brag, but my net worth is considerably north of 'comfortable.' My investments have been *very* good to me. The company's doing well, my parents' charities are in fine shape, and...I mean, I've got to do *something* with my assets. My will names Kenna as my primary heir, of course, but I've made bequests to Aurie, Dec, Cici, Edie, and Gaw, too. Wanted to look after them when I'm no longer here," he murmured.

Ed's jaw briefly tightened, and then he reached across the gap between them to grip his companion's arm. "You're a good man, Ennis Hayward."

"I don't have any plans for the property," he continued. "I promise you, I'll keep it wild, and that'll protect your nexus point. And...I guess I'll be here by myself to watch over it."

"What do you mean?"

"The compound's emptying, right? You're all moving away, either here or to your old castle, so that's me alone in the cabin, eh?"

"Surely you need not be alone," said Ed. "Kenna will

be here, I assume, and if she belongs to either Coileán's or Val's court, you'll have an in."

"Right," he said, chuckling, "the guy who can't do jack shit with magic—"

"You saw the Fringe community, didn't you? Most of them are weak at best, and some are outright mundane. I don't think they would turn you away, especially not if there's wine involved. Or if you'd rather remain in the mortal realm, I'm sure I could find a use for your skillset. Think about it," he said as he stood. "And Ennis?"

"Yes?"

Ed nodded deeply. "Thank you for sheltering us all these years. It's not every friend who becomes family."

The two men smiled with shared understanding, and the TV switched to a view of a distant lake—my signal to take a much-needed nap.

Feeling stronger on Sunday afternoon, I watched through the gate Toula had opened near our compound—the massive, stable gate, I noted with faint envy—as every available wizard got to work. Leaving Maria to oversee Edie and Dec's training, Toula joined Ed and Bert to begin construction of the pocket dimension, the scaffolding of which began to arise in the meadow near the runway like a fever dream of glowing neon tubes. Untrained as I was in higher-order spellwork, I could only appreciate the scope of the project—that, and the fact that all three of its architects seemed to be tethered to their work by dozens of energetic tendrils.

Reinforcements were on the way. The few wizards remaining in the compound stood by to take orders and bring refreshments, while Ennis had flown off before dawn to retrieve the ones who'd been staying in Fairbanks. As evening approached in Fauxlaska and the sun began to climb in the real version, Bert paused his work to take a quick call, then opened a gate that disgorged a dozen people. A few I thought I recognized from old Away Team photos, but though some were complete strangers to me, Toula seemed to know and enthusiastically welcome them all. Then again, given how much of the casting burden she was carrying, I doubted she would have turned away help from any corner.

The oddest event of that first day of construction was a surprise gate from Conota, a hole barely a yard across. Raurit's father popped through, then shrank the gate to a pinhole behind him—considerate, I thought, in light of the generally deleterious effects of magic and dark magic when they clashed. "I heard reports of a large-scale project here," Arik explained in his oddly accented English as Toula and Ed paused to greet him. "Just curious."

Once they explained, his expression lightened. "A fine idea," he concurred, then glanced to his left, where an observer invisible to the others waited to murmur a quick message. "And Arnold says to tell you that you need at least another half-dozen stacks around the weakest joints. He's seeing strain already."

"I'm *aware*," Toula muttered, not looking anywhere near Arnold. "Got my hands full, here."

Arik waited while Arnold spoke again. "If I may?" he asked Toula, who nodded warily. A gesture toward his throat amplified his voice, and Arik called across the meadow to the wizards congregated around the snack table. "Daphne! Madison! You're needed for stack work!"

I wondered if Gaw could see Arnold loitering on the periphery of the project, studying the construction with a critical eye, or if that was just my weird talent acting up again.

Occasionally, the feed would switch from Alaska to Toula's practice room or the field outside of Coileán's palace that we'd quickly grown to hate. Training continued in full force, judging by the bruises I could see. Though my friends' performance seemed sufficiently impressive to me, Maria called Edie out after a shield broke and snapped at her to focus. "Sorry," Edie retorted, matching her tone, "but I'm just a *little* distracted today. Can't imagine why."

"You're not ready to help with the pocket dimension," said Maria, "nor will you be until you master far more than the basics."

"I was talking about *Cici*," she countered. "It's been a freaking week. When's she going to wake?"

As much as I wanted to reassure her that I was alive and well—or rather, improving—I had no choice but to watch in silence.

I abandoned my bedroom and fixed up a nest on the couch, the better to catch snippets of interesting activity on the television between Gaw's visits. My sleep became erratic, bursts of napping between long stretches of inactivity, but sloth seemed to be what the doctor ordered. By Monday morning, I was strong enough to putter around the kitchen and make a meal more complicated than toast, though the exercise left me vegetating until well into the afternoon.

I drank my tea and observed as Avus and Coileán met in Coileán's office to discuss the future of Faerie. Neither of them had slept more than a few hours in the previous days, Avus because he was still reaching out to find the realm, Coileán because he'd taken the lead in the repatriation project. Magic was spreading in the mortal realm, diffusing through the gates that Gaw continued to punch open, and more and more faeries were finding their way home by the day. After spending twenty-five years stranded in a magicless world, getting by however they could, few of the refugees had any qualms about abandoning their lives in the mortal realm. But no one among the returned had information on Irem's whereabouts, and so those members of her court who'd reappeared in Faerie were left leaderless and unsettled.

Given that one of Irem's last moves before the closure

had been to lay siege to the Fringe settlement, Coileán had sent some of his available guards to help protect them, and Avus promised to do likewise. But neither could send as many as they'd have preferred: with no boost from the realm to strengthen them and no indication that it would ever return, they needed guards for their own protection. Avus worried about attacks on the villa, though it was remote and he was relatively powerful. Coileán, who was considerably younger, spoke frankly about his concerns. "If Toula stays in Alaska for now, she's probably safe," he said. "I have half a mind to send Dec with her, just to keep him out of sight. And Aiden."

"Your brother," replied Avus, "has a room full of steel components at his disposal. I wouldn't fret."

Coileán snorted. "Oh, yes, of course, he can just toss bits of old computers at anyone who wants to kill him. Silly me."

"He's resourceful."

"So is your sister, but you still keep peeking at the construction site."

"I'm concerned that she will overexert herself," he protested. "You know Toula."

"Well enough to know that she neither needs nor wants your supervision," he retorted with a smirk.

Suddenly, the view cut away from the office to a gate deep in a forest—where, I had no idea, given how little I'd seen of Faerie to that point. To my surprise, I spotted my brother standing on the other side, waiting with his arms folded. "Gawain?" he called. "A word."

Gaw might not have been able to vocalize yet, but I heard him all the same, like a whisper in my mind. *She's safe.*

It wasn't just my talent, then—Gaw was seeing what I'd seen all my life. I wondered how awkward their meeting had been.

"*Oh?*" said Publius. "That's not what I hear."

Unconscious for her own good. She's improving, but she's not ready to wake yet.

"You could let Bee make that determination."

Cici's injuries aren't in Doc's wheelhouse. What, you think I'm keeping her down just for funsies?

"I think we're into her eighth day, Ed and Toula are worried, and personally, I'm with them."

Gaw seemed to sigh. *You know me, yes?*

"Well enough," Publius allowed.

Have you ever known me to intentionally hurt Cici?

"You did have that hair-pulling phase…"

Yeah, when I was five. I'm trying to help her. Please trust me— she's on the mend.

He seemed unconvinced, but he let it go. "Arik continues to visit. If you'd like, one of us could pass on word of your condition through him."

Please don't, Gaw replied. *I have enough on my plate right now without getting slammed with questions from the kings.*

Publius grimaced in sympathy. "And the missing queen? Do you know of her whereabouts?"

Yes. Another problem to be addressed once I pull myself together.

He sounded closer to frustrated than exhausted, which I took as a positive sign.

"Before you go," said my brother, "would you do me a favor? Tell Cici I hope she feels better soon."

She's watching us right now. You can tell her yourself.

He perked. "Truly?"

I'm trying to stay on her good side, man—I'm not going to lie to you.

Publius chuckled, then looked almost into the middle of my view—not quite, giving me an idea of how it felt on his end of the conversation whenever anyone other than a medium tried to speak to him directly. "Take care of yourself, little sister," he murmured. "I miss you."

"Miss you, too," I whispered at the TV, though he couldn't hear me.

"And I *suppose* the boy would make a suitable match for you, considering your stated interest—"

"Damn it, Publi!"

I wasn't sure whether Gaw's laughter was audible only to me or to my brother as well, but the picture quickly switched to a calming mountain vista, and I buried my face in a throw pillow. Though I'd made no secret of my feelings for my boyfriend—hell, if Gaw was in my head, he knew damn well how I felt about him—unrequested fraternal assistance in my love life landed near the bottom of my wish list.

The following afternoon—early morning, Alaska time—I watched like a kid awaiting a rocket launch as Toula stood with Ed, Bert, Maria, and the other wizards outside the finished pocket, which floated just above the wide meadow like a blimp. The pocket was at least a quarter-mile across, and Gaw, who'd visited that morning, had explained that it could be expanded once it was anchored. For now, the important task was to put the ship inside the bottle.

In her hands, Toula cradled the snow globe I'd seen on a bookshelf in her office all my life, a glass globe surrounding a gray castle mounted to a plaster base sculpted to look like a green lawn. In lieu of snow, tiny flakes of glitter fell atop the castle whenever the globe was shaken, which wasn't often. The model castle was no model at all, but rather the Arcanum 2 installation, hermetically sealed and protected. Each time I'd sneaked into the room to give it a shake, I'd wondered if I was inadvertently tossing books and furniture around, the detritus of the lives uprooted by the sudden loss of magic.

Unable to see her face from my vantage point, I could only imagine what was going through her mind as she dissolved the glass globe and tipped the water into the grass. Freeing the castle from its base, she held it in her palm, then gave it a tiny nudge, as if trying to coax a baby bird into flight. The castle rose above her hand and floated into the pocket, where it came to rest roughly in the middle of the space.

"Here goes nothing," said Toula. Her lips moved…

…and in a flash of purple, the castle exploded to full size. A few pieces of glitter caught in the spell, now rendered as large as hockey rinks, slipped from the towers and struck the ground with a series of dull thuds.

"Should have brushed it off first," she muttered, but Bert and Ed offered her congratulatory backslaps all the same.

"And whoa, where are you going?" Maria asked, catching Ted as he started toward the bubble of spellcraft.

"To see what's left of the old place," he replied. "There's bound to be some cleanup ahead of us—"

"*Priorities*, Ted," Bert interrupted. "This thing is currently visible to anyone who happens to fly past." With a nod to Toula, he said, "Looks stable to me. Whenever you're ready."

Maria and Ed likewise nodded their assent, and Toula held out her hands like she was cupping an invisible balloon between them. Quickly, she clapped her hands together, and the pocket vanished. In its place, glowing a brilliant red in the magical spectrum, was an otherwise ordinary rock.

The four of them approached, and then Ed, after a long exhalation, said, "Moment of truth."

When he touched the rock, he vanished.

I held my breath until he reappeared a minute later, none the worse for wear. "Stable," he announced. "The nexus point is identical on the inside, so that won't be difficult. So, uh…" He paused and regarded the pack of hopeful wizards, who'd been creeping closer during the trial run. "Who's ready to inspect the damage?"

As the others rushed into the pocket to begin the restoration work, Ed pulled Toula aside and said, "I'm going back to our place for a little while. Call me if there's an emergency."

She frowned. "You've left the stove on for twelve days?"

"Goodness, I hope not. No, I'm going in search of the rest of the Arcanum." Tapping his temple, he explained, "Haven't been sleepwalking in a long time. Let's see if I still have the knack."

"Okay," she said cautiously. "Don't try to talk to anyone who's driving, remember."

"Of course," he replied, and started toward the compound.

"And be nice, Ed!"

He glanced at her over his shoulder. "I wasn't planning on beginning my new reign of terror *just* yet, Toula."

The view cut away to a rapid tour of the gates Gaw had created in the last two days, through which magic flowed like water from a pipe. Gaw's attention was diverted when someone *else* created a gate near one of the many empty mansions I'd noticed on his oversight tours of Faerie. A disheveled brunette ran through, fell to her knees, and kissed the grass, then picked herself up. Her mismatched attire transformed into an opulent gown, her hair unsnarled itself and rose into a perfect coiffure, and her stubby, grimy fingernails lengthened and reddened to glossy perfection. She dropped her plastic cup with a snarl of distaste, and a few bills and coins spilled onto the ground as she swept toward home, a panhandler no longer.

"She's full-blooded," said Gaw, appearing on the couch beside me, "and she's not the only one. Her neighbor returned yesterday, and those two have a feud going back…oh, at least three hundred years."

"Can you get word to Coileán and Avus?" I asked.

"It's not critical at the moment, and the neighbors aren't in either of those courts, anyway." He sighed and absently ran a hand through his hair. "But it's going to escalate."

"You need to make yourself known. Ask Publius or my

grandmother to tell Arik the next time he visits the pocket site. Or Arnold, you know he wouldn't mind."

"I'm not quite to that point—"

"Then put me on the back burner and get there," I protested. "I'll be fine."

Gaw reached for my hand, and I squeezed his. "Soon. Patience, Cici. But here, something happier."

When the picture switched, I saw a massive tree apparently deep in a forest, surrounded by tiny lights in a rainbow of colors. "What's that?" I asked.

"That," said Gaw, "is the heart of piq territory. The ones who escaped have been finding their way back. Word's spreading. And *that*," he added as the view zoomed in on an opening in the trunk of the tree, "would be Kuni."

I watched his golden glow zip toward the tree, where a taller, purple-glowing figure in a pink gown stood waiting for him, her tiny arms and violet-patterned wings outstretched in welcome. As he landed, the two embraced, and both began to laugh as they cried.

"His aunt, Lailu," Gaw explained. "High queen of the piq. She just returned yesterday."

I didn't know more than a few words of Piq, but even if I'd been fluent, their rapid, high-pitched conversation would have been impossible to follow. Regardless, I didn't need to understand them to see the joy on their faces.

Tuesday night, I watched from Gaw's perspective while he met Conota for the first time as equals. The two couldn't occupy the same realm—neither could leave his respective domain—but they solved the problem by opening gates into the mortal realm that faced each other. The gates were set a good ten feet apart, a necessary precaution, as magic and dark magic never played nicely together.

"I admit," said Conota in Fae, "I'm surprised to see you." He flashed a fanged smile, an expression that set off all my primal alarm bells. "A rare experience, surprise."

I'm well aware.

His green head tilted slightly to the right in query. "You cannot manifest?"

Not yet. It's on my to-do list.

"What could be more pressing?"

For starters, keeping my girlfriend alive.

Conota's brow knit around his third eye, and then he shrugged. "Irojans. You would be better served if you could find a way to suppress that part of yourself."

On the contrary, Gaw replied. *It's been the realm's experience here that those with human heritage have more successful tenures. And seeing as the kings want to reestablish ties with the rest of the magical community, a little of the—what do you call it? "Irojan madness"?*

"Precisely."

"Empathy," to those of us so afflicted, and it goes a long way. You chose Arik as king for his mixed blood, did you not?

"True," Conota allowed. "Sometimes, I regret that choice."

I think it'll be beneficial to us all in the end.

"Perhaps. I'm willing to be surprised." He paused, then said, "You feel different than your predecessor. Stronger. More like the first Faerie."

I am. And now that my people are coming home, I have work to do. The opposite gate seemed to shrink as Gaw withdrew. *Wars to stop. You know how it is.*

"Why bother? They'll sort matters out on their own."

Good old Irojan madness strikes again, he thought, and sealed his gate as Conota rolled his eyes.

And so, when Gaw found me on the boulder the next morning, I wasn't entirely shocked to be given the option to cut my vacation short. That he'd suggested it when I hadn't completely healed told me how much he needed my help on the outside, and I decided I could deal with a little discomfort while we steered the realm away from absolute chaos.

"Let's get to work," I said, sliding off the boulder and onto the shore. My feet crunched against the damp gravel at the lake's edge, and I took a final look at the peaceful wilderness. Sure, it was all in our heads, but Fauxlaska was beautiful, and I'd miss it.

Dropping down beside me, Gaw led me around to the forest side of the boulder. "This is going to hurt, and I'm so sorry."

"Grabbing you hurt, too, and I survived that."

"Not easily." He squeezed my hands, then drew them to his lips and kissed the backs of my fingers. "I hate to do this to you. Trust me, you are *not* going to feel good when you wake."

"Frat party hangover not-good?"

"Enraged Mina not-good," he replied, and I winced. "Listen, as soon as you're conscious, you need to get Val to numb you. He knows how, and he can do it more effectively than most faeries can. Don't let your dad try to do it in his place—Marcus is good, but Val's got the experience to make the construction solid."

My stomach flopped. "Okay..."

"Once he finishes, you're going to want to supplement the numbing with chemical assistance. Call Dr. Bee."

"Is that not overkill? If I'm numb, then why do I need painkillers?"

"Because even as strong as he is, I don't think Val's going to be able to do enough on his own." He held my gaze and smiled grimly. "Are you ready?"

"Sure."

Gaw didn't need to be in my head to know *that* was a lie, but he had the grace not to call me out on it. "Deep breath. In...out...in again..."

I closed my eyes and expanded my lungs.

"Hang on, Cici," I heard him say. "See you on the flip side, I hope..."

Before I could release my breath, I felt like I was plummeting through space, only to slam into concrete. I tried to cry out, though the best I could do was a moan of pain. Every fiber of my body ached, and not until my fingertips grazed the sheet beneath me did I realize I was in bed.

Awake. I was awake, and oh, *shit*, the agony of movement was a torment best avoided. I might as well have been inhaling rusty knives—it wouldn't have hurt any worse.

Maybe, I mused, the pain would lessen if I opened my eyes.

Bad idea. The daylight that filtered through the gap in my gummy eyelids stung, and I screwed my eyes shut again.

This was less than ideal. The simple act of breathing left me whimpering, sunlight felt like a blast furnace on my eyeballs, and I desperately needed to pee, but getting out of bed seemed as impossible as raising the lost continent of Atlantis.

Finally, after several interminable minutes, I heard my mother softly call my name. "Baby?" she murmured. "Can you hear me?"

"Avus," I whispered, forcing my cracked lips to move. "Get Avus."

"Oh, thank God," she breathed, but I screamed as she tried to lovingly brush my disgusting hair from my face. "Oh…oh, sweetie, I'm sorry, did I hurt—"

"*Avus*," I begged while tears rolled past my ears to drip onto the pillow.

I forced myself to keep breathing through the pain while my door slammed open and Mom's voice echoed across the courtyard, yelling for my grandfather to come quickly.

My eyes were still leaking when he ran into the room with my parents on his heels. "Cecilia?" he asked. "Can you hear me?"

"Numb," I managed.

"Be still," he told me, and had it not been so excruciating, I would have laughed at the notion of voluntary movement. But soon, I felt the sharpest pain begin to dull, while the lesser aches faded to uncomfortable throbbing. Risking the assault of daylight once again, I opened my eyes and found myself cocooned in a tight mesh of enchantment—and looking past the erratic lattice, I saw Avus bending over me, coaxing the numbing construction into existence. When he noticed me gazing blearily up at him, he smiled. "Welcome back, little one. How does that feel?"

"Better," I croaked. "Thanks."

When he patted my shoulder, I yelped, and he withdrew his hand in surprise. "Are you *still* in pain?"

"Uh-huh. Could someone call Dr. Bee, please?"

"That enchantment should have left you virtually insensate to touch—"

"It's not enough. Gaw said I'd need drugs, too."

Avus's jaw dropped. "You found Gaw?"

"Yeah. He's okay—"

"Let her *rest*, Val," Mom snapped, phone already to her ear. "Bee, hey. Are you in the compound or the castle?...Oh, good. Cici's awake, and she needs strong pain meds. Do you have anything on hand?"

Pa stepped out into the garden to open a gate for the doctor, who bustled through five minutes later with her black kit and a take-no-prisoners attitude. "Move," she ordered Mom and Avus, who backed away from the bed while she took their place. After shining a penlight in my eyes and asking me a few orientation questions, she dug in her bag and produced a vial and syringe. "Morphine," she told me. "One never knows when it might be needed."

"Where the heck did you get *morphine*?" Mom asked. "How old is that stuff, anyway?"

"I made it last night. Simple replication spell on one of my old doses. The potency may be slightly off, but it should do the trick." She drew up the liquid into the syringe, then pulled back the covers and gave me the injection through my pajama pants in the thigh. "There, love, let's see how you handle a baseline dose," she said to me. "You'll probably feel drowsy in a few minutes. Nothing to worry about."

"What happened to you?" Pa asked from over Dr. Bee's shoulder. "Why are you in such pain?"

"And *where* is Gaw?" Avus demanded.

I lay motionless while the doctor tucked me in again. "I had to get Gaw's attention," I told my father. "Left me pretty sore. And he can't manifest just yet," I added, looking at my grandfather, "but he's working on it…"

Glancing past Avus, I noticed Gaw lingering against the wall, nibbling his lip as I began to relax. He didn't seem fully there, more like a spirit than a living entity, but I could clearly pick him out of the shadows.

"You were right," I mumbled.

"Who was right, sweetheart?" Mom asked.

Gaw hissed in sympathy. *I'm so sorry, Cici. Relieved that you can see me, but I'm sorry about the discomfort.*

"Discomfort?" I echoed.

Torture?

"Closer."

"Honey," asked Pa, "to whom are you talking?"

I wasn't sure you'd be able to sense me, Gaw continued, *but I had a good feeling about it.*

"I've been seeing invisible people all my life. You're nothing special," I teased, then started to laugh before a flash of pain sobered me.

Sleep. Tell Val that if you're up for it, we can talk tonight.

"Gaw says we can talk tonight, if I'm feeling strong enough," I told Avus. "He's here."

Avus huffed in impatient frustration. "If he's here, then let's talk now…"

His voice faded as the lights in the room began to flicker, then flared and went out.

"He says that 'tonight' means 'tonight,'" I relayed, then closed my eyes and slipped into true sleep.

CHAPTER 16

I found Gaw sitting at the foot of my bed when I woke hours later to waning afternoon light. "Hey," I grunted, and gave my fingers a test wiggle. Yes—the pain remained, but weaker now, even after the morphine had worn off.

You're improving, Gaw told me, speaking to my mind as he smiled. *Val added some healing work to that enchantment after you crashed. I'd say you'll feel much better by morning.*

"Great." Gingerly, I sat up and slid my legs off the bed, then tried to stand.

Careful, he cautioned as I wobbled on my unsteady feet. *You've been horizontal for a week and a half.*

"How has my bladder not exploded by now?" I muttered.

Magic, but I wouldn't push my luck much longer, were I you.

Suddenly chilly in my tank top and thin pants, I spotted a bathrobe draped over a chair across the room and decided to see what I'd retained of Mina's lessons. All I needed to do was focus on the object and will it into my hands—surely I could manage that much.

But when I motioned the bathrobe toward me, the chair burst into flame. I yelped and staggered back, and the nightstand rocked as it broke my fall.

Gaw barely looked at the chair before the flames vanished, and in seconds, the fabric was whole unblackened once more. *Here*, he said as the robe floated across the room to me. *You might not want to play with magic just yet, eh?*

"What the hell was *that?*" I demanded, clutching my

chest as my heart began to slow.

Your talent's not what it was the last time you tested it. Nothing's wrong, he assured me before my lips could form the question. *You're just monstrously powerful and minimally trained, so for your own safety and the integrity of this building, maybe you could do things the old-fashioned way for now.*

I stared at him incredulously as I reached for the thick robe.

Pretty please?

"Where did that come from?"

Do you remember when I said there might be unintended consequences to getting up close and personal with Faerie's raw essence?

"Yeah. It hurts like hell."

More lasting consequences, he amended. *You're stronger than you were. It's not a bad thing, just a tiny bit worrying until you get some lessons in power management.*

I slipped on the robe, flinching as my stiff arms twisted, then padded toward the bathroom. "Let's not tell Mom and Dad about this right now, okay?"

No worries there. You're the only living person in this realm who can hear me.

When I started to close the door, he waved from the bedroom. *Take your time, enjoy. I'll be waiting.*

"You meant it when you said you're aware of everything that goes on here?" I asked.

Gaw nodded. *For good and ill.*

"So then, when I get in the shower…"

I'll be a gentleman and focus on something else. Unless you want company…

"Nice try," I said, and shut the door in his face.

Half an hour later, I emerged in a cloud of shampoo-scented steam with my wet hair twisted up in a towel. "I've really got to get a hairdryer if I'm going to be staying here," I grumped, scanning the room for my stuff. "Uh…where's my bag?"

Your mom took the liberty of cleaning your clothes and putting them in the closet.

"Nice of her." I looked through the few items on offer and chose jeans and a barely wrinkled lilac T-shirt. "What's the plan? You want to talk with Avus and Coileán, right?"

Bingo.

"In an official capacity?"

That would be the idea, yes. And there's not a hairdryer because most people around here manage it with magic.

"If I tried that, I'd probably set my head on fire. Wet ponytail it is," I said, tossing my ensemble across the rumpled bed before returning to the closet to hunt for my underthings. "Not what I'd choose for anything official, but unless you want to take a crack at it—"

Call Bonnie. She'll fix it for you.

"Bonnie's got better things to do than play beautician."

You need to speak with her anyway—she's Val's chief of staff.

I poked my towel-turbaned head out of the closet. "So?"

Bonnie knows how to make arrangements, he replied, leaning against a bedpost with his arms folded. *Tell her I want to talk to the kings at sunset. She'll take care of summoning Coileán, so you won't have to try to make a gate to the palace and inadvertently create a black hole. Plus, I need you to do me a favor once you're decent.*

"Yeah? What's that?"

He grinned. *Get Bonnie first. Daylight's burning.*

As the sun sank and the lanterns lit themselves, I led the way through the villa to Avus's office. Thanks to Bonnie, who'd taken one look at my wet hair and casual ensemble and facepalmed, I looked more the part of the official interpreter in tailored black pants, a flowy beige silk top, and a French braid. True, walking still left me winded and wincing after my brush with Faerie's core, but at least I was closer to presentable, which was more than my companion could say.

Neither of us knew why Gaw had asked me to snag

Kenna on her way in from a day of practice. As pleased as she'd seemed to see me awake and mobile, Kenna hadn't even hugged me because of her sweat-soaked clothing. She'd done what she could in a hurry, but Mina and Kiet had focused their lessons more on issues of combat and self-defense than on aesthetics, and the best Kenna could manage was a damp T-shirt that *didn't* stink.

Though I kept it to myself, I had a theory as to why Gaw wanted her included in his meeting with the kings. Kenna had to belong to *someone's* court, and if he announced her affiliation with both of them present, there'd be no argument. If Kenna wanted, she could probably switch allegiance then and there without stirring up hard feelings. Still, considering the layer of salt drying on Kenna's bare arms and legs, Gaw could have worked on his timing.

Pausing outside Avus's office, I knocked twice. The door swung open on its own, and I found Avus and Coileán waiting, sitting at opposite ends of Avus's green couch. Both seemed oddly tense, and I saw the question in their eyes as they rose to greet me. "Gaw asked for Kenna to be here," I explained. "That's all he would tell me."

"Come in, then, both of you," said Avus. "Sit down. How are you feeling, Cici?"

I glanced at the faint lattice of his handiwork, which was barely visible above my skin. "Better, thanks."

"Have you eaten?"

My empty stomach chose that moment to growl, and Coileán chuckled as he gestured into existence atop the coffee table a crudité and bowls of olives and nuts. Two glasses of water appeared in easy reach of Kenna's and my chairs facing the couch, and he shrugged as we sat. "I'd offer you something stronger, kid, but not with morphine in your system. Bee would kill me."

"I'm probably dehydrated, anyway," I replied, and drained my glass. It refilled as I returned it to the table, and he winked when I caught his eye. "Okay, that's a useful trick."

"Why can't we study *that* instead of getting tossed around?" Kenna complained. "There's bound to be more to magic than breaking bones."

"Plenty," Coileán agreed. "But focus on priorities…and speaking of which," he continued, glancing at me, "is the guest of honor joining us?"

I looked past him at Avus's unlit fireplace, where Gaw leaned against the elaborate mosaic, nodding. "He's ready."

"And *Gaw* is the realm?" Avus asked.

"That's right. He knows you've been trying to reach him, but he's had his hands full with me of late," I added. "Which is why he hasn't yet gotten the hang of manifesting. So, uh, here's how this is going to work. Since I can see and hear him, I'm going to be acting as his mouthpiece for a little while. I'll tell you whatever he says, and if you could bear with me, that would be great."

They nodded, and I turned to Gaw. "Whenever you're ready."

Since Cici is still on the mend, he began, *I want to keep this brief, and I don't want to repeat myself.*

"I think I speak for both of us when I say that we have questions," Avus replied once I fell silent.

Understandable, but there will be plenty of time for that later. Right now, I want to make my first official communication—he paused, waiting for me to finish—*and I thought it only proper that it should be to all of the Three at once.*

Coileán and Avus jerked like they'd been goosed, then stared at Kenna with her wet clothes and salt-stiffened hair. "I'm sorry, *what?*" Coileán asked.

"You're joking," said Avus.

I looked to Gaw for an explanation as Kenna, who'd been nibbling a baby carrot, swallowed the wrong way in her shock and began to cough. "Hold on," I muttered, and rose to pound Kenna's back until her airway cleared. After a moment, she was still red-faced and watery-eyed, but at least her choking had served to distract the others from Gaw's revelation. "Okay," I told him, "everyone's breathing now. Want to continue?"

He waited until I'd taken a sip of water, then thought, *To answer the question that's been on your minds since Faerie reopened, I intend to honor the arrangement that Kura made with the original Three and my mother maintained. Before you leave this room tonight, you'll have your boost.*

Relief washed over Avus's and Coileán's faces, though Kenna's expression veered toward queasy.

Yeah, Kenna, it's going to hurt. A lot. I'm not going to try to sugarcoat that. It'll hurt less than what Cici's been dealing with, and it'll be over in a matter of seconds, but there's no way for me to make it a pleasant experience.

Unsure of where to look, she focused on me instead of Gaw. "Why would you think that I'm—"

I don't think, I know, he interrupted, and I hurriedly interjected to cut her question short. *Don't argue with me on this. You're the heir. I'm absolutely sure of it.*

"But *how?*" she demanded, flabbergasted.

Only I could see Gaw's satisfied smile. *Oberon's heir was Eleanor, who never had kids. When Irem killed her, Irem was the next eldest of Oberon's children, so she inherited. I rummaged through the memories of Irem's returning associates to see what became of her. One of her guards killed her a few weeks after they fled to the mortal realm, once everyone was convinced that Faerie was gone forever. Irem proved to be insufferable.*

"Which guard?" Avus asked.

Killed himself shortly thereafter, so no need to worry. Anyway, when Irem died, her eldest living child was a son, Sangun. He held on for a few years longer than his mother did, but he died in a fight with one of his cousins more than twenty years ago. Sangun had several children over the course of his life, none of whom survived him…except the youngest. That would be you, Kenna.

She stared at me, the color draining from her face. "I…but I…I don't know…"

I'm sorry to give you the news of his death like this, Gaw continued, *but trust me, you're not missing anything. Sangun was an absentee sperm donor on his best day. I'm sure he never knew that he'd gotten your mother pregnant, nor would he have cared. And that's a shitty thing to tell someone, I know,* he thought as her eyes welled. *You've always felt weird about your family situation, and I get that. But having seen what I've seen, trust me when I tell you that you dodged <u>such</u> a bullet. Ennis would walk through fire for you. He's a better dad than Sangun could ever have been, had Sangun shown the slightest interest in any of his offspring.*

Kenna's lip trembled, but she nodded.

By the terms of the old agreement, it doesn't matter that he never knew you, Gaw told her. *It doesn't matter that he never knew he was the king in exile. You've been a queen since you were two years old. It's time for you to step into that role.*

"But…but I don't know anything about being a freaking *queen!*" she protested.

You're young, sure, but you'll figure it out. We're in similar boats, you know? Besides, Coileán and Val didn't entirely know what they were doing when they got the gig…and they'll help guide you along. <u>Right</u>, gentlemen?

I must have put just enough edge into my voice, as both were wise enough to murmur agreement.

A suggestion to you two: hold off on the fireworks for a few days. Give Kenna a chance to adjust and properly call her court.

"That could be arranged," said Avus.

Great. And I'm going to ask you to work with her, Val. You have the training experience.

"I can do that," he replied as Kenna once again looked slightly sick. "Whatever you need."

Thank you, thought Gaw. *And Kenna…* He sighed in my head. *You're terrified. It's okay—this is a ton to thrust onto anyone's shoulders. My life plans have shifted lately as well.*

She cracked a tiny grin at that.

But right now, exiled faeries from all three courts are finding their way back across the border. In the months before the closure, things around here went to hell in part because Irem let her court run wild. They need to be reined in, and you can do it. I'll give you what you need to keep order, and you know those two aren't going to hang you out to dry.

Kenna glanced toward the couch, and Coileán lifted a crystal tumbler half-full of amber liquid—scotch, I assumed—in brief salute.

They've watched us grow up, Gaw told her. *Now that there's no pressing need to, say, destroy me, you're all on the same team. Welcome to Team Keep the Peace. You get a tiara instead of a T-shirt.*

Avus and Coileán nodded vehemently when her worried eyes flicked toward them again.

Coileán, I want you to get Nico on board. He'd be willing to serve as Kenna's captain, and she'll need someone experienced. You both know he can play nicely with Kiet and Mina.

"He *did* swear fealty to me…" Coileán began.

And you're not going to raise a stink when he defects, right?

"I'm old, kid, not stupid."

I could hear him laughing in my head. *Glad we can reach an agreement. Kenna, I can't make you choose a captain for your guards—*

"I have guards?" she interrupted.

You will, and you'll need them. Nico served Oberon and Eleanor, and he knows his stuff. If you listen to him, and if you can be slightly smarter about your personal security than Eleanor was, then you should have no problem.

"Hold up," I told Gaw, and paused to drink. The siren song of the snacks made my stomach rumble all the louder, but I had a job to do first. "Okay," I said, putting the empty glass down. "Hit me."

I'm going to get the boost going again now for you two, Gaw told Avus and Coileán. *And Aiden—why not? His is small, anyway. Okay, brace yourselves.*

Each clutched an arm of the couch, but aside from a grunt from Avus and a brief hiss from Coileán, the only effect I could see was that both gained a soft white corona. As they relaxed their grip on the furniture and studied each other, Avus murmured, "That's not nearly as bad the second time."

"Third for me, remember."

"That's it?" asked Kenna, screwing up her face. "Shoot, that looks easy."

The kings traded glances as their glow faded out. "*Easy*, she says," Coileán muttered. "Such unwarranted confidence."

"Youth," Avus concurred.

"Gaw says to tell you that the first time is miserable," I reported to Kenna. "And because you're so young, he's going to have to make yours huge to put you on par with them. Go stretch out on the couch—this should be easier if you're horizontal."

The others stood, and Kenna warily lay flat. "Now what?" she asked.

Tell her to brace herself, but for real, Gaw told me. *And as for you, Cici, once I start this, you cannot touch her. I'm serious.*

Kenna clenched her fists and screwed her eyes shut once I relayed the message. "I'm ready."

Like hell you are, Gaw muttered, but before I could decide whether to share that word of encouragement, the boost hit her.

Kenna's back arched like she'd grabbed a high-voltage line, and her head flew backward as she howled in pain. Instinct made me reach for her, but Gaw snapped me away. *NO!* he yelled. *Don't do it!*

"But—"

It's almost over.

He wasn't lying. Within twenty seconds of the first jolt hitting her, Kenna's screaming ceased, and she lay panting and shivering on the couch, a quaking form with damp clothes and a newfound radiance. It was another full minute before she began to open her eyes. Avus offered her a hand to help her sit up, and she groaned as she switched positions. "I take it back," she said, then noticed her glowing fingers and fell silent. Slowly, she rotated her arm, examining the strange light. "Uh…hey, guys?"

"That's normal," Coileán reassured her. "Concentrate. It'll fade."

After a few deep breaths, the light dimmed, then extinguished itself, and Kenna rubbed her head. "How do you feel?" he asked.

"Like I just hugged a lightning bolt."

"Sounds about right. The worst is over."

"God, I hope so."

But Avus made a face. "Don't get too comfortable. You and I are going outside to work."

Kenna raised her head and moaned, "*Why*? Can't we wait until tomorrow?"

Having lived with us kids as long as he had, Avus had grown immune to whining. "No. If you lost your temper right now, you might accidentally blow someone up. Is that what you want?"

"Of course not!"

"Then get up. We're wasting time. Gaw, are we finished here?"

"He says yes," I replied.

"Good. Nice to have you back, boy. Rest well, Cici. Coileán, you know your way home," he added, and shepherded Kenna through a fresh gate into the dark meadow.

As the gate closed behind them, I sank onto the couch and tossed a cherry tomato into my mouth. My stomach bellowed for more, and so I grabbed the bowl of nuts and started cramming handfuls down, manners be damned. Coileán sat beside me in Avus's vacated seat, beckoned his scotch to his hand, and finished it as I fed the starving beast within. When I came up for air, he floated my water glass toward me, and it refilled before it reached my hand. "Those nuts are dead. They're not going anywhere," he teased while I washed the salt out of my mouth. "Do you want something more substantial? I'm no gourmet, but I can put together a mean ham sandwich."

"I'm okay, thanks," I replied, reaching for the baby

broccoli florets.

"*Are* you?"

I glanced up and found him watching me intently. "You've been comatose for days," he continued, "Val said you were a wreck this morning, and somehow, you're the only person in the realm who can talk to Gaw—who is, in fact, alive. I'll take the good news, of course, but what the hell happened to you?"

Too hungry to share, I picked up the bowl of ranch from the middle of the veggie tray and held it close for dipping as I scarfed down my impromptu dinner. "I heard Ros—not the real Ros, but the part of her that's the realm," I explained between bites—"calling me, and—"

"Yeah, I got that much of the rundown from our Ros. What happened while you were unconscious?"

He waited until I'd swallowed a trio of carrots. "Got way too close to the source of Gaw's power. Super-concentrated raw magic, I guess. Old Ros and her posse warned me not to touch him, but it was the only way I could see to wake him up, and...well," I said, reaching for the cucumber slices, "let's just say that no one told me true love's kiss is *quite* so excruciating."

"Moon and stars," he muttered.

"Yeah. It left me pretty battered. I'm feeling better now—"

"Because you're swaddled in a healing construction."

"I'm improving," I insisted. "But, uh..." I hesitated, then looked to Gaw, who'd taken one of the open chairs.

Tell him, he urged.

"I think I'm stronger than I was," I said to Coileán. "More powerful, I mean. Gaw thought there might be side effects, and I set a chair on fire when I woke up this afternoon—it's okay," I hastily added, seeing his expression shift, "Gaw fixed it."

"I'm not concerned about a damn *chair*," Coileán replied. "How much stronger do you feel?"

I laughed in disbelief. "You're asking *me*? I've barely

begun to work with magic, so I'm probably not a good judge."

"That's fair. Want to find out?"

"What, now?" I asked, grabbing another handful of tomatoes.

"Val's busy, I have time, and as long as your parents don't catch me putting you through your paces when you really ought to be in bed, we should be fine." He stood and motioned open a gate. "And Val's got ample space out there. Shall we?"

Giving the food a last longing look, I followed Coileán into the night.

We trekked through the mountain meadow until the lights of the villa had faded to bright pinpricks in the darkness. Calling a halt, Coileán held out his hand, and a blue fireball blazed to life in his palm, casting an eerie glow on his face. "Let's start with something basic," he said, stepping back a few paces. "Show me yours."

I thought of the violet flame I'd conjured days—no, I realized, almost two weeks ago—remembering how easy it had been to call forth the fire even before Mina and Kiet had begun battering me in their practical seminars. *Piece of cake*, I reassured myself, then mimicked Coileán's stance and sent forth my will.

My vision was suddenly obscured by the sphere of purple fire that bloomed around my body. Though the flames didn't hurt, I cried out, shocked, and Coileán jumped back in alarm. Remembering the lessons my tutors had beaten into me about focus, I concentrated until the fire vanished, then caught my breath and looked at Coileán, whose fireball seemed so well-behaved by comparison. "You see?" I said. "It didn't do that before."

"It's okay, little one. No harm done," he soothed, though he kept his distance. "Try again, but not with so much power behind it. You want to gently tap the gas, not floor it."

Steeling my nerve, I tried again…and though the air

around me still went up in flames, they were slightly smaller that time.

Over the next hour, Coileán coached me until I could produce a fireball without turning into a torch. "Good. *Very* good," he said as I extinguished my latest effort, then produced a half-dozen glowing white baseball-sized orbs and tossed them into the air to free his hands. "Let's try shielding."

"Can you please not break my bones tonight?" I begged. "It's been a long few days."

"I'm not going to break anything."

"Yeah, until my shield fails. That's Mina's go-to line, too."

He chuckled, shaking his head. "I mean it. We're going to do this gently, Cici."

"In that case, petition to change teachers?"

"Mina is a fine instructor," he replied, "and I'm sure Kiet is equally talented. But when one is playing with an unknown talent, it behooves one to not risk anger-fueled flares. Right, let's see your shield."

That, at least, gave me no trouble. It burst forth at a thought, chaotic in its internal construction but ten feet in diameter. Coileán approached to inspect it, then declared. "That's a beginner's effort. Messy, but impressive in size." He surprised me with a quick bolt to the shield, which bounced off and fizzled out in the grass. "Solid. Nicely done. You can drop it," he added, then rubbed his chin in thought. "Let's see…"

A new orb appeared in midair between us, this one the size of a basketball, then floated up above my head. "I want you to get that for me," said Coileán. "Any way you like, just don't destroy it."

Thinking of my flambéed bathrobe, I hesitated to try to call the orb to me for fear of disintegrating it. Instead, I stood there awkwardly and considered the problem, looking for a solution that wouldn't end in fireworks. Coileán had created the enchantment holding the orbs aloft—should I attack that? But what if I attacked him by accident? What if I set *him* on fire?

Frustrated, I jumped, just to prove to myself that the orb was out of my reach. But instead of landing, I continued to rise, and I gasped when I looked down and saw the ground receding. Maybe this wasn't the solution Coileán had in mind, but it was working, and I steered myself toward the orb. Soon, my fingers grazed its cool surface, and I hugged it to my chest as I hovered some twenty feet off the ground.

"How does that feel?" Coileán asked.

I took stock of myself—tired, still hungry, sore, but not exhausted by the effort. "It's not bad," I called down. "Kind of nice up here. There'd probably be a good view if it weren't dark."

"You know, levitating an object isn't a difficult skill to master. *Self*-levitation is another matter entirely."

"Oh?"

"It's almost impossible without concentrated effort. You seem fairly relaxed," he remarked. "Can you land?"

Focusing on the ground, I slowly lowered myself until my shoes touched the grass. As I returned to the comfortable sensation of dirt beneath my feet and tossed the orb to Coileán, the truth suddenly hit me.

I could *fly*.

As I tried to process that, I looked toward Coileán and spotted Gaw standing beside him, softly luminous against the night. He watched as I struggled for words, then thought, *Told you.*

What does this mean? I managed to reply in kind.

Do me a favor and don't tell Val and Coileán yet—they've got their hands full straightening Kenna out and putting the courts back together, he replied—*but you're now the single most powerful person in the realm besides me.* He spread his hands and offered me an uncertain smile. *Surprise?*

You...boosted me, too?

No. This is all an unintentional result of our contact. I haven't given you anything extra, which means that I can't take this power away from you. It's yours, and it'll only grow stronger with time. And you might find that your temper runs hotter than it used to. Nodding at Coileán, he added, *Honestly, you're the bigger danger right now than Kenna, and judging by the slightly frantic thoughts running through his head, he knows it.*

So what do I do? I demanded.

You keep working with Coileán until one of you gets tired tonight, and then you get up tomorrow and do it again. I'm afraid I can't help you control it. You'll figure it out, he hastened to assure me, *but I can't just snap my fingers and fix this for you. Sorry, babe.*

As he began to fade even from my view, I asked, *Where are you going? Aren't you going to make sure I don't kill Dec's dad?*

Gaw snorted. *He's a big boy, and I've got my own work to do…and a certain brother of yours who demands regular reports as to your well-being. Can't imagine why.* With that, he blew me a kiss and vanished.

I found Coileán waiting for me to snap out of my apparent stunned silence. "Sorry," I muttered, "got caught up with Gaw. So, uh…where were we?"

CHAPTER 17

Though telling time in Faerie is more of a guessing game than a science, it had to be close to midnight before Avus and Coileán released Kenna and me for the evening. Maybe they were old enough to go without sleep, but Kenna and I certainly weren't, and we dragged ourselves through the corridors of the villa as we slunk toward bed. Seeing as my room was closer, Kenna followed me in, kicked off her shoes, and flung herself facedown into the pillows.

"You want to shower first?" I asked, stepping into the closet to find my pajamas.

"Nope."

"Whatever." Wincing as I wriggled out of one set of clothing and into another, I soon rejoined Kenna and climbed into bed beside her. "Scooch over," I mumbled, and she rolled away from me. "Want to get the lights?"

"Can you do it?"

"Fifty-fifty chance that I'd set the room on fire if I tried from here."

She groaned but sat up and waved at the lights until they shut off. "What were you two doing, anyway? Playing catch-up for all those days you left me alone with Kiet and Mina?"

"Take your glasses off," I reminded her.

I heard the soft clatter of the frames as she dropped them onto the nightstand. "Okay, I'm blind again," she said. "So why was Coileán working you tonight?"

"Because I got a little too close to Gaw, and now I've

got more power than I know what to do with."

"Join the club, I guess." Kenna sighed and pulled the blankets over her, then whispered a rather pointed, "*Fuck*."

"Yup."

"I'm a goddamn faerie princess."

"Faerie *queen*," I corrected.

"Not helpful," she began, but was interrupted by rapid knocking.

My bedroom door cracked open, revealing Edie on the threshold with a flashlight. "Hi!" she whispered as I started to sit up. "I heard you were awake and, like, Gaw's freaking *alive*. How're you feeling? How's he?"

"He's okay, and I'm drained," I said, motioning her into the room. "Long night."

"Tell me about it. I finally got a chance to work with Bert Wold, and it's close to lunchtime over there, and he realized how late it was on this end, so…wait, is that you, Kenna?"

Kenna groaned and raised an arm.

"Ooh, slumber party," said Edie, slipping off her shoes. A moment later, she crawled into bed between us, and Kenna and I made room as she snuggled in.

I thought of all the times the three of us had done this as children, most often during the long winter nights. We'd tell stories and giggle for hours until a parent or two ordered us to sleep, at which point we'd simply turn our volume down. Upon reaching adolescence, we'd begun to prefer our privacy, and the slumber parties had petered out. Still, I felt comfort in the familiar warmth of my friends' bodies next to mine, even if everyone smelled like sweat that night.

"You've been at the castle?" I asked. "How's the pocket holding up?"

"Pretty well, and how'd you know about the castle?"

"Gaw showed me while I was recuperating. So how are things going over there?"

"Well, Mom and Dad let me come over for the first

time today," Edie explained as she curled onto her side. "Everyone's been busy putting the castle back together, but Bert had time to tutor me for a few hours. And he took me to the library—you won't *believe* how many books they have!" She sounded like she'd been handed the keys to a new Ferrari.

"Nerd," Kenna mumbled.

"Dork," Edie fondly retorted. "Anyway, Mom said she'd show me around. Dad's been busy sleepwalking on and off since yesterday. He's already made contact with a bunch of wizards—the ones who sided with Toula before she got kicked out of office, I think. They're supposed to be joining us soon. And he found a group of Fringers in California," she added. "They're *thrilled* to be going home."

"Is Dad going to be running flights, or what?" Kenna asked.

"Actually, with the number of gates that have spontaneously opened—"

"Gaw's doing," I interrupted.

"Huh. Nice of him. There's enough of an outflow of magic that Bert thinks the other wizards will be able to make intra-realm gates within a few days. Oh! And we're going to have an ambassador of sorts from Conota," she added, speeding up with her excitement. "Dad and Toula talked to Raurit's parents, and they said he could stick around the castle and observe."

I frowned in the darkness. "Like…glamoured?"

"I don't know. But Mom says he's human enough to get along with people, and his parents want to build a working relationship between Conota and the Arcanum, so that's the plan for now. And since we're getting someone from *that* realm," she added, her tone shifting toward persuasion, "it would only be fair if we had a similar ambassador from *this* realm, too."

My mom did that once for Coileán, said Gaw, speaking to my thoughts. *And then Eleanor sent my dad. There's precedent.*

Have you invited yourself to the girls' slumber party? I asked.

He didn't answer me, but I could sense his amusement and slight embarrassment.

"Toula suggested Dec, at least for Coileán's interests," Edie continued, unaware of my silent conversation. "He could use the casting training, and he and Raurit got along well on the RV, so this could be fun. Toula just has to convince Coileán, but it's not like Dad's going to let anything happen to Dec."

"And you'll be there?" Kenna asked.

"That's the idea. Toula and Dad said they want me to start learning how to be grand magus," she said, and laughed to herself. "Honestly, I don't know if I want that job, but I'm willing to learn about it, especially while I'm still figuring out how to use a wand." Poking me in the shoulder, she said, "You could go for Val, Cici. That would be three of us and Raurit—"

"I'm not leaving Gaw," I insisted.

He sighed in my head. *Just because I'm stuck in Faerie doesn't mean you need to be. It sounds like fun.*

And who are you going to talk to if I leave?

I'm close to figuring myself out, he replied, *and then I'll have a direct line to the Three. They won't be able to shut me up.*

"How's Gaw doing?" Edie asked. "Everything I heard today was pretty vague."

"He's getting acclimated," I replied, declining to mention that he was listening in. "Overwhelmed. But now that he's not having to worry so much about me—"

Ha.

"—he's got time to focus on himself."

"He's really the realm now?"

"Yeah."

"Weird," she said.

Tell me about it.

"But I think he's okay," I said to her. "Or he will be. It's a big change, and he's got, like, *politics* and crap to think about now, but he's still Gaw," I added, and smiled to myself. "That much I'm sure of."

"Speaking of politics," said Edie, "does he know anything about where Irem might be hiding? I think Toula and Dad are getting anxious."

At that, Kenna let slip a brief bust of laughter that sounded only slightly this side of hysterical.

"What's so funny?" Edie asked, rolling toward her.

"Irem's dead," said Kenna.

"*What?*"

"And this doesn't leave the room," I interjected.

"Okay, sure. Fine. What happened to her? Who's in charge of that court?"

"Gaw said one of her own guards killed her," I explained. "And that left one of her sons in charge, but he probably never knew it, and...um..."

"It's me," Kenna groaned.

The mattress creaked as Edie sat up in bed. "Wait. *You...*"

I squinted at the sudden reappearance of Kenna's corona. Sighing, she sat up as well and considered her glowing arms. "It's official," she muttered. "But it's not public knowledge yet, so if you could keep this quiet for now—"

Edie cut her off with a fierce hug, and the light faded. "My lips are sealed," she promised. "Are *you* okay?"

"I don't even know. I never got dinner tonight, and I'm gross, and I'm trying *really* hard not to freak out, and... shit."

"Want me to run to the kitchen?" Edie offered. "Or back to the castle? There's food around."

"Honestly, I think I might throw up if I tried to eat, but thanks." She flopped back into bed, and Edie followed suit.

"Not like you don't have enough on your mind, but you could pick an ambassador, too."

"I love you, Edie, but that's way on the back burner right now."

"Oh, I get it," Edie replied, readjusting the blankets. "I

didn't want you to think Dad was being unfair. He mentioned getting someone in there from Irem's court, whenever she showed up again, so I'm sure the offer extends to you."

Silence fell in my room, and I stared up at the ceiling, its intricate mosaic lost in the shadows.

"Hey, guys?" Edie murmured. "Think it's too late for us to run away to Bora Bora after all? We could sneak out tonight, grab Dec…Aurie could come…hell, Raurit's friendly enough."

"What about his cousin?" Kenna asked. "Or whatever she is—Lilian, right?"

"Ooh, yeah," said Edie. "She was pretty. Purple, but pretty. And they're not actually cousins—their dads were raised as brothers, but they're not related."

Kenna snorted. "Is that the excuse he's going with?"

"I have no idea—I haven't seen him since we left Kentucky. All I'm saying is that it wouldn't be completely scandalous if they starting dating. And yes," she added, "Lilian can come when we run off to Bora Bora."

Dibs on the window seat.

Kenna and Edie gasped, and I realized I wasn't the only one who'd heard Gaw. Chuckling, I sat up as he appeared in the corner of the room. Given his translucence, I assumed he remained invisible to the others, but he looked mightily satisfied with himself.

"Not bad," I said. "Of course, you realize that if you stick around the slumber party long enough, there's a non-zero chance that you'll leave with a pedicure."

Seeing as I haven't fully explored corporeality, I'd like to see you try, he retorted. *And if you do run off to the South Pacific, I want at least one rum-based drink as a consolation prize. Preferably served in a coconut. A big coconut.*

"Gaw, hey!" Edie called, kneeling on the bed for a better look. "Where are you?"

That's a surprisingly difficult question, but since you're all exhausted, let's just say…hmm. He plopped into the chair I'd set on fire that afternoon. *Chair by the bathroom.*

"Okay, thanks." She crawled to the foot of the bed, then faced his perch and yelled, "Why the *fuck* didn't you say goodbye, Gawain?"

I saw him flinch with the force of her question. *I'm sorry, okay? I didn't want to make things worse than they were—*

"We thought you killed yourself!"

Exactly. I thought I was about to be obliterated, but it needed to happen, and I knew that if I dragged the rest of you into my mess, I'd just keep stalling. But I'm fine, he insisted. *I'm sorry for putting everyone through that, and I'll assemble a body eventually, and then, if you need to slap me across the face for being an asshole, I'll give you a free shot.*

Edie huffed, but her voice softened. "I don't want to *hit* you. Just promise me that if you ever plan to off yourself again, you'll give us fair warning."

Deal, but I'm not going anywhere. By the way, Kenna, you know that weird feeling in the back of your head?

"Yeah…"

It's not your imagination, and it's not going anywhere, either. That comes with the boost, and it'll grow stronger once I get a handle on everything.

"What *is* it?" she asked.

We're linked now. Val and Coileán have it, too. I've got a direct pipeline to the three of you, and vice versa.

"What about privacy?" Kenna demanded. "I mean, can I shut it off when I want some alone time?"

Nope. Sorry. But on the other hand, it's a two-way street, and I can't cut myself off from you, so…consolation prize?

"No! That's just awkward!"

Before they could squabble, I rolled out of bed and felt on the nightstand for my phone. "As long as we're staying up all night, I'm calling the rest of the pack," I said. "Gaw, how the hell is my reception this good, anyway?"

He offered me jazz hands in reply. *Magic.*

Unlike poor Kenna, Dec had gone back to his dad's place for a shower, dinner, and an early bedtime once Kiet and Mina released them that afternoon, and my call woke him from a sound sleep. Once my voice pierced his grogginess and he registered who I was and what I was asking, however, he threw on clothes, woke Aurie, and picked her up outside her grandfather's house. Edie met them outside the villa and hurried them in, I turned some lights on, and finally, there we were again—the six of us, exhausted and sore but garrulous with the hour and with each other's company. Naturally, Aurie and Dec had a million questions for Gaw—and they expressed the same sentiment as Edie had about his grand plan to quietly disappear—but once they were satisfied that Gaw was alive and I was conscious once more, Kenna confessed her news, which set them off again. Edie sneaked to the kitchen to grab snacks and returned with a few bottles of unlabeled red wine, which turned out to be surprisingly sweet. We sat around my room on whatever furniture was available—Gaw willingly yielded his chair to Aurie—to eat, drink, and commiserate about the insanity of the last month. We toasted to Gaw not being dead, to Ed's grand nepotistic plan of succession for Edie, to the hope that Mina and Kiet might be needed far, *far* away in the near future. Kenna endured more than her share of faerie princess jokes—though to be fair, she'd earned them for the ribbing she'd given Dec and me.

Eventually, Dec said, "This doesn't have to be a one-off thing. I've got the hang of gates now, Edie can do it wandless—freak of nature, that one."

She grinned at the praise.

"And Kenna should have it down," he continued, but she held up a hand to pause his spiel.

"I've got kinks to work out," she replied. "Could open a gate, might open a wormhole to another dimension. Who knows, really?"

"Or we could just pick you up," said Edie.

I glanced at Kenna, but she said nothing about the fact that I was also in extra training.

They think you're behind because you've been sleeping, Gaw told me. *Kenna's not going to say anything.*

No? I asked him.

Nope. I asked her not to. Let them believe you're doing remedial work.

They wouldn't say anything, I replied, watching Aurie toss reheated meatballs into the air and catch them in her mouth.

Probably not, but Dec, at least, would want a demonstration if word got out that you could levitate, and there's no need to freak out Val's guards, is there?

Point. I grabbed the bag of chips and sighed with pleasure as the oil and salt coated my tongue. *If you want snacks, you'd better hurry up and materialize.*

I don't actually get hungry anymore.

Too bad for you, then, I thought, and poured myself more wine.

Maybe it wasn't perfect. Gaw was still barely more than a ghost to everyone but me. We'd all been uprooted from the lives we'd known, and the ones we'd imagined embarking upon had gone up in smoke. Our hometown was toast. Edie and Dec were being groomed for leadership, while Kenna had come in that evening to find a court dumped into her lap. As far as I knew, Aurie's father still wasn't speaking to her grandmother, and her power was laughably weak beside the rest of ours. And as for me…well, on top of everything else I'd been through in the last weeks, acquiring massive, uncontrolled power wasn't the worst that had happened.

Sure, my life was still a mess, but for a few hours, laughing with my friends and getting tipsy on Avus's wine, I felt almost normal again.

Whatever else we were, whatever else our elders wanted us to be…we were together again.

When Bonnie stopped by to check on me around dawn,

she found more than she'd been expecting: Edie, Kenna, and me in bed, Dec and Aurie snoring on cots he'd managed to enchant into existence, and the remains of our midnight meal stashed atop my table, complete with empty bottles. I woke to her hand on my shoulder, and as I tried to focus on her face in the pale light, she whispered, "You know, hon, there are plenty of other rooms here. Y'all don't have to cram in like sardines."

"Safety in numbers," I whispered back.

"Uh-huh. Well, your grandfather asked me to rouse you and Kenna, so hit the shower, missy."

Half an hour later, when the pack of us trooped in for breakfast, Avus barely batted an eye as he glanced up from the stack of papers beside his plate. "Truly, I don't mind houseguests," he said, refilling his coffee, "but Declan, be sensible and tell your father where you're going, eh?"

"I'm almost twenty-three," Dec protested. "I don't need to tell Mommy and Daddy where I am."

"I have shoes older than you," he replied, and turned to the next of his papers. "Sit down and eat."

A few minutes after we tucked in, Coileán arrived, ruffled his son's hair in passing—and ignored the sour look Dec shot him in return—then nodded to Avus. "Same arrangement today?"

"That was my thought, yes."

"Good, because I asked Aiden to give you a hand."

Avus grinned and sipped his coffee. "I suppose he does still owe me a favor."

"That, and daylight and fresh air are good for him on occasion. Have fun." Glancing down the table at the rest of us, he asked, "Kenna, did you sleep at *all*?"

She was sporting an impressive set of dark circles that morning beneath her turquoise frames, and she radiated surliness as she clutched her coffee close. "Eventually."

"How many of you need a hangover cure?" Avus asked, and smirked when he saw our surprise. "Come, now, you think Bonnie wouldn't tell me about the state of your room?"

"Bonnie narced?" Edie muttered.

"She tells me what I need to know…" He paused and smiled as Maria strolled in. "Welcome back. How's the castle?"

"Messy but intact," she replied, and snagged a piece of toast. "Edie, Dec, you're starting with me today…and *whoa*," she said, taking a closer look at them. "Did we not sleep last night?"

"They camped in Cici's room," Avus began, "and—"

"Yeah," Edie cut in, "because Cici finally woke up, we got to talk to Gaw, and Kenna's a freaking *queen*, apparently, so we had a late night."

Coileán and Avus stiffened, and Maria quirked a brow. "Seriously?" she asked.

"Yeah," Kenna mumbled into her coffee. "And Edie, remember the part about how that information wasn't supposed to leave the room?"

Edie grimaced. "Oops."

"Does your dad know?" Maria asked Kenna. "He hasn't mentioned it to me…"

"I haven't told him yet."

"You should," she replied, then pointed to Dec and Edie. "And you two are going back to bed. I'm no use to you unless you can focus on your casting, and you look like you pulled an all-nighter, so why don't we try again in the afternoon?"

Dec dropped his fork with the shock. "*Really?*"

"Yeah. We've been working you to death, anyway. Step away from the caffeine and go have a nice lie-in. As for the rest of you, I'll make your excuses to Mina and Kiet."

"Kenna will be with me today," Avus told her, "and Cici's with Coileán. If you'd like to try to convince the captains to release Aurie, be my guest."

Maria folded her arms. "Come on, Val, they're exhausted. If nothing else, Kenna needs to have a long chat with Ennis."

"Your opinion is appreciated, carissima filia, but training will proceed on schedule."

"But—"

It sucks, Gaw interrupted, *I know, but trust me, they need training more than sleep.*

"Man, whose side are you on?" Kenna grumped as Maria, surprised by the mental intrusion, regained her composure.

I'm on the side of public safety. Chug that coffee—your tolerance is impressive. But Val, Maria's right—she should have time with her dad, too. Why don't you push the schedule back an hour?

Avus turned his attention to his papers. "Your opinion is appreciated as well, Gaw, but—" He hissed in sudden pain and reached for his temples, and Coileán winced in sympathy.

That wasn't a suggestion.

Kenna and I shared a brief, knowing smile as we finished eating, and Coileán hustled me outside while she wandered off in search of her father.

That day, Coileán took me to a remote patch of wilderness to work, explaining that I didn't need an audience, especially as my go-to trick was levitation. Avus did likewise with Kenna and Aiden, though he chose a different site. By sunset, I'd learned enough control to manage gates again, and I noticed with satisfaction that my end product was far more stable than it had been before my close encounter with Gaw. It seemed Avus shared Coileán's idea, as Kenna arrived on her own steam just as I was sealing my gate. She looked as gross as I felt after a day in the woods—sweaty, disheveled, grass-stained, wearing a sprig of leaves in her hair, and sporting fresh bruises on her bare arms—and she waved wearily as I approached.

"Lessons over for the day?" I asked.

"Yeah, thank God." As we started into the villa, she

asked, "Is your aunt still staying here?"

Quick process of elimination led me to Artur, as Beth had already accompanied Ed to the castle. "Last I saw. Why?"

"Could you take me to her room? I want to ask her a few questions."

"Do you want to *shower* first?"

Kenna stopped and screwed her eyes closed. A few seconds later, she seemed impeccably put together—even the smell had vanished. "Convincing enough?"

"Seriously?" I said, laughing. "You're going to glamour up instead of bathing?

She tossed her hair over her shoulder. "Think of it as dry shampoo."

Though I was still red-faced and dripping, I led Kenna to Artur's room and knocked. She opened the door remotely and called to us from the garden, and we found her sitting in the light of an orb, reading a paperback from Mom's voluminous stash in a lounge chair. Briefly, she inspected our appearance, then draped the book over the armrest to hold her place and sat up. "What's wrong, girls?"

"Plenty," I muttered, rubbing a knot in my shoulder. My shields were good, but Coileán's aim was better.

"Mm. Can you be more specific?"

Kenna glanced around, but seeing the three of us alone, she blurted, "Irem's dead, and I'm the new queen, and I'm about *this* close to a nervous breakdown." She held her finger and thumb a hair's width apart for emphasis. "*Help.*"

"Interesting," she replied, unfazed. "This hasn't been announced, I take it."

"Not until I have a little more control over my power."

"Ah. Wise. You want to come in with a show of strength—don't give your detractors fresh ammunition at the outset. And you *will* have detractors," she said. "It comes with the position. Then again, seeing as the Three rule almost absolutely in this realm, that shouldn't present you with an insurmountable problem, assuming you don't get yourself killed." She paused to give Kenna's face a long look. "I don't know any particulars concerning ruling in Faerie—let's be clear about that. Why come to me instead of Coileán or Val?"

"Because I don't think either of them remembers what twenty-two feels like," said Kenna. "And they act like this should be no big deal for me, but I barely know who *I* am, much less what I'm supposed to be doing with a court, and…I mean, you've been in this boat, right?"

Artur nodded. "King at ten. High king at fifteen."

"What do I do?"

"You grow up very quickly," she replied with a sad smile, and gestured to the other lounge chair in the garden. "Sit, let's talk. Cici…"

"I need a shower," I said, scrunching my nose as I caught a whiff of myself.

"Thank you," Artur murmured, and I showed myself out.

CHAPTER 18

For Kenna, Friday went much as Thursday had gone, except that Aiden dragged Mal's dad out of the Fringe settlement to assist him and Avus. Both Aiden and Rufus had served as surrogate kings for a year, and as Rufus was relatively young and Aiden had come to the job with no prior magical training, the two understood Kenna's hesitations and questions in ways that Avus didn't.

My training, however, took a backseat to Coileán's other concerns. He worked with me for an hour that morning, but he called a halt well before breakfast to deal with the security situation. With Avus busy whipping Kenna into shape, Coileán had taken the lead on mitigating the chaos of the returning faeries, and Mina and Kiet alike took orders from him. Every available guard was put into rotation—some at Coileán's place, some at Avus's, a few patrolling the occupied lands to look for hotspots, but many pulling shifts at the settlement. The little town had been under siege when Faerie collapsed, and Avus and Coileán feared that some of the faeries whom Irem had let loose upon it might still have a taste for blood after their forced exile. Thus, the guards joined the town's regular security force to watch the gate and the decorative wall, with Nico and Ned, one of Mal's many uncles, coordinating the effort on that end.

With Mina and Kiet occupied, Aurie had been freed from her lessons and left to her own devices. Maria took over Toula's practice room and kept Edie and Dec trapped in there all day, and while I could have just pretended to stay out in the wilderness and keep practicing without Coileán's supervision, Gaw discouraged slacking. *You need this*, he insisted as I blew up a football-sized rock. *More than Kenna does, if you want to be particular about it.*

"Then why am I zapping boulders by my lonesome?" I muttered as my next victim burst into gravel.

What, I'm not fun enough?

"You know I love you," I said, shielding myself against the onslaught of splinters from the dead tree I'd shot, "but it'd be nice to work with someone who can teach me how to control this."

You're improving, Gaw insisted. *And they're in triage. The Three need to formally call their courts and lay down the law before this place devolves into skirmishes again, but Val and Coileán aren't going to do that until Kenna is minimally competent. So let her have her tutors, and keep at the independent study.*

Sighing, I leapt and landed on a sturdy branch forty feet above the ground. From my perch, I could see little but leaves—the forests of Faerie were *old*, and my chosen tree barely reached the canopy—but I appreciated having a seat.

I stayed out until sunset, then caught Kenna slouching her way into the villa. "Having fun?" I asked.

I wasn't sure then if looks could kill, but judging by the glare Kenna had aimed my way, I'd be toast if she tested the theory.

Saturday proceeded in the same fashion: Kenna was pummeled by her trio of tutors, Dec and Edie studied stack techniques until their eyes crossed, Aurie hung out in her grandfather's library, and I roamed the wilderness, rendering large items into rubble and trying not to start a forest fire.

Sunday, however, brought a respite.

"You can take the afternoon off," Coileán told me as I threw bolts at his shield. "Val and I are heading back to Alaska for an early-morning meeting."

"But won't it be close to midnight there if you leave

here at lunch?" I asked.

His shield bowed but absorbed my latest blast, and Coileán grunted approvingly at my effort. "Closer to ten, actually—the time difference is slipping. You'll acclimate," he added as my face crinkled. "Anyway, we're coordinating with Ed first, having a pre-meeting chat to be sure we're on the same page. And there was a snafu with the scheduling, so we'll be kicking off this show at close to three in the morning local time. Come on, kid, you can hit harder than that."

The bolt I forced his way almost knocked me off my feet, but Coileán nodded. "Again."

"How do you mess up scheduling that badly?" I asked.

"You tell a bunch of wizards that you've got Arc 2 up and running, but you forget to mention that it's no longer in Glastonbury. Live and learn."

Gaw gave me the details once Avus and Coileán left. *Ed wants to get everyone around the table. He's brought in many of the former magi—the friendly ones, I mean—and extended invitations to the Minor Arcanum through their sleepwalkers. And wouldn't that be a nightmare*, he added, laughing to himself. *Picture it: you're asleep, having a nice evening, and then you're interrupted by Simon freaking Magus.*

"With an invitation you can't refuse?" I asked between bites of pizza. Avus's kitchen staff had worked wonders over the last few days, but my favorite offering thus far was their thin-crust pies, and I helped myself while Kenna washed off the grime.

He tried to be non-threatening, but that was never going to be an easy sell.

"Is that what he told you?"

Nah. I picked his brain when he came over yesterday.

"Gaw..."

I can't help it! And if you'd seen some of the memories in there, you'd pity me.

"Aw, poor baby," I teased. "Is omniscience no fun?"

Less fun than you might imagine. Anyway, Ed coaxed a few of the Minors to join them, and he used their contacts to reach out to the Dark Company. Arik and Hope are coming, too.

"Quite a crowd."

He's trying to do this right. I just wish he'd have the meeting here, he grumbled. *Whenever they leave the realm, it puts me on edge.*

I picked up a fresh slice of pizza and tucked in. "Maria and Toula are going, yeah?"

Yeah. Edie and Dec should be here soon—I told them there was food.

"Edie wasn't invited?"

Ed doesn't want to make her perform for a crowd until she's comfortable with her talent, he explained. *So no, she got the afternoon off, too.*

As predicted, Dec and Edie popped in a few minutes later, and Kenna joined us fresh from the shower, her hair pulled into a dripping tail. We lingered in the dining room, enjoying our freedom and the prospect of a few hours to ourselves, when suddenly, Dec's phone rang.

"Please don't be Mom or Dad, please don't be Mom or Dad," he muttered, pulling it from his pocket, then checked the display and sighed with relief. "Hey, Aurie," he said, putting the phone on speaker mode. "Hungry? There's pizza at Val's."

"No, thanks. I want a lift and backup, and Gaw told me you folks aren't busy."

"Did he, now?" said Dec, rolling his eyes to the ceiling as if expecting to find Gaw hiding in the mosaic. "What's going on?"

"I'll tell you when you get here. Put the gate well away from the windows—I don't want Dad and Granddad asking questions."

Edie leaned closer to the phone. "Is this going to get us in trouble or killed?"

"Just be a friend and bring the wand, eh?"

Curiosity got the best of us, and within minutes, Aurie was sneaking out of her grandfather's stately manor and running across the manicured grounds to our hiding place just inside the woods. "Thanks for coming," she said as she caught her breath. "I don't think they'll miss me for a while. Chess," she muttered, and stuck out her tongue.

"Where are we going?" I asked.

Her mouth tightened into a thin line. "I was hoping one of you knew the way to the dragon barn."

The rest of us traded brief, uncertain glances. "Uh…why?" I pressed.

"Because I want a word with my grandmother," she replied, absently rubbing her stumpy arm. "And in case anyone gets a crazy idea, I want backup with more than nominal magical talent. Please?"

We weren't about to abandon one of our own, and so, a moment later, I opened a gate near the huge barn, which was no less forbidding in its scope by daylight. The sheep in the fenced pasture nearby continued eating, unbothered by the lightning-rimmed rift in space, and I was wondering if they'd simply grown acclimated to gates when I saw one pause, lift its head, and bleat as its front and back legs walked in opposite directions. The sheep that had calmly split in half was now two identical sheep, and both resumed the first's attack on the grass.

"The *fuck*?" I hissed, pointing to the flock. "Did anyone else see that?"

They replicate by budding every few hours, Gaw explained. *It's the only way to keep their numbers high enough to sustain eleven dragons.*

"This place has magical freaking sheep, too?" Kenna demanded.

You can blame Coileán for that.

Dec's nose wrinkled as we watched another sheep reproduce. "Disturbing, Dad," he muttered, and looked away. "How are we playing this?"

"Simple: if anyone tries to eat me, start shooting," Aurie replied, and strode off.

As we rounded the pen, a pair of purple dragons

emerged from the barn, snapping at each other's neck, then lunged together into a ball of scales, teeth, and wings. A roar from within the barn called a halt to their wrestling, and the two shook themselves and stepped into the pasture, where they began picking off the oblivious sheep.

"Please tell me that was play fighting," Edie mumbled behind me.

"I think so," said Aurie, pausing to observe. "And I could be wrong, but those might be my cousins. Dad said one of his sisters had a clutch two years before I came around, so those are probably hers…and since Faerie was frozen all this time, I guess they're only about three years old. Still dragonets."

Kenna peered at the dragons as one of them flung a sheep skyward by the back leg and caught it before it descended. "*Big* kids."

"Think older teenagers." She took a deep breath, then squared her shoulders and led us onward.

We'd almost reached the wide expanse of trampled dirt in front of the barn when another dragon stepped outside, blinking in the afternoon light. Unlike the pair in the pasture, this one had the black-and-white coloration of a Holstein cow, and its long neck rose as it noticed us. *Hi*, came the alien voice in my head—fortunately, in Fae instead of in pure thought. *Who are you?*

"I'm here to see Georgie," Aurie replied.

Though Coileán had shown me the rudiments of looking into another person's thoughts, I had no need to pry where Aurie was concerned. Not only was she a natural telepath, but she was emotionally ramped up and making no effort to guard her mind. The set of her jaw belied the fear I sensed washing through her, and beneath that, the anger.

The dragon cocked its head. *But who are you?*

"Just get her for me."

I felt the dragon's mental shrug as it returned to the barn. Sidling close to Aurie, I gripped her shoulder and murmured, "You don't have to do this. Feeling like you do—"

"I feel like I want to either punch something or puke," she muttered.

"Exactly. We can come back later."

"Running's not going to make this any easier." She paused as the tremors in the ground increased in strength, then planted her lone hand on her hip as Georgie emerged from the shadows.

It's possible, I suppose, to reach the point where one is no longer awed and slightly on edge to be in the presence of a full-grown dragon. One can acclimate to almost anything through long exposure. But my occasional glimpses of shifted Frank hadn't been sufficient to silence the primal mammalian fear of coming face-to-face with a carnivorous lizard the size of a jet plane. Georgie was maybe two-thirds the length of a football field from nose to tail, horned, and solid black but for her huge red eyes. The claws visible on her front feet put those of my worst nightmare grizzlies to shame.

A little voice deep in my mind—one I certainly wasn't proud of—expressed relief that she seemed to be fixated on Aurie instead of me.

I felt more than heard it when Georgie started speaking to her, a rush of thought conveying sense and emotion in a tangle too knotted for me to unravel, but Aurie, slipping into Fae, cut her off with a curt, "Tell me why I don't deserve to live."

Georgie hesitated, then adjusted her approach. *I never said—*

"Bullshit. I'm missing wings and a hand," she snapped, raising her left arm for emphasis. "So what? I've done all right for myself."

You grew up.

"Yeah, thanks to Dad. And my granddad's pretty great, too. But you know, it would have been so nice to think that the rest of the family didn't want to eat me."

Perhaps wisdom cautioned Georgie to hold her peace in the face of Aurie's naked anger.

"Dad told me what you did," she continued, reddening. "You wouldn't even look at me before you sent me away. Am I that disgusting to you?" Furious tears started to roll down her cheeks, and she blinked to dispel them. "Well, I'm here now. Go on, tell me to my face."

I felt the warning rumble of my own rising temper but forced it down. Much as my anger on Aurie's behalf wanted an outlet—maybe a few practice bolts—releasing it would only make matters worse.

A few other dragons began to appear near the door to the shaded barn behind Georgie—red Horus, black Rego, a smaller green one I took to be a sister—and Aurie turned her rage upon them in turn. "What the fuck is *wrong* with you?" she screamed. "You tell a guy you want to kill his kid, and then you're surprised when he doesn't want to speak to you ever again? For fuck's sake, what sort of psychopaths *are* you?" By then, she'd begun to tremble with the force of her fury. "I'm the one with a faerie in the family—at least I have an excuse. But hey," she said, twisting her expression into a saccharine smile, "this is great! Now that you're all here, you can tell me why I need to die. Go on! I'm all ears."

I heard telepathic echoes of the other dragons' surprise and bewilderment even as another two, blue and purple, joined the pack. Finally, Georgie looked behind her and thought, *The root of this problem is that Frank isn't your full brother.*

Five heads cocked in confusion.

Though she parsed her communication into words, I could still feel her discomfort. *After I left your father, I was chased and injured. Kura...* She hesitated, her embarrassment mounting. *Kura transformed me to hide me instead of just giving me an escape. I don't know why. But the man who found me took me in and tended to my injuries, and when I felt better, I was...curious,* she thought with reluctance, *and I did something I shouldn't have, and…*

Wait, thought one of the other dragons—I didn't know their mental voices well enough to reliably distinguish them. *So Runt is…*

His father is half fae, Georgie replied. *And Frank takes after him in many respects. I should have seen it years ago, but…* Her wings shifted and refolded, almost like a shrug. *We were trying to help him after Ione died, and I know you all meant well, but it went over like a lead balloon. A flaming lead balloon*, she added, glancing back at Aurie. *And it seems that Aurora takes after her father.*

Standing as close as I was to Aurie, I began to catch flashes of the pain she was hiding beneath her shield of anger.

The other dragons made no sudden moves. *Is that the hatchling?* one of them asked after a moment.

Yes, thought Georgie.

How? She's far too old—

"I'm twenty-six," Aurie snapped. "The world went on without you."

And this has been festering all along. Carefully, Georgie curled up outside the barn and rested her head near Aurie. *I'm sorry, little one*, she thought. *I thought I was doing the right thing. Obviously, that was a mistake.*

Aurie's face crumpled as she struggled to hold herself together.

I told Frank to take you away because I wanted him to provide a better life for you than what you could have had here. If you were anything like your father—which you seem to be, she allowed— *then you could handle a world in a body you were never meant to inhabit. In that form, at least, you can walk.*

Despite her best efforts, Aurie's tears spilled over once again.

I never intended to push you or your father away forever, Georgie continued. *Not even for twenty-six years. It's only been a year here, you understand—*

You live with them, Aurie retorted, jutting her short arm

toward her cousins in the pasture. *And you couldn't be bothered with me for a year?*

Georgie flinched at the force of her thought.

I know you only through Dad's memories, she continued. *All this time, I thought this side of my family had been wiped out, but I didn't even know you to miss you. I missed the <u>idea</u> of you because you never cared to know me.* Her lip quivered as her face contorted. *Just tell me why.*

I was giving Frank his space. I was hoping he would return, send a message, anything, but—

You threw us out! Why would you expect him to come crawling back to you?

I was wrong, Georgie told her again. *I hurt him when I was trying to help him. He was so lost that summer, so…fragile. Desperate. You wouldn't have been happy or safe here, and he needed to take you to Glastonbury. I thought a firm push would give him direction.*

Aurie took a steadying breath, then managed to verbalize again. "I never knew my mother," she said, unable to fully master the tremor in her voice, "but I know that Dad loved her. *Very* much. He lost her. He lost my brothers. And I came out with all sorts of fun defects, so he got to deal with a baby with a bad heart for a while. I was kidnapped," she continued offhandedly. "Might have died. Guess you never heard about that. Probably don't care."

That's not true—

"What I'm getting at," she said as an angry spark danced in her wet red eyes, "is that Dad *needed* support. His family. So thank goodness for the Away Team, because he sure as hell didn't have a family here he could count on." Looking past Georgie at the silent dragons, she spat, "I grew up with a bunch of wizards and faeries and who-knows-what who've been aunts and uncles to me because you bastards wouldn't. Well, now's your chance to explain. Tell me to my face why I don't deserve to live. Who wants to be first?"

You deserve life, Georgie replied. *And I'm so sorry for hurting you. I've thought of you often over the last year, you and Frank both. All I wanted was for him to be happy and for you to be safe.*

Though I was admittedly no pro at telepathy, nothing about Georgie's answers struck me as insincere. I felt sadness in them, and plenty of guilt, but no mendacity.

But Aurie...

Though she kept her mind fairly well locked down, I'd caught flashes of her mood before, but never anything like this. For once, Aurie was wide open, and what radiated from her was raw and ugly. Beneath the veneer of anger lay the deep hurt of an abandoned child, through which flowed a current of self-loathing. She was the defective one, she was the reason her father's family had cast them out...so maybe they were right about her.

My blood boiled as I sensed her pain, and it was all I could do not to lash out when she turned away from Georgie and finally broke down. She covered her mouth with her hand to muffle her sobs, but her shoulders shook, and as I traded glances with the rest of our pack, I saw my sentiment mirrored in their faces.

As Aurie wept, Georgie's head slid closer over the dirt until she nudged Aurie's back. Gentle as it was, the touch still almost knocked Aurie off her feet, but she caught herself and wheeled around to find Georgie inches away from her. *I was wrong, and I hurt you, and I'm so very sorry*, Georgie thought. *That was never my intention.*

Of course you didn't want to hurt me, Aurie shot back through her tears. *All of you wanted me dead instead.*

"To be fair, that's draconic instinct," said a familiar voice, and I spun on my heel to find Gaw approaching, glowing but seemingly solid. "They're hard-wired to kill or abandon hatchlings who aren't going to make it. More resources for the rest of the clutch, see?"

Aurie pulled up a corner of her shirt and swiped at her eyes. *What, you're suddenly an expert?*

"Actually, yeah. There've been a *ton* of dragons in this

realm over the millennia, and I've picked up a lot of information over the last few days. A small percentage of it is actually useful," he added, rolling his eyes. "Aurie, you have every right to be hurt and furious, but Georgie means what she's saying. She feels like shit."

"I know," she mumbled.

As Aurie sniffled and wrestled herself back under control, Gaw rested his hands on her shoulders, then hugged her. She squeezed him back, closing her puffy eyes and whimpering as she fought her tears. *They were wrong*, he told her, though he was apparently broadcasting. *You aren't the problem. And your dad would die a thousand deaths to save you. If it's you or them, he'll choose you every time, because there is nothing in the universe more important to him than you are. He doesn't regret you, so don't tell yourself that this is all your fault.*

She remained in his embrace, resting her face against his shoulder as he rubbed one hand up and down her back.

Do you know why Georgie wouldn't take a look at you on the night you were born? Gaw asked.

"I can think of a few reasons," Aurie muttered.

Not the right one, though. She was afraid she'd lose her nerve. She knew you needed to leave this place, but she worried that if she let herself get too close, she'd find a way to rationalize why you should stay.

Aurie straightened, and as Gaw released her, she turned to Georgie and sniffed. "Well?"

It's true. She hesitated, then asked, *May I see your real face?*

"This *is* my real face."

"One of them," said Gaw. She shot him a glare, and he shrugged. "Where's the lie?"

Though she wavered, after a moment, Aurie said, "Give me room."

We backed away—I wasn't at all displeased when Gaw joined me and wrapped his arm around my waist—and Georgie retreated toward the barn. Aurie closed her eyes and exhaled, then said, "One of you had better know how to make clothing."

Before we could take a poll, she shifted.

I'd seen Aurie's full draconic form just once before, when we'd been little kids playing near the runway and Aurie, babysitting, thought she spotted a bear in the woods. She was maybe only three-quarters Georgie's size—far smaller than her uncles hiding in the barn, and even smaller than the curious cousins who'd stopped eating to investigate the commotion—but small for a dragon was still huge by most standards. Where Georgie was glossy black, Aurie's scales were blue-green, a perfect transposition of her natural hair color, and she bore horns and claws similar to her grandmother's. But her back was smooth, unmarred by wing joints, and her left front leg ended around the knee. She'd thrown her weight to the right before shifting, and so although she wobbled a little, she managed to stay upright and stared at Georgie. *Well?*

Georgie ventured close again. *You're beautiful, little one. Like your mother.*

When Aurie tried to take a step, she fumbled, and Georgie darted in to support her. She braced Aurie with her body until her granddaughter regained her balance, then began rubbing her neck against Aurie's. As Aurie followed suit, their conversation from that point became incomprehensible to me, a stream of pure thought.

"Are they making up?" I whispered to Gaw.

"Getting acquainted," he whispered back. "But it's a good sign." He looked over my head toward the far side of the sheep pasture, then said, "And here comes Frank."

"*What?*" I said, turning in time to see the flash of an opening gate. "How did he find—"

"I told him. Thought he might want in on this."

"That wasn't the plan."

"Easier this way. Now she won't have to sneak over here."

Frank vaulted the rail fence and sprinted across the pasture toward the barn, dodging oblivious sheep. His panic echoed in my mind as he neared, and Georgie looked up and thought reassurance. Frank froze in his tracks, and when Aurie turned to see him, she nodded.

I'm so sorry, Frank, Georgie told him as he stared at the pair. *I was trying to do the right thing for you both, and I failed miserably.* When he didn't answer, she added, *I know we don't always understand each other, but I love you, son, and I never meant for you to feel abandoned.*

He didn't reply in words, but rather with an overwhelming wave of hurt and loss.

She slumped at the onslaught. *I'm sorry. I didn't know how to be the mother you needed, but I could have been better. I should have been better*, she amended. *Owain told me the truth last week. Frank, I had no idea, and I see now that our approach after Ione was…*

"Cruel?" he suggested. "Heartless?"

Misguided. I only wanted to help you.

"By killing my children and kicking me out?"

Her head sank lower. *Horribly misguided.*

They watched each other for a long moment, mother and son, and then, in a burst of confettied clothing, Frank shifted and approached. Leaving Aurie balancing on her own, Georgie met him at the fence. Whatever passed between them then was hidden from me, but as they rubbed their heads and necks against each other, I glanced back at the gate through which Frank had run and saw Owain standing at the edge, smiling.

After a moment, Frank carefully stepped over the fence, rumbled at his daughter, and took up a place at her left side in case she lost her footing. While Georgie returned her attention to Aurie, Horus sidled out of the barn and started toward his brother, but Frank stopped him with a flash of fangs and a warning growl. *Let me make this crystal clear*, he thought. *If any of you so much as hurt my daughter's feelings, I'll kill you.*

They were trying to help, Georgie interjected.

They can start by not threatening Aurie. What the hell is wrong with you? he asked his siblings.

"Nothing," said Gaw, wandering dangerously close to several tons of agitated lizard. "You're the one bucking the norms, Frank. You know that."

He growled but didn't deny it.

"Look," Gaw continued, stopping between Frank and the pack in the barn door, "now that everyone's on the same page, maybe there can be some mutual understanding. Yeah," he told the group, "Runt acts weird, but it's for a good reason. Frank doesn't always get you because he's missing some of that hard, instinctive drive, and you don't get him in turn. And Frank," he said, looking in the other direction, "I know you're hurt, but think of all the times you felt terrible because you thought your family was dead and you never got to clear the air. You've got that chance now."

Come here, Gaw.

He obliged, and once he was in striking range, Frank lowered his head until Gaw was looking up into a mouth full of sharp teeth. *We all know you're plugged into the realm now*, Frank told him, softly broadcasting, *but try to pretend that we still have privacy, okay, kid?*

"Keep telling yourself that," Gaw replied with a grin, then waved as Owain began to cross the pasture toward them. "Your dad's coming up behind you."

Could do without an amateur family counselor, Frank hinted.

"I know. See you around, Aurie," he said, then rejoined me and opened a gate back to Avus's. "She's in no danger," he told our group as the others neared. "And since it's Frank's birthday tomorrow and I'm feeling generous, let's give them some peace."

CHAPTER 19

I awoke to light on the other side of my eyelids, but it wasn't morning peeking through the curtains to the garden.

"Hi," said Gaw as I opened my eyes. "They're back."

"Who?" I mumbled through my fog.

"Val and Coileán. Just got in from Alaska. *Long* morning over there," he said, and whistled low.

Reaching the point of sufficient consciousness to understand polysyllabic words, I sat up and squinted at him. "Did the meeting not go well?"

"It went in unexpected directions. Before things kicked off, Ed went sleepwalking, and he thinks he's found Leander Kirby."

"The guy who got Faerie sealed off? He's still around?"

"Outside of Chicago. Anyway, the talk turned pretty quickly to what they want to do with him. Every faction in the community has a legitimate grievance, except maybe the Company…"

"Sure." Shifters didn't need magic to go back and forth, but I suspected that even they wanted a word with the former grand magus.

"Well, the Arcanum's claiming dibs. Some of the magi want to try him for treason, just like James Mulligan and his cronies. On the other hand, Toula and Bert are pushing for leniency."

My face scrunched. "*Why*?"

"Because Leander was a dumb, arrogant guy still shy of thirty when he got his chain, and he wasn't intentionally treasonous—he stupidly thought he could seal off Faerie and still keep magic, which would have made things simpler in the mortal realm. The real traitors are Francine Leighton and—"

Catching himself, he swallowed the end of that thought, but I knew where his mind was going. "My grandmother. You can say it."

"Eva," he murmured. "They were the masterminds who tried to destroy the other realms out of spite, and Leander was their convenient pawn. Bert, especially, is pushing for leniency—he was a young, dumb grand magus once, too."

"So where are Eva and Francine?"

Gaw shrugged. "Ed hasn't located them yet. And since they're still in the wind, the magi who've just spent twenty-five years without magic are *quite* interested in bringing in the guilty party on hand. They've been bickering about how to do it—do they grab him now? Put him under surveillance? Try to negotiate a surrender? And the other complicating factor is that Ed thinks Leander has a family to consider. The cooler heads don't want to bust down his door and risk hurting untrained wizards in the crossfire."

"What have they decided?" I asked.

"For now, surveillance. While Ed keeps looking for Francine and Eva, a few of the sleepwalkers from the Minor Arcanum are going to keep an eye on him, just in case he gets paranoid now that magic has returned."

I rubbed the gunk out of my eyes, which had begun to smart less as they adjusted to Gaw's brilliance in the dark. "Kind of surprised that Avus and Coileán didn't jump at the chance to drag him in."

"Politics," he muttered, then smiled when I patted the sheets. "Don't mind if I do."

The mattress creaked under his weight, and as I stretched out under the covers again, Gaw joined me. "What politics?" I murmured, scooting closer to the middle of the bed. "Surely they have a claim against him."

"Absolutely, but since the Arcanum wants the first crack, they're trying to play nice. I wish they wouldn't— too much concern for politics is what got them into this mess—but it's not my call. There *is* good news, though."

"Oh?"

He grinned. "Discussions are continuing this evening in Alaska, which would be morning here, so you and Kenna get another reprieve."

"See, now," I said, "if you're going to wake me in the middle of the night, you should lead with that." Reaching toward him, my hand found his beneath the blankets. "You seem stronger."

"I've been practicing. Went to see Mom and Dad after dinner last night, and Mom gave me some pointers. Honestly, it's freaky," he continued, entwining his fingers with mine. "I've got a version of Mom in the group mind, right, and then there's the real one, and they're not synchronized in terms of what they know. I mean, there's a lot of overlap, except for the last quarter-century, but I definitely prefer my real mom to partial Ros. Maybe that should go on my Mother's Day card this year," he joked.

"If you keep going at this rate," I told him, "you're not going to need me around much longer."

"Fat chance of that."

He hesitated before moving closer to kiss me, which I appreciated—recent experience set off all sorts of warning bells about being in close proximity to Gaw. But there was no pain that time, nothing but the comfortable familiarity of his lips on mine, and my internal blatting klaxons ceased. I kissed him back, lingering and deepening as the flutter in my belly stirred to life. He didn't seem to be breathing, but he was warm and solid, and I knew the scent of him.

"I've missed you," I whispered.

His kisses trailed lower, down the curve of my neck toward my tank top. I'd always had a decent sense for Gaw's moods, but now, I found myself awash in the sensation of his naked hunger…which might have been overwhelming, had I not shared his eagerness.

"Are you strong enough?" I asked as he slid his hands beneath my shirt.

"I'd better be," he almost growled, and I laughed as I helped him fling the shirt onto the floor. The rest of my clothes quickly followed. As for Gaw, he didn't waste time—his form was suddenly nude, and I ran my hands over his bare chest. "Convenient trick."

"Let's just hope I can keep this together," he said, easing me onto my back, then slid atop me and started to kiss me again…

…until he stiffened, but not the part of him I'd been expecting to. "*Shit*," he muttered, and vanished.

"Gaw?" I sat up and searched the room for him, but he'd disappeared without any clue as to the cause. "Too soon?" I asked. "We don't have to force this tonight—I'm in no rush. Come back to bed." I paused, hoping he'd answer me, but Gaw remained silent. "Honey, it's okay," I tried again. "If you can't hold a body together just yet, that's fine. I'm not upset. There's no need to be embarrassed…"

A sudden pounding at the door cut short my attempt at reassurance, and before I could say another word, Kenna pushed her way inside and turned on the lights. "We've got trouble," she said as I yanked the blankets over my bare chest. "There's about to be a fight at the Fringe settlement…" Her eyes narrowed as she considered my state of dishabille. "And was I imagining things, or is there a reason why that brand-new little presence in the back of my head just seemed incredibly *aroused*?"

"What does it look like?" I snapped, willing my shirt off the floor and into my hand. "Shut the door."

Kenna closed her eyes and groaned as I hastily dressed. "*Really*, Cici?"

"You're awfully prudish all of a sudden," I replied as my pants flew back onto the bed.

"Because it never involved me before!" Shoving the door closed, she muttered, "So every time you two go at it from now on, I'm going to get notified?"

"I don't know how this works!"

"Because if *I'm* aware of this, then I can guarantee you that Coileán and your grandfather are as well."

I paused, pants half on, and stared at her. "Oh, *shit*—"

Look, Gaw interrupted, *this is humiliating and awkward for everyone involved, but can we discuss it later, please? Priorities.*

"A little warning would have been nice!" I protested.

I'm sorry, I'm still figuring this out, too. Dec's on his way, and Edie's awake. I'll open a gate for you once they get here.

"What about Aurie?" Kenna asked. "She can't make it here on her own."

Let her have family time. Cici, babe, you're going to want shoes.

Five minutes later, dressed in my pajamas once again but still flushed, I stepped through Gaw's gate to a meadow a short distance from the settlement. Once my eyes adjusted to the orbs, lamps, and fireballs in the distance, however, I shoved thoughts of my newly complicated love life to the rear of my queue of problems.

The town was under siege.

Someone inside—perhaps several people, judging by the haphazard construction—had thrown together a shielding dome over the settlement. As the only other defensive structure was the waist-high brick wall around the perimeter, whoever was powering the shield had their work cut out for them. Outside, the floating lights and flickering torches revealed a swarm of faeries in the darkness, who shouted at the guards standing on the wall, just within the shield.

"Come on," Gaw muttered, and we slipped closer to the action, staying low and hidden in the shadows as well as we could.

Nearing, I could pick out familiar faces on the wall:

Mina and Nico, plus a few Stowes. Kiet stepped up beside them with a firm nod for the others, and Mina touched her throat.

"Go home!" her voice rang over the cacophony of the crowd. "You are ordered to disperse."

"What's going on?" Edie murmured.

Gaw's sigh echoed in my thoughts. *There's been an influx of returning faeries in the last days, and they've compared notes. That's a chunk of the full-blooded part of Irem's court.*

I cut my eyes to Kenna, who looked sick at the sight.

"The settlement is under the kings' protection," Mina continued as the crowd held its position. "Guards await inside, and our orders are to use them as necessary. I would rather end this peacefully."

Someone within the mob amplified his voice in turn. "My queen gave me leave!" he shouted back at Mina, and his fellows yelled encouragement. "We were denied magic for decades. Why should the mortals enjoy it now?"

"They are under the kings' protection," Mina insisted. "Stand down."

"This is *our* realm," he retorted. "The queen wants it cleansed. Get out of the way."

Dec stepped close to Kenna and gripped her taut shoulder. "How do you want to play this?"

"I...I don't know," she stammered, her eyes saucer-wide. "I haven't announced myself yet, I can't just tell them Irem's dead, and...and my power's not totally controlled..."

Neither was mine, of course, but Kenna had far more on the line than I did. "Dec," I said, "I need a favor."

"If you want a bazooka, no one's taught me how to pull one from the ether yet."

"Can you make me louder?"

He frowned. "Sure, I guess. Why?"

"Just do it."

Shrugging, he touched my throat, and I felt a warm pulse as the enchantment took hold. I gave him a thumbs-up, then motioned for the three of them to stay put and started toward town. "Hey!" I bellowed. "Hey, you! Angry mob!"

The captains, at least, could hear me, and the looks on their faces suggested that they expected me to end up dismembered in short order.

"Go home!" I yelled over the din. "Get out of here, or I'll turn you assholes into a crater!"

A few of the attacking faeries began to titter and guffaw, and the crowd parted to allow their apparent leader to step out and face me. "Who are you?" he asked, his voice still amplified. "A *child?*"

I stopped in my tracks, nervous energy surging within me, then leapt and hovered. "I'm the reinforcements," I said, and let the violet flames explode around me.

By the time I called forth a pair of fireballs, the edges of the crowd had begun to unravel with the unorganized retreat. I rained down fire from above as I flew toward the mob, and the leader—who by then was standing *very* much on his own—threw together a shield around himself. When I shot a bolt through the shield and shattered it, he ripped open a gate and ran.

I remained aloft until the last of the attackers had turned tail, then extinguished myself and landed in the grass, shaky but unhurt. As I caught my breath and let my heartbeat slow, Kenna jogged up and hugged me. "Thank you," she whispered, her arms trembling as badly as mine were. "I owe you one."

"No problem," I boomed, and she yelped at my unintentional shout.

"Let's just take *that* off," Kenna muttered, touching my throat, and I nodded when I felt the enchantment break. "How does that feel?"

"Fine," I replied, my voice once again at a normal volume. "And I'm okay, no one managed to shoot me—"

"What the *hell* was that?" Dec demanded as he and Edie marched up. "How did you—"

"That's what happens when you get too close to Gaw," I replied. "And thanks for the amplification—I don't trust myself with delicate work yet." Glancing toward the wall, I found the captains and the Stowes waiting, and I led the way. "Hi," I called, waving at the defenders. "I know it's early, but I could really go for breakfast right now. Like, I would legitimately kill for caffeine. Is there somewhere in town that's open?"

"And doesn't have an anti-pajama policy?" Edie quipped.

"Ned?" Nico muttered.

Ned, the eldest Stowe brother, a brown-haired man with wide blue eyes, pulled two of the others closer. "Get Luce out of bed," he ordered. "*Now.*"

As the messengers ran off, Nico stepped down from the wall and headed for me. "Are you a queen, then?" he asked, his brow knitting in the light of the floating orbs around us. "Surely not, unless something's befallen your grandfather and father…"

"I'm not," I replied. "But you should know that Irem is dead."

"Then who—"

"Her replacement will reveal himself or herself in due course, and that's all I'm at liberty to tell you," I said, and slammed together my mental shield. I couldn't yet manage blocking to Coileán's satisfaction, but it was better than no defense at all.

Fortunately, Nico didn't press the issue. "What have you become, little one? How—"

"Side effect of finding Gaw. And that's why Coileán has been working with me alone," I told Mina and Kiet as they joined us. "Don't worry, you don't have to train me."

Mina made no effort to disguise her sudden relief at the news, but she looked ill again just as quickly. "You're not fully in control yet?"

"Crater blasting, yes, but not everything."

Mina, Kiet, and Nico traded looks, and she cleared her

throat. "You know, in light of that information, I think it might make everyone feel better if the four of you ate *outside* the walls today."

I wasn't in the mood to argue, especially once Kiet produced a suitably large table a few yards from the gate and created a massive pot of hot coffee. As I poured a second cup, Luce Stowe, a short blond in a red bathrobe and matching silk pajamas, hurried through a fresh gate with a train of covered dishes floating along behind him. "I heard someone was in need of an early breakfast...or would this still count as a midnight snack?" he mused as the dishes deposited themselves on the table. The cloches lifted to reveal fluffy scrambled eggs, a platter of thick-sliced bacon that would have made Aurie weep for joy, a towel-lined bowl of biscuits and muffins, a steaming dish of diced potatoes with peppers and onions, and a massive serving bowl filled with chopped-up fruit. Plates, flatware, salt and pepper, and butter and jam appeared in the appropriate places, and Luce concluded by lifting the lid of the coffee carafe and taking a deep sniff. "Passable," he declared, "but let me do that next time, eh? And does anyone need tea?"

"What," Ned asked, "no omelet station?"

Luce shot him a withering look. "The Michelin star means I find minions to make omelets for me. Would you care to try sometime? Of course, seeing as boiling water is at the upper end of your culinary repertoire, we might need to begin with something a bit simpler."

Ned pulled a short bronze sword from a holster on his belt. "I'll remind you that I have knife skills."

"That's not a knife," Luce replied, and opened a tiny gate. I caught a glimpse of a granite kitchen countertop on the other side before he reached through and returned with a wooden box, which he opened to reveal a long blade that glinted in the orbs' light. "*This*, you ignorant barbarian, is a knife."

"Is that...*steel?*" Nico asked.

"Damascus steel. Accept nothing less." He snapped the box closed with a smirk, then nodded to us. "Bon appétit," he said, the French only slightly mangled by his British accent. "Which one of you is the flying fireball?"

I raised the hand that wasn't rooting through the breadbasket.

"Ah. Do us a favor and don't burn down the town. I rather like it," he said, then nodded to the others and took his leave.

Had Luce stuck around, I might have kissed him. The food was incredible, crispy and fluffy and tender in all the right places, seasoned to perfection, and abundant, and I inhaled it. While I worked through a third helping of potatoes, Dec said, "Just curious, but what *did* you do with Gaw that left you like this?"

"Not what you're thinking," I retorted once I managed to swallow.

"Could we not talk about that, please?" Kenna muttered.

I'm sorry, okay? Gaw cut in, then materialized—fully dressed, I noted. *Mom tried to warn me, but I didn't pay enough attention.*

Judging by the surprised looks on Dec's and Edie's faces, I guessed that he'd limited his conversation to Kenna and me. *How do we get any privacy?* I asked.

He grimaced. *I can't give you full privacy, unfortunately. Not from the Three. It's not like they're getting a ringside view, but because of our connection, I'm sensitive to their moods, and they're aware of mine. Which means…* He left the thought unfinished, but I didn't need further clarification.

It's not that I don't want you two to have fun together, Kenna interjected, *but I don't need to know when sexy time hits.*

And I'd really rather not announce it, Gaw replied, *but the situation is what it is. At least it's equal-opportunity embarrassment.*

"Is this a private conversation, or does someone want to loop us in?" Edie asked.

Gaw folded his arms and stared off toward the distant

trees to avoid her gaze. "Long story short, I've got a permanent hookup to the Three. I'm constantly in their heads, so I have a steady feed of what they're thinking and feeling. But this goes both ways, so when, say, I try to have a private moment with my girlfriend…"

Dec took one look at Kenna, who was flushed to her ears, and snickered. "Oh, no—*really*?"

"Why don't you go ask your dad how much fun this is?" she muttered.

"Yikes." He resumed his breakfast, then paused and lowered his fork. "Hey, Gaw?"

"Yeah?" Gaw asked as a fifth chair appeared for him.

"When you say you're connected to them, does that mean you get their current thoughts, or do you have access to their memories as well?"

"Everything they've ever thought, felt, sensed…and don't ask me to explain how I can process it. I'm still adjusting to that. But, uh…" An evil little smile creased Gaw's face. "What this means for you is that if you piss me off, I can show you, in *excruciating* detail, your own conception."

"Bro," he muttered, pushing back his plate. "Not cool."

Satiated and once again cognizant of the hour—a faint paleness stretched across the eastern horizon, portending the sunrise yet to come—we did the sensible thing and went back to bed.

As I kicked off my shoes, Kenna knocked and let herself in. "Got a second?" she asked, closing the door.

"Sure." Unshod, I flung myself onto the bed and groaned. "Bonnie had better not come around to wake us today."

"Beat you to it. I asked Gaw to pass the word that we're sleeping in."

Seeing Kenna linger awkwardly by the wall, I sat up and

rubbed my shoulder. "Is this about Gaw and me? Can we save it for full daylight?"

"It's not." She took a deep breath, then slowly exhaled. "Thank you for covering my ass out there."

"No problem."

"It *is* a problem. That's my court causing trouble, and if I had my shit together, I could do something about it."

"It's over," I insisted. "Angry mob dispelled. Crisis averted."

"For now."

"Now is good enough for me. You'll be ready soon, and then you can do what you like with them. But as for today, no harm done, right?"

"I guess," she muttered, her tightly folded arms betraying her agitation. "But today could have gone sideways, and that would have been my fault."

I shrugged. "It didn't—"

"But it *could* have. It's not your job to corral my court, and I…should have taken the lead. I panicked."

"Look, Kenna," I said, "this is uncharted territory for all of us, okay? I don't remember taking any classes on riot control. Mina didn't drill us on siege tactics."

She snorted, but when I slid off the bed and hugged her, she squeezed me back.

"We're in this together," I murmured. "And if that means covering each other's asses, so be it."

"Until I call my court, and you sticking up for me turns political."

"Screw politics," I said, pulling back to look her in the eye. Her glasses were smudged and perched slightly askew on her nose, and the shadows on her face spoke more of worry than of the long night. "We've been friends for the last twenty-two years. Nothing's going to change that."

Marginally reassured, Kenna slipped off to her room, and I burrowed beneath the blankets with a long, contented sigh.

I'd quashed a fight. Flown on my own power. Kept my

fire contained.

Sure, my life was still a jumbled deck of cards tossed into the air, and I was frantically trying to arrange them into a house as they fluttered down. No job prospects, my childhood home on the verge of abandonment, my boyfriend selectively corporeal and *far* too connected to Avus for my taste…but for the moment, I was quietly pleased with myself.

I'd taken the lead when the others hung back. Taken *control.*

As I drifted off, my mind replayed the frightened crowd's dispersal, people fleeing on foot or through gates they frantically opened like holes being punched in the night, and something within me smiled with satisfaction.

I'd discovered that sleeping in was often the best medicine, and that morning proved to be no exception. With Avus and Coileán back in Alaska with Maria and Toula, and Kiet and Mina warily watching the settlement for trouble, there was no reason for any of my posse to rise before midmorning, and only my bladder's complaining eventually roused me from my warm bed. Brushing my teeth, I contemplated my reflection: mussed and sleep-puffy, to be sure, but unbruised. I felt surprisingly good—competent, even. Hungry, but that could be fixed. A little too greasy for comfort…

Morning, beautiful.

I spat and rinsed the toothpaste from my mouth. "Hey, yourself. How long does our vacation last?

Undetermined, but at least a few more hours, judging by what I've overheard. Val wants to talk to you once things quiet in Alaska.

"Something wrong?"

He's come to the realization that you might require a bit of guidance as to how things work in this realm.

My shoulders tightened, and I reached for the floss.

"Oh?"

Yeah. Technically, it's problematic when you start attacking people from other courts without his permission.

With my mouth occupied, I switched to mental communication. *If Avus thinks he suddenly has the right to tell me how to live my life, he's delusional.*

Technically...

There's no "technically" about this, Gaw. I didn't sign up for any of this, and if I'm past needing permission from my parents, then I sure as hell don't need it from him.

Believe me, I get it, he replied, *but step back and look at the broader picture for a minute, okay?*

My reflection arched a brow.

This realm is home to a race of assholes with short tempers, long memories, centuries-old grudges, and reality-warping power. The only system that has ever maintained peace here for more than a few weeks is the courts, and only because Faerie makes the kings or queens the biggest dogs in the room. You can't appeal to a full-blooded faerie's sense of decency and altruism because that does not compute. The only way to keep them in line is threatening them with a big stick.

"Okay..." I mumbled as I went for my molars.

This realm isn't a democracy—it's three more or less absolute monarchies, with me drafted into the role of occasional referee. So while Val has no right to meddle in your day-to-day business, he can crack down in other respects.

A clenching jaw was no help in my quest for oral hygiene. *Such as?*

Well...last night, for starters. He's not upset, especially since he'd sent Kiet and guards to help with the riot, but that's the sort of thing that should go through him.

You're the one who sent us out there! I protested.

Because I knew he wouldn't be opposed to it in the end, and because the shield situation in town was less than ideal.

All right, I thought, *what else?*

Gaw hesitated. *Before the closure, the Three put in place restrictions on movement. No crossing into the other courts' territory without permission, no going to the settlement without permission…no leaving the realm without permission.*

My eyes widened, and I tossed the floss into the wastebasket, where it instantly vanished. "He can't force me to stay here! If I want to see Kenna or Dec or Edie or…or fucking Timbuktu, I *will*!"

Cici—

"We've lived under everyone's thumbs long enough! God," I sighed, glaring at the mirror, "we should have never left Anchorage."

He appeared behind me, and I turned around to hug him. "I know," he muttered, rubbing my back. "And if you flee the realm and never look back, I'll understand."

"I'm not leaving you," I mumbled into his shoulder.

After a moment, Gaw said, "There's a bit of a wrinkle in the system now, you know?"

"What's that?"

"Well, I said that the Three have to be the biggest dogs in the room, right? I give them that power."

"Yeah…"

He pulled away from me, and I looked up to see his sly smile. "There's never been anyone quite like you to consider. Technically—"

"*Again* with the technicalities?" I interrupted.

"You'll like this one. Technically, you're stronger than they are. I suppose I could increase their power to compensate…"

I waited for him to finish the thought, then prompted, "But?"

"But nah."

My brow furrowed. "What are you saying?"

"I'm saying that Dec may be stuck taking orders from his dad, and Aurie's going to do her own thing, because that's how the dragons roll, and Kenna's about to have a freaking court to consider…but I love you, and you almost *killed* yourself for me, and so, as far as I'm concerned, when it comes to you, Val can ask nicely and deal with it." He kissed me, and as we lingered there together, our foreheads touching, he murmured, "I'm going to ask you, as a personal favor, not to burn Faerie to the ground. Other than that, if you need to tell Val to back off, I'll be with you."

"Wouldn't that go against your agreement with the Three?"

"You know, Kura withheld the court from Val for decades, despite the pain to her, because she was still pissed about his mother. I'm *pretty* sure I can handle it."

I grinned, then kissed him again. "Love you."

"Love you, too. And, uh…you know, Val and Coileán are away, so my connection to them isn't as strong right now, and Kenna's still sleeping…"

"Mm. I *did* just freshen my breath," I began, then laughed as he swept me off the bathmat and strode back to my bedroom. "*Someone's* eager this morning."

"This someone has had several weeks' drought, only just regained his body, and would very much like to get back to exploring yours."

As he laid me on the mattress, I whispered, "Kenna is going to *hate* us."

"She's having a nice dream about that blond soccer player in our first-semester English class," he replied, climbing up to join me. "I don't think she'll mind terribly if it goes in an unexpected direction."

Kenna and I were lounging in one of Avus's courtyards, enjoying the blissful combination of late afternoon sunlight and not being punched, when Edie ran up, panting. "*There* you are!" she said as she caught her breath. "Mom just called from Alaska. Big news."

"How big?" Kenna asked, sitting up on her chaise. "Is it even dawn yet over there?"

"Doubtful. Dad's been sleepwalking all night with some of the Minors. When they checked in on Leander a little while ago, they found him packing. Looks like he's getting jumpy."

Kenna frowned. "Are they going to grab him now or wait until he bails?"

"I don't know, but Mom says there's a meeting about to kick off. More of the old magi have come in, and there have been talks going on all night over there, but this is going to be another mass sit-down. Sounds like everyone wants a piece of this guy."

I pushed my sunglasses atop my head and rolled a crick in my neck. "Is your mom going to call us with an update when they finish?"

Edie snorted. "Forget *that*. I've got a way to listen in, if you're game."

Eavesdropping on a magical summit seemed like the sort of opportunity that might not present itself a second time, and so, within ten minutes, Kenna and I had thrown on long-sleeved T-shirts against the familiar chill of early August mornings and summoned Dec to join us. As we prepared to depart, I heard Gaw in my head: *Okay if I ride shotgun?*

I thought you couldn't leave Faerie.

I can't, but part of me can go a little past the gate if I'm riding along, he explained. *It won't hurt.*

Hop aboard, I replied, smiling to myself, and his presence at the back of my mind seemed to almost imperceptibly solidify.

Edie did the honors—her gate, I noted with a twinge of jealousy, was a beautiful specimen—and we stepped through to a large office. I saw nothing but darkness beyond the windows, while the room itself was a mess. The desk's former contents lay scattered on the rug, and while a few books had managed to remain on the shelves, most had landed in a pile. The desk and guest chairs, less sturdy than the other furniture, were overturned on the floor.

"What is this place?" Dec whispered as Edie closed the gate.

"Magus office, I don't know whose. They all ended up like this after twenty-five years of getting tossed around inside a snow globe." She shot me a reproving look, and I grinned sheepishly. "Come on, this way. No talking."

After peeking into the corridor to see whether the coast was clear, Edie hustled us into a small office a few doors down. Considering its size and the lack of decoration, I assumed it had once been assigned to some poor junior Council aide. Edie listened for a moment, but with stillness in the air, she aimed her wand at an unmarked spot in the stone and muttered. An opening began to form in the wall, and as the last stones stacked themselves on the floor, a purple face appeared in the hole.

"Hi," Raurit whispered. "They're just beginning. Something about coffee?"

"Necessary, I'm sure," Edie whispered back, and motioned for us to follow her into the dark, unfinished room.

Once inside, I could make out the faint glow of a ward in the far wall. Again, Edie began to cast, and I watched as a few of the ward's channels opened and realigned themselves—and suddenly, the wall became transparent, revealing a stone-walled room hung with tapestries and filled with people.

"It's just a visualization spell," Edie reassured us. "Whoever put up the privacy ward around the conference room did it sloppily, and I found a way through."

"Where *are* we?" Kenna asked.

She shrugged. "Probably a former closet that someone forgot about, judging by the dust in here. Try not to sneeze, okay? They shouldn't notice us if we whisper, but anything more than that might sound suspicious." Pointing to the visualization, she added, "That's the Council's main conference room."

I settled in and looked around the large circular table, trying to pick out familiar faces. Spotting Avus wasn't hard, and Coileán sat beside him. Ed had taken a spot near the door, with Toula, Bert, and Maria bridging the gap in the ring. Iris Johansson sat on Ed's other side with a few elderly strangers—magi, I assumed. A few chairs down from Coileán sat Raurit's parents, both of whom appeared to be nursing steaming mugs. Beside them was a middle-aged woman with dark skin and a complex updo of silver braids, who kept one hand on her coffee and the other on the computer in front of her. I'd never met her, but I knew her from catching the occasional video chat between her and my mom: Yolanda Ford, the mortal realm's lone Fringe coordinator. A tenured archaeology professor at Stanford, she'd devoted most of her time to mundane matters after the closure, but she'd kept in touch with the scattered survivors. Everyone else was a stranger to me.

As if reading my mind—possible but unlikely, as I'd learned what that felt like—Edie whispered, "All the players are there. Faerie, Conota, the Company, the Fringe, the Minor Arcanum…"

Kenna stared at the wall for a long moment with her arms folded across her chest, then nodded. "If you'll excuse me," she said, heading for the hole. I caught her arm and gave her a questioning look, but she smiled. "It's okay," she whispered. "I've got this."

I watched the visualization while she sneaked out of the closet. Shortly thereafter, someone knocked on the conference room door, and Ed frowned. The other participants looked on curiously as he rose and opened the door, and I caught his double-take in profile when he found Kenna standing on the other side in her slouchy best. Before he could ask what she was doing there, she said, "As long as everyone is meeting, I'd like a spot at the table."

He cleared his throat. "How did you—"

"I'm not doing my court any favors by twiddling my thumbs on the sidelines."

She held his stare, and his eyebrows rose as the realization hit. He glanced over his shoulder at Coileán and

Avus, but they had eyes only for Kenna. I couldn't hear what, if anything, passed among them—Edie's spell allowed visual and audio espionage, but telepathy was another matter, and the three of them managed impressive poker faces. But after a moment, Coileán said, "You're quite right, and welcome." He pulled out the chair beside him and beckoned her into the room. "We hadn't troubled you with these discussions because of everything else on your plate right now."

One of the gray-haired magi peered at her as she made her way around the table. "Who is—"

"Lady Kenna," said Coileán, cutting him off. "Who has every right to be here."

Judging by what I could see of the others' reactions, it seemed that most caught the gist that Kenna was the new queen. But the old magus wouldn't quite let it go. "*How* old are you, girl?" he asked as she pushed her padded chair up to the table.

Kenna grinned, straightened her glasses, then gestured the coffee urn and a clean cup into her hands. "Hasn't anyone ever told you not to ask a lady her age?"

That earned a chuckle around the table, and Toula nodded when Kenna cut her eyes that way.

Resuming his seat, Ed gestured to the Conotan delegation and said, "Kenna, I believe you've met Arikol and Imaranta."

"He knows she has," Raurit whispered beside me.

I glanced at him and shrugged. "He's being polite."

"And Dr. Yolanda Ford," Ed continued.

Yolanda looked up from her computer long enough to exchange nods with Kenna.

"Let me introduce Meghan Pomeroy," Ed continued, moving clockwise around the table. The middle-aged blonde sitting near Hope, who seemed sturdy enough to play tackle, lifted a hand in greeting. "Head of the Dark Company."

Kenna smiled. "Lupine?"

"Ursine," Meghan replied in a voice that hinted at rich contralto.

"I'm sorry, the only true shifter I've ever known—well, half shifter," she allowed—"goes wolf…"

The older woman gently laughed at her discomfort. "No need to apologize. It's not like we walk around with identifying badges."

"And this is the delegation from the Minor Arcanum," said Ed, slipping into the brief silence. "All sleepwalkers. Alvaro de la Costa, in from Buenos Aires."

A man with a shaved head and thick black mustache nodded to Kenna.

Ed extended a hand to a woman in a pale blue hijab on Alvaro's left. "Heer Hassan from Cairo, so we've done terrible things to her sleep schedule. And last but not least, Ujarak Ashoona."

I couldn't clearly see the face of the dark-haired boy beside her, but he seemed like a teenager, and I assumed he was Inuit.

"Ujarak has been especially helpful in keeping watch over Leander while sleepwalking," Ed told the table. "He's the one who caught our target packing this morning. Drink your coffee," he added to Ujarak. "You've earned it. Need a refill already?"

As the young sleepwalker tanked up, I kept my eyes on Kenna. Superficially, she appeared serene, but I knew her well enough to recognize the veneer over her nerves. Kenna was scared, but she was hiding it well, and I had to give her credit for her composure.

"In brief," said Ed once Ujarak was clutching a steaming mug, "Leander is preparing for departure. He waited for his wife and two daughters to leave home early this morning, and he began packing. The evidence is hidden in the trunk of his vehicle."

"He's going alone, then?" Iris asked.

"That would be our supposition, yes. And soon. The concentration of magic in this realm is rising—he must suspect that someone will be searching for him. My guess is that he's trying to put distance between us and his family."

Meghan drummed her fingers on the table. "Are they mundane?"

"The wife appears to be, but the daughters glow in the dream space. Untrained, I suspect, but that's a problem for another day. Anyway," he said, picking up his train of thought, "as I see it, we have two options: grab him soon—either this morning or in the next day—or wait until he takes to the road, then snatch him as he flees. Thoughts?"

After several suggestions were put forth around the table, Kenna raised a finger for Ed's attention. "There's no need to grab him immediately and put people in danger as long as you can keep eyes on him. Let him stew for a while—he'll make a dumb move if he's panicking. And then, if you think he's really about to bail, snatch him before he gets a chance to leave a note. *That's* important."

"How so?" he asked.

"Because if he's any sort of decent father and husband, he'll know that his family's worried sick about him. That'll discombobulate him, and you can pump him for information while he's off his game."

"I doubt that would be enough to throw him," said one old magus—a gray-haired stranger with a strong Australian accent. "Whatever else can be said for him, he *was* grand magus."

"But was he any good at it?" Kenna countered. "Also, that was twenty-five years ago. He's married now. He's got kids to think about, right?"

"True," said Ed.

She smiled grimly. "So how do you suppose he's going to react once he realizes that the sleepwalkers can track his kids? I mean, maybe he's a lousy father," she allowed, "but *my* dad moved to the middle of nowhere to do the best thing for me. If Leander's half as good as he is, then he'll do what's necessary to protect his family. Offer him amnesty," she suggested to Ed. "Tell him you'll train his kids and won't keep him in a dungeon for the rest of his life if he cooperates. Surely he knows where to find some of your missing wizards—maybe even Eva and Francine. Could be a starting point."

Kenna settled back in her chair, a little pink in the face, but Ed sipped his coffee and considered her suggestion. "I like it," he finally said. "I think that's a workable plan. Any opposed?"

"You're entitled to your opinion," said the old Australian magus down the table, "but I hardly think you have the right to call for votes. You're not even a member of the Council."

An uncomfortable silence fell over the table when Ed turned to stare him down. As the man began to shift in his chair, Ed quietly said, "I am Simon *fucking* Magus. I built the Arcanum. And because its most recent crop of illustrious magi have proven catastrophically inept at choosing a leader, I'm stepping in to superintend for now. Have you got a problem with that, or do you and I need to step outside and settle our differences…Norleigh, was it?"

"Connor Norleigh," Toula offered.

"Well?" Ed pressed. "Do we need a private moment, Magus Norleigh?"

He silently shook his head.

"Good."

"Perhaps the Arcanum can deal with its internal…*hiccups*…at a later time," Arik interjected. "Looking around this table, I must say I'm pleasantly shocked to find us unified behind a common purpose."

"Common enemies are useful like that," Val replied.

"True. Still," he continued, folding his hands on the tabletop, "I hope this sort of communication, if not cooperation, can be continued once we lack an enemy to neutralize."

As the talk turned, Dec and I excused ourselves,

leaving Raurit and Edie to eavesdrop in peace. Dec sneaked us back to Faerie, and Gaw materialized as soon as the gate was closed. "Ugh," he muttered, rubbing his neck. "Being quiet that long gets on my nerves."

I frowned. "You could have talked to me."

"It's harder past the border, especially without an open gate nearby. And since I'm going to be twitchy until the Three are back, you don't want me griping in your head."

"How do you think it's going?" Dec asked.

"Pretty well. Kenna seemed to hold her own," said Gaw, then folded his arms. "She's right—Leander's not the main target. Ed and the rest can use him however they like, but I want Francine and Eva *dealt* with."

Dec shrugged. "I think that's the common sentiment…"

"That may be, but I'm going to make myself perfectly clear when the Three return. Those two tried to kill my mom—this is personal."

I thought I caught a flicker of guilt in his eyes when he glanced my way, but if he'd expected me to protest, he was disappointed. Eva might have been my grandmother, but given the way she'd treated my mom and Beth—not to mention the time she'd tried to flat-out murder Maria—I felt no compulsion to beg for mercy on her behalf.

"We'll find them," I murmured, and rubbed Gaw's back. "I'll be sure to tell Kenna when I see her."

"Don't worry about it," he said with a little smirk. "As long as the Three are here, they *have* to hear me out."

CHAPTER 20

The meeting in Alaska didn't break up until close to eight a.m. local time, when the sleepwalkers, who'd been working all night, began to crash. For Kenna, however, there was no respite. As soon as they returned to Faerie, Coileán and Avus took her out for a training session in the dark, it having become evident to all three that practice time was drawing to a rapid conclusion. At least we'd had a rest day for most of Monday, as they pushed on through her exhaustion until dawn. When I wandered into the dining room for breakfast Tuesday morning, I found her slumped in a chair, inhaling scrambled eggs like she hadn't eaten in a week.

I'd hoped to avoid her fate, but my luck had turned. With the Alaska group taking a wait-and-see approach to Leander and continuing the hunt for wayward wizards, Avus crashed for a few hours, but Coileán found time to squeeze me into his morning schedule—and the work he'd done with Kenna the night before only seemed to have warmed him up. His bolts came hard and fast, but my shields were improving, and by midmorning, the land around us was pocked with craters from his deflected shots.

"Tighten up your aim," he said during a water-break critique. "You're not playing horseshoes." Wincing, he rolled his shoulders—I'd given his shield a workout as well—then suggested, "What if we put the physical lessons on hold for a bit and worked on glamour? Far less painful."

"If you need me to go easy on you, just say so."

My shield materialized an instant after the bolt left his hand, and I laughed as it fizzled out against a tree. "Don't get cocky, girl," he chided, but he grinned as he tugged my ponytail. "Incidentally, Mina told me about your little stunt at the settlement yesterday morning."

I braced myself for a rebuke but tried not to let on. "She didn't like my form, huh?"

"Actually, I believe the phrasing was 'unexpectedly terrifying.' Flying fireball? That's your response to a riot?"

"It worked, didn't it?"

Coileán paused for a long drink of water, then pulled a sweat towel from the ether and dabbed at his neck. "Lots of bad solutions 'work,' Cici. If a light goes out, you can change the bulb, or you can throw the whole lamp away and buy a new one. But you're not going to chuck the lamp unless there's a problem in the wiring that you can't fix, right?"

"Yeah…" I mumbled.

"And throwing it out wouldn't be the first step. Start small and escalate."

"You weren't there!" I protested. "There was a mob outside town, and Gaw said the shield wasn't great—"

"I got the play-by-play," he said, cutting me short. "All I'm suggesting is that you wait for your opponent to escalate before you go into 'burning death' mode. Some problems only require the threat of consequences to be resolved, especially where there are political considerations. Okay?"

I nodded and drained my water bottle. When I came up for air, however, I found Coileán watching me with a curious expression.

"You know, I used to get on Greg Harrison's nerves *so* badly," he said. "Poor guy became grand magus in"—he squinted at the puffy clouds in thought—"1970, I think it was, and we started crossing paths. He didn't mind me most of the time, especially since I was handling faerie issues before they could affect the Arcanum, but our methods didn't always align. Greg was slow to act, cautious. He had the Arcanum's welfare to consider, of course, but he also had to keep the Council happy if he wanted to hold on to his position, and sometimes, balancing those interests wasn't as easy as it should have been. Me?" He shrugged. "All I had to do was take care of myself. My mother seldom bothered me directly, your great-grandmother was nowhere to be found, and Oberon was down in the Keys, trying to be Jimmy Buffett without a guitar. In other words, most of the time, I could punch as hard as I wanted to without major repercussions."

"Nice."

"Well, yes and no. Once I took the throne, Greg finally decided to clue me in to Aiden's existence, and I saw that the poor kid was an ambulatory punching bag. I protested, and Greg gave me this spiel about how I'd been acting like Batman for too long, while he was the mayor of Gotham with civic responsibilities to consider beyond crimefighting. He'd let Aiden grow up in a shitty situation because that seemed like the most political solution to the problem of basically finding a high lord in a basket on his doorstep. I didn't buy it."

I thought of Dec's uncle, who'd made us learn to build computers when we were thirteen and was the first to step in whenever our playground arguments turned physical. Aiden was gentle with us, a touch on the geeky side, and always eager to show us new video games. I could see where Coileán might be upset to find that he'd been abused.

"But I was new to leadership, and Greg had been at it for forty-odd years by then," Coileán continued. "In retrospect, he wasn't entirely full of shit."

That took me aback. "*Huh?*"

"Oh, he was still an asshole for what he allowed to happen to Aid," he assured me, "but he did make a good point, and now that I've had time to see life from the mayoral perspective, shall we say, I understand where he was coming from. The thing is—and I'm not sure that Greg ever came to terms with this—Gotham needed both sides."

My eyebrows rose.

"Any regular town would be ill-served by having a masked vigilante running amok at night, smacking around ne'er-do-wells with thematic weaponry. Let the police do their jobs, eh? But Gotham's not an ordinary town—it's beset by an incredibly high number of criminals with some combination of superpowers, money, and good old-fashioned psychopathy, and there's not much the police can do against, say, a mastermind with a giant freeze ray. So while the mayor may well be annoyed, Gotham needs the guy who jumps in at a moment's notice and fights crazy with crazy."

"Okay…" I allowed.

"What I'm getting at, the long way around, is that Greg was bound by rules and considerations that didn't apply to me, and I could step in quickly when he couldn't. He didn't always approve of my methods, but he knew that, more or less, we were working toward similar ends. A few decades later, I'm now in a position like Greg's, and I'll be honest, kid, it *chafes*," he said with a soft chuckle. "Your grandfather's in the same boat, and Kenna's climbing aboard. The thing you need to understand is that sometimes, no matter how much one of us wants to leap into action, we have to stop and think about the ramifications."

I folded my arms. "Like not killing Leander when he was grand magus?"

"You had to go there, didn't you?" he muttered.

Shrugging, I said, "Isn't that the textbook example of being overly cautious?"

Coileán gestured, and a pair of stools appeared for us. Sinking onto one, he replied, "The Leander situation was a series of bad events, all hitting at once. Irem killed Ellie and set that court loose, which led to a child abduction. Toula stepped in and handled it off the books, but word got back to the Council, and the magi who'd been looking for a reason to get rid of her for years used that as a pretense. Leander was a dumb little shit looking to make a name for himself and taking advice from all the wrong people, and that landed us in Alaska."

"But you could have stopped him," I pointed out. "Don't tell me he's stronger than you are."

"He's not. Toula could easily have taken him out—hell, Maria probably could have managed it. But assassinating the grand magus with one court already running wild would only have made matters worse between us and the Arcanum. Val, Toula, and I were trying to preserve the peace. In retrospect…" He made a face. "Maybe we should have taken him out. Maybe Ed should have found a way to get out of his arrangement with the Minor Arcanum and take office by force. Or we could have blown up Arc 2—that would have put a temporary stop to the problem."

I had to smile at the absurdity.

"The events that led to the closure were a grade-A cluster, and I'm not going to sit here and say we did everything right. We've had years to think about our mistakes. But look at what Ed's doing now—he's assumed control, sure, but he's bringing everyone to the table and trying to find a solution to the problem of a generation of untrained wizards who are about to wake up and discover magic. We're under no obligation to play along," he continued. "It's the Arcanum that got the community into this mess. Conota has a grievance, *we* certainly do, the Minors have a grudge going back to Ed's first life…if we worked together, we could wipe out every Arcanum member on the face of the planet and let their kids stumble through magic on their own. It'd be nice to never again have to face an organization that thinks the only good faerie is a dead one. But as I see it, this is the best solution. The *safest* solution. I don't want unnecessary wars, Cici. You think I want to see you and Dec in the front lines?"

"Mina might complain if you tried to put us there."

He rolled his eyes. "Mina's only hard on you kids because she knows you can handle it. Take the pain as a compliment. Anyway, all of that said…you need to understand that there are times when the three of us and Ed and Arik and the rest can't act. Not because we don't want to, but because we have to balance the consequences. Sometimes, the mayor's hands are tied, you know?"

I studied his face. "But?"

"*But*," he echoed, and slowly smiled as he held my gaze. "From time to time, Gotham needs Batman. Understand?"

I nodded.

"Good. And should you tell Val that we ever had this conversation, I'll deny everything." Winking, he stood and returned his stool to the ether. "All right, ready to tackle glamour?"

Before I could answer him, a flash of lightning heralded the opening of a gate, and I turned to see Kenna limp through, freshly showered and wrapped in sloppy healing enchantment—her own work, I suspected. "Hi," she said, and peered at me. "What, no blood? What sort of training *is* this?"

"There wouldn't be blood during yours if you were quicker on the draw," Coileán replied. "Need something?"

"Actually, yeah. Can I borrow Cici for a bit?"

"Well, we were working," he began, then paused to stifle a yawn. "I could do with a nap, I suppose. How long do you need her?"

"Couple hours?" She flashed me her best pleading smile.

"Sleep is very important to a healthy body and clear mind," I told Coileán with mock gravity, and rose from my stool to follow Kenna. "I'd hate for you to do without on my account."

He snorted. "Such magnanimity. Fine, go on," he said, waving us on our way. "You're not hurting my feelings."

Kenna grabbed my wrist and pulled me through the gate, which deposited us in a lush meadow atop an apparent cliff. I could see the ocean before me—the smell of salt on the breeze was a dead giveaway—and I watched a pair of seabirds dip as Kenna closed the gate. "Nice spot," I said, turning around. "Are we picnicking today or...*oh*. Oh, my."

The cliff extended for quite a ways behind us, an elevated peninsula above the western sea. An avenue lined with mature oaks began near the base of the peninsula and cut through the middle of the headland, but before it could reach the edge of the cliff, it ran smack into a godawful pink palace. The monstrosity perched at the end of the lane like a translucent plastic dollhouse castle blown far out of proportion.

"Hideous, isn't it?" said Kenna, glaring at the cotton-candy confection. "It's made entirely of rose quartz. I took the self-guided tour and got lost three times, since the floorplan makes zero sense, but there's a huge throne room. Still...*ugh*."

"Whose is that?" I asked.

"Mine. Irem razed Ellie's mansion, which apparently was still massive and overdone with marble but less...*pink*," she said, scrunching her nose, "and she put that up in its place."

"Jesus," I muttered.

"Jesus wept, more like. I need your help."

"With what? Paint?"

"I wouldn't like it any better in beige." Turning to me, she said, "Keep this quiet for the moment, but I need to call my court, and I want to do it tomorrow...but I *really* need a suitable base of operations first, and there's no way in hell that I'm settling in there."

"I don't know. Could be a starter palace," I teased. "A little fixer-upper."

"Do you *want* me to push you off the cliff?"

I leapt, putting about ten feet of air between us. "Got to catch me first. But seriously, what can I do?"

"I mean, you can start by helping me blast that thing…"

Working in tandem, we reduced Irem's palace to a pile of pink rubble within a minute, and a final burst from me rendered it a mound of glittery sand. As the palace began to blow away over the water, I said, "Now what?"

"Now," Kenna replied, "I've got to figure out what to put there. Any ideas?"

"I don't know, but that's a nice little pond behind the debris—"

"*Focus*, Cici. I've never built a house before! Like…where do you begin? Something in brick? Stone? I could build a castle out of literal diamonds, you know."

"You *could*," I said, "but why?"

"Exactly! But I've got to put something up that's sufficiently impressive if I want any shot at convincing the court that I'm not completely in over my head, so…ideas?"

I considered the cloud of quartz drifting off to sea for a moment, then nodded. "Yeah, I've got an idea. Stay here."

"Where are you going?"

"Just wait." Carefully, I opened a gate to the settlement and slipped through.

A quick enquiry at the wall led me to a high-ceilinged office building off the main square, where Robbie Stowe kept his studio. He looked up from his paper-strewn desk as I entered to the tinkling of the overhead bell. The second-eldest of Mal's uncles wasn't a large man, brown-haired like Ned but thinner and with a kindly twinkle in his dark eyes. "Hello, Cici," he began, tossing paperweights onto the corners of a set of plans. "What brings you out here?"

"I heard you'd been slammed," I replied, taking in the exposed brick and gray wooden floors. A pair of blue, brass-studded leather armchairs occupied the space in front of Robbie's long mahogany desk—which seemed closer to a table, given its dimensions—and an abstract copper chandelier hung overhead. The place had a decidedly masculine feel to its decoration, though not aggressively so.

"And how. So many homes and buildings here suffered damage during the closure. They were repaired when Gaw did his thing, but all of that breaking and shaking has given people an opportunity to reconsider their design choices. To be fair, there are houses here I've not touched in seventy years, so they're due for an upgrade. Tea?" he asked, nodding to the black kettle on a repurposed end table behind him. Twenty-five years in Alaska had done little to alter Robbie's British accent or his love of the national brew.

"I'm fine, thanks," I told him. "But I've got a rush job if you could spare the time today."

One eyebrow quirked. "How rushed are we talking?"

"Needs to be finished by tonight. And, uh…it's *big*."

"Well, I don't mind taking a look." Grabbing a leather binder from his desk, he gestured toward the door. "Lead on."

I opened a gate back to the cliffs, and with a bemused frown, Robbie followed me through. When he stepped across, he glanced from Kenna in her T-shirt, leggings, and smudged turquoise glasses to the rapidly dwindling sand pile, then stiffened. "Is that…*was* that…Irem's palace?"

Sealing the gate, I said, "Robbie, we're going to swear you to secrecy, okay?"

"I can swear to whatever you like, girls, but once Irem returns, she won't have much difficulty learning what you've done—"

"She's not coming back," Kenna interrupted. Before Robbie could argue, her corona flared, and he retreated two steps toward the nonexistent gate.

"Like I said, we're swearing you to secrecy," I told him.

He pointed to Kenna, tried to speak, then cleared his throat and managed, "*You?*"

"Surprise," she muttered.

"My lady. I, ehm…this is certainly unexpected…"

"Here's the situation," I said, interrupting his mumbling. "Kenna needs a residence. I know you guys all switched allegiance to Coileán when Irem took over, but you're the only architect we have, and…"

"Please?" Kenna asked with a hopeful smile.

"We're not trying to cause trouble," I continued, "and if you could throw something together, we'll give you whatever oomph you need to erect it."

Robbie ran one hand up and down over his chin in agitated contemplation as he considered the site. "Let me get this straight," he finally said. "You want me to design a *palace?*"

"Whatever you like," Kenna replied. "As long as I can have it by morning and it's not tacky."

"Dear girl," he said, giving her a long look down his nose, "I don't *do* tacky."

She grinned up at him. "So you'll do it?"

"Of course I will. One doesn't get the opportunity to design a bloody palace every day."

"I'll be happy to explain to Coileán—"

"There's nothing to explain. You may not be my queen," said Robbie, "but you've been one of the kids underfoot for the last two decades. If you need a palace, I'll put one together." A table appeared before him with a gesture, followed by a stack of long paper and a neat pile of pencils. "Right, let's start with the important questions. Are you thinking something more along the lines of Balmoral or Versailles? Or do you want a properly defensible castle?"

"Uh…" She glanced from the blank pages to Robbie's expectant face. "Do you have any pictures?"

He huffed a soft sigh. "You've got no idea what you want, have you?"

"None whatsoever."

"Well, at least you're honest, my lady. And here," he said, pulling a soft cloth from thin air. "Clean your glasses. I can't show you details if you've got fingerprints all over the lenses."

As Robbie had the palatial problem well in hand, I took my leave and returned to training with Coileán after lunch. He chuckled when I explained the crisis. "I wouldn't deny Robbie the opportunity to build something that grand," he said, pouring a drink at his office bar. "No need for pointless cruelty. Thirsty?"

"Just water, please."

He *tsk*ed but brought me a glass as he joined me with his bourbon. I hadn't expected to resume training in Coileán's office—personally, I wouldn't have trusted me not to set a fire—but he felt confident enough that I wouldn't destroy his nice couches with only glamour on the schedule.

The afternoon passed painlessly for a change, albeit awkwardly as I tried to manage the increasingly complex illusions Coileán dreamed up, and he smiled when he called a break. "You're doing well," he said, refreshing his tumbler. "Excellent progress all around."

"You don't have to flatter me," I replied, rubbing my forehead as a headache threatened.

"I'm not blowing smoke, kid. If you were flailing, I'd tell you, but you seem to be intuiting nicely. Reassuring, that," he added, and drank. "This is the start of a new day for us all."

"Sure. If you three can work with Ed and the Fringe and Arik's folks, all at the same time—"

"Oh, that's good, but it's not what I was talking about."

Putting his glass on the coffee table between us, he sat forward and held my stare...which, considering the age in his eyes, was more than mildly disconcerting. Coileán might have been Dec's dad to me, but there was no getting around the fact of what *else* he was.

"The most powerful being in this realm, bar none, is now Gawain," he said. "The most powerful being who's not a manifestation of the very soul of Faerie is you, Cici—Gaw confirmed it," he added before I could protest. "And since the two of you are assumedly on the same team, that's a lot of weight you're slinging around."

"We don't *always* agree…"

"You say that, but if it comes down to choosing, oh, Val or his girlfriend? Come on, I'll give you one guess as to where Gaw's loyalty lies," he said, smirking. "So that's you two. Kenna's one of us now, so that's an entire court in her corner, and if Ed has his way, Edie will be grand magus in a few years. Kid, that's a *massive* power bloc, and that's before Dec tells me I've screwed up and drags Aurie in for good measure."

"Again," I said, "it's not like we always move in lock-step."

"Naturally. I've seen you fight," he said, "but you fight like *siblings*. You may have your internal squabbles, but if someone from Leander's wing of the Arcanum were to pick on Edie, I'm fairly confident that the rest of you would present a united front. Hell, you're all blood, anyway."

"Gaw and I aren't—"

"Not you two directly, but everyone in your little clique is tied together. You and Edie are first cousins, you and Dec are first cousins once removed, Dec and Aurie are first cousins twice removed, and both of them are distant cousins to Gaw…uh…" He frowned and started counting on his fingers, then gave up. "Gaw's my fourth great-grandnephew. You do the math. And Gaw and Kenna are cousins, too, through Oberon. You're *family*, and incredibly for a family with so much fae blood, it seems like you genuinely love each other."

"Well…yeah," I admitted.

"Beats the alternative," he said, lifting his glass. "But it does put the rest of us in an unusual position."

We're not planning a coup yet, Gaw interrupted.

"Oh, good."

Though if the rest of them want to move farther away than Anchorage, I don't think you get a vote anymore.

Coileán sipped and smiled to himself. "You're forgetting something, kid. We've got access to gates and blood traces now. Unless they go to Conota, we *can* find them—and if they got that far, I'm pretty sure Arik and Hope would lend a hand."

You're going to let Dec live a little, Coileán.

"Hey, I've agreed to send him to Ed. Give me some credit."

And how much of that was Toula's doing? He's an adult—you can't keep him locked in his bedroom forever.

Coileán looked at me again and sighed. "See what I mean, Cici? *Brand* new day."

The first glow of dawn had just sneaked past my curtains on Wednesday morning when I heard Kenna's voice echo across my mind: *Come. Your queen commands it.*

"The hell?" I mumbled into my pillow.

Sorry, said Gaw. *That wasn't aimed at you. More of a general message.*

I groaned and rolled over. "She's up early."

She barely slept last night and threw up once, but the new palace is nice. Robbie's good.

"Mm. What happens now?"

I've sent the message out into the mortal realm, so with any luck, the stragglers will make their way back across. Her palace is open, so her court can stop in to meet the new queen, and she'll address them later today. He laughed to himself. *Poor Ennis is trying so hard to be supportive. He got up hours ago and made Kenna breakfast—Robbie got a couple Stowes in to stock the kitchen—but she's too nervous to eat. So that's Ennis stuck with a mound of chocolate-chip pancakes, and he's currently chowing down with Nico, who is not complaining.*

"Shouldn't Nico be making sure Kenna doesn't get shot?" I asked.

Eh, no one's arrived yet, and Nico's got a long day ahead of him. Since he's in charge of keeping Kenna unperforated, Ennis doesn't mind feeding him. At least someone's enjoying breakfast, he added wistfully.

"You make it sound like you can't materialize and steal food."

It would be rude to poach.

"Poor baby."

Burrowing deeper into the mattress, I closed my eyes and tried to drift off. But before I could slip back to sleep, Avus's summons jolted me out of the pleasant twilight. "*Why?*" I whined, staring at the mosaic ceiling in the dusky light. "Why does it have to be freaking sunrise?"

Coileán's next on deck, so you may as well give up on sleeping in, Gaw replied. *Shower?*

"Is that a suggestion for my well-being, or are you angling for an invitation?"

If you'd like company…

"Perv," I said, throwing off the blankets. "All right, I'm going to go steam up the bathroom. You coming?"

He manifested with a towel around his waist, then kissed me good morning. "I'll get the water hot. Just shuffle in here whenever you make it out of bed."

By eight, Avus's villa's central courtyard was swarming with the returned. A few I knew from Alaska, but many were strangers to me, faeries who'd run when the realm collapsed and struggled alone without magic. I overheard snippets of conversations as I walked around the courtyard, nibbling canapés to distract myself from the sheer insanity of the event.

Avus—a man who'd told me bedtime stories and

taught me to navigate by the stars during the long winter nights, who'd taped my crayon drawings to his fridge and read over my college essays for the fun of it—looked positively regal. He wore a dark tunic and pants, nothing flashy, and he didn't seem to have a crown. Then again, judging by the glances people gave him, the deferential radius, and the murmured *my lord*s, he didn't need one. He carried himself with calm confidence and welcomed newcomers with politeness, if not effusive warmth, and when he seated himself on the throne in the middle of the courtyard, the crowd fell silent to hear him speak.

Honestly, it was bizarre, but the truly awkward part of the morning was yet to come. As Avus concluded his remarks, he made a point to draw the court's attention to Pa, Mom, and Maria…and then to me, where I skulked near a table of wines in a long-sleeved dress. I wanted to blend into the gardens around me when so many eyes turned my way, but I forced myself to wave, then hid behind a pillar as soon as their attention had shifted elsewhere.

Once Avus finished and rose to work the room again, I tried to sneak out, but the going was slow. I could barely make it a few feet before someone else in the court wanted to stop me for a word—and the *my lady* refrain soon left me on the edge of either hysterical laughter or snapping, and I wasn't sure which.

Finally, I made it back to my room, locked the door, and snatched my phone off the bedside table to call Dec. He answered on the fifth ring, and I could hear the muted sounds of a crowd on his end of the call as well. "Cici?"

"Oh, my God, this is so weird," I said.

"*Thank* you! I thought I was the only one." A door slammed behind him, and I heard rapid footsteps on stone. "Sorry, I had to get out of there. The throne room's fancy, but the reverberation is pretty bad."

"We have snacks."

"Yeah, Astrid put out a spread, but Mom told me it

would be poor form for me to hang out by the bar, so…"
He exhaled loudly. "*Shit*."

"That bad, huh?" I asked, flopping onto my bed.

"I mean, it wasn't torture or anything, but I think it's
finally hitting me that I'm next in line for a fucking throne,
and…you know?" he finished lamely.

"You're in line for two, don't forget. After Pa and me,
it either goes to Maria or your mom, and then—"

"*Stop*," he begged. "At least you've got your dad as a
buffer. I'll be honest with you—I don't think I'm cut out
for this faerie prince gig."

"Same." I rested my free arm over my eyes and listened
to the muted noise of Avus's court beyond the walls. "You
want to sneak off?"

"Thought you'd never ask. Where to?"

"Is Aurie there?"

"Yeah…"

"Grab her and meet me in the field outside the villa.
We're going to crash Kenna's party."

Five minutes later, Dec, Aurie, and I joined the stream of
latecomers wandering up the oak-lined lane toward the
palace on the headland.

"Robbie built that *yesterday*?" Aurie asked in disbelief.

I took in the new construction—graceful,
symmetrically placed limestone towers topped with
burnished copper, walls studded with tall, arched windows,
a gate wide enough to admit a small airplane—and
nodded. "He's good."

"Mom said he's a master mason," Dec offered. "Not
the Scottish Rite kind—he actually apprenticed as a
stonemason once upon a time."

"I'd believe it." Nudging Aurie in the good arm, I
asked, "How's the fam?"

"It's all a little awkward," she replied after a moment's
thought. "Georgie's eager to reconcile with Dad, Dad's

twitchy, Dad's siblings are giving him a *wide* berth, and poor Ros and Granddad are trying to mediate. But my cousins and I are okay," she added, brightening. "Neve's kids, I mean. "It's possible that Horus and Rego have fathered kids, but they don't have anything to do with them."

"Nice guys," Dec muttered.

"They're playing by different rules. Doesn't make it any less distasteful, but acknowledgement is a path to understanding, right? Anyway, Neve's got five kids. They're two years older than me, but physically, they're three, and they're still adolescents…which is weird," she admitted, "and they're not quite sure how to deal with my missing limbs, but since I'm the only one of us who can throw fireballs, they've decided I'm not intolerable. Come with me to the barn sometime—I'll introduce you."

"Are *you* okay, though?" I pressed.

Aurie grinned. "Not going to lie, clothes itch after a few days in the buff, but…" She shrugged and nudged me in turn. "Could be worse. No one's tried to kill me yet, so I count that as a win."

Soon, we passed through the massive gate and into the courtyard of Kenna's new palace, which was already beautifully landscaped. Following the crowd, we headed inside, up a flight of stairs, down a few corridors laid with thick rugs and hung with tasteful tapestries, and finally reached the throne room, a space with a soaring ceiling, at least a dozen chandeliers, and a delicate golden throne set on a high dais against the back wall.

"Well, damn," Dec whispered, snagging a shrimp off a table of hors d'oeuvres. "This is…different."

And so was Kenna. Dressed in a dark blue gown with a train that wouldn't have seemed out of place on a red carpet, she wore her brown hair in an upswept style held in place with golden ornaments. A coordinating necklace—sapphires set in gold—filled the space left by her fairly conservative neckline. Then again, Kenna had little chest to speak of, and achieving deep cleavage would have required a feat of either engineering or enchantment. But what struck me even more than her dangling sapphire earrings—this from a woman who seldom sported more than studs—and matching tiara was the absence of her familiar glasses with their bright resin frames. She'd exchanged them for a pair of frameless oval lenses held together by a thin gold bridge, and they perched on her face without earpieces. Unless the light glinted off the glass, her eyewear seemed to disappear.

I smiled to myself at her handiwork. With her lifelong host of ocular issues, Kenna had never tolerated contacts, and she had to find the new glasses somewhat freeing.

"Hi, guys!" said a familiar voice—in English, which sounded odder the longer I hung out in Faerie—and I turned to find Ennis approaching, a mug of coffee in his hand. Though the court seemed to have no problem with day drinking, I laughed to myself that the winemaker apparently found the hour too early. "I didn't know you were coming," he said, giving us brief, one-armed hugs in turn. "Kenna's going to be thrilled," he added, dropping his voice barely above a whisper. "Poor kid's been worried sick about this. So...did we escape our own festivities?" he asked with a conspiratorial wink.

"We needed air," Dec told him. "And, uh…"

"Yeah?"

"Don't take this the wrong way," he said in a rush, "but I'm kind of surprised to see you, um…here…"

Ennis laughed. "I wasn't planning on it. Maria explained what was going on, and I was going to hide out at the settlement today in case of collateral damage—I got the warning spiel about what can happen when there's a critical mass of faeries."

"You could have stayed at Avus's," I protested. "There's plenty of room to avoid people."

"Oh, sure, but there's a *nice* little coffee shop in town, and I forgot how much I missed those…" He shook his head, snapping himself back on track. "Anyway, Kenna asked me to be here, and if she wants her old man around, I'm not going to say no. How's Maria holding up?" he asked me.

"Still alive and making nice with the court, last I saw."

"Good to know. We're sneaking off to town for dinner, once the ceremonial stuff's over—I owe her a proper date night, and at least three Stowes swear there's a quality Italian restaurant."

"Not afraid of what the actual Italian will think?" Aurie teased.

"The woman eats frozen deep-dish and mozzarella sticks. I'm not overly concerned." Glancing to his left, he spotted Kenna and waved to her. "Look who stopped by!"

Kenna swept across the stone floor toward us and offered us a polite, oddly reserved smile. "I wasn't expecting to see you here today," she said in Fae as Dec hurriedly swallowed the last of his pilfered shrimp. "Is something wrong?"

"Came to see the new place," I replied. "Sorry, we didn't bring a housewarming gift…"

An apparent aide appeared at Kenna's elbow and gave the three of us a brief once-over, then spared a glance for Ennis. "My lady, shall I escort these uninvited—"

Kenna held up a hand to stop her. "That won't be necessary. Lady Cecilia, Lord Declan, Lady Aurora…my office, if you will." Segueing into English, she added, "Back in a few minutes, Dad."

The aide stepped aside, and we followed Kenna across the throne room, out a side door, and through a gate she opened in the middle of the hall. On the other side was a spacious office. To the left, an abstract stained glass window cast a shimmering rainbow onto her blonde wooden desk. The right side of the room included a trio of curving blue couches around a raised glass firepit filled with aqua-colored stones. A modest bar sat against the far wall—nothing nearly as impressive as Coileán's, which could give a pub a run for its money—and some of the shelf space was occupied not with bottles, but rather with tins of coffee beans and loose tea.

Kenna closed the gate, locked the office door, then plucked a pillow off the nearest couch, held it over her face, and screamed.

"And *there* she is," said Aurie. "I was wondering."

"You're doing well," said Gaw as he appeared behind her and patted her shoulder. "And you can kick them out soon. Just ply them with booze and send them on their way."

"You look really polished," I offered. "The tiara's a nice touch."

She groaned into her therapy pillow.

"Hang on," said Dec, "I'll make this better." He opened a gate into his dad's office, slipped to the bar, and returned with a bottle of amber liquor. "There, housewarming gift. He'll never miss it. Should I put a bow on this or start pouring?"

"Double for me," she muttered, and waved one hand toward her little bar. "Glasses are over there. Get a couple extra down, eh?"

"You're expecting more company?" he asked, heading over to fix the drinks. "And do you have ice?"

"Robbie fixed the copper bucket so it keeps refilling itself, and maybe." Reaching into the folds of her gown, she pulled her phone from a hidden pocket and dialed. "Hi, Edie? Sorry, did I wake you?"

"Nah, I'm in the castle, teaching Raurit how to play poker," she replied through the tinny speaker. "Why, what's up?"

"You want to come drink with us? Raurit, too—heck, if he's willing to jump in an RV and drive halfway across the freaking continent, he gets an invitation."

"Sure. Can you make a gate to that empty magus office I used? We've commandeered it for poker night."

Kenna did the honors, and Edie laughed aloud when

she saw her. "Didn't know there was a dress code," she said, slipping across the border in her flannel pajama pants and Seawolves sweatshirt. "What's going on?"

"Called our courts," she replied, and pointed to Dec. "He'll hook you up."

Dec hoisted the bottle in salute, and Edie grinned. "Is this the new wardrobe?" she teased. "Faerie princess couture?"

"*Hell*, no. This is going in the very back of the closet as soon as the palace is empty. And this is my new palace," she said offhandedly. "Came with a bonus tiara."

"Maybe we could move poker night here," Raurit suggested, accepting a glass from Dec. "Feels odd…"

"Lack of useable magic," said Edie.

"Obviously. But as long as no one cheats…"

I helped Dec pass the remaining glasses around, then lifted mine. "To not killing each other."

We drank to that, and Kenna lifted hers in turn. "To an end to the increasingly obnoxious 'faerie princess' jokes."

"Come on," said Gaw, chuckling, "you started those."

"And I *deeply* regret it," she replied through clenched teeth. "Truce?"

The rest of us turned to Edie, who smirked and raised her glass. "I suppose I could be merciful."

CHAPTER 21

We had barely polished off the bottle, and Dec was already talking about sneaking back to his dad's stash for more, when Edie's phone rang. She glanced at the readout and frowned as she answered, turning on the speaker mode. "Hey, Mom. I'm over at Kenna's new place, don't worry."

"Hi, Beth!" Kenna called from the couch where she'd sprawled in her finery.

"Hi, yourself, Kenna," Beth replied. "And Edie, honey, you might want to get back over here. Like, *now*."

Edie's brow furrowed. "Am I in trouble?"

"No, no," Beth hastily reassured her. "Bert and a few of the other magi just returned from Chicago with Leander. Your dad said he was trying to sneak out of the house in the middle of the night, and they grabbed him before he got to the train station. Little weasel looks like he's about to shit himself."

"You've seen him?"

"Yeah, when they hauled him in. Interrogation's going to be in the conference room, if you kids want to watch."

As we traded looks, Beth's chuckling broke the awkward silence. "The privacy wards around the conference room are *just* visible if you concentrate. I noticed the faint glowing when someone with a wand—and I'm not naming names, Edith Hilda—made changes, and then Toula and I found your hidey hole."

"Shit," Edie whispered, holding the phone well away from her.

"Look, the bottom line is that your dad is *well* aware of

what you're up to, but he doesn't mind—for now—as long as you keep it quiet. And he's absolutely tightening the wards once he gets a moment to breathe again, so don't get used to this."

Edie hesitated, then said, "So…we can watch the interrogation?"

"Your father thought it might be educational," Beth replied with a little smirk in her voice. "Come on over. He doesn't mind."

When Edie hung up, Kenna sighed and pushed herself off the couch. "I should probably get back to my own party," she mumbled. "You guys have fun without me, but I want a full report."

"I'll give you the highlights once they get back," Gaw promised, and shooed us on our way. "Go on. I'll tell your folks where you are."

I kissed him as Edie opened a gate, and the five of us without pressing business in Faerie slipped across the border to watch the show.

We secreted ourselves in the forgotten closet with no time to spare. Edie had barely triggered the visualization spell when two middle-aged wizards—not magi, I assumed, but maybe former Council aides—marched Leander into the conference room and sat him at the table. "The grand magus will be with you shortly," one of them snapped, and they exited, leaving Leander alone at the big table.

He looked…disappointing.

I'd grown up on the story of how young Leander Kirby, with his disarmingly charming smile and unflappable charisma, had swept into power, kicked Toula and Maria off the Council, thrown anyone who wasn't entirely a wizard out of the castle, tried to have Ed brought up on charges of treason, and then oversaw the disastrous mass spell that had seemingly destroyed Faerie. He'd been a handsome bogeyman in my younger years, a monster hiding behind a mask of blond-haired, blue-eyed wholesomeness.

The man slouched at the table was, at best, a sad shell of the Leander I'd imagined. Oh, he was tall enough and had broad shoulders, but whatever youthful physique he'd once enjoyed had softened into middle age. *This* Leander was in his mid-fifties, his blond hair going gray at the temples, his blue eyes sunken above puffy bags and hidden behind horn-rimmed glasses, his cleft chin partially obscured by his midnight salt-and-pepper scruff. He wore a ratty gray sweatshirt and jeans with well-used sneakers, a far cry from the ceremonial magus robes Maria had described. But what struck me most was the bind on him, a tight network of spellcraft wrapped just above his skin, almost hidden within his natural aura. Leander wasn't handcuffed—bound as he was by magic, the best he could have done in his own defense would be to throw a punch, a poor option in a castle full of pissed-off wizards.

After Leander had been left to stew for a few minutes, the door opened again, and Ed strode in. Given the hour in Alaska, I could understand why he, too, had dressed like he'd thrown on whatever clothes were convenient to step outside in the dark and bring in more firewood. He pulled out a chair near Leander and sat, and the two men eyed each other for a long, quiet moment.

Finally, Leander broke the silence. "Kidnapping? Really?"

His accent sounded vaguely Midwestern, though his voice was gravelly.

"I prefer to think of it as an arrest," said Ed, motioning the coffee tray onto the table between them. "Call it whatever you like. Doesn't matter to me."

"You have no right—"

"Bullshit," Ed snapped. "Incidentally, Faerie's open again, no thanks to you. So…Chicago, eh? Left Glastonbury for a fresh start?"

Leander's jaw clenched as Ed fixed himself a mug. "How'd you find me, anyway?"

"Were you a better student of Arcanum history," he replied, measuring out sugar, "you'd recall that I'm a sleepwalker of *particular* talent."

Though Leander kept his chin high, even I could detect the threat in Ed's calm response. "I heard Simon Magus could kill in his sleep."

"True."

"Then why am I sitting here?"

"Let's just say I've mellowed the second time around. Also, I'd like to give you an opportunity to be useful for the first time in your miserable existence. Coffee?"

Leander hesitated until he saw Ed drink, then reached for the urn and the cream.

"I *am* curious as to what rock you've been hiding beneath all these years," said Ed as Leander poured. "Tell me, how was your time after leaving office? Had to have been better than mine was."

He frowned. "Your hit squad said you'd been in Alaska—"

"No, *before*. I ended my tenure with a nearly five-year stint of torture in Faerie, and as soon as I returned, I retired to Ireland. Ignominious, but I suppose I deserved it. Still," he said, raising his mug, "it was tricky for a while to look Coileán in the eye, considering what his mother did to me in the end." He drank as Leander looked on in bemusement. "Castration. I don't recommend it."

Leander's eyes widened. "You—"

"Got better, but really, it's nothing I'd care to relive. Now, surely Chicago wasn't that bad."

I wasn't sure whether Leander was shaken by Ed's nonchalance or merely thrown by the late hour and his abduction, but he offered Ed a straight answer. "Started over with the money and the credentials the Fringe pulled together," he replied between sips. "I didn't have any marketable skills—not much call for wizards in Chicagoland, especially without any magic to draw upon—so I enrolled in a community college and got an associate degree in IT."

"Useful, I suppose."

"Put food on the table. I got a job, got promoted, made a few lateral moves, met my—"

Ed smiled as Leander's mouth snapped shut. "Your wife? She's pretty. Mundane, certainly, but quite handsome."

Leander stiffened. "I swear, if you hurt her—"

"I have no intention of doing so. She's in IT as well, I gather."

"Manager at another company," he grudgingly revealed.

"And how do you suppose she'll take it when she wakes and finds you gone?" asked Ed. "What will she tell the girls?" A flicker of panic crossed Leander's face, but Ed shook his head. "That's not a threat to your kids. I'm not in the business of killing children. Not anymore, at least."

"I thought they'd be safer if I weren't around," Leander muttered. "In case some maniacs with wands came after me, oh, in the dead of night."

"Well, I gave those so-called maniacs strict orders not to harm the girls, so calm yourself. By the way, they're both wizards."

Leander eyed him suspiciously. "How do you—"

"Know?" Ed finished. "A neat feature of the dream space is that talented individuals seem to glow. Your two are talented—maybe not to the extent you are, but I'd say those are solid wizard signatures. Have you warned them?"

"About what?"

"About magic's return. What's going to happen when one of them gets overly excited or angry and suddenly blows a hole in the wall? I trust you've not trained them."

"Didn't see the point," he muttered into his coffee.

"Too bad—they're dangers to themselves and everyone around them until they learn control. And I assume your lovely bride has no idea that you're a wizard, does she?"

"No."

"Mm. That's bound to be a delightful chat."

Leander stewed for a moment, then glared back at Ed. "Look, you can cut the conversational crap. I'm not afraid of you."

"That's because you're either a liar or an idiot," Ed replied. "I'm leaning toward the former, but if you'd like to sway my mind, by all means, please continue."

"You have no right to haul me in here like I'm some sort of criminal! I'm still the grand magus—"

Ed's cackling killed his protestation. "*You?*" he said once he'd begun to sober, dabbing at the corners of his eyes. "You left us cut off from magic for a quarter-century, and yet you claim the office?"

"At least I was legitimately elected. You have no claim to it."

"The scales are tilting toward the idiot side," said Ed with another chuckle. "Leander, I am *very* much aware of the Ivanovich Rule. Do correct me if I'm mistaken, but when the succession is unclear, any potential grand magus may challenge the other candidates in single combat for the chain. Employed by Alexei Ivanovich and Toula Pavli to great effect, isn't that right?"

"Yeah," Leander grunted.

"In that case, if you'd like to fight me for the office, I'm amenable. But before you act rashly," he said, lowering his voice, "bear in mind that I literally wrote the book on spellcraft. Several of them, in fact. There's also the little matter of my diary to consider. And you should know that I'm stronger now than Simon ever was." He smiled as Leander began to lean away from him. "Funny thing about that rejuvenation spell I threw together. It didn't kill me, it merely…rewound me, for lack of a better term. I may not look it, but for an ostensibly mortal man, I am very, *very* old. And since talent only increases with age…"

By then, Leander looked like he'd rather have had the protection of the table separating them, but Ed's stare pinned him to his seat.

"Since you may, in fact, be an idiot after all, permit me to put this in simple terms," Ed murmured. "I can fuck you up with both hands behind my back. Now, shall I make the arrangements to publicly kick your miserable ass into the next millennium, or will you yield now and save face?"

I glanced at Edie, whose eyes had widened to saucers in the light of the projection's glow. Her surprise was understandable—I could count on one hand the number of times I'd heard Ed even raise his voice. For him to threaten bodily harm with that odd little smile was like discovering that your kindly neighbor had a dozen bodies hidden under the basement floor.

"I'll yield," Leander mumbled.

"Smarter than you look." Ed leaned back in his chair and sipped his coffee. "Here are my terms. You won't be brought up on treason charges, which means you won't face execution. You'll be allowed to live out your life, *unbound*—hell, if you want to return to the castle, I'll find a place for you. And your daughters will be given the wands and training they so desperately need. In return, you'll give me names and addresses. I'll find my targets eventually, but leads would speed the process along."

Leander swallowed hard. "Who do you want?"

"Your supporters, certainly. Any magi still out there who didn't kill themselves once they saw what they'd accomplished. But my first priority is locating Eva Stanhope and Francine Leighton." He smiled and crossed his legs. "I'm all ears."

"There's not much I can tell you," Leander replied. "My supporters scattered, and most of them haven't spoken to me since. I messed up—"

"That's obvious, but what else do you know?"

He sighed and stared grimly into his mug. "I can't tell you where Eva and Francine are. Take a look, if you think I'm lying," he added, tapping his temple. "Not like I can keep you out with a bind on me. But…"

"But?" Ed prompted.

"I, uh…I did meet Francine's daughter some years ago. Professionally. Dahlia Leighton."

"Go on."

"We both work for Bruton Singh," he explained. "It's an international law firm, offices on four continents. She heads up IT for the parent office in London."

"Have you got an address?"

"The main office, yeah, but not Dahlia's place. We're not *that* close. Unless there's a problem, I only talk to her quarterly, when we get on group calls to discuss updates and whether we want to change vendors."

Ed nodded. "Tell me about her."

Leander's cheeks puffed, and he released the breath in a long exhalation as he stared past Ed at the heavy wooden door. "She's about sixty, a few years older than me. Pavli put her on long-term probation when her mother was locked up. I lifted that, but she never came around any of the installations before…you know…"

"You sealed off Faerie?"

His face began to redden. "Yes. That," he said curtly. "Look, Dahlia's not a threat. She hacked into the Arcanum's network during the end of the Conclave era, but that's it. She keeps her nose clean—she's not even a white-hat hacker these days, as far as I know. Never married, no kids, no drama."

"London, you said?"

Leander hesitated. "Hampstead, I think."

"That'll do."

As Ed rose, Leander asked, "When can I go home? I left a note, but Ophelia's going to worry, and she'll call the cops before long…"

"I'd make myself comfortable, were I you," Ed replied. "Nothing personal, but I don't trust you not to make phone calls to people I'd rather surprise. And I wouldn't be concerned about…Ophelia, was it?"

"If she thinks I've been kidnapped—"

"We'll bring her and your daughters here once it's decently morning in their part of the world. No sense in leaving them to wonder about your safety."

Leander's eyes opened wide with alarm. "No, no, that's a *bad* idea. She's going to flip—"

"You need to tell her the truth—might as well do it now and get it over with. And I assure you," he said, leaning over Leander, "man to man, father to father, your children will not be harmed." With that, he walked over to the door and rapped twice, and it opened to reveal a pair of waiting aides. "Take Mr. Kirby to an available suite, please," he told them. "A three-bedroom, if you will. Post a guard."

Leander didn't struggle, and after he was on his way, Ed finished his coffee and tidied the conference room before leaving. A moment after he departed, I heard a knock on the wall behind me, and Edie moved a few stones to find him waiting in the tiny aide's office. "*Really*, kids?" he said, rolling his eyes.

"We're your backup," Edie improvised. "In case he tried to flip the table, you know?"

"Is that so? Well, understand that the wards *will* be tightened in the near future, so don't get any ideas."

"Are you going to bring Dahlia in?"

He glanced at his watch. "It's already a little after seven tomorrow morning in London, I think, so I suspect she's bound for the office. We'll need to wait until night." Stifling a yawn, he said, "I'm going to go sleepwalk and see if I can't track her. Stay out of trouble and be back here after lunch—we'll try to retrieve her then."

"You're inviting us along?" I asked.

"And does Mom know about this?" Edie pressed.

Ed smirked and patted her head. "Simon started conquering the world when he was twenty-four, my girl. I dare say you're old enough to help with one little abduction."

Noon in Alaska was then about three in the morning in Faerie—Gaw promised the day alignment was shifting back toward synchronization, but he couldn't do much to hurry it along—and so I grabbed a nap after dinner while waiting for the appointed hour. My parents weren't thrilled with the news when they caught wind of it from Beth, who was *definitely* not thrilled with her husband's great idea, but they told me to be careful and to listen to my uncle if I truly intended to try my hand at kidnapping. I could tell they wanted to say more—Mom, especially, kept biting her lip and shooting me worried glances over the dinner table—but they held their peace. As for Avus, he simply reminded me that not every problem needed to be solved with fireballs and suggested a waterproof jacket.

The last was solid advice, as the gate Ed opened revealed a quiet street of brick duplexes and apartment buildings, all slick with rain. I considered the precipitation in the glow of the nearest streetlight, then put up my hood and stepped into the drizzle. Frankly, it was a disappointing first impression of England, but as Aurie, Dec, Edie, and I slunk near a wall to hide ourselves in the shadows, Ed remained on the sidewalk, eyes closed and faintly smiling.

It was, I realized, the first time he'd returned to his homeland in decades.

After a moment, Ed joined us, wiped the water off his face, and pointed to the left side of the duplex up ahead. "She's in a semi-detached house, which isn't ideal—I'd prefer distance from the neighbors on all sides—but my snooping suggests that the neighbor with whom she shares a wall is an old woman. Here's hoping she turns off her hearing aids when she goes to bed."

We fell in line behind him like overgrown ducklings, but as we crept up the street, a knot tightened in my gut. I wasn't afraid that we'd be detected—well, I mean, I *worried* about being caught skulking around a nice neighborhood in the middle of the night, but that wasn't the primary source of my anxiety.

My grandmother had been a sort of faceless monster when I was a kid, still young but old enough to ask why Avia came around but my mother's mother never visited. Gradually, I learned about Eva. An ambitious magus in a poorly matched marriage, she'd wound up pregnant with Mom after a one-night stand with a stranger she hadn't known to be fae, then abandoned the baby with her husband half a country away—out of sight, out of mind, and no one the wiser that her child was witch-blooded. But Granddad had died when Mom was ten, shortly after Eva gave birth to her only marital child, Beth, and Eva had sent Mom out of the country to boarding school at Arc 2 in Glastonbury. She'd virtually abandoned Mom, done everything she could to prevent her daughters from forming a relationship, and never lifted a finger when some of the old-blooded kids began bullying Mom to drive the apparent witch out of their midst.

It was Maria who'd come to Mom's rescue when those kids—led by Dahlia Leighton, another magus's daughter—had pummeled Mom until she was black-eyed and bloody. Maria and Mom had named names, and Toula had warned the aggressors against further action…but Dahlia's mother, Francine, had taken offense and broken Mom's arm in class, and she might have killed her had Arnold not arrived in time. Francine was removed from the Council, and her family had run off to Alaska to join the Conclave, a splinter group of wizards angry that the grand magus was also a witch-blooded high lady. Working together, and with a technological assist from Dahlia, Eva and Francine had tried to murder Maria and frame Bert for the crime. Unfortunately for them, Maria had survived her injuries, and Toula had sentenced the conspirators to life in prison.

And there they would have remained, had Leander not come to power three years later, pardoned them, and reinstated them to the Council. So eager had he been to prove himself that he'd listened when they'd told him they could seal Faerie off but still keep magic flowing into the mortal realm. Had it worked, Leander would have been a hero to a large chunk of the Arcanum. Instead, his foolishness had cost the realm all magic, sent the scattered Arcanum into hiding, and even led some of his supporters, horrified at what they'd done, to commit suicide.

While Eva and Francine had been the biggest monsters in my childish imagination, Dahlia had held a place in that pantheon, too, both for her violent cruelty to my mother and for her participation in the plot that had left Maria barely more than a burned corpse impaled to the floor. Logic reminded me that I was in possession of considerable power, accompanied by a similarly gifted team with a singular purpose, but the irrational voice in the shadowy corner of my imagination reserved for creatures beneath the bed whispered that Dahlia might be stronger still. Meanwhile, the part of me that was eternally five and scared of the dark wished my big brother were there. I hadn't seen him in more than a week—longer if I didn't count my observation from Fauxlaska.

As we crept into the driveway and behind a new cherry-red coupe, Ed pointed to the front door and whispered, "Camera on the doorbell. See it?"

We nodded.

He beckoned Edie closer with a crooked finger. "Try to hex that. Don't destroy the door, just disable the camera." When she started to protest, he shushed her and patted her shoulder. "You've got this, Edith. Try for me."

Edie's stomach had to be twisting as badly as mine was, but she reached under the back of her shirt and extracted her wand. Bracing her arm against the car's hood, she aimed and began to whisper. I saw the magic near the door brighten as it activated, and then, with a soft pop, the light of the doorbell camera winked out.

"Well done," Ed told her, and slunk toward the house.

"Couldn't we just go invisible or something?" Dec whispered.

He paused, pressing his back to the shrubbery to avoid the light on the stoop. "I'd rather not bother with the hassle of maintaining that sort of glamour, but by all means, if you'd like to manage one…"

Dec shut his mouth and shook his head, and Ed turned back to the task at hand. "No sign of an alarm ward," he murmured. "Either she's incapable of building one or she hasn't yet made time." Tutting, he walked up the three brick steps to the door and held his hand over the lock until it clicked. Motioning for us to join him, he waited until we were in position, then eased the door open.

I'd taken only two steps into the house when the hiss and yowl of a cat stopped me in my tracks.

An adorable orange kitten in Dahlia's foyer bowed up and fluffed out like it had touched a live wire. The kitten's green eyes glowed in the porch light, but when I edged closer, it finally decided that I was bad news and skittered out of the room.

I sighed as the cute little thing ran for cover. "Sorry," I whispered to Ed. "It's hard to be sneaky around—"

Another hiss interrupted me—the light spilling in from the stoop showed a black cat with golden eyes deeper in the foyer—and then a third cat hidden in the shadows picked up the chorus. Somewhere inside the house, a dog began to yap, followed by a buddy, the two barking back and forth like asynchronous percussion. As the dogs chorused, one of the cats crept closer, teeth bared and tail twitching. Before it could lunge, Aurie stepped up to greet it with a quick jet of flame that singed the rug and sent the cat scrambling for the staircase.

"Nice," Edie murmured.

Aurie held up her finger and thumb like an imaginary pistol, but in lieu of blowing the invisible smoke away from the barrel, she substituted more fire. "Man, I miss this in Faerie."

"Let's focus, please," Ed chided, and glanced toward the stairs as the ceiling creaked twice. "Right, we've got movement. Stay behind me."

We headed upstairs single file to find a narrow corridor leading from the first landing. By the light of the orb Ed tossed above his head, I saw four rooms branching off the corridor…and only one of them had a closed door. He motioned for us to hug the wall, then eased toward the target room, held out his index finger, and whispered. The lock and the door's hardware disintegrated, and after waiting a beat for return fire, Ed kicked the door open and stormed into the room.

First in after him, I found the room's occupant ready for battle: a gray-haired woman wearing an oversized T-shirt and flannel pajama pants printed with glasses of wine, holding a golf club like a baseball bat as three more cats voiced their displeasure from the corner.

"I'm no golfer," said Ed as the woman's grip tightened, "but even *I* know your form is terrible, Ms. Leighton. Put it down."

"Who are you?" she demanded, her voice quavering— with fear, I decided, not from a tremor of age.

"That's a surprisingly complicated question," he replied, "but why don't you just call me Eadwig? Grand Magus, if you prefer."

Even in the pale light of his orb, I saw her chin begin to tremble.

"I'm not here to hurt you," he continued. "But we need to talk about your mother."

The golf club started to twitch as Dahlia's shaking spread. "I made a mistake, all right? One stupid mistake as a kid. I haven't spoken to the Conclave crowd in years."

"I understand—"

"And I wrote off Mum after that. I had nothing to do with whatever happened to Faerie."

"Then you'll be pleased to know it's been undone," he said. "But my questions remain. Now, will you come peacefully?"

Her eyes scanned our faces for a few seconds before

she muttered, "Don't have a choice, do I?"

Ed shrugged. "Not a good one, no. Would you like to put on proper trousers before we leave?"

Edie, Aurie, and I had watched Dahlia as she dressed, but to my surprise, she hadn't tried to run. Maybe, I reasoned, as she settled in at the conference room table in the previous day's dress pants and a purple blouse, she didn't have the talent for it. Wandless casting wasn't possible for every wizard, so perhaps Dahlia lacked the ability. True, she'd magically beaten up my mother, but Mom had been barely more than mundane back then—any wizard would have outclassed her.

While Ed took a seat at the table, the rest of us leaned against the walls in the gaps between the tapestries, unsure whether to sit or retreat to our espionage closet. As I considered the coffee and tried not to think of how late it was in Faerie, my brother appeared by the door and hurried toward me. "Finally," he said, all smiles. "I was concerned."

I'm still in one piece, I silently replied, grinning back at him. *More or less. I've been thrown around too much of late.*

"Gaw continues to insist that you're whole and healthy, but I prefer to see the evidence for myself." He gave me a quick once-over, then nodded. "No visible bruising. Is that due to magic, or are you black and blue under your clothing?"

A little of both. I've missed you, Publi.

"Missed you, too," he said, taking the spot beside me, then raised a hand in greeting to Raurit. If he brushed up against the old tapestry, he'd do it no harm. "Training, yes?"

Too much of it. And everything still feels like it's going to fall apart if I look away, I admitted. *Kenna's got a court now, and Avus's acting like a king—it's _weird_*, I insisted as he chuckled—*and Gaw appears and disappears whenever he likes…*

"Who's she?" he asked, pointing to the subject of the imminent interrogation.

Dahlia Leighton. Her mom and my grandmother were the masterminds behind the closure.

"Ah. That explains her boundless delight in being here. Were you planning to watch, or do you want to talk elsewhere? I need details."

Before I could answer him, Ed waved and whispered, and a full tea set manifested on the table between them. "Help yourself," he offered. "I left out the poison."

Dahlia didn't react to his weak attempt at a joke, but she did pour herself a cup of strong tea, which she took black. "What do you want to know?" she muttered. "Why me?"

"Because I'm searching, and Leander gave you up as a potential help," he replied. Her dark eyes flashed at the news. "But I meant what I said—I mean you no harm. Live your life in London, for all I care. Just tell me how to locate your mother and Eva, and I'll let you get back to sleep."

She laughed once, harshly, and sipped her tea. "If you want to talk to Mum, I'd suggest finding a psychic. She and Eva killed themselves right after they fucked up Faerie."

Ed seemed taken aback by the news. "Are you certain?"

"Absolutely." She drank again, the picture of nonchalance until I noticed her free hand clenching. "They got their revenge, you see?"

"Explain."

"What is she saying?" my brother asked.

I gave him the quick recap and braced myself for real-time translation.

Dahlia kept her silence for a long moment, then licked her lips and stared into the distance past Ed's shoulders. "I cut ties with Mum after she and Eva tried to kill Corelli. Stealing books is one thing, but what they did to her…" She shuddered. "I'm not perfect, I've made mistakes, but murder was a step too far for me."

But beating up a little kid's okay? I added to Publius, biting my tongue to stop myself from shouting at her.

"Patience," he soothed.

"My dad came 'round a year or two after Mum was locked up," Dahlia continued. "Finally saw her for what she was. We moved to London, I started a legitimate job, Dad worked when he could find it—not much we could do as wizards, being bound and all, but we got by. I started with Bruton Singh, and that turned into a career. We learned what Mum and Eva had done the day after it happened, and we returned to Glastonbury only long enough to get fake credentials and cash."

She sipped her tea while she collected her thoughts.

"Dad lived with me until he died of a heart attack five years later. He never spoke to Mum again. I'm the one who found her body."

"Did she leave a note?" Ed asked.

"A text, actually. I'm not entirely surprised she did it. She had no one, Eva had no one—not like her daughters wanted anything to do with her—and they'd got their revenge by taking magic away from everyone else, so what more were they going to do with themselves? Two former magi without power or even families?" She sighed and pursed her lips. "About a week after everything went to hell, just as the last of the magic was going, Mum sent me a text from a burner phone telling me not to visit this particular bit of Shapwick Heath, a place where she used to take me walking as a child. Curiosity got the better of me, and I went the next day."

The hand holding her mug began to shake.

"I found a burnt-out car in the woods with two charred corpses in the front seat. They were blackened beyond recognition, but I saw melted gold around their necks. Magus chains. I called the police and claimed I'd found them on a hike, and I believe they've been anonymous victims ever since. But I know damn well that was my mum and Eva. That bloody text was her suicide note. She *wanted* me to find them there. Twist the knife, you know? I abandoned her, so she got even. And that's my last image of my mother: a burnt corpse in a stolen car, twenty-five years ago."

"They're not dead."

I looked at my brother, who shook his head. "They're not dead," he repeated. "If they were, I'd know. I'd have taken pains to keep Eva away from you." Frowning at Dahlia, he mused, "She seems sincere—perhaps she was truly deceived."

"They faked their deaths," I blurted, making Dahlia jump.

Ed was unbothered by the interruption. "You have that on good authority?"

"Yeah," I said, and Raurit nodded.

Recovering, Dahlia blotted a splash of tea off her hand and scowled. "How would the girl know anything about—"

"She's a medium," Ed interrupted. "So is he," he said, pointing to Raurit, "in case you've never had dealings with the cynaeli. And if word from beyond the veil is that your mother staged that scene, I'd believe it."

Dahlia's eyes widened. "'Beyond the veil'?"

"The point is that Francine is still breathing," said Ed, "and as such, I intend to find her. Any idea where she might be hiding?"

For the first time since we'd nabbed her, Dahlia looked truly stunned. "I...no, I haven't got the first idea where she would be. We're an old-blooded family—it's not as if she had mundane cousins who would have hidden her all this time."

"Mm." Pausing to drink his tea, Ed mulled that over, then said, "Bottom line, I *will* find them. Now, I can continue to search for them as I did Leander and you, or we can make this easier."

"I'm listening."

"Your mother and"—he grimaced—"my mother-in-law aren't stupid. They're magi, they have access to my work, and now that magic's back, I assume they're taking precautions to block blood traces and hide themselves in the dream space." The smile he flashed over his mug wasn't friendly. "I can work around those blocks. Unfortunately, they had the foresight to steal their blood samples from the Archives before they left, but if I could convince you to part with a donation…"

"Take it," Dahlia muttered. "If they're really alive…if Mum let me believe she'd died like that…then you'll have what you need from me."

"Thank you, Ms. Leighton," said Ed. "Your cooperation is appreciated. I'll ask that you remain here until they're located—"

"You can't! My pets—"

"Will be brought shortly," he assured her. "I won't leave them to starve. If you'll wait here a moment longer, I'll send for the doctor to draw blood."

The logical part of me knew that Ed was doing the right thing by showing her kindness, by *smiling* at her, but as I'd listened to Dahlia, something red and raw within me had forced its way to the surface.

When Ed headed for the door, I stepped up to the chair opposite Dahlia's and forced my face into a mask of polite neutrality. "Before I leave, I just wanted to introduce myself," I said.

Her eyebrows rose. "Oh?"

"Yeah. I'm Cici Connolly," I replied, then sent a blast of force toward her, gripping her by the hair and slamming her face into the wooden table. Dahlia screamed as her nose broke, then clutched at her bleeding face and stared at me, too shocked to speak.

"*That's* for my mom," I told her. "You remember Kitty, right?"

"*Cecilia*," Ed snapped. "Enough!"

I wheeled on him, hands on my hips. "You said that *you*

wouldn't hurt her. I never signed on to that."

"Out," he barked, motioning me toward the door.

Edie made a face in sympathy as I passed her, but as I marched from the room, my brother murmured, "Was that really necessary?"

Yes.

"In that case, I think we should have a chat about the meaning of the word," he replied, following me down the hallway.

Free of the conference room, I was able to push the ugly thing inside me back into its hole, but as it retreated, it whispered a truth.

Taking action—taking control of the moment, disapproving elders be damned—felt *good.*

CHAPTER 22

I'm sure my mom wasn't thrilled to get up at dawn to give Dr. Bee a blood sample, but she understood Ed's rush to begin. Blood traces work vertically—they can reveal a person's living ancestors and descendants—and since both Mom's and Beth's fathers were dead, it wasn't like the trace would hit on their paternal line. Really, as long as Edie and I stayed out of the mortal realm while the trace was running, a sample from either of Eva's daughters could have led to her. But Ed was taking no chances, and before breakfast time in Faerie, he'd begun setting up the complicated spells that would allow him to work through the protective barriers that Eva and Francine had surely thrown together in the last days.

Joining Pa and me for pancakes, Mom gave me a long, hard look as she settled in at the table with a bandage taped to the bend of her elbow. "You broke her *nose?*" she asked, reaching for the platter of bacon.

I kept my face blank. "Whoops."

"Cecilia Maria."

Pa snorted in a vain attempt to hide his laughter, and Mom rolled her eyes. "If I needed you to fight my battles for me, young lady, I'd ask." She loaded up her plate, then glanced my way and barely grinned. "It's going to take quite the spell to get the blood out of that blouse."

"I can tell you're heartbroken."

"Crushed. You'll be pleased to know Dahlia's on the mend." Mom paused, and her smile grew ever so slightly wider. "Of course, the poor thing's nose is all swollen, and she'll have a pair of black eyes for a bit…and she did shrink away from me in the infirmary like I was about to shoot her…"

"How terrible," Pa deadpanned.

"I know. Wish Maria had been there. By the way, I saw Toula going in to help Ed," she added, drowning her breakfast in syrup. "Guy's on a mission."

Pa sawed off a chunk of his short stack and chewed. "What does it say about the quarry when Simon Magus is calling for reinforcements?"

"That he's not underestimating them, and he's no fool—Toula's a technical caster par excellence. They're proceeding on the assumption that Mom and Francine still have a digital copy of his diary, so that's two blocks to get around: the blood trace and the dream space."

"I'm still not entirely sure how the latter works…"

"I don't think anyone is—the Minors don't do much with theoretical thaumaturgy, and the Arcanum has overlooked sleepwalking for the last millennium. The important thing here is that it *is* possible to hide yourself from sleepwalkers. Mulligan either figured it out or got lucky when he hid the Fringe. Talk to Badger sometime— she still kicks herself for not realizing that they could have been hidden that well. Anyway," she continued between bites, "suffice it to say that Ed and Toula have their work cut out for them, and they don't want to be disturbed. So no sneaking off to Alaska, yeah?" Mom told me. "You can entertain yourself here for a few days."

"What about Dahlia and Leander?" I asked.

"Leave them alone. I don't want you going ten rounds with either of them."

"Fine," I sighed, "but Ed's keeping them there, right?"

She nodded. "Dahlia's menagerie was being delivered as I left. Ed said they picked up Leander's family before y'all went after Dahlia, and that was no fun. Had to blast the phone right out of his wife's hand, and then she freaked out when they showed her actual magic, and…"

She shook her head and attacked her breakfast. "Leander's got some serious explaining to do, though part of me is slightly giddy at the fact that the old-blooded little shit married a mundane girl. Their kids are new-blooded—what a tragedy," she said, her voice thick with sarcasm.

"I don't see what the big deal is," I replied. "They're wizards—who cares if their mom can't cast?"

Mom and Pa traded knowing looks, and then she said, "Sweetie, if you hang out around the castle long enough, you'll discover a neurotic community full of ancestor-obsessed wizards, half of whom don't even want to let you in the club unless you've got nothing but wizards five generations deep. Of course, the snootiest of the lot trace their ancestry to Simon Magus, who's about as new-blooded as they come, but no one seems to grasp the irony."

"On the plus side," Pa offered, "with Ed taking over, they have a new-blooded grand magus who must look at their pedigrees and laugh, so…progress?"

"Let's hope. I pity the first moron who insults Edie's bloodline."

After breakfast, my parents slipped off to work on the house they'd begun building while I'd been busy with Coileán. Avus wasn't thrilled that they were moving out of the villa—he'd insisted that they could have their own wing, and surely they could live in proximity without stepping on each other's toes. But Mom and Pa had grown accustomed to having their own space during their time in Alaska, and I couldn't blame them for wanting to put distance between themselves and the heart of court affairs. I accompanied them out to the site, and I had no complaints—they'd selected a modest estate bordered by forest with a creek running through it, and the house, while at least twice as large as our home in the compound, wasn't palatial.

As Pa gave me the tour of the kitchen, which they'd designed to easily accommodate the two of them working in tandem, Mom said, "We're putting in a room for you, of course. And your own bathroom."

"No pressure," Pa quickly added, "but we didn't know what your plans were, and we didn't want you to think you were stuck at the villa. Unless you want to be there—it's certainly a nice residence, and having the kitchen staff is convenient…"

"But if you don't want Bonnie checking up on you forever," Mom finished, "just know that you have options. Or you could build your own place…assuming you want to stay here, of course. There's a wide world out there beyond the border."

I stared at my parents, weighing the odds that they'd been replaced by pod creatures in their sleep. "You *want* me to go exploring? Since when?"

They shared a look, and Pa replied, "Now that we can reach you in case of emergency, and we're not stuck in the middle of the wilderness, hoping Ennis's plane can get off the ground…if you want to travel, Cici, it's your right."

"It's time," said Mom. "I know it pissed you kids off when we brought you home last spring, and in retrospect, we were—"

"Overprotective and clingy?" I volunteered.

"Ooh…how about 'concerned for your safety but could have gone about it better'?"

"Mm. Suppose I could compromise."

"You're growing up, whether we like it or not," she said. "When I was your age, I had the Away Team and a place of my own in the castle. I know we haven't been able to give you the freedom you want, but…you know, times are changing. Edie's going to have a job with the Arcanum, Gaw's doing his thing, Kenna has her hands full…" She shrugged. "We want you to be safe, but we're really not trying to be your jailers, baby. If you're ready to see what's out there, then we'll stand back and ask you to call every few days. Promise."

I searched their faces, looking for the catch. "This

wouldn't have anything to do with keeping me away from my boyfriend, would it?"

Pa shook his head. "We're not that stupid, dear girl."

"So you're going to stop nagging me about Gaw? All of this 'you're too young' crap is going to end?"

Mom made a face. "It's not *crap*, Cici. You're young, end of story. But seeing as you're both adults…maybe we could back off a little."

It wasn't perfect, but it was a start. "Thanks," I told them.

Pa pointed to the ceiling. "Your room's upstairs, but we haven't touched it yet. Do you want to put it together? Just in case?"

Mom and Dad made a bedroom for me, too, Gaw whispered to my mind. *Not that I use it. And my grandparents still keep a room for Mom, even though she literally lives on the other side of the barn.*

"Sure," I told Pa.

"Would you be amenable to minor parental supervision in case of fireballs?"

"What, you don't want me burning your house down?" I teased.

He slung an arm around my shoulders and said, "I remember what it was like to suddenly come into a great deal of power. Accuracy can be *slow* to develop."

"He's not wrong," said Mom, and shooed us toward the staircase. "We've been working hard. Don't torch the place, baby."

By midday, Pa and I had come up with a passable bedroom for me, which was convenient, as I desperately needed a nap. I'd been going strong since the middle of the night, and my new bed, tricked out with a deep mattress and silky sheets, begged to be broken in.

While my parents worked downstairs, negotiating over color schemes and furniture placement, I snuggled in and tried to pass out. But exhausted though I was, sleep eluded me. When I closed my eyes, I saw Dahlia at the conference room table, a gray-haired, mostly harmless woman with shock on her face and blood dripping from her nose.

My reaction left me unsettled.

Sure, it had felt great at the time—there I was, swooping in to avenge my mother—but Publius was right that it hadn't been *necessary*. Dahlia was in Ed's custody, she'd come along peacefully, and he'd assured her that she wasn't in danger from him...so yes, I could see why he'd been peeved with me for the sneak attack. On the other hand, what I'd done to her was no worse than what she'd done to Mom...albeit years ago, when they were children.

It was my rage that worried me. As a kid, I'd been taught to control my red-hot temper before I lashed out, but that was before my temper had been given teeth. In the last month, I'd stood defiant while my friends pulled guns on our families, I'd attacked Avus, and now I'd beaten up a prisoner who'd already surrendered. This wasn't like me.

Unless it was. Unless the control I'd once exerted was a flimsy veneer for the rage boiling within me.

And I couldn't deny the rage. Exacerbated by the turmoil of recent weeks, by my mounting frustration with my family, by the loss of Gaw and of my home and of life in the bachelor pad, of our little commune of six with our petty problems and our dreams of Bora Bora, my soul felt frayed.

The world would calm down, I reassured myself as I rolled over. I'd find breathing room again. A place where I belonged. I'd have control over my life and my future, and then maybe—just maybe—my finger would come off my internal trigger.

Someday. When the monsters from the closets had been dragged into the light and we were all safe again.

My afternoon nap was broken only by the promise of dinner back at Avus's, and once satiated by roast beef and potatoes, I fell into my bed at the villa to continue my interrupted slumber. Avus chuckled at my half-closed eyes—"Oh, little girl, you are *young*," he said as I jerked myself awake over dessert—but with no one insisting that I step outside for a few hours of physical punishment, I intended to make up my sleep deficit.

Edie, who was staying over while her father and Toula worked, invited herself into my bed, and I relaxed with her familiar warmth beside me. "You still have a room here," I mumbled as she scooted closer in the darkness.

"But if I'm in here," she said, "Gaw will leave you alone and let you rest."

Ha, ha.

"Shut up," she muttered. "Girls' night. No boys allowed."

He fell silent, but I felt a soft sensation like lips peck my cheek, and I smiled as I drifted off.

The peaceful transition between consciousness and sleep made it all the more jarring when the bed started shaking and Gaw yelled for us to wake up. Groaning, I opened my eyes to find him standing near the door, filling the room with his peculiar radiance. The world beyond the garden door remained dark, and groggy as I was, I couldn't tell whether I'd slept for ten minutes or ten hours. "Wha…?" I managed, squinting at him as my gunky eyes adjusted.

"Kenna's in trouble. You need to get up."

"What?" said Edie. "What's wrong with Kenna?"

"She's under siege. Feet on the floor, let's go."

I forced my legs to slip out from beneath the blankets and tested my balance. "Under siege by whom?" I asked. "Who would attack her?"

Gaw sighed impatiently as he dealt with the reality that he was the only being with near omniscience in the room. "Her own damn court. And they've taken Ennis hostage, so get a move on." A gate opened in the middle of my bedroom, and I recognized Coileán's office on the other side. "I'm calling a meeting. Book it."

Five minutes later, I found myself huddled between Edie and Aurie as a crowd filled the office. Dec joined us, barefoot, shirtless, and stunned by the rude wakeup, as the last of the summoned filed in and closed the door.

"I'll make this brief," said Gaw, standing in the middle of the room as the group, a mixture of our friends and family and Coileán's and Avus's guards, pressed closer. "Ennis took a walk alone tonight. Insomnia. Some of the court saw him and acted on the spur of the moment. They're holding him hostage, and they've surrounded Kenna's palace."

"*Why?*" Frank asked.

"Because they didn't like what they saw of her yesterday. She's young, inexperienced, quite obviously half fae. And Ennis didn't make any secret of the fact that they've been living in Alaska all along. So now the full-blooded chunk of that court that was enjoying Irem's loosening of restrictions comes back to find that their new queen grew up listening to you two," he said, pointing to the kings, "and since *you* three dropped in on her," he continued as he looked at Dec, Aurie, and me, "the logical conclusion is that Kenna's *way* too buddy-buddy with the other courts. One thought is that she's probably no more than a puppet, and she's going to clamp down again."

"Did you tell her any of this?" I demanded.

"Not yet," he admitted. "I was hoping it would die with time, but—"

"*Gaw!*"

"She's nervous enough as it is! I didn't want to ramp up her paranoia—"

"What *paranoia?*" I snapped. "If they've snatched Ennis—"

"Is he hurt?" Coileán interrupted. "Is Kenna?"

Gaw grimaced. "Ennis is a little banged up, but he's

intact. Kenna's just panicking."

"What's their endgame?" Avus cut in.

"They want her off the throne. Of course, I'm not going to allow that—"

Dec snorted. "Shitty of you."

"It's for the good of the realm," he replied, gritting his teeth. "To prevent this sort of situation. The only way out for one of the Three is death. My concern is that they'll try to use Ennis as a bargaining chip—keep him in captivity and use threats to his safety to sway her. A few of them have floated the idea of asking her to leave the realm and let them do as they like in her absence."

Avus frowned. "Could she *do* that?"

"Technically?" Gaw shrugged. "That's not much worse than what Oberon did. It would be a disaster for stability here…but look," he hastily added, "Kenna needs to take charge now. This is important. She needs to go out there with her guards and make a stand, show that she's not a little pushover. And she needs to do it *herself*," he stressed, looking to Avus and Coileán. "If you two come riding to the rescue, that'll just solidify the suspicion that she can't handle the court alone. But…"

"But?" Coileán echoed.

"But they've got her dad, and she's desperate to avoid getting him killed." He lifted his hands and let them flop to his sides. "So you see the problem."

"The *problem*," I interjected, "is that you could stop this right now."

Gaw turned to me, his face tense. "It's not that simple—"

"It is! That's Kenna and Ennis! *Do something*!"

"I'm not a king, okay?" Gaw snapped. "You've got to understand that. I can arbitrate, and I might be the weapon of last resort, but this is something Kenna needs to do. If she can't prove herself, this'll just escalate."

I looked to Ros, who was standing with Sam and her parents near Coileán's desk, but she was nodding silently.

As my anger threatened to boil over, Artur stepped from the pack, her hand creeping to the hilt of the sword buckled at her hip. "The politics are simple, yes?" she said. "The other courts should not come to her aid?"

"It wouldn't look good if the Arcanum meddled, either," said Gaw.

"Very well. I answer to none of them, and I'm going."

"Artur, wait—"

She marched up until she was almost on his glowing toes, then gave him a hard, withering stare. "I do not answer to you, Gawain. And I care nothing for court politics tonight. Ennis is helpless, and he's in danger, and I'll be *damned* if I do nothing. Stay out of my way."

"You're not going alone," Pa said from the other side of the room.

Gaw wheeled on him. "If *you* get involved, that drags Val in—"

"Nonsense. Magus Corelli?" he called, and picked stricken Maria from the crowd. "You're the supervisory magus for the Away Team, are you not?"

"I, uh…" she began, stammering, "I *was* until Leander—"

"Fuck Leander," Pa interrupted. "Are you our magus, yes or no?"

They locked eyes, and after a second's pause, Maria straightened. "Yes. Yes, I am."

"Then you'll authorize a rescue mission?"

"You're damn right I will," she said, and began pointing to those of the former Team gathered around her. "Marcus, Kitty, Mal, Frank…uh…Artur, if you're doing your own thing…"

"I don't mind having backup," Artur replied.

"Wait a minute," Gaw tried, "this is still problematic. The Team is an Arcanum group—"

"The Team is the *Team*," said Avus, then nodded to Maria. "And if Magus Corelli wishes to intervene, I won't stop her."

"Are you accepting recruits?" Aurie called from our corner.

Gaw sighed and rubbed his forehead. "Guys…"

"Screw it," I said. "We're going. How can you not—"

"You think I like this?" he retorted, his voice rising. "You think I want to see either of them hurt? This isn't about us—this is about the *realm*. The big picture, Cici. Kenna's got to show that she can kill, if that's what it takes. That she can keep order—"

"This *is* about us!" My arms shook with my mounting fear and fury, the jagged-edged panic looking for an escape valve. "I lost you. I'm not losing anyone else."

"Cici—"

"*No.*"

I barely noticed that I'd begun to glow as well until Edie and Aurie slid away from me.

"Cici," Gaw tried again more gently, "this isn't a game. If Kenna can't take control—"

"*I* am taking control," I muttered. "Here. *Tonight.*" Looking at the kings, I found Avus's face a careful blank, but Coileán faintly nodded. "Unless you can tell me right now that Ennis will be just fine if we do nothing."

His shoulders slumped. "I can't."

I saw the turmoil in his shifting expression—fear for Kenna and Ennis, worry for the realm, guilt over the bind into which he'd put us—but I was in no position to offer comfort.

"I'm with you, Artur," I said, and opened a gate to the base of the peninsula, revealing orbs and flickering torches in the distance. "Lead on."

She squeezed my shoulder in passing as she slipped into the night, and I waited while the rest of our small force followed her. Before I could step across, Gaw murmured, "Cici?"

I shot him a sharp glance. "What?"

"Be careful," he said, and vanished.

Sealing the gate quickly in case the flash of its opening

had attracted unwanted attention, I hurried to join the huddle.

"As long as Kenna is inside with her guards, she's not in immediate danger," Artur was telling the others as I squeezed in. "The first priority is Ennis. We find him, we extract him, and *then* we see about Kenna."

"I'm down for extraction," said Mom, "but I don't like the odds of the six of us against however many of them are massed out there—"

"*Ten*," Edie protested. "There are ten of us."

"And you're staying back," Maria told her. "Let the ones with full training take the lead." Returning her attention to Artur, she said, "The difficult part is going to be finding him, especially in the dark…"

As they plotted, I fought to keep my emotions in check, but the frustration of being shunted to the sidelines made my temper spike. *Gaw?* I asked.

Yes?

At least he didn't sound upset, I noted—concerned, maybe frustrated in turn, but not angry. *Where is he?*

In the thick of their line. Close enough to be in danger if Kenna starts shooting.

Can you guide us in?

I could almost feel him cringe. *Hell, I could give you a neon sign, but all that would do would be attract attention. He's guarded well.*

Look, I know you're in a weird spot, I thought, trying to reason with him, *but this is for Ennis. If you help us, the odds are better that we'll all make it out intact.*

I know, and I hate this—his frustration rang almost as clearly in my head as my own did—*but I can't just toss them off the cliff and give you a clear run at him.*

What about a gate? I pressed. *Could you open a gate for us near him?*

Yeah, he replied after a moment's hesitation, *but again, that would be like a neon sign. You'd be mobbed coming through.*

Unless we had a distraction.

Cici—

Just be ready, I replied, and interrupted Artur's mutterings. "Gaw can give us a gate to Ennis, but we need something to draw attention."

"Can do," Frank rumbled. "No fire, unfortunately, but—"

"If you go up alone and unshielded, you'll be a giant target," Maria protested.

"Which is why he's not going alone," said Mom, and Frank nodded. "I can shield us, maybe shoot a little. If the rest of you could offer something in the way of ground cover—"

"Can you carry two?" Pa interrupted, looking to Frank.

He snorted. "Can you stay on?"

"If you avoid acrobatics up there, then probably yes. You shield, I'll shoot," he told Mom.

"And we'll wait for the gate," Artur concluded. "Frank?"

"Just give me space," he said, and ran away from the palace toward a meadow. Dark as it was, I couldn't really see him shift at that distance, but the moonlight glinted off his scales as he returned, his footsteps shaking the ground. *Saddle up*, he thought.

Mom quickly constructed a tandem saddle, the seats comically small in comparison to the long straps necessary to hold them in place, and Frank stood still while she hooked it on. "Comfortable?" she asked.

It's not chafing yet. Let's do this. He lowered his body, and they scrambled up his front leg and onto the seats at the base of his neck. A shield burst forth from Mom, covering about three quarters of him, and with a few running steps and a leap, they were airborne.

Beside me, Aurie muttered, "Have you ever felt somewhat useless?"

"They're the distraction. We're here for *extraction*," I replied, and watched to see whether the ploy would work.

At his full size, there were nothing subtle about Frank.

His wings cracked like flapping sails, and he roared as he flew circuits around the palace with his passengers, their location made evident by the glow of the shield around them. I watched as a few bolts left the ground and fell from the sky in turn, but judging by the lights I could see, most of the mob seemed to be holding their position. They certainly weren't running from the aerial danger…but then again, how much danger were they in? Pa wasn't exactly raining death upon them.

My heart raced. This wasn't working. If they couldn't break up the crowd, if we couldn't get to Ennis…

Cici, you've got to calm down, Gaw tried. *Deep breath. Focus.*

But it was too late for meditative breathing. Fear seized my internal controls, and right behind it came anger.

How *dare* they?

"Cici?" Edie asked as my shoulders tightened. "Are you okay?"

"No," I said, almost growling in a voice I barely recognized as my own. "Be ready to move."

"What are you—"

I jumped and called upon the purple flames, then flew toward the line as Frank and my parents disappeared around the back of the palace. Hoping I wasn't about to punch a hole through my own throat, I summoned the tiny burst of power necessary to amplify my voice as I sped toward the mob. "Let him go!" I yelled. "You let him go *right now!*"

The flaming fireball approach appeared to have lost some of its efficacy, however, as the nearest faeries clumped together beneath thick shields instead of fleeing. More and more of them in my path did likewise, forming a shield wall like a turtle shell. And then, as I hovered at the edge of the line, someone down below taunted, "What are you going to do now, girl? Take your little light show home!"

Breathe, Cici, Gaw begged.

But all I could see was red as they laughed. The force

building within me finally reached its limit, and my arms shook with my rage as they rose. I opened my clenched fists and turned my palms on the smug faeries still jeering at me below.

No more. *I* was taking control now.

I barely felt the pulse that shot from my hands, the bolt of power that lit the ambient magic around it like an electric current, but it penetrated the shield wall and turned the ground beneath me into a crater.

The taunts switched to screams, and for one brief, crystalline moment, I smiled.

Seconds later, the return fire began.

Practicing with Coileán, I'd learned to block one bolt at a time, maybe two. Now I had two dozen coming at me from the ground, and since I was a hovering, glowing target, the aim from below was *very* good. My arm ached as it pressed against the inside of my shield, pushing back as the construction tried to fall apart under the barrage, but rather than send me into retreat, the pain only amplified my anger.

The bolts coming at me were strong, but they were pistol fire next to the bombs I dropped onto the crowd. The dust in the air, thrown up when chunks of earth and unlucky faeries went flying, turned the streaking lights of our respective bolts into a laser show. Finally, prudence screamed at me to move, and I began to streak back and forth over the mob, crying out when the strongest bolts hit my shield and returning fire whenever I could.

But I was tiring. My arms felt like burning gelatin, my chest heaved, and the haphazard lattice of my shield was fraying. I ducked and wove, dodging fireballs and even a few small bolts of lightning, fueled by my rage but running out of gas.

As I shot a long burst of fire into the crowd, setting a few of the attackers ablaze, Frank and my parents emerged from behind the palace and saw what I was up to. *Cici!* Frank shouted into my mind. *What the hell are you doing? Get out of there!*

Distraction! I thought back at him. Suddenly, my shield failed, and a bolt clipped my left shoulder before I could patch the hole. Screaming with fury, I dropped another explosive blast.

Cici, stop! he cried.

Retreat, Gaw interjected. *Artur found Ennis. It's over, fall back—*

No.

People talk about a red film coming over your vision when you're enraged. I didn't experience that, but rather a narrowing of my focus until all I could see was the torchlight below me and the bolts flying for my head. Those bastards were shooting at me, and now, with Ennis out of the way, there was no reason for me to hold back.

I poured myself into the blasts, aiming them at the areas with the most concentrated fire below me and counting every pained cry as a win. Gates flickered open and closed as some of the siege force made their escape, but those who stayed faced my wrath. They'd threatened Kenna, they'd kidnapped Ennis, and now that I had taken the field—taken *control*—they would pay.

Light and movement at the palace drew my attention, and I looked that way in time to see the massive gates open and Kenna, glowing brilliantly, emerge with her army and go to work. Thus distracted, I missed the bolt that found the lucky opening in the rear of my shield and hit me in the back of the head. It wasn't a particularly strong bolt, but it struck hard enough to knock me out.

I don't remember the world graying or going black, or even the pain of impact. My last sensation before consciousness failed was Gaw's voice shouting through the chaos: *Get under her, Frank! Now!*

I don't need help, I started to tell him, but the thought escaped me as the world winked out.

CHAPTER 23

I learned later that as my fire extinguished itself and I tumbled from the sky like Icarus unwinged, Frank caught me across his back and carried me to the ground while Pa held me in place. I recall barely waking, the feeling of grass beneath my palms, the air thick and stinking of blood and ozone, my aunt's blazing eyes inches from mine as she demanded an explanation I couldn't give her. Then I threw up, adding the pungent, acrid stench of my vomit to the noxious odors around me, and lost consciousness again.

When the gaps were filled in, I learned that my parents had hurried me back to Avus as Kenna took her vengeance on the court that had defied her. As Avus put me to bed, Mom called Dr. Bee, who found a hairline fracture at the back of my skull, diagnosed me as concussed, and started a drug drip to reduce my mild cerebral edema. The combination of medicine and healing enchantment kept me stable, but I slept until nearly noon, when I woke to a splitting headache and found Pa sitting by my bed with his computer. He put it on the floor as soon as I moaned and stirred, then held me down to keep me still.

"You're safe, baby," he soothed as I tried to fight his arm. "It's over. Don't move, you're connected to an IV."

That pierced my mental fog, and I looked up to see his dark, worried eyes above me and a gray IV pole parked beside my bed. "Kenna—"

"She's fine. So is Ennis. A broken arm, no permanent damage."

I considered that for only a few seconds before I rolled over and threw up again, splashing the bedding and the rug.

"It's all right," Pa told me, enchanting the soft surfaces clean once more and creating a glass of water. "How's your head?"

"Sore," I mumbled.

"As predicted. You're not leaving your bedroom until tomorrow, so try to sleep while the enchantment works."

I drank, but my tongue felt like thick sandpaper in the foulness of my mouth. "What…where…"

"You were hit—do you remember? That was last night. Everyone's safe, and Bee will be back in an hour or so to adjust your medication."

"Mom…"

"Napping. She took the first shift," he replied, and smoothed my hair from my clammy forehead. "Sleep, Cici."

I could feel my eyes growing heavy even as he suggested it, but fear and dread prodded me awake for a moment longer. "Did I do okay?" I croaked.

Pa hesitated, then tucked the cleaned blankets around me. "It's over, little girl. Sleep."

Twilight had descended before I woke again. That time, I found myself alone in my room, but a glass of water on the nightstand sat beside a note informing me that all I needed to do was call for my parents if my pain was worse. I didn't want to bother them—my head felt better, and though the world briefly swam when I struggled upright, I didn't puke, which I counted as a victory. The bar was low that day.

I was wrestling with the idea of venturing to the bathroom to rinse the lingering funk off my tongue when a quick double rap at the door heralded a visitor. "Feeling better?" Ed asked as he let himself in. "Gaw said you'd awakened."

Seeing him there surprised me. "Aren't you busy with Toula?"

"Took a break. I wanted to look in on you," he replied, and pulled up a chair. He sat, lightly crossed his legs, and leaned back against the padding with a curious little smile on his face. "How many people did you kill last night?"

"Huh?"

He chuckled. "You weren't throwing softballs, Cici. What did you think was happening?"

Horror flowed like ice water into the dry well where my rage had boiled. "I…I mean…"

"Suppose it was dark," said Ed, who seemed as relaxed as if he were discussing an inoffensive but unmemorable movie. "You couldn't see the field. I heard they carried you off unconscious, so I assume no one debriefed you." He paused, but when I could manage nothing more than a low stutter, he said, "I saw it before Kenna fixed the damage this morning. Craters all over the place. Limbs, too. I found a lower jaw by itself, but the head—"

"Stop," I begged.

Ed stared at me while I took deep breaths to calm my roiling stomach. "It gets better," he said in an unexpectedly conversational tone. "Easier, I should say. Now that you've got your first kills under your belt, the next will come more easily."

"They were going to hurt Ennis!" I cried. "They went after Kenna!"

"You misunderstand. I wasn't suggesting that your actions weren't at all justified," he replied, shrugging. "Of course, Ennis's captors would have been foolish to kill him—they may have snatched him on the spur of the moment, but I doubt they would have been so stupid as to do away with their bargaining chip. His life wasn't in immediate danger, though that *was* a nasty break in his arm. He'll be in a sling for a few days yet, Val thinks."

"Is Kenna—"

"A little bruised but otherwise fine. Now, credit where it's due, you *did* put down that rebellion fairly quickly. Killing the problem was the most expedient way to end it. And the next time a similar situation arises, you'll know what to do." He steepled his fingers and held my stare, the expression in his blue eyes inscrutable. "Eventually, you'll start to overlook questions of justification. The calculus will turn instead to expedience, which, on the whole, is a far more effective way to achieve your ends. But really, my dear, it does grow easier with practice. That nausea you're feeling right now won't bother you forever."

"I saw Kenna come out before I got hit," I said in a rush, trying to push away the blame. "Maybe she made those craters and…uh…"

"Oh, I don't doubt that she fought like an angry Fury, given the damage left behind," he told me. "Honestly, I didn't know she had it in her. Kenna talks a good game, but she's never been particularly *aggressive*…then again, they took her dad. I suppose that court just learned a valuable lesson: don't mess with Ennis."

I started to relax. "So then *she* made—"

"She made plenty of her own kills, and most of her wounded are enjoying Coileán's hospitality this morning. Having also been a guest of his mother's secure cells, I assure you they won't be escaping until Kenna's ready to deal with them. But her damage path is clear, and it's concentrated by the palace. Yours, on the other hand, starts far away from the palace and works inward. You two almost met in the middle…at different times, I suppose, since you'd been carted off by then. Incidentally, she saw you fall, and she's been worried, but her task today has been tracking down last night's escaped combatants and hauling them in."

A scene came to mind—courtesy of Gaw, I assumed—of Kenna in a black tunic and leggings, her brown hair tucked back in a bun, one hand holding a shield before her while the other blasted death into her adversaries. She was snarling at the mob, and in the light of the orange fireballs she flung from her fingertips, I saw that her new glasses were spotted with someone else's blood.

"Kenna's a queen now," said Ed, as if he'd been privy to my mental movie. "Some of that violence comes with the throne—she must prove that she's capable of war before she can forge peace. But that's not your burden, girl. And it wasn't Kenna who started the bloodshed last night." When I said nothing, he uncrossed his legs and scooted closer to my bed. "Talk to me, Cici. What happened out there?"

I couldn't answer him for a moment, but flashes of memory returned as I stared at the wall—lights, explosions, screams…the coppery stench of blood…

By then, there was nothing left in my stomach to vomit up, but Ed conjured a bucket from the ether as I tried my best to turn my guts inside out. He held it for me while I retched, then while I sobbed in terror at what I'd done.

"May I hazard a guess?" he murmured as I wiped at the tears and snot and bile on my face.

I nodded.

"Let's see if this sounds right. The life you knew is in its death throes. You've discovered impossible power within yourself and don't fully know how to wield it. In a matter of weeks, if that, the place you've always known as home will be nothing more than a ghost town, *if* we leave the houses standing. You're desperate for independence but lack clear direction, and you're feeling your way through adulthood, lashing out every time you perceive a parental hand holding you back, even if it's keeping you from the edge of the cliff. Court life is new and foreign, and I'm sure it chafes to find yourself with yet another layer of authority over you. You don't know Faerie's rhythms, you don't know most of the people in this realm, and your peers are dealing with their own personal upheavals. Declan and Aurie are suddenly tied to a foreign power, Kenna *is* a foreign power, Edie will be spending most of her time in another realm, and Gawain…" He laughed once, softly. "For God's sake, you stood there and watched him kill himself. Maybe he's back now, in one fashion or another, but the memory of that loss *must* haunt you. Even though everyone around you is excited to tell you about the wonderful things you're gaining, you've lost so much. The world tilts now in…*unpredictable* directions."

He arched an eyebrow, and I nodded again, my eyes and nose still leaking.

"There's a storm inside you," he continued. "Fear of the unknown, of loss. Sadness, frustration…anger. You feel like you're spinning out of control, don't you?"

"Yeah," I whispered.

"Mm. Then last night happened. A threat to two people you care about—a true threat," he allowed, "not something imagined. You tried to regain control with the weapons at your disposal. And when that toxic cocktail is as strong as it must be in you—because, like it or not, my dear, you are undeniably fae—the weapon you reached for wasn't diplomacy. Fire is so much more effective than mere exhortations, am I right?"

"I didn't mean to—"

"You did," he said firmly, though there was no anger in his tone. "Perhaps you regret it now, but in the moment, you meant to do what you did."

Ed paused while I cried again, then handed me a washcloth. "I understand, Cici," he said once my sobbing had quieted.

I tried to refute that, but all I could produce were garbled syllables of denial.

"Little girl, I know what it is to be where you're sitting. To be young and out of control and desperate to force the universe to make sense again." He hesitated, and when he next spoke, his voice was almost inaudibly low. "I wasn't yet twenty-three when my village burned. Twenty-three the first time, I mean. And it wasn't *my* village—it wasn't home. It was *so* far from home, and I had no one from my old life there—not my parents, not my brothers and sisters and their families, not a wife, no one. I'd been shunted into the priesthood to hide my gifts, and I didn't understand why I'd been made this way, why I couldn't stay with the people I loved without endangering their lives. Don't get me wrong," he added, "the education I received was so much greater than I'd ever have had as a farmer's son, but the life to which it led me was *lonely*. My order took my name and my home from me, and left me to fend for myself in a priestly guise in a little town that should have mattered to no one."

I sniffled while Ed's jaw clenched and unclenched.

"I had nothing but my books and the occasional visit from another member of my order, but there were good people in that town. Simple people. And when I was your age, after I'd had two years to come to know them and care for them, I floated at sea in Grivam's arms while they were slaughtered and the town burned to ashes. They had done *nothing* wrong—their deaths were meant as a warning to my order. Had I settled anywhere else, they'd have lived. Men, women, children, the aged, babes in arms…they'd have had their lives. But they died because of me."

"It wasn't your fault," I murmured.

"Then whose was it?" he asked with a mirthless smile. "Who do I blame? God? Providence? Dumb luck?"

"How about the guys who set the freaking town on fire?"

"Perhaps. But…" He struggled briefly, then said, "I remember that panic and fear and sorrow and guilt while I watched the fire. My life was out of my control, and I was desperate to right that. So when I came ashore again, once I could focus, I decided that I would destroy the people who had slaughtered my town. And I did," he said simply. "But that didn't kill the fear—that nagging dread of the next threat hiding in the shadows. I *never* again wanted to feel like I'd felt that night, so I pressed on, reassuring myself every time I killed another wizard or broke an arcanum beneath the might of my own that I was taking control. Preventing another catastrophe. I seldom stopped to consider whether *I* had become the catastrophe, but…you know, I had the power to make myself feel safe. Secure. Until I didn't."

Holding my stare, Ed murmured, "I justified the violence at first as a necessary evil. I was eradicating problems, and unfortunately, war was the best tool in my arsenal. But by the end, I didn't need true justification to do what I did. I didn't even need to lie to myself about why I murdered thousands of people in lands I thought I'd never see. It was *expedient*, a balm to my paranoid fear that they might find a way to rise up and leave me bobbing in the shallows once again while my world burned."

I didn't resist when Ed took my hand, though his grip was unusually tight.

"I don't want that for you, Cici. You are *so* strong—and don't try to deny it," he said as I opened my mouth. "Gaw came clean about you when your parents demanded answers, and they told me. You're stronger than I ever was, stronger than the Three…little girl, you could be the greatest tyrant the world has ever known if you put your mind to it. Start your own fifty-year war for supremacy, build a blood-soaked throne, and tell yourself that you are, now and forever, the master of your own life. But I don't think you want that."

I shook my head and whispered, "No."

"Then what *do* you want?"

I thought of our apartment in Anchorage, laughing over teriyaki takeout and drinking cheap beer. Of the bachelor pad and our stupid, unrealized trip to the tropics. Of waking up snuggled against Gaw on a dark winter morning, nearly blind but safe with the smell of his shampoo and the soft warmth of his breath beside me. Of the boulder by the lake, sunning and splashing in the cold water and shrieking during the endless chicken fights with my friends who were family. Of the walled compound, which, no matter how much of a prison it had seemed of late, was still the home I saw when I closed my eyes.

"I don't know," I told Ed.

"I think you do. I think you want to wake up and find everything back to normal."

"Might be nice."

"But not possible," he said gently. "Change is seldom easy, especially when you feel the earth shaking beneath you and can't make it stop. So you save what you can from destruction…which, for you, means lashing out to save Ennis and Kenna. You'd do it for Edie, I have no doubt," he said, squeezing my hand. "For Aurie, for Dec…you almost killed yourself for Gaw, but I bet you'd go on a rampage for him in a heartbeat if you thought it meant life or death."

"What do I do?" I mumbled.

Ed released me, sat back, and sighed. "Wish I could tell you. I suppose you could start by accepting the fact that none of us is nearly as much in control as we'd like to be, but that's not overly helpful today." He considered me for a moment in silence, then said, "Edie shares some of your fear and frustration, but not quite to this degree. And she has a massive library at her disposal now, plus time to read and study—she'll be fine. Whether she admits it yet, the magus gig will suit her. But you?"

I shrugged helplessly.

"Knowing you as well as I do," said Ed, "I don't see full-time court life as an appealing option for you, just as it never has been for your parents. You want to get out, see the world, make your own way—correct?"

"Maybe."

"*More* than maybe. Have you given any thought to the Away Team?"

"Not really," I confessed. "It's been gone for years…"

"Sure, but most of the original members are still alive, and I think it would be a good and useful thing to reinstate. There's probably plenty out there that the Team never found before the closure—certainly no one else in stasis, thank goodness, but books, objects, weapons…" He rubbed his short beard as he thought. "Ted might opt to stay in Faerie, and I can't blame him—he's seen better days—but I bet he'd be willing to assist remotely. I imagine Artur would be interested, and after that little stunt your father and Maria pulled last night, I think those two, Kitty, and Frank would be game. Maria would need to be the supervisory magus again, naturally—I can't see anyone else wanting that job. And before you turn up your nose at working with your parents," he continued, "it wouldn't be all the time. Any decent leader would know to mix up the senior and junior members, drawing on strength and giving the newcomers a chance to improve their skills. Something to think about, at least," he said as he rose. "But not tonight. For now," he murmured, staring down at me, "remember who you are, Cici. Don't make my mistakes."

Ed was almost to the door when he paused and looked back. "Seven."

I frowned. "Come again?"

"According to Val, that's how many you killed last night. Gaw kept a tally, I suppose."

When the door closed behind him, I burrowed back into bed. As the last of the light faded outside, I curled up as if I could compress myself to a point so small that the world might forget I'd ever existed.

The bed sagged behind me after a time, and I opened my eyes to see sharp shadows on the wall. Though I couldn't smell Gaw, I knew he was behind me. Closing my eyes again, I rolled over and buried my face against his shirt, and he held me until sleep returned.

I didn't want to leave my room at Avus's. I didn't want to face my family, to see their shock and disappointment at the monster I'd become. But by dawn Saturday, I was wobbly with hunger, and Gaw nudged me toward the small dining room. "I could come up with room service," he said as I brushed my teeth, "but hiding isn't going to do you any good."

To my surprise, the first person I encountered as I followed the smell of bacon was Ennis, who'd had the same idea. Truth be told, he'd had better mornings—he sported a black eye shifting toward green, his lip was busted, and his swaddled right arm hung against his chest in a sling. I could see the fine mesh of enchantment around him, and I wondered how badly he'd been hurt to still be so banged-up when Gaw reminded me that faeries heal more quickly. *I can speed things along for you*, he said. *Ennis, not so much.*

Rather than shrink away when he saw me, Ennis beamed and hurried closer. "Hi, sweetie," he said giving me a one-armed hug. "How's the head? Heard you got a nasty crack."

"I, uh…it's better," I replied, thrown by his greeting. "Are you—"

"Nice and numb." He pulled back, still smiling. "Val's *good*, and I've got a wonderfully attentive nurse here who's probably already draining the coffee, so shall we?"

"Uh…sure." I walked with him toward the dining room, still anticipating an explosion. "I thought you'd be with Kenna."

"That was her plan," he said, laughing sadly, "but the poor kid's got her hands full, and Maria said there's no reason why I shouldn't convalesce here, where she can keep an eye on me. Security's nice and tight, I guess, so that's a plus."

"Welcome to Faerie," I muttered.

"Got to admit, I've never been taken hostage before, but I'm okay," he insisted. "And thanks for coming after me. I know Kenna's grateful for what you and everyone else did."

Maybe, I thought, Ennis didn't know the extent of it,

and I wasn't about to go into gory detail before breakfast.

I braced myself as I opened the door, but Maria, who indeed had the coffee carafe in her hand, just looked up and nodded. "Hi, Cici. Hungry? Ennis, sit down, I'll fill a plate."

"I'm not an invalid," he protested, pulling out a chair.

"You say that, but I've seen you eat left-handed."

I'd barely staked a seat at the table when my parents arrived. "Mom, Pa," I said as they headed toward me, "I'm sorry—"

"Shh," Mom interrupted, pulling me into her arms. "It's all right, baby."

"No, it's not." I looked at Pa, who joined the huddle as soon as Mom loosened her grip enough to let me catch my breath. "I'm sorry, I shouldn't have—"

"Do you really think you're the only person in this room to have taken a life?" he murmured into my ear.

I stiffened, frowning.

He silently pointed to Maria, Mom, and himself. "When Nath attacked Glastonbury, did you think we sat it out?"

"I shot a raider after Frank crisped him," Mom added. "Hell, Frank *eats* his kills."

"And as long as we're talking body counts," said Maria, "I'm confident that Artur has everyone in this room beaten. *Collectively.*"

"Not everyone."

I turned at the sound of my grandfather's voice and found him in the doorway. "Not even by a narrow margin," he continued, holding my gaze.

"Seven, Ed said," I murmured.

Avus shrugged. "I've cut down more than that in five minutes. Sometimes, it's the best of the bad options."

"Well, now," Ennis muttered as Maria slid a plate in front of him, "*that's* reassuring."

"That's the reality of managing the occasional uprising in this realm," Avus replied. "Negotiation, in my experience, is seldom a viable alternative." He sank into his chair as an espresso cup manifested on the table before him. "So, Cici," he said, regarding me as he lifted his drink, "what do you feel like doing today?"

He delivered the question simply, but I couldn't miss the subtle shift it implied.

Briefly, I debated how to answer him. I could do the responsible thing and say I was feeling well enough to continue my training, assuming someone was available to teach me. I could continue my sick day and return to bed, and no one would bat an eye—not after my concussion.

"I'm going home," I told him.

For a second, the room seemed to hold its breath, but Avus just nodded. "For how long?"

"Don't know."

He glanced out the window at the beautiful morning—whatever else could be said for it, Faerie rivaled southern California for nice weather—then squinted in thought. "Late afternoon there, I would guess. Possibly early evening. You should have several hours of sunlight left if you leave now."

I glanced at my parents, but neither moved to stop me. "Might be back for dinner."

"Okay, sweetie," said Mom. "Give us a call if you need anything."

"Thanks," I murmured, and I meant it. Wrapping a handful of bacon and a roll in a napkin, I opened a gate and slipped away.

By design, I'd landed in the den of our bachelor pad. Familiar though the space was, the unusual silence was eerie—the hum of the refrigerator and of the dying kitchen fluorescents we'd left on before making our RV escape were all I could hear. I dropped my breakfast on the coffee table, then took a deep breath and slowly turned around, as if I were a camera trying to capture the details of the den in a perfect panoramic photograph. Honestly, it looked like Fauxlaska but for Dec's kitchen calendar, which still announced the month as July.

Four weeks. We'd fled on a warm Saturday in mid-July, and though everything had changed in the intervening days, the house seemed frozen on the edge of that precipice.

I walked into the kitchen and opened the refrigerator, then immediately regretted my decision. We hadn't exactly disposed of the leftovers before going on the run, and the cold had only been able to do so much to stave off the spoilage. I made the rotten vegetables and moldy meat vanish, leaving me with little more than condiments and the open box of baking soda. When the stock was that low, it was time for a grocery flight to Fairbanks…but Ennis would never make that run again.

I closed the refrigerator, willing myself not to cry at the stupid empty shelves.

Munching on my pilfered bacon, I gave myself the slow tour. The laundry room, where Dec's last load had been mildewing in the washing machine all month. The downstairs bedrooms, their comforters still bearing the impressions of the bags we'd packed that night. The upstairs bathroom, where I could picture Gaw curled up on the thin rug, pale and sweating. His room, the bed barely made, the blackout curtains drawn. My room with the painted stars on the ceiling, the clothes I'd pulled from my dresser but left on the bed unpacked, the tack board covered in photos of the six of us, my modest collection of interesting rocks from the lake, the bookcase overloaded with my haul from Anchorage, my graduation tassel hanging from a hook on the wall.

I wiped my hands clean on my leggings, pushed the discarded clothes aside, and curled up on my bed. The world still glowed beyond the curtains, but the sun was shining on the other side of the house and not knifing its way into my eyes—decent napping conditions. But I wasn't sleepy, just…weary.

Melancholy, perhaps.

Sure, you can't ever truly go home again, but I'd been expecting home to *exist* in some fashion once I grew up. This place had been full of life only a month ago. Now, the silence of the compound meant that I might as well have been hanging out in a mausoleum.

As I spiraled deeper into my thoughts, the front door squealed open and slammed. "Cici?" called Kenna. "Are you here?"

I scrambled off the bed and ran downstairs to find her, and as I jumped the last two steps, she caught me in a rib-crushing hug. I hugged her back, and we stood together in the empty house, pressed against each other like magnets.

"Thanks for going after my dad," she finally whispered. "I don't know what I'd have done if…" She cleared her throat. "If he hadn't made it out of there."

"I'm sorry."

"For *what*? You didn't break his arm."

"For…you know, how I went about it."

Kenna pulled back, but she held on to my shoulders and looked me in the eye through her crooked glasses—the turquoise pair, I noted, not the fancy new ones. "I executed twelve for treason yesterday. Here's hoping the rest of them got the message."

"Yeah, but you're their queen, and I—"

"Inflicted collateral damage?" She laughed harshly. "Half the court wants me dead and someone more worthy on the throne in my place. Going after me is bad enough, but they went after *Dad*. He's never hurt anyone in his life, you know? So as far as I'm concerned, they got what was coming to them." She paused, brow furrowing. "Did Val give you shit?"

"No," I said, "but Ed gave me a lot to think about."

"Well, for what it's worth, I'm grateful, and I know Dad is, too. How's the head?"

Before I could answer, a gate opened in the den, disgorging Aurie and Dec. "Edie's walking over from the castle," he said by way of greeting. "So, the old place still stands?"

I smiled to see them. "You're going to want to redo your clothes in the washer. They stink."

"*Shit*," he muttered as he hugged me, "I knew I forgot something."

As the sky finally dimmed that night, the five of us sat on our boulder and watched the stars pop out over the lake. Though Gaw couldn't physically join us, he opened a gate in midair beside the boulder and sat at its edge, attracting moths with his unnatural radiance. The mosquitoes buzzed and died under our slapping hands, and the boxes and bags rattled as we passed around chips and cookies, disposing of the pantry leavings in a binge of salt and sugar. Though the Perseids had peaked for the summer, we caught a few faint meteors as they streaked across the sky in their silent immolation, then lingered while the bats emerged to swoop around us as they feasted.

In some sense, the night felt like a wake—not a truly solemn wake, but more like a party in honor of the departed. Though it was barely lunchtime in Faerie, we drank the last of our beer and opened several bottles of Hayward's finest chardonnay, even passing one through the gate to Gaw. He couldn't get drunk any longer, but he played along as we drank to mourn the death of our hometown.

Sometime after night truly fell, we stumbled back to our house for the real work. Using a technique Toula had shown her, Edie shrank our possessions down to the size of dollhouse furniture, and we divvied up the spoils in cardboard boxes. Edie took her favorite recliner, Dec claimed the fridge, Kenna wanted the TV, Gaw didn't care. Finally, having passed our boxes through the gate to Gaw for safekeeping, we took a last look around the empty house, then stepped outside.

"Should we lock up?" Kenna asked. "It feels weird

leaving it open like that…"

"We're not leaving it," I replied, and gestured. With a burst of my will, the house shrank until it was only a few inches across, then floated into my hand. I created a base mimicking our sad, weedy lawn, then anchored the house, set a few lights glowing inside, and encased it all in a glittery snow globe.

Dec examined my handiwork as I gave it a test shake. "You totally cribbed that from Mom."

"Guilty. You want it?" I asked.

He patted my shoulder. "Keep it safe, eh? Just in case."

And with a last look at our empty lot in the streetlamps' glow, we went our separate ways.

CHAPTER 24

I spent the rest of the day alone, first sobering up in the garden behind my room at Avus's while I watched the mosaic fish swim in the fountains, and then, once restlessness set in, returning to the wild places where Coileán had tutored me to let off steam. By nightfall, I was damp with sweat from my exertions—not so much due to the rocks I'd shattered, but rather from the cross-country run on which I'd embarked. Mina might not have been breathing down my neck, but long years of conditioning had birthed in me a paranoia that she might emerge at any time and demand pushups.

By nightfall, my head was clear, and the run had helped put me more at ease. Flushed and sore, but in a good, familiar way, I headed back to Avus's place to wash off and investigate dinner options.

I'd just stepped out of the shower and tucked a towel around myself when Gaw warned, *Incoming*.

"Huh?" I began, but before I could press him, a gate cracked open in my bedroom, and Edie ran through, bathrobe flapping and feet bare. "Cici!" she called, looking around, then spotted me dripping on the mat and barged into the bathroom. "Get dressed. You need to come with me. And where's your phone?" she asked, glancing about the steamy room. "I left mine by my bed…"

"*What* is going on?" I demanded, clutching my towel.

She paused, coming up for air, then seemed to reset herself—typical for Edie, whose train of thought sometimes ran two steps ahead of everyone else's when she was overly focused on a problem. "Dad and Toula found them. They broke through the blocks overnight and tracked Eva and Francine."

My jaw dropped. "They're alive?"

"Yeah. In Florida, apparently. Dad sleepwalked and followed them around this little town—Windward Beach, looks like one of those fancy resort communities. He got enough detail that they were able to map it with pictures online," she explained. "The road signs have this distinctive starfish logo—"

"Forget the road signs! Is Ed going to bring them in?"

"I don't know, but he's called an emergency meeting in half an hour, and I thought you might want in on this."

"Phone's on the nightstand," I said, sweeping past her into my room. "Call Dec and Aurie, I'll—"

Two fresh gates opened behind me, and they hurried through, wide-eyed. "Gaw said something about the missing magi?" Aurie began, then took a step back when she saw my state of undress. "Sorry, interrupting?"

"Edie can tell you," I replied, and hid in my closet to make myself decent. *Seriously, Gaw?* I thought as I rummaged through my pile of underthings.

Well, you weren't going to answer the door. Time's wasting.

Shortly thereafter, having thrown on clothes and, with some trepidation, willed my hair dry, I stepped through the gate Edie had opened into the empty magus office with Gaw riding shotgun in my mind. But as we headed for the corridor, a middle-aged redhead in a smart navy suit blocked our way. "Excuse me," she said to Edie as we stumbled back, caught red-handed. "Are you, uh...*his* daughter?"

Edie plastered on a winning smile, presumably going for a charm offensive to bluff our way out there. "Edie Stanhope," she said, extending her hand.

The woman shook it, but she regarded Edie as one

might a pacing wolf. "Lana Berry. I was an aide to Magus Johansson, um…before. *Wow*, you've got his look…" Catching herself, she cleared her throat and straightened. "Your father said to tell you that you and your"—she sized up Aurie, Dec, and me—"friends? You can come into the conference room if you behave yourselves." She hesitated, then said, "I was told there might be a purple guy…"

Edie whispered open a gate, and Raurit, who'd been pacing in the den of an institutionally bare apartment on the other side, grinned and hurried through. "That's us," she said cheerily. "And thanks."

The aide stepped aside, watching with unease as our motley crew filed past. Once she was out of earshot, Edie whispered, "Who puts on a suit at three a.m.?"

"Someone who wants her old job back," I muttered. "And where's Kenna?"

Coming on her own steam, Gaw told me. *She doesn't need to be skulking around the Council offices.*

"Gaw said he'd pass the word," Edie replied, and pushed open the door to the conference room.

As the table was already filling with people who seemed to belong there, we staked out spots against the wall behind the magi's section. Raurit's parents were seated and waiting, and Kenna waved at us as she breezed through the door a moment before Avus and Coileán arrived. At least their bit of the table was alert. Given the hour in Alaska, the magi barely took their seats before reaching for the caffeine, and some arrived bearing mugs and insulated tumblers. Two of their number sported full regalia— formal robes in black or dark green over business attire, all topped by ornate gold chains of office—but the rest appeared to have thrown on whatever was convenient. Iris Johansson, an insomniac who claimed to be concerned about glaucoma at her age, trailed more than a hint of pot smoke on her ratty bathrobe when she swept into the room.

Last in was Ed, who closed the door behind him and

ensorcelled the lock. "Right, then," he said, energetic despite the hour. "The short version: we've laid eyes on Eva and Francine. Toula, if you'd be so kind..."

She gestured toward the table, and a projection of the country appeared, quickly zooming down to the far eastern edge of the Florida panhandle. A red dot appeared along the Gulf and began blinking.

"Thank you. We broke through their blocks early last night and ensorcelled a map for the blood trace. Surprisingly, the traces converged in a residence, and a sleepwalk confirmed it. They're alive and cohabiting. We kept watch overnight until about half an hour ago," he continued, nodding to the Minor Arcanum sleepwalkers, "when they left the house, heading toward a downtown region."

"It's a planned community," Toula explained. "Houses, a hotel, shops and restaurants, beach access. Looks kind of chichi."

"It's possible that they're merely visiting," said Ed, "but given the state of their closets and baths, we think it's far more likely that they're residents. There was definitely winter clothing in the closets—not much," he allowed, "but then again, Florida. Hardly the sort of thing one would need in August, I'd wager."

Coileán and a few of the better-traveled magi nodded vehemently.

"How do we want to proceed?" he asked the table. "Wait for nightfall and try to corner them in their home, or see if we can't locate them within the town?"

"Home might not be the safest plan," said Heer Hassan from the Minor Arcanum. "I cannot see spells within the dream space..."

"Nor can I," Ed replied when she cocked an eyebrow at him in query.

"A pity. But as the two of them have already put blocks on tracing attempts, I would assume they've warded their home. Not an insurmountable obstacle, to be sure—"

"A few good bolts would probably do it, depending on the ward strength," said Coileán. "If it's shoddy, we might be able to set the house on fire."

Ed winced. "Yeah, not subtle. I'd like to bring them in with as little collateral damage as possible. Hitting them at home would seem to be attacking their base, and if anything's fortified, that's probably it."

Meghan Pomeroy, the Dark Company's leader, lifted a finger to take the floor. "I don't have anyone in the area, so recon's not an option unless one of you wants to work the gates for us, but instinct tells me they're probably going to be close to home today. It's a little after…what, seven a.m. there, right?"

"Bingo," said Toula.

"Okay. We've got two women in their eighties living together in an upscale beach community, leaving home around seven and heading downtown on a Saturday morning. Did they eat before they left the house?"

"Yes," said Heer. "Eggs and coffee."

"So they're not going out for breakfast," Meghan continued. "Presumably, they're not living on government benefits alone. I don't know, maybe they made themselves a small fortune before magic dried up, but let's assume they've got a source of income. At least something to pass the time." Lifting her steaming mug, she said, "They're working or volunteering, one or the other. Maybe some sort of civic committee, maybe tourism, maybe a shop. I doubt they're working in a restaurant—too much time on their feet. If you'd help us, we could send someone in for recon."

"A shifter?" one of the magi asked. "You want to set a wolf loose on the Redneck Riviera?"

She stared at him over the rim as she sipped her coffee. "You know, surprisingly, we don't deploy lupine shifters in *every* situation. This wouldn't be a job for me, either. I've got a guy in Tokyo who goes housecat—he could cover some ground without causing much of a fuss."

"Unless he ends up at a shelter," Iris pointed out. "Some do-gooder might call in animal control."

"Fuck the cat," interjected Connor Norleigh, the Australian magus, as he turned to Ed. "Can't you kill them in your sleep?"

"I could," Ed replied with a shrug, "but in light of what happened the last time I allowed myself to do that, and out of respect for our colleagues," he added, giving the Minor Arcanum trio a pointed glance, "I think that would be unwise. Best to bring them in for formal proceedings. Give them an opportunity to explain themselves, if they can. Let's be civilized about this, eh?"

A flush crept into my face, but I maintained my silence.

"I've got an idea."

The table looked at Kenna, who seemed far more relaxed to be the focus of attention than she'd been at her first such meeting. "August in Florida—it's tourist season," she said. "School hasn't started back yet. No offense to the Company," she continued, nodding to Meghan, "but we don't need a shifter to scope out the area. If this is a beachy tourist town, then a group of college kids with sunburns would work." Smiling, she pointed to Edie, Aurie, and me. "And we've got a posse on hand. Three of us just graduated in May—I'm *pretty* confident that we could pull this off."

"Or," said Toula, frowning, "we could send in someone with a little more experience—"

"Like who? *You?* They know you," Kenna retorted, "and even if you glamoured yourself, they might catch on. They could probably figure Ed out pretty quickly. Any of the magi should be familiar. Kitty and Beth are out. Minor Arcanum...I don't know," she admitted, "but what's wrong with sending us? No one will look twice at a bunch of twenty-something girls window shopping, especially if we behave ourselves."

"Wait," said Dec, "I want to go, too."

"Okay, four twenty-something girls and one boyfriend

to carry the bags," said Kenna. "We'd barely even need to glamour—just a little fresh redness to make it convincing, yeah? Throw on some T-shirt and shorts, slap on sunglasses, and we'll blend right in."

Ed gave her a long, hard stare.

Kenna grinned.

"It's not a bad plan," said Meghan from down the table. "Assuming you can keep your cover story straight."

Some of the magi nodded, though Toula appeared to be less than thrilled with the idea. Ignoring her, Kenna looked at us and raised her thumbs. "What do you say?"

Dec pretended to mull the question over. "I mean, it's not *quite* Bora Bora…"

"Oh, shut up, we're going to the beach," she snapped playfully, and rose from the table. "Come on, back to my place. We need to *accessorize*."

Raurit offered to help, but we turned him down. It wasn't that we didn't appreciate the offer, we explained, but that we wanted to limit our glamour as much as possible. Making ourselves slightly rosier wouldn't be difficult or noticeable in our auras, whereas hiding Raurit's violet complexion and adding fingers would require less subtle work. We were dealing with magi, after all, and if they knew how to block blood traces and hide themselves in the dream space, we didn't want to do anything to set off their alarms—they had to be somewhat paranoid already. Plus, there was the significant problem of Raurit's English. The five of us could pass as Alaskan—I sincerely doubted that the average resident of a Floridian tourist town had the linguistic expertise to notice that none of us sounded quite like our college peers whose parents hadn't been transplants to the area—but Raurit spoke with an unplaceable but decidedly foreign accent. In the interests of simplicity and security, he stayed behind and wished us luck.

It had been a long day already. Two o'clock on that Saturday afternoon in Windward Beach was closer to one in the morning in Faerie, and between strategy sessions with Ed, Coileán, Avus, Toula, and Meghan and wardrobing discussions at Kenna's, I'd been too wired to nap. But adrenaline kept me going as we strolled down the main street, stopping to peer in shop windows and step inside to peruse the trinkets on offer.

I'd thought that July in Kentucky was unpleasant, but it paled beside August in Florida. Too far from the water to receive the full benefit of the sea breeze, we sweltered in the hot, humid air, which settled around us like a moist hug. An afternoon storm was approaching from the Gulf, but not quickly enough for my taste. At least the summer weather offered an explanation for my nervous sweat. Walking into stores provided only a brief respite from the heat, as well as a fresh problem: with the buildings kept at meat-locker temperatures by their powerful air conditioning, sweat quickly chilled and left my clothing clammy. I even caught myself with goosebumps in a candy store before I excused myself to eat my saltwater taffy on the sidewalk.

The good news was that after an hour of wandering, having been dropped off behind a Dumpster with the help of some street-level photography, we hadn't attracted undue notice. We'd opted for T-shirts—all but for Dec, who'd come up with a white tank top with an airbrushed Jolly Roger across the chest—and shorts, added color to suggest insufficient sunscreen application, and pulled our sandals out of storage. Kenna had thrown on a floppy blue bucket hat and braided her hair into pigtails, while Aurie had borrowed my Seawolves baseball cap. We hadn't bothered to color her naturally blue hair, and at Toula's suggestion, she'd clipped in a nose ring to make herself seem ever so slightly edgier. If shopkeepers gave us a second look, it was Aurie who drew their attention, but they quickly looked away—hoping, I suspected, not to be caught staring at the girl with half an arm missing.

Keyed up though we were, we did our best to make a day of it. As former Arcanum security personnel, Minor Arcanum volunteers, and even a few faeries filtered into town and took up positions on benches and in the windows of cafés in case of trouble, the five of us moved from store to store, coming away with Windward Beach–branded apparel, a crab-print bowtie, a pair of stuffed dolphins, some *fantastically* ridiculous mermaid ornaments, and enough candy to make us sick.

As I threw away the dregs of my much-needed strawberry slush and wiped the fresh perspiration from my forehead, we paused around the trash can—which, like everything else in town, bore a starfish logo and seemed a little too clean—and took stock of our remaining targets. "Toy store behind you," murmured Kenna. "The next one down looks like children's clothes, and then I think there's an ice cream parlor past that."

Looking over her shoulder, I said, "Knives behind you, and I think they're sharing space with a Christmas decoration store—"

"I'm sorry, *what?*"

"Probably better not to ask. Something called The Boozy Olive beside that."

"I see wine bottles in the window," Edie offered.

"Okay," I said. "And past that…" I squinted at the sign, which had been rendered in script. "Earthly Treasures."

"I vote we start there," said Aurie. "And if that's another bust, we step next door and see if they're offering wine tastings."

Edie snorted. "You know, we're not *actually* on vacation."

"Surely I'm not the only one here who could use a drink," she retorted.

The rest of us grudgingly conceded.

"Fine," said Dec. "We check the shop, we hope for

cheap booze, and we press on…"

Lightning flashed over the Gulf, and I studied the darkening horizon. A spirit I didn't know loitered a few yards away from us on an otherwise empty bench, a teenage girl in board shorts and a tank top. She thumbed one hand toward the clouds massing over the water and called, "This is going to be gross. Do you have umbrellas?"

No, I replied.

"Stu and Stacy's sells a few, but they're, like, *ridiculously* expensive," she informed me, and rolled her eyes. "There's a drug store about a quarter-mile down the road from the entrance to Windward. If you're planning to be out this afternoon, you might want to swing by there before the storm hits."

Thanks, uh…

"Mary Hannah." She approached with a curious smile. "You're a medium? Cool. My cousin reads palms in PCB, but she wouldn't know a spirit guide if one came up and smacked her between the eyes."

True, we were on a mission, but I hated to disappoint. With so few mediums in the world, I couldn't blame the random spirits I encountered for trying to get my attention. *Is there something you need?* I asked her. *A message passed along?*

"Who, me?" She grinned and shook her head. "Nah, I just like the people-watching here. Vacationing?"

Not exactly, I thought, then paused as inspiration struck. *You come here often?*

"Well, my mom and dad own the ice cream parlor," she replied, pointing to the seafoam-green shopfront down the way, "so yeah, I hang around. Looking for a recommendation?"

People, actually—

"Earth to Cici," Kenna interrupted, snapping her fingers in front of my face. "Are you with us?"

"Just a minute," I said, and turned my attention back to Mary Hannah. *I'm looking for two women. Both would be in their eighties, but I don't know what they look like these days.* Ed couldn't exactly take photos in the dream space, and his artistic ability was nowhere near the level of a sketch artist. *One's American, one's British.*

Without missing a beat, Mary Hannah pointed to Earthly Treasures. "The only Brit I've ever known to live here owns the weird shop. Her business partner is American, I think, but not from around here. They're nice enough, but they keep to themselves."

What's weird about the store?

Mary Hannah chuckled. "Crystals and shit. They bring in a guy to read your aura on Wednesdays and a past-life regression 'psychic'"—I could hear the irony quotes—"on the first Saturday of the month. I sit in sometimes, and you'd be *amazed* how many people were once Cleopatra." She cocked her head. "Friends of yours?"

Something like that. Hey, thanks.

"Sure!" she chirped, and pointed again to the sky. "Seriously, this isn't going to be a half-hour shower. Take it from a local and get somewhere you want to be before the clouds open."

Once she had wandered out of earshot, I turned back to the waiting huddle and murmured, "Sorry, getting intel."

"Ah, yes," said Edie, "nothing creepy at all about the 'I'm having a silent conversation' thousand-yard stare."

"I'll just talk aloud to thin air next time, okay?" I countered, and drew closer to the others. "Only British woman in town runs Earthly Treasures, but it's an esoterica store. You don't think any self-respecting wizard would be caught dead with that stuff, do you?"

Edie shrugged. "I don't know—might make good cover. No one's going to ask too many questions about the wand you keep lying around if you're selling books on witchcraft and aliens and things."

I thought of the similar store in Anchorage, which Edie and I had visited only after a mutual dare. It had smelled like patchouli, one of the flyers pinned to the announcement board had offered a lecture about the extraterrestrial origins of the pyramids, and when I stared too long at one of the display tables, trying to figure out what was on offer, the proprietor had tried to sell me a tiny ceramic door bedecked with toadstools and flowers so that I could make my garden a welcoming space for the fae.

"Maybe," I allowed, "but whatever we're doing, we need to move. My source says the storm's going to be messy."

Aurie thumped me on the back. "Esoterica it is, then, followed by whatever's on offer at The Boozy Olive. Come on," she said, and strode off down the sidewalk.

Earthly Treasures' windows weren't promising, a cluttered showcase of crystals, candles, and a sun-faded dreamcatcher, but I followed Aurie through the wooden door to the cool interior. Mindful of the steel doorknob, Aurie gave Kenna and me space to pass without burning ourselves, though the tinkling windchimes that served as a doorbell set off my alarm with their proximity to my head. I pushed my sunglasses into my sweaty hair and took in the wares: mismatched tables and glass cases practically sagging beneath the weight of the geodes and mineral specimens for sale, pine bookcases along one wall loaded with titles no legitimate wizard would ever deign to read, a display of vaguely "ethnic" drums festooned with feathers and painted with what were surely misused symbols.

And then, as my eyes adjusted to the weaker light, I spotted the woman dusting a shelf behind the jewelry counter.

She was perhaps a hair shorter than me—age had stooped her—and birdlike in her thinness. She wore her white hair in a sensible bob, a professional but low-maintenance style, and sported a summer-weight pink cotton sweater over her chinos. A pair of gold-framed reading glasses hung over her chest on a braided green cord. Her lips, thin and dusky pink in her wrinkled face, spread into a warm smile, crinkling her dark eyes, when she found us loitering in the entryway. "Come in, come in!" she said, motioning us deeper into the shop. "Welcome. Take a look around. Is there anything I can help you with today?"

Her accent was American—and if my ear wasn't deceiving me, fairly close to my aunt's silo-bred intonation. But something about her reminded me of my mother, albeit a funhouse-mirror version. It wasn't her looks— Mom told me she favored her father, with her pale blonde hair and green eyes—but her stance, the way her chin barely rose as she examined us, struck a chord of familiarity.

I realized I was staring at my grandmother and quickly glanced away before my expression could alarm her.

Fortunately, Edie stepped to the plate, dripping with charm. "Hi!" she said, shifting her shopping bags. "We're just passing though…okay if we look?"

"Oh, be my guest," said Eva, then frowned at the sliver of dark sky visible through the window. "Getting ready to rain?"

"Looks like it," said Edie, and thrust her things into Dec's arms. "Sweetie, would you mind…"

Dec heaved a sigh and settled into the old armchair by the door, and the rest of us left our packages at his feet.

Eva laughed. "Poor dear. Are you being a good sport?" she asked him.

"A *very* good sport," Edie replied, planting a kiss atop his head. "Because he knows he's going deep-sea fishing all day tomorrow, leaving his girlfriend *alone* on vacation."

"Outlet shops," Eva told her in a stage whisper, while Dec, feigning boredom, pulled out his phone to play a game. "Anyway, you kids take your time. Let me know if you need information on anything…oh, and we have refreshments," she added as a gray-haired woman emerged from a back room carrying a plastic pitcher.

The newcomer was about Eva's size but softer, pudgy

about the midsection and in her rouged cheeks, and her blue eyes, pale with age, lay at the center of a web of crow's feet. Instead of a sweater like Eva's, she wore a shawl patterned with colorful swirls against the chill of the air conditioning. "Hello, there," she called from across the shop, her accent unmistakably British. "Would you like some tea? It's a detoxifying blend—proprietary, you know," she added with a wink.

The fact that a Brit was offering me iced tea was disturbing on its own—not to mention that said Brit had to be Francine Leighton—but Kenna took her up on it and asked polite questions while the rest of us browsed.

As esoterica shops went, even in my limited experience, the place was largely inoffensive. Besides the copious quantity of crystals, all labeled with their supposed uses and directions for charging them, the store offered a dozen loose-leaf teas in glass apothecary jars, which promised health, healing, and a load of what I strongly suspected to be hogwash. A table near the front held a display of sage bundles, incense sticks, and oils in dark-tinted vials, while one in the back, behind a selection of candles, showcased chunks of pink salt and translucent selenite hollowed out and formed into lamps. Between two bookcases, an open door led into a side room filled with yoga accessories, but the main draw of the space, at least judging by the other patrons in the store, was the variety of windchimes hanging from the ceiling. Every few minutes, a fresh jangle of steel pipes over the Andean soundtrack playing behind the counter announced that another curious browser had stepped into the next room.

While I studied a tray of necklaces in the display case, Eva slipped closer to me and smiled again. "Something you'd like to see?"

"Maybe that one?" I said, pointing to a copper-wrapped green pendant on a brown leather thong.

She pulled it free and offered me a mirror while I tried it on, then nodded her approval as I centered the polished stone over my shirt. "Oh, now, *that* suits you," she said. "Brings out your eyes, dear."

I tried to force my expression into polite interest, though my guts roiled to be so close to Eva. "What's the stone?"

"Aventurine. It brings good luck and connects with the heart chakra. That means it promotes harmony and helps calm your negative emotions," she explained.

If it did, perhaps it had a delayed effect—it certainly wasn't helping me in the moment. Still, the necklace was only twenty dollars, and I passed her the cash.

"Where are you kids from?" she asked, making conversation as she rang up my purchase. "Looks like you've been out on the beach."

"Yeah," I said, feigning an embarrassed laugh. "I've never seen sun quite like this before. SPF 15 was *not* enough."

"Not for a full day out there, with a complexion like yours. Didn't you reapply?"

She had a point. I'd inherited precious little of Pa's olive undertones, and I'd earned my share of sunburns as a kid. "I didn't feel it until it was too late."

She *tsk*ed. "Skin cancer is nothing to mess around with, even at your age. Daily sunscreen, that's the trick. Now, we do have a lovely salve in the back that'll help your burn—and in travel size, if you need to get on a plane."

"Actually, yeah," I said, segueing into our practiced story. "We're heading back to Anchorage on Wednesday. *Long* flight. I'll probably be peeling by then, with my luck."

Eva's jaw dropped. "*Anchorage*? My goodness! What brought you down here?"

I glanced over my shoulder at the rest of my crew, who were busily examining rocks and, in Dec's case, frowning at his phone. "We're about to be seniors at the University of Alaska, and this is our last real summer vacation, and the four of us have been roommates for years. He's the tagalong boyfriend," I murmured, cocking my head toward

Dec, "but he's okay. Almost a roommate by now."

She glanced his way with a knowing twinkle in her eyes. "Ah."

"Anyway, we've been talking about doing something crazy for the last hurrah, and we thought we'd go see a beach where the water's actually warm."

"It's like bathwater out there," Eva agreed. "Never a good sign during hurricane season, but oh well. You kids mind the warning flags, now. We've lost people to riptides, especially after a storm."

I thought of Mary Hannah and wondered how she'd met her early end. A watery grave sounded terrifying.

"Excuse me," Edie interrupted, showing Eva a rainbow-colored column of stones. "Is this a chakra wand?"

"That's it exactly," she replied. "Great for reiki. What's your practice?"

"Well," said Edie with a little chuckle, "honestly, I'm a complete beginner, but I've watched some videos about crystal healing, and—"

"Come with me," said Eva, stepping from behind the counter. "I have some *wonderful* books for beginning practitioners…"

While Edie distracted Eva and Francine helped another group of browsing tourists, Aurie, Kenna, Dec, and I silently coordinated while we faked interest in the merchandise. Though I still wasn't entirely confident in my newfound ability to speak directly to another mind—yet another facet of my power on which Coileán had drilled me—Aurie had the natural ability and practice to simplify the process for the rest of us.

I don't think they're suspicious, Kenna began.

No, Aurie agreed, *but have you noticed what's hiding on Eva's back?*

I cut my eyes to where she stood by a bookshelf with Edie. Though it was faint beneath her sweater, I suspected that the bulge along her spine was a wand slipped into her waistband. No matter how grandmotherly Francine and Eva looked, I reminded myself, these were magi.

The magi who had tried to destroy two realms and kill everyone within them.

Who had set Maria on fire, impaled her, and left her to die.

Francine, who had broken my defenseless mother's arm and would have done worse, if given the chance. Who had led her own daughter to a charred corpse as part of her escape.

Eva, who had abandoned Mom, turned Beth against her, and then dropped Beth as soon as she was no longer useful.

Maybe they'd changed in the last quarter-century. Maybe they'd learned their lesson. Or maybe everything I was witnessing was nothing more than an act they put on to ensure their survival in a world without magic.

Careful.

I glanced at Aurie, who was watching me from the other side of the candle display. *I'm fine*, I told her.

No, you're not. You're ramping up.

My fingers sought the cool stone around my neck, but the aventurine did nothing to calm my simmering anger. *It's under control*, I insisted, though the look Aurie shot me told me she knew I was lying.

What's the plan? Dec asked, still studying his phone.

Have you alerted anyone? thought Kenna.

Meghan. She's marshalling the troops at the ice cream parlor, just in case. He jumped as a clap of thunder sounded overhead and looked out the window as the heavens opened up. *And they may be there a while…*

Last time I checked, wizards don't melt, and neither do shifters, Aurie replied. *Right, we need to split them up. Wait for the other shoppers to leave. Kenna, you go to the other room and see if you can't get one of them to follow you. Think you can handle a magus on your own, or do you want my help?*

I can handle it, she replied.

Okay. Disable that magus, and we'll work on the other. Dec, stay by the door. If anyone tries to come in once we're alone, lock them out.

Even as we plotted, the other customers began to head off—probably bound for The Boozy Olive to wait for a break in the storm, I guessed, regretting that we hadn't checked there first. As Eva and Edie had progressed from books to chakra kits, Kenna meandered into the adjoining room...and shortly thereafter, Francine followed.

Fate was on our side, as the booming thunder and a sudden, violent uptick in the precipitation muffled the noise as Kenna incapacitated Francine. *Everything okay?* I asked after a moment.

Yeah. I choked her out. She's breathing, but I'm holding her unconscious.

How...

You'd be surprised what your granddad knows. Just let me get her onto this stack of yoga mats for safekeeping, and I'll be right there.

When Kenna emerged, she seemed completely calm, almost bored, and not a hair was out of place. With a faint nod to Aurie, she resumed idly examining a shelf of amethyst chunks.

But when Francine didn't follow her, Eva took notice. Having been surreptitiously keeping an eye on my grandmother, I saw her stiffen and leave Edie to browse alone as she retreated behind the counter. Her hand started to go to the small of her back, but she caught herself and left the wand where it was hidden. "Excuse me, dear," she said to Kenna, "have you seen my partner?"

Though she maintained her grandmotherly tone, the façade appeared to be cracking.

Kenna glanced up, all innocence. "I think she was straightening something in the back."

"Oh?"

The two locked eyes for a long, silent moment, and my heart began to pound against my ribs as I waited for one of them to blink.

Finally, Eva murmured, "*No one* goes into the windchime room without trying them, even just brushing a finger against a set of chimes on the way out. I suspect it's human nature when confronted with that many noisemakers. So since you seem to have avoided the temptation, what, pray tell, are you?"

I looked toward the door as Dec threw the bolt and tucked his phone into his pocket.

"It's over, Eva," said Kenna. "Will you come quietly?"

With that, Eva's control splintered, and she whipped her pine wand out from beneath her sweater just as Edie pulled hers from beneath her loose, camouflaging T-shirt. "Who are you?" Eva demanded. Answer me *now*."

If Kenna was worried to find a wand aimed at her face, she disguised it well. "Kenna Hayward," she replied, showing Eva her empty hands. "That's Declan Pavli over at the door, there"—Eva twitched at his surname—"and I think you may have met Aurie, but she was quite a bit smaller the last time you were at Arc 2 together."

Aurie made no sound, but the twin curls of smoke rising from her nostrils and her faint smirk spoke volumes.

"And those are Edie and Cici," Kenna continued, pointing to us in turn. "Your granddaughters. So maybe you want to watch where you're waving that stick."

As Eva turned to us, she noticed the wand in Edie's hand, and her lip curled into a snarl. "I suppose you're Beth's, then?" she asked, her voice hard and sharp. "And do you honestly expect me to believe that's a *pine* wand you've got, kid?" she scoffed. "Your mother was never a great talent, so who do you think you're fooling?"

Edie settled into a fighting stance. "Maybe Mom's not an exceptional wizard, but you're not taking my dad into account."

"Well!" she replied with feigned surprise. "Tell me, then, who settled for Beth?"

My cousin flashed a grim smile. "He answers to several

things, but he's been using Ed Stanhope for a while. Eadwig, if you're feeling fancy. And Dad thinks I'm pretty handy with one of these," she added, tightening her grip on her wand.

Eva's cheeks, which had flared red, began to pale. Still, she looked at me and sneered, trying to recover her lost footing. "You—no wand? I suppose that means you're the mongrel's spawn."

Careful, Aurie warned again, but the disgust in Eva's voice acted like a match on my temper's short fuse.

"What do you think you're doing," Eva continued, unaware that my muscles were clenching with my building rage, "trying to assault your betters? *You*? Some little witch-blooded brat? Do you know what I am?" she demanded as flecks of spittle landed on the glass countertop.

"A murderous traitor," I managed through clenched teeth.

"A *magus*," she retorted, and fired at me.

I blocked the killing bolt, sending it into the ceiling in a shower of dust and debris. And then, as my fury washed over me, I flung Eva against the wall, shattering the glass shelf behind her and flinging crystals everywhere. Tight bands of enchantment pinned her arms and legs to the brick, though I shot a bolt into her wand wrist for good measure, splintering it. She screamed in pain, but I cut that off with a band around her throat, which I slowly began to squeeze as I advanced on her with my arm outstretched.

"Yeah," I said as she struggled for air, "I'm witch-blooded. So is Dec. So's his mom, and you know what Grand Magus Pavli was capable of, right?"

Cici, control yourself, Aurie snapped across my thoughts, but louder in my head was Gaw's wordless presence, and his bloodlust was raging as strongly as mine was.

"She's about to pass out," said Kenna. "Cici, it's okay…"

I turned to her and snarled, and she retreated a pace.

"Listen to me," she said with forced calm. "The danger's almost over. We can bring them in, just like we planned."

But I was past worrying about the damn *plan*. I was stronger than Kenna, and I was *certainly* stronger than the old bitch in my grasp. I knew what she'd done to Mom, to Beth, to Maria, to the whole fucking Arcanum…

She tried to kill my mom, Gaw growled deep within my mind, his anger as bright as the lightning flashing outside the store, even with most of him stuck in Faerie. *She tried to kill my mom.*

My rage beat against my resolve like a swollen lake spilling over a dam, and it felt *so* good to release it, to direct it at a target and make her scream. I looked at Eva, red-faced and choking, but all I could see in my mind's eye was the moment of Gaw's disappearance.

She was the cause. She and Francine were the cause of so much chaos, so much destruction and loss. The exile to Alaska, my parents' stifling overprotectiveness, Gaw's apparent death—I laid *everything* at her thrashing feet.

Why did we need to bother with a trial? Why did *she* deserve that courtesy?

"Cecilia," spoke a familiar voice, and I glanced to the end of the counter to find my brother standing there. "Enough."

Stay out of this.

"No. This isn't you. *Control* it."

I'm in control!

"No, you're not. Look around you," Publius ordered. "No one is moving to stop you, not because you're doing the right thing, but because they know you're out of control, and you're just as likely to kill them as Eva. Is this what you want? To be so damn terrifying that not even your friends will stand up to you?"

She needs to die—

"Not by your hand, little sister. Yes, she's done horrible things. Let the Arcanum bring her to justice. You know Ed won't show mercy. All you're doing here is giving her a quick death before the Arcanum can administer justice. You're giving her an easy escape. *Think*, Cici."

You know what she did—

"Of course I know what she did," he said, stepping through the counter and approaching me. "But have you appointed yourself her executioner? Is this really what you want?"

Yes.

"*No*. Stop and think about this! Look to your future—if you cannot control yourself, what choice will you leave the ones who love you but to hunt you down? If you can't control your own anger and no one can stop you when you rage, then you're no better than a mad dog. Cici, that's not you."

I cut my eyes to the others and found them staring at me, Edie still armed but shaking, Kenna standing between Dec and Aurie and me with a shield in her hand, ready to defend them.

Eva's head lolled to the side as she passed out, and my brother continued to press me. "You can stop this," he murmured. "Be stronger than the anger."

He stepped into my path, directly into the enchantment I was shooting at Eva, and reached for my hand.

And when I reached for his in turn, to my shock, our fingers touched.

"What…" I whispered.

Publius's eyes widened, but he gripped my hand, then grabbed my other one while I was still too stunned to comprehend what was happening. "Fight it," he said. "Let her go."

I stared into his eyes—older and darker, but otherwise so much like my own—then took a deep breath. Rage still surged through me, a floodtide poised to scour the land clean.

Publius was wrong—this *was* me. This potential for destruction was all mine, the curse of fae blood exacerbated by my panic as the old, familiar world shattered and reformed. I couldn't control the return of magic or the end of the compound or the shifting ground beneath my feet, but I *could* control my reaction to my own fear and anger.

I forced my fury down until my head began to clear, and then I released my hold on Eva. As she fell onto the pile of broken glass on the carpet, I was suddenly gripping nothing but air, but my brother smiled at me. "I knew you were strong," he told me as Edie and Kenna ran up to check on her.

"Still breathing," Edie announced a few seconds later. "Let's get out of here. Kenna, get Francine. Cici…"

"I'm sorry," I mumbled.

"It's okay," she soothed, but her brow furrowed. "Uh…was I seeing things, or was that, uh…your brother?"

"You saw him, too?"

"Just for a few seconds. Huh…"

As Dec sent a message to our waiting backup, Kenna waved open a gate to the Council's conference room. "Hey!" she yelled down the hall. "I need security, *pronto!*"

I stood with Publius, catching my breath, as they floated our unconscious prisoners through the gate to Alaska. Aurie lingered at the edge, waiting for me to follow, but I waved her on and sealed the gate. With Publius watching, I did the best I could to repair the damage, restoring the shop to its former state, turning off the lights, and drawing the blinds. The storm raged overhead, a few shoppers squealed outside as they ran through the deluge, and after a time, with the music turned off and the ceiling fixed, I was once again able to face my brother.

What the hell just happened? I asked.

Though he shrugged, he smiled. "I'm not sure, but I'm proud of you."

CHAPTER 25

Ed didn't hold the trial that afternoon—not because he wasn't eager to put the matter behind them, but because Toula insisted that these things took time to do properly. She'd been given barely two months to prepare for the Mulligan regime's mass trial, which had left her exhausted. Even Eva and Francine's first trial had been the culmination of eight months' investigation into the rest of the Conclave's activities. He wasn't thrilled with the idea of a delay, but as he'd drafted Toula to present the Arcanum's case, and as she was more experienced with such matters than anyone else on the rebuilt Council, Ed stepped back and let Toula run the show. Besides, the prisoners were once again securely locked in the castle dungeon, and the Arcanum faced far more pressing matters.

Arc 2's numbers were swelling by the day. Every Arcanum wizard who heard the news made his or her way in, even those who had never visited the castle in its previous location, and many brought families. Some came with leads on other wizards' hiding places, and the sleepwalkers stayed busy as they reached out and passed the word along. Surely, Ed joked, they wouldn't all stay once the Arctic winter set in—with August passing, the first snows were only a month away—but as the climate within the artificial pocket could be manipulated by simple spellcraft, many of the returning wizards saw no reason to leave. Those who had grown up within the Arcanum and then been thrust into a decidedly mundane world just wanted to come home.

The Glastonbury installation had never been the largest of the seven, and with the castle running out of room, Ed knew he needed help. And so, on the first of September, while the Council aides busied themselves updating biographical information for the newly returned, the lately born, and the confirmed dead, Ed met Robbie Stowe outside the pocket and ushered him inside. He presented Robbie with the blueprints to the castle—or the best approximation thereof, having been drafted decades before by an enterprising archivist and left in storage. Robbie studied them over a table he created from the ether, listened as Ed described the swelling population, then winced. The castle simply couldn't be expanded to fit that many people—not without creating apartments completely from magic, building pocket dimensions within the pocket itself—which meant a total overhaul.

Robbie passed the day designing a castle with room to grow that preserved much of the aesthetic of the original. The final plans included forty towers instead of the twenty-four in existence, each considerably wider and taller than the previous iterations to accommodate necessary living space, offices, and storage. He divided the towers into five connected rings of eight, then aligned the rings in an X shape. Each ring was designed with a substantial courtyard for recreation—he knew as well as anyone how unforgiving walks outside the pocket would be in a matter of weeks—while the central courtyard would be large enough for an amphitheater. One tower was earmarked as dormitory space for Minor Arcanum students and other young wizards whose parents opted not to move in. He designed a substantial complex with an eye toward the school itself, sketching out a huge competition room with thick walls deep underground to minimize structural damage from stray bolts and dozens of smaller, padded practice rooms. A cavernous dining hall and a comfortable infirmary were penciled in, and whole towers were given over to the Archives and the library.

While even I understood the elementary thaumaturgical principle that spellcraft and enchantment tend to be explosive when used in combination, Robbie and Ed coordinated carefully. By the next morning, when they began the building project, Ed and a veritable platoon of aides had plotted the destinations of the old castle's rooms and warned occupants to put their furniture and breakables in neat piles for safe transit. As Robbie erected the towers, anchoring them with several subterranean floors and sealing them against drafts, Ed and his crew painstakingly moved belongings into new apartments using a relay system of gates. For the library and the Archives, whole rooms of books and artifacts were floated along, pulled from their shelves and whisked onto duplicated shelving in the new building. The worst of the build had concluded by nightfall, though Robbie continued to work late into the evening by the light of a dozen orbs, landscaping and touching up his stonework. Few noticed at first that one of the many gargoyles he affixed along the high roofline was shaped like a dragon, and while the wolf several spots down the line might have left the average wizard bemused, anyone who had seen Robbie's nephew shifted knew that the architect had left a copy of Mal up there.

Some of the magi muttered that it seemed unwise to give a *faerie* intimate knowledge of the Arcanum's stronghold, but Ed was unconcerned. "I've known Robbie for quite some time," he reportedly told them, "and he's no child. If he wants to sack the place, I assume he'll blow a hole in the door and patch it once he's finished."

This might not have been entirely convincing to the skittish Council, but as Robbie was hardly the sacking kind, Ed could sleep easy.

Arc 2's remedial school of wizardry opened its doors on September 15. While the ten-year-olds had been wand-

tested in advance and were primed to begin with the
basics, their elders born during the closure were tested one
year at a time, with Toula and Bert overseeing the
festivities. Edie told me later that the day was absolute
chaos but no one really seemed to mind. Parents who'd
lost magic as children and grandparents who'd never
imagined they'd see the day cheered from the bleachers in
the competition room while the nervous kids waved wands
at cubes and tried to coax them into motion. Some could
barely manage to move the smallest blocks, while others
accidentally set their targets on fire or tossed them
spinning around the room. Several kids managed to scare
themselves, with one nervous girl stumbling backward into
the table and sending a huge pile of wand boxes tumbling
to the floor. Everyone was applauded, no matter how
strong or weak the talent. They had magic back, and that
was enough.

Toula tested Arcanum and Minor Arcanum children
alike, equipping all with Levey wands. As the cohorts
progressed in age, a few of the candidates merited pine
wands, though Dec confided later that none of the others
managed anything quite so spectacular as Edie's wand test.
Once each class was outfitted, they were dismissed with
their new teachers to begin instruction. While the ten-year-
old first-years could afford to spend time on magical
theory, history, and politics, the older students focused
first on wand safety and casting basics, and their early
lessons consisted of little else. By October, however, the
frantic work of the early days gave way to calmer schedules
in which magical subjects shared space with the mundane.
High school students reluctantly began studying calculus
and Russian literature along with shielding and focus
techniques, while the eldest of the bunch—the twenty-
somethings born after the closure and the thirty- and forty-
somethings who'd been left with a partial magical
education or less—settled in for lectures and seminars
more appropriate to their experience. With most of the

Arcanum having abandoned their mundane employment, they had time for classes, and the magi sent to educate them likewise evaluated them for positions within the castle. Young Council aides needed to be drafted— generally the most promising of the talents—while those with a scholarly bent were nudged toward the Archives or the library. A few of the remedial students who'd been teachers in their own right were put to work immediately.

Not without cause, Toula had worried that the Minor Arcanum kids might be harassed. All were living in the dorm, which set them apart from most of their classmates, and they kept to themselves at first. But the scuffles she'd feared failed to materialize. Caught up as they were in the novelty of a new school in a new community—not to mention their newly acquired skill at spellcraft—the kids soon mixed and bonded. With every resident of the castle having been magically given English fluency as needed—it worked as well as anything as a common tongue—the youngest of their number ran in the halls of the castle, started pickup games of soccer in the courtyards, and studied together. The older students, who'd grown up unhampered by the norms of magical society, simply said to hell with their parents' politics and got acquainted. After all, who cared about councils when you could *cast*?

As for the Council itself, Ed had his work cut out for him. Unlike Toula, Bert, and Arnold, he took a hardline approach: those magi who had supported Toula were welcome to their old jobs, while those who had advanced Leander's cause could apply their talents elsewhere. Though the ousted magi might not have liked it, few dared complain. Simon Magus was back, he'd taken the big office, and he remembered well which of them had run like lemmings toward the precipice. Some of Leander's former supporters quietly left the castle in disgrace, but most remained, accepting positions as instructors or assisting with the necessary logistics of managing the complex. Dahlia Leighton even decided to stay once Ed prevailed upon her to head up the much-needed IT unit. As for Leander himself, the former grand magus taught computer science, while his daughters, having overcome the shock of learning they were wizards, made friends and generally impressed their instructors. His wife, I heard, was less than thrilled to find herself in remote Alaska, but she soon joined a support group of other mundane spouses and gradually acclimated to a world in which just about anything could happen.

It didn't take much convincing for Ed to lure Maria back onto the Council. The fact that Magus Corelli couldn't cast didn't mean that she couldn't teach the mechanics, and she enjoyed working with the younger kids. Toula, however, required slightly more persuasion. She'd done her time as grand magus, she'd been kicked out, and she refused to return to a position that meant hiding her personal life. Finally, Ed said, "I will throw a company picnic just so you can walk in with Coileán draped on your arm, if that's what it takes. For the good of the Arcanum, I need someone at my right hand who will look me in the eye and tell me my ideas are terrible."

He knew he needed her more than she needed him. Ed might have had the pedigree, but Toula understood what the Arcanum had become since his first time as its head. Leaders of other magical factions who would have balked at dealing with him directly knew her personally or by reputation and trusted her. The Arcanum's patriarch and its problem child might have seemed an odd combination, but Ed leaned on Toula, and she had the grace to guide him. If the rest of the Council took offense that Toula spent most of her nights away from the castle, they were wise enough to keep their mouths shut.

With the youngest seated magi in their fifties, however, Ed needed to fill the empty slots on the Council. Taking Toula and Bert's suggestion, he drew from the former aides, choosing those who understood the mechanics of Arcanum governance and could be trusted not to stage an immediate coup. And then, in mid-October, he asked Edie to come aboard.

Edie still wasn't sure whether magushood was her ideal career path. Unlike Dec, she was too powerful a wizard to safely spar against the other remedial students our age, and so she divided her time between private instruction with Ros's mother, Helen—another former grand magus—in Faerie and independent study in the Arcanum's expansive library. Edie had all the makings of a solid archivist. Plus, she recognized how nepotistic it looked for her own father to put her on the Council, especially given her youth and the fact that she was still learning casting techniques. She protested that she wasn't qualified.

To that, Ed quietly arranged a little practice session with Edie and some of the newly elevated magi. By the end of the afternoon, it was clear to all present that what Edie lacked in finesse, she more than provided in raw power. With a little encouragement from Beth, Edie accepted her chain and began sitting in on Council meetings at the end of the month. She came prepared and listened far more than she spoke, but one morning, when she backed up her position on a procedural nuance with reference to a volume of nineteenth-century Council minutes that she'd been reading in her free time, her new colleagues began to view her as more than Ed's talented daughter.

"Give her another year to get her bearings, and she'll be well on her way to running the show," Toula reported to Coileán on one of her frequent trips back to Faerie. "Plus, think about how many wizards consider it a point of pride to trace their lineage to Simon Magus. That kid's got a better claim than *anyone*."

Edie brought me over one evening to show me her new magus portrait, which hung in the executive wing with all the others. I spotted Toula's and Maria's in the mix, and then, at the far end of the hall, Ed's. Edie laughed as she told me about his trip into the Archives to move the deceased magi's portraits into storage. "He found the section of the gallery for the *really* old magi," she explained. "They only started doing portraits around 1350, so someone in the eighteenth century went back and painted the first three hundred years of magi based on whatever little details were available. Dad's looks absolutely nothing like him, but it's got a great chiseled jaw." Grinning, she added, "He took a picture of the painting, and now he uses it for his avatar in the Council's online chat."

"You have a chat?" I asked.

"Dahlia worked it up, but it's mostly for the aides to send each other memes. Mine shares the good ones with me," she added.

I elbowed her as we headed toward her new office. "Oh, we have an *aide* now?"

She stepped into her suite, then rapped on a door and poked her head inside. "Were you planning to go home tonight?"

The man inside, a strapping ginger our age who'd been assembling a flatpack bookcase on the rug, looked up and flashed a sheepish smile. "Eh, eventually."

"Want me to, like…put that together?"

"Thanks, Magus, but building it's half the fun."

"Okay, then," she replied, though she sounded unconvinced. "Have a good evening."

Once we were safely back in the hallway and out of earshot, she waggled her eyebrows. "That's Kiernan."

I whistled appreciatively. "Not bad, but you can't actually date your *aide*, can you?"

"True," she admitted, wrapping her arm around my shoulders as we headed for the stairs. "But who says he's going to be my aide forever?"

While the Arcanum restarted itself, life began to settle in

Faerie.

As she adjusted to her position, Kenna leaned on Nico, who had the sense necessary to keep her alive, and Rufus, the only other person around who'd ever ruled that court. Even if the Stowe clan had switched their allegiance to Coileán before the closure, those who'd fled to Alaska remained on friendly terms with the new queen, while the two who'd stayed behind took their brothers' word for it. Rufus had spent much of his life as a history professor, Kenna told me, and so floundering twenty-somethings were old hat to him. He'd considered Eleanor a close friend, but having learned of Kenna's background, he didn't hold her murderous grandmother against her.

Fortunately, no one mounted a second attempt at a siege. The court, perhaps shocked to discover that their apparently hapless queen could be vicious when provoked, stood down and stayed quiet—well, relatively speaking. Kenna's desk was soon loaded with complaints, just as Coileán's and Avus's were, and the Three began gathering every few days for a group venting session.

Naturally, Kenna set up an expansive apartment in her palace for Ennis, and she begged him to stay. By the end of October, having come to appreciate that he'd never age another day as long as he remained within the realm, Ennis had resigned from the company that bore his family's name, settled his affairs, and sold his California property for a substantial sum. The assets went into a trust with Kenna and Edie as the named beneficiaries, and Ennis put off for another day the question of how best to eventually fake his death. In the meantime, though he'd moved in with his daughter, he spent much of his time in the Fringe settlement. Few there knew anything about Hayward Wines or his family's generous bequests, nor did they care. No, Ennis quickly became one of the more popular people in town because he'd brought his plane with him from Alaska, and after Aiden finished with it, it would never need fuel again. With nothing but time on his hands and a community of people who had either not seen a real airplane in decades or never at all, he passed long afternoons in the air, taking up passengers for the thrill of the ride. Sure, there was nowhere to go but in lazy circles, but Aiden had connected the plane's onboard computer to the aerial maps that he and Ros's father, Joey, had spent years producing, and Ennis could stay up for hours. Soon, the drone of his engines overhead was no longer a cause for alarm to the people below, and a dragon or two occasionally joined him, much to the delight of his passengers.

I'd worried at first that Ennis wouldn't be able to resist the lure of the mortal realm, especially not with Maria spending so much time in the castle. Gaw reassured me, however, that the two of them were making the situation work. Like Toula, Maria frequently slipped off to Faerie, though *where* she ended up was never a certainty. Unlike my parents, she'd never built her own place, opting instead to keep her childhood room at Avus's. This meant that when Maria and Ennis had their sleepovers, it was either under Avus's roof or in Kenna's palace, and all parties tacitly agreed to keep the doors *locked*.

They couldn't keep Gaw out, of course, but gradually, he learned the art of discretion. All he would say of their time together was that every so often, just for fun, Maria would glamour Ennis back to the way he'd appeared when he'd first wandered into the compound. He couldn't decide whether he wanted to keep the glamour on a more permanent basis, and though he asked her to choose for him, she refused. Maria loved Ennis, no matter what he looked like, and the feeling was entirely mutual.

Though Edie, Kenna, and Gaw had their hands full, the other half of our posse continued to try to figure ourselves out as the fall arrived.

At his father's insistence, poor Dec was forced to

continue training with Mina when he wasn't attending remedial classes in Alaska. I couldn't blame him for trying to stay away—Mina didn't understand the concept of mercy—though I missed him. I knew I'd see little of him, as he'd agreed to serve as his dad's liaison to the Arcanum. Politics aside, however, Dec didn't want a whole apartment to himself, and so he, Edie, and Raurit grabbed a spacious unit on the top of a tower. It was far larger than the three of them needed, but Edie explained that this way, they could have guests. Every so often, they sneaked in Raurit's friend-with-potential, Lilian, while I crashed on a spare bed when I needed a change of scenery. Even Kenna popped by on occasion with wine when the walls began to close in around her.

They had ample room for Aurie, too, but in those early days, she spent most of her time at the barn, getting to know her extended family. Frank was a less frequent visitor, and relations remained strained between him and his mother and siblings, but Aurie got on well with her cousins, and Joey—who was also her kin—gladly showed her around. But Aurie almost always remained in human form for the sake of mobility, and she whiled away the hours sitting atop the fence or on a hay bale, chatting while avoiding being accidentally squashed. Her cousins didn't mind—as far as they were concerned, Aurie was weird but interesting—and Aurie never protested when they flew off on hunting excursions. Still, she watched wistfully as they soared, and Georgie, who'd taken pains to study her odd little granddaughter, saw everything.

One morning, when the dragonets flew off with their mother, Georgie came up behind Aurie as she stared after them and nudged her in the shoulder, almost knocking her off her feet. *You've never been up, have you?*

I've flown with Ennis, Aurie told her. *He used to make jaunts to go shopping.*

The airplane, which Georgie had only observed from a distance, didn't impress her. *But you've never _flown_.*

Tricky to get off the ground when you're missing wings, you know?

Frank never took you up?

She laughed. *Dad shifted only in case of emergency. We didn't take unnecessary risks over there.*

Georgie snorted, then turned and headed for the barn. *Joey! Get the tandem saddle!*

Having been tidying the mess the dragonets left inside, Joey poked his head out the massive opening and frowned. "Why the tandem?"

Because I don't trust Aurie to hold on by herself.

Aurie protested—she'd never even ridden a bicycle, much less another being, and as Gaw confided to me, her stomach had flip-flopped at the thought of going up. But Georgie persevered, and in a matter of minutes, before Aurie had time to think of a good excuse, she was seated in the front of the two-person saddle in a duster and goggles against the wind. "Nothing to worry about," Joey assured her as he slid in behind her and wrapped a strong arm around her waist. "Hold on to the saddle horn, that's a girl…now adjust your knees, get your legs steady…"

"It feels weird," she told him as Georgie patiently waited on her belly.

"Oh, it's *going* to feel weird, and your legs are going to hurt in new and exciting ways tomorrow morning, but don't worry about that now. Try to loosen up a bit—I've got you, honey, I'm not going to let you fall."

Aurie, who'd been sitting as stiffly as a mannequin, tried to comply, with minimal success.

No barrel rolls, Georgie promised her, and then, as Aurie fought down a scream, Georgie rose to her feet, thundered across the field, and took to the sky.

Within five minutes, Aurie was laughing with delight as she clung to the saddle horn for dear life. *This is amazing*, she told Georgie as they circled the barn, *but carrying riders can't be comfortable for you—*

Georgie interrupted with a burst of amusement. *I can*

barely feel you back there, she insisted. *And even if you were burdensome, hatchling, this is the least I can do.*

Aurie smiled to herself as her hair, tied back at Joey's suggestion, fought to escape her ponytail. *That's what Dad calls me.*

She rode in silent wonder for a time as the world grew smaller beneath them and Georgie turned toward the coast, then thought, *Thank you.*

What passed between them after that needed no words.

As for me…well, if I were being kind to myself, I was an anxious mess.

My little stunt in Florida, coupled with my much larger and far more fatal stunt outside of Kenna's palace, left me shaken. Finding myself possessed of a hair-trigger temper was awkward enough without the possibility of my unchecked rage leading to actual death, and for a few days after we hauled Eva and Francine away to Alaska, I retreated into my new room at my parents' house, afraid I'd snap and literally take someone's head off. Gaw tried to reassure me that I could manage myself, but I felt like I was clinging to control by a fraying thread.

It was Avus who finally came to me, once I'd been sitting on my bed for four days, staring at the wall. He closed the door and sat beside me, then said without fanfare, "Gaw told me everything."

"*Shit,*" I muttered.

"One may seize control over external forces, if one is fortunate," he continued quietly. "Political power, military might, an obscene display of enchantment that brings enemies to their knees, and so forth. *Self*-control requires patience and practice to master. That's why we made you meditate as children—the fae temper is a hazard at best, and I'm sorry you inherited it."

"It's gotten worse since I bonded with Gaw."

"Unsurprising. If I may make a suggestion?"

I nodded.

"For the last weeks, you've been running from crisis to crisis. Of course it must feel like your world is completely out of control." Avus hesitated, then said, "Perhaps we could have better managed the transition. The problem with triage is that the matter you deem most urgent may not ultimately be the one with the most lasting consequences if left unattended."

With a sigh, I leaned against him, and he pulled me closer. "I'm fucked up."

"You're in transition," he replied. "As I was saying, you feel panicked because of factors beyond your control. Start focusing on what is *within* your control."

"I can't control my temper—"

"But you did."

"Only because Publius stepped in!"

Avus snorted. "Perhaps he was persuasive, but you and I know there's not a thing he could have done to stop you. If you lost control for a moment, *you* recovered it."

"Not quickly enough," I protested.

"And that, my dear, brings us back to practice. There's a technique used to great effect to work on managing your temper. It won't stop the rage," he cautioned, to my disappointment, "but it will help you resist the urge to kill everything in a fifty-foot radius." When I turned and met his eyes, he smirked. "What, you thought you were the only one?"

"What do I do?" I asked.

"Basically, I provoke you until you learn self-control. It's not fun, and it may be painful, but I believe it would help. And you need to do it with Coileán or me," he said before I could ask. "Your parents aren't strong enough to defend against you."

"I don't want to hurt anyone—"

"It's an accepted risk. And I have time now, if you're interested."

I mulled that over for a moment, trying to sort through

the roiling ball of fear and sadness and anger deep within me, then nodded and slid off the bed. "Okay. Let's do it."

Avus hadn't lied to me. Training involved dredging up my triggers and shoving them in my face to see how long I could go without trying to incinerate someone. Years before, when he'd done the same for Aiden, he'd produced copies of Aiden's bullies and his parents. For Mom, Mina had conjured forth Eva to send her into a fresh rage. Pa had been subjected to the wife and cousin who'd had him buried alive.

As for me...well, Avus had material to work with.

He produced a version of Pa and Mom, their voices pulled from the night on the phone the previous winter when they'd insisted I move home after graduation. A perfect rendering of Gaw at the moment of explosion. Eva's twisted features as she insulted me to my face. He got me worked up, then showed me the compound being reduced to rubble in a blink. He couldn't locate in my memory any of the faces of the faeries I'd killed outside of Kenna's palace—the night had been dark, and I'd barely been paying attention—but he found enough to cobble together strangers who pinned down an illusory copy of Ennis and broke him, piece by piece, while the poor man screamed. And it wasn't always Ennis in their grip. Avus cycled through the faces in my mind, training me to control myself as I watched horrors befall my friends and family. When I snapped and blasted lightning at his creations, he simply gave me a moment to collect myself, then restarted the scenario.

"I know it hurts," he told me after the third session, when my body was trying to decide whether it wanted to burst into tears or vomit first. "It's tantamount to forming a callus over your emotions, and the only way to do that is to expose you until you know your reactions well enough to subdue them."

"Did you go through this?" I asked as he handed me water.

He nodded. "Many do. All of the guards have."

"So...these things I'm seeing, they won't affect me when we're finished?"

"Oh, child," he said, and chuckled sadly. "They will *always* affect you—and that's not a bad thing. What will change is how you allow yourself to respond to them."

It took a week of practice sessions before Avus was satisfied with my progress, and he announced after the last one that he'd give me a few days off to work on my own. "You could practice precision bolts," he suggested. "Or rest—whatever you need to do."

Instead, after breakfast the following morning, I headed back to Alaska—not to the pocket dimension, but rather to the empty compound. Wandering the gravel pathways in the waning afternoon light, the sounds of my crunching shoes and the rustling of branches and drying leaves in the nearby woods the only accompaniment to my thoughts, I walked the perimeter, avoided the place where the bachelor pad had been, and wound my way to the house in which I'd grown up.

I found that Mom and Pa had cleaned it out, leaving the rooms bare. The only sign of habitation was the darker rectangles on the walls, hints of where pictures had once been hung. The overhead lights still turned on, and the water still ran from the tap—no one had yet bothered to shut down the compound's homemade utilities—but the place echoed queerly, a bleached shell washed up on a distant beach, bearing no trace of its former occupant.

"Looking for privacy?"

I turned from the kitchen sink and found Publius standing in the empty den. "Depressing, isn't it?" he said, considering the denuded space. "Understanding that all things end and witnessing the end for yourself are vastly different matters."

I was hoping you'd come around.

He grinned. "Missed me already?"

I'd have been back sooner, but Avus has been working with me.

"Ooh," he replied, wincing. "How many bruises?"

Fewer than Mina used to give me, so...progress, I guess. Leaning against the wall, I folded my arms and faced him. *All right, be honest with me. What happened in Florida?*

"I heard you'd returned to this realm for more than a few minutes and stopped by to find you—"

How did we touch?

"*Ah.*" My brother shrugged. "Honestly, I'm not certain. Surprised me, too. If I had to guess, you were expending a large amount of energy in a concentrated stream, and I stepped in the middle of it."

Did it hurt?

"Not at all. Odd, but not painful."

Do you want to try again? For real, this time?

His face brightened. "You think you can replicate that without blasting a hole through the house?"

I think it comes down to focus and control, but since we don't appear to have any breakables left here... After a pointed glance at the empty room, I cobbled together a pair of wooden chairs, which, though hardly impressive, were strong enough to hold my weight. *Have a seat*, I told him, then pulled my chair closer until our knees were mere inches apart. With a deep, centering breath, I raised my hand, waited for his to almost touch mine, and closed my eyes. *I make no promises...*

A long two minutes after I began gently ramping up the power, the familiar coolness against my palm suddenly solidified into pressure against my fingertips. When I opened my eyes, Publius seemed marginally more solid, and he pushed my hand, experimenting with our novel connection. "How does it feel?" he murmured.

I slipped my fingers to lace them between his, and I tightened my grip until my knuckles whitened. *It feels...*

Suddenly, I was holding nothing at all. "*Shit!*"

"Lost focus?"

Yeah. Hang on, let me try again…

Publius had ample patience with me as I tested and tweaked. By twilight, I'd worked out how to keep a steady flow going into him, even from across the room. Playing with his newfound materiality, he hesitantly flipped on the overhead lights, then grinned like a kid at the result before sobering. "We should stop, Cici."

I'm sorry, I said, dropping the connection, *I've kept you—*

"No, no. I have nowhere exciting to be," he assured me. "But I know what a strain this must be to you. Ask Uther or Kei when you see them next about what happened to Hope when she overextended herself."

Frowning in bemusement, I took stock of my condition, but other than a few bumps from the previous day's work with Avus, I felt fine. *I'm not tired.*

"No?" His expression morphed toward mine. "This is always taxing to the cynaeli…"

Not cynaeli, am I?

He stepped closer to me, as if he could sus out untruth by proximity alone. "Are you *certain*? This isn't me trying to be overprotective—if they push too hard, it can kill them, and I'm speaking only of power enough to make one of us visible. That's why I never asked for more than a few minutes from Hope…"

Really, I feel fine.

We regarded each other for a moment, considering the implications of these new facts.

"Screw it," I muttered, and sent a burst into Publius again. As I picked out the subtle signs of success, I threw my arms around him, and he hugged me back, squeezing until my ribs ached.

Got plans tonight? I asked, resting my head against his shoulder.

"My wife will understand."

Then wait here. Releasing him and severing our connection, I stepped back and opened a gate.

A few minutes later, I led my puzzled father into the

empty house and closed the gate behind us. "What did you want me to see, sweetheart?" he asked, and peered at the chairs I'd made. "Oh, did you come up with those? Not bad. If we added a bit of finesse to the legs—"

When he gasped, I knew that my new party trick was working, and my brother and I traded smirks while Pa's mouth opened and closed like a landed fish's.

"Salve, Pater," Publius said to him with a smile.

It took Pa a few seconds longer before he recovered sufficiently to whisper, "Salve, Publi," in turn.

Pa barely knew what hit him when his son hugged him, though the strangled noises he produced in the moment were simple enough to interpret. "Another of my little side effects from Gaw," I explained as they held each other. "Don't mind me, I'll be outside."

I couldn't give them full privacy, but at least I could offer them a semblance of a normal conversation without me as a mouthpiece. While I sat on the porch steps, watching the early stars pop between the patchy clouds overhead, I caught snippets of muffled voices and bursts of laughter through the wall, and I smiled to myself.

On the first Monday of December, as a blizzard raged across northern Alaska and the pocket dimension enjoyed a perfect sixty-eight-degree day, Eva and Francine's trial kicked off. Ed had ordered bleachers erected in the central courtyard, giving both the Arcanum and their guests ample room to watch the proceedings. The Minor Arcanum had sent several dozen of their senior members, as had the Dark Company. Toula maintained a gate into the Fringe settlement, giving Ted, Ennis, and the curious a window onto the affair. But of those in Faerie who could safely make the trip, most opted to appear in person.

My mom sat between Pa and Beth on a row near the front, and Artur glared at anyone who so much as looked at them askance. Dahlia was easy to find; she'd scoped out a spot near the aisle leading from the holding cells to the platform, and she made a point to spit as her silent mother marched by. Edie sat in the section reserved for the magi, while Kenna shared a bench with Avus, Coileán, Arik, and Hope, but Dec, Aurie, Raurit, and I claimed a row of our own with a decent view. Dec joked that he should have brought popcorn, but Aurie glowered him into silence and patted my back.

Toula's first witness, the star of the Arcanum's case, was quietly contrite Leander. The bluster I'd seen in him months before had evaporated, and he answered her questions plainly, offering a full recitation of the events that had led to the closure: his elevation, his decision to pardon the pair as a jab in the eye to Toula, the discovery of a massive power source in Toula's storage closet, and the plan that Eva and Francine had insisted would make him the greatest magus since Simon himself.

Glancing around, I noticed that Arnold Lowe had appeared and was nodding along as Leander confessed. *Is that how it went down?* I asked.

He turned, picked me out of the crowd, and wiggled one hand back and forth. "He was more of an ass than he's letting on, but otherwise, that's largely how I remember it."

Do you want to say a few words?

Arnold chuckled but shook his head. "I left it in Bert's hands," he said, pointing to the empty seat beside Maria, "and I trust he'll do well. Besides, if you give every magus a chance to speak, we'll be here long past midnight."

Leander concluded with the most damning piece of the story: the immediate aftermath of the closure, when the magi noticed that magic and dark magic alike were draining, and the culprits laughed and announced what they'd done in retribution for their few years of incarceration. Francine barely winced when Leander finished his testimony, but my grandmother kept her head high and stared at the crowd with defiance.

Bert took the witness chair next, corroborating much of Leander's story with his own account, including conversations he'd overheard through means of magical bugging. More importantly, he produced a copy of the plan that Eva and Francine had made, and he explained every elementary flaw. "This wasn't designed to allow an outflow of magic from Faerie," he said after reading a particularly egregious example of bad thaumaturgy. "This was designed to destroy the other two realms. They *knew* they were selling Leander an impossible bill of goods."

A few other magi followed him, each presenting more or less the same story from slightly different angles, but by that point, the case against the defendants for treason had been made. I'd expected Toula to wrap up after Iris left the platform. Instead, she pulled her phone from the pocket of her formal robe and murmured, "You're on."

The crowd rumbled as Ros opened a gate and strode for the front. "I can't give you a neat, essay-perfect explanation of the spellcraft involved in the closure," she said after a few preliminary questions, "but I *can* tell you that it almost destroyed Faerie." Keeping her voice low and level, she described the destruction as the realm fractured and her personal agony from the attack, then spoke of how she'd done her best to warn Faerie's denizens of the impending apocalypse, knowing full well that many—especially those refugees from the Fringe who'd fled to Faerie during the Arcanum's Mulligan regime—couldn't leave. "I would have been annihilated," she concluded, "and all of them with me, had Beth Stanhope not pulled me out." Ros glanced toward Eva, her mouth curling into a small smile. "Yeah, Eva. It was *Beth*. The kid you deemed a disappointment helped save magic as we know it."

Eva stared daggers at her daughters, but bound as she was, she was powerless to retaliate.

Toula's next witness left the chair empty. A small gate appeared on the platform beside it, and Gaw, who'd actually cobbled together a blazer for the occasion, stood at the edge as light spilled through. "I don't have much to say," he told her, "except I know the state in which their actions left this realm. And as they absolutely tried to kill my mom," he added, glancing toward Ed, "I'd *appreciate* it if that were taken into consideration."

Ed nodded, and Gaw offered his brief testimony.

As he spoke, I noticed Arik slip out of his seat and disappear, but I didn't have to wonder long about his sudden departure. As soon as Gaw took his leave, another gate opened in his gate's place, disgorging Arik, who stepped aside to give Conota a clear view. I looked to Raurit, but he seemed as surprised as I was to find his grandfather called.

"I will keep this brief," he said to Ed, not bothering to wait for Toula to introduce him. "Your prisoners tried to destroy my realm. How do you intend to deal with them?"

"Just as we are now," Ed replied. "The question I have is are you absolutely certain you were attacked?"

"Of course I'm certain," Conota scoffed.

"And were they successful?"

He snorted. "No. I sealed our border as a precaution." Pointing to Eva and Francine, he asked Ed, "You have a plan to prevent further *inconvenience*?"

"I do."

"Good."

With that, the gate closed, and Toula shrugged. "At this time, we rest."

The defendants refused to speak, and no one offered to say a word on their behalf. With that, Ed opened the proceedings to anyone whose grievances had yet to be addressed.

What followed spanned several hours of testimony. Older Arcanum members spoke of the destruction of their homes and communities following the necessary eradication of the installations before their camouflaging wards failed. Some complained of being thrust into mundane society with money and faked credentials but few useful skills, left to fend for themselves in a world they weren't equipped to navigate. Others spoke of wizards who had died after the closure, those who had taken their own lives rather than face a future without magic and those who had succumbed to conditions that might have been treatable with spellcraft. A few younger adults talked about the remedial education they were receiving, the best the Arcanum could do to make up for the lost years.

By the time that members of the Minor Arcanum were getting up to have their say, I noticed that Carey Jones had joined Arnold in the crowd—and the tall, muscular man with the dark ponytail standing beside them had to be Zeb Jones, I reasoned. The longer the aggrieved spoke, the more spirits appeared around the bleachers. A few, I noticed, seemed to be wearing magus chains.

As the afternoon light turned golden, and with Gaw having joined the watchers from Faerie, Ed rose to address the defendants. "Your guilt is beyond question. Your confessions have followed you all these years, and the myriad harms of your treasonous actions cannot be fully encapsulated in this proceeding. You sought not only to destroy the Arcanum but the other two realms besides, without concern for the lives that might have been lost. Have you nothing to say for yourselves?"

The security personnel waiting around them prodded them to their feet, but the two held their silence.

"Very well," Ed continued. "Then I will say only this. In my prior lifetime, I made many terrible decisions, and I killed thousands without cause. I've done my best to learn from those atrocities and live in peace this time around. But I'm willing to make an exception when one is warranted."

With that, he sent a pair of bolts flying toward their heads.

The two died quickly, cleanly, and as far as I could tell, painlessly. As they collapsed to the platform, he turned their bodies to ash with a whisper, and a sudden wind—his creation, no doubt—lifted the remains and carried them through a fresh gate, scattering them unceremoniously in the snowy wilderness.

I looked then from Ed's impassive face to Mom and Beth, who sat with their arms around each other. They didn't seem to be celebrating, but their eyes were dry.

About a week later, after the hubbub of the trial had begun to fade, I received a message from Ed in the middle of the night asking me to stop by his office the following morning. Our times had come into alignment in mid-October, but they'd since slipped past each other again, and Alaska was by then a good seven or eight hours behind Faerie. I rolled over and went back to sleep, but once morning hit in my part of the realm, I called Dec to compare notes. He'd likewise received the invitation, as had Aurie. Brushing my teeth while I puzzled over the note, I thought, *Gaw?*

"He wants to get the Away Team back together," Gaw replied, manifesting in the bathroom behind me.

I spat and rinsed my mouth. "You think, or you know?"

"Well, seeing as he's already been in touch with Ted, your folks, Artur, and Frank..." He hopped onto the counter and grinned. "Really, you *can* just ask me. There's not much I'm going to hold back from you."

"Hm." I kissed him, then willed my hair clean and detangled. "Girlfriend perks?"

"Absolutely. And you should hear him out. I mean it," he said, and laughed as I cocked an eyebrow. "You can't blow up shit in the woods for the rest of your life. You're *bored*, babe. I know you too well."

"I'm adjusting," I protested.

"You're drifting. I can tell you here and now that you're not going to find purpose flitting between parties. You're already near the top of the court's social ladder, so there's no challenge there for you. Unless grad school is calling your name..."

"Not really."

"Hear him out," he repeated. "Everyone here who's been on the Team has good memories of it. Just see what Ed has to say, eh?"

"And what about you?" I countered, taking his hand.

Gaw kissed me again. "I'm not going anywhere, Cici. And I meant what I said: go out there and see the world, then tell me about the best parts. With any luck, we've got a *long* time together ahead of us. There's no rule that we have to spend every minute of it in the same realm, is there?"

"I guess not," I murmured, "but I don't—"

"You're not abandoning me, and I'll be fine."

"But—"

"Cuthbert is the only crafter who truly knows how that big battery that Francine and Eva used was made, and I know *damn* well that he's not talking. The only living crafter with the skill to reproduce his work is Amy Levey, and if you think a Fringer who lost her family to Mulligan is about to hand over a massive power source to the Arcanum—"

"Okay, *okay*, I get it," I cut in, "but I still worry..."

"And you'd be the first person I'd call in a crisis," he replied. "But since nothing's burning, why don't you go have a little fun?"

A few hours later, Ed had to make more chairs to accommodate the crowd in his office: my parents, Beth, Artur, Frank, Antony, Mal, Daphne, Lakshmi, and Maria from the original Away Team, plus Dec, Edie, Aurie, Raurit, and me. Last to arrive was a middle-aged woman with silvering brown corkscrew curls and large gray eyes fringed with thick lashes. "Look who wandered this way," Ed said as he presented her to us, and several of my elders leapt to their feet.

Mom beamed and hugged her, Beth waved as she hurried across the room, and Frank lifted her off the floor and spun her around. Laughing, she regained her balance and noticed Aurie, then caught her breath. "Oh, my goodness, baby, you grew up!" she cried, and darted between the chairs to embrace her.

The newcomer, I quickly learned, was Quinn Dellucci, who'd saved Aurie's life and spent the next year cursed for her pains. An art conservationist by trade, she'd returned to her parents' home outside of Chicago after the closure, then migrated to New York for work. There, she'd run into another displaced wizard, a suddenly unemployed junior archivist who was pursuing a degree in conservation to make himself employable, and they'd hit it off. Bonding over their brief time in the Archives had turned into dating, and they were the proud parents of three teenage wizards. While their kids lived in the dorms, they'd quit their jobs and sold their home. Quinn's husband preferred the detailed work of a conservator, a necessary skill in the Archives, but Quinn's career trajectory had taken her into management—and Ed, who was sorely in need of a new head archivist, had snapped her up.

"Here's the deal," said Ed once we were seated again. "The Team was a great initiative, and it needs to return. Now, I've spoken with Ted, and he's retired to Faerie, but he's willing to help with research. He said it's not his place to choose someone to head things, but if he were to be asked his opinion, he would recommend Frank."

I cut my eyes across the room. Frank's expressions were often difficult to read, but even I could tell he was pleased.

"That makes sense," Lakshmi interjected. "I'm ninety, and I finally have *grandchildren*—and a great-grandchild on the way. I'm not returning full-time."

"I think I speak for Antony as well as myself when I say we'll be on the research side with Ted," Daphne added, and Antony nodded fervently. "Even with magic to ease the joint pain, we're not as young as we once were."

"If you want to join Ted in the settlement—" Pa began.

"Not just yet, but I appreciate the offer. Besides," she said, looking at the younger end of the room, "*someone* has got to train the newbies."

"If you're interested," said Ed, turning our way. "Maria will stay on as the supervising magus, but Edie, I want you to work as her understudy for now."

"We could vary up the assignments," Mom suggested. "Especially once you get enough experience to go out on your own—I mean, it's not like your father and I would constantly be breathing down your neck," she told me with a grin. "But seeing as our field crew's down to Frank, Artur, Beth, Mal, Marcus, and me," she said, turning hopeful eyes on the rest of our pack, "we could use some new blood in the ranks."

"And you'll have real support from the Archives this time," Quinn offered. "I'll give you whatever assistance you need. Maybe we could even work up a formal training situation—we loan you a promising junior for a few months, you give her hands-on experience and send her back."

"That's not a bad idea," Frank mused. "Cooperation would be a novel development…"

"I've spoken to your parents," Ed continued, pointing to Raurit and Dec. "There's not much for a liaison to do on a daily basis, and they think this would be good for you. Aurie—"

"Hell, I'm in," she interrupted.

Mom and Pa looked at me, and Artur cocked a brow.

"Sure," I said, "I'll give it a try."

"But we have one condition," Frank told Ed. "And this is non-negotiable."

Ed sat back and folded his arms. "Oh?"

"No more subbasement. We get a suite with windows and proximity to an elevator."

"You drive a hard bargain," he replied, cracking a smile. "But I believe we have a deal."

The large suite that Edie, Dec, and Raurit had claimed soon gained a couple more quasi-permanent residents, as Aurie and I wanted a place to crash in the castle. As we were working in that time zone, we needed to adjust to the local clock. Frank snagged his own apartment in another tower next door to Mal's and Artur's, and while my parents opted to commute to the house they had just finished decorating, they spent as much time in the Team's spacious new office suite as they did in Faerie. Lakshmi, who remembered the former layout and amenities better than anyone, had taken charge of the setup, even including an office for Quinn's first victim, a thirty-three-year-old junior archivist who was still in remedial classes but eager to get his hands dirty. If the fact that most of his temporary colleagues were partly fae concerned him, he hid it well.

On the first Saturday of the new year, less than a month after the Team's restoration and four days after I'd returned from a trip to Egypt with Beth and Raurit in search of a cache of papyri, Kenna sent a group message shortly before six a.m.: *Are you guys awake? I'm making pizza rolls.*

We are now, Dec wrote back, and I threw a stress ball at the wall between our bedrooms to express my displeasure.

Cici's definitely awake, was his next text.

Still, despite the defiled sanctity of Saturday morning, the five of us trooped over to Kenna's. One of her guards led us to a lovely courtyard decorated with floating lanterns in anticipation of sunset, where we found Kenna in jeans and a sweatshirt, waiting with the promised pizza rolls—plus beer. "Breakfast of champions?" she asked, grinning sheepishly. "Or I could find something more appropriate. I'm sorry, I've been swamped for two months, and I missed you."

Gaw appeared a few minutes after we tucked in and produced coffee, then settled down as Kenna peppered us with questions about our new jobs. She promised to visit if we'd sneak her in, told Raurit to invite Lilian by the next time she came to Alaska, and griped about the insanity inherent in trying to convince five-hundred-year-old psychopaths with old grudges to play nicely. As the patchy clouds overhead began to turn golden, Gaw casually said, "There's something I've been working on. Anyone want to see?"

Curious, we scarfed down the last of the pizza rolls and followed him through a gate…and as soon as we saw what he'd been up to, we stopped in our tracks.

Had it not been for the lovely weather and the concurrent lack of mosquitoes—and the fact that it was January—I'd have thought myself back in Alaska. There was no sign of the compound, but I recognized the mountains and woods around us. It even *smelled* like home, a bouquet heavy with pine. Where the compound should have been was a beautiful stone mansion, rising from the middle of the meadow like a slightly rustic version of Pemberley.

"What *is* this?" I asked.

Gaw rubbed the back of his neck and smiled. "I don't really have a place to store what's left of my stuff except at my parents' house, and that's awkward. You five have an apartment now, but…I thought it might be nice for you to have a crash pad here, too."

My jaw sagged. "This is for *us*? Are you serious?"

"Suites for everyone. I put in a media room, but if you want a real television, we'll need to get Aiden out here—you don't want me messing with electronics. And I realize you're not hurting for space," he added, turning to Kenna, "but in case you need to get away for a bit and clear your head…"

As she hugged him, Dec asked, "Where are we? Whose turf is this?"

"No one's."

"Huh?"

Gaw shrugged. "Before Mom became the realm, the western sea just went on. She added a far shore, but she didn't really do much with the terrain. I found a nice spot and…got creative, I guess."

"It looks like home," Edie murmured. "Not the house, but the rest of it…"

"It's perfect," I said, and kissed him. "Version two of the bachelor pad?"

"Eh, something like that," he replied, beaming. "I just wanted us all to have a place if and when needed. We've got this, we've got each other…"

Whatever further sentimentality he'd hoped to express went out the window when Kenna grabbed his hand and started tugging him across the meadow toward the door. Gaw turned on the lights as we neared, and by the time we reached the wide stone staircase, we were almost running. Aurie threw open the wooden doors, and we oohed and aahed over the surprisingly tasteful foyer. If I had to guess, I thought Gaw might have been quietly picking Robbie's brain for design ideas.

While I gave myself a tour, I heard cackling from down the hall and followed it to find a massive kitchen done in marble and copper…and Dec, wiping his eyes. A quick perusal of the room revealed the cause of his mirth: a copy of our tropical beaches calendar on the wall, updated for the new year. "Nice touch," I told Gaw, wrapping my arm around his waist. "Doesn't match the décor in the slightest."

"It's too bad we never made it to Bora Bora," said Dec, "but I'm glad the calendar lives on."

At that, Gaw pointedly cleared his throat, and a fresh gate appeared by the long kitchen island. "Will this do?"

Dec poked his head through the hole in space. "Oh, man! Where did *this* come from?"

"As I said, Mom never really filled in the details," Gaw replied. "It wasn't *that* challenging to throw together a beach."

For the moment, the new house was forgotten as we shoved each other through the gate to get a better look. The last of the sunlight reflected off the clear, shallow water lapping against the white sand of an unspoiled stretch of coastline. A fire flared to life in a shallow pit above the tidemark, colorful orbs burst into view in the palm trees, and the water began to glow with an eerie bluish light.

"Bioluminescent coral," Gaw explained. "I thought it might make night swimming more interesting. There's a protective reef out a few hundred yards, and I just put up a shield—no one's getting eaten in there tonight."

Not bothering with the formality of trunks, Dec stripped off his shirt, pushed his sweatpants up over his knees, and ran for the water. "Whoa, this is warm!" he called back to us as he plunged in. "Come in, you've got to see this!"

The others hastened to join him, but I stood on the shore for a moment as Gaw pulled me close. "Thank you," I whispered. "It's beautiful."

"It's ours," he whispered back. "No one else knows the way here or to the house. It's not quite what we had in mind last summer—"

"*Nothing* is what we had in mind last summer," I said, and leaned my head against his shoulder as a soft wind carried to me the smell of brine and the shrieks of my friends, who'd started a water fight. "But I think I could get used to this."

And I did. Slowly, and not without a bit of mourning for the life we'd lost, I acclimated to the weirdness of living in two realms, to my new job, to parents who'd finally decided to stand back and let me fly, to my own power. Over the long winter and into the spring, I continued to work with Coileán and Avus when our schedules permitted. But as the months passed and novelty faded into routine, I found my flashes of rage subsiding—and when one occasionally flared, I had tools at my disposal to calm myself.

It wasn't until February when I woke without the coil of anxiety in my gut, though I did have a splitting headache. The night before, the original members of the Team had decided that we newbies were ready to come off probation, and Lakshmi added our initials to the giant wall calendar of field excursions. Unfortunately, it was tradition to celebrate the induction of new members with the cheapest sparkling wine available, and Frank had come prepared, using the Arcanum's new permanent—and well-hidden—gate into Fairbanks to do a little shopping. (Other cities had been considered, but Fairbanks was relatively close, and as many of the castle's residents could pull money from thin air, Alaskan prices weren't exactly prohibitive.) The wine that Frank procured would have made a frat boy turn up his nose, but we gamely chugged it down before retiring to our apartment to sleep it off. Waking with a hangover wasn't a joyful experience, but as I carefully applied Coileán's time-honed enchantment to ease the symptoms and chugged a quart of water, I took stock of myself and realized what was missing. I wasn't *worried*—hungry and dehydrated, sure, and excited about my increased freedom at work, but I no longer felt like something predatory was lurking in the shadows just over my shoulder.

I was…*okay*.

Better than okay, really. Content.

Before I could mull over the ramifications, Edie emerged from her room, bed-mussed, puffy-eyed, and begging for coffee, and I gave myself permission to enjoy the day.

By then, I wasn't always sleeping in the apartment. As much as I liked the convenience of having a place in the castle and appreciated the camaraderie, it was seriously difficult to beat the house that Gaw had hidden away. My suite was bigger than our Anchorage apartment, the fridge was always stocked, and I finally had privacy with my boyfriend—or the closest thing to it in Faerie. The others came around on occasion, especially as our clocks drew closer to synchronization again, but much of the time, Gaw and I had the place to ourselves, and if my grandfather suspected what we got up to out there, he never said a word about it to me.

I'd made plans to spend the weekend in early April, having nothing immediately pressing in my schedule and a trip to Argentina to share with Gaw. Having turned off my computer, watered my new spider plant, and said goodbye to my brother, who'd taken to hanging out on my office couch in recent weeks, I headed to the house with my overnight bag and flopped onto my bed.

"Tired?" Gaw asked as he manifested.

"Just grateful for Friday." I sat up and considered the light in the sky. "Are we in synch?"

"About as close as we're going to get." He sat beside me and grinned. "What are you feeling for dinner? I want to cook."

Gaw grilled a pair of perfect steaks—a skill he'd learned from his dad, who'd grown up on a cattle ranch—and while they were resting, he cheated and pulled my favorite sushi platter from the ether. "My roll technique is terrible," he said by way of explanation, but the version he'd made from memory tasted as good as anything we'd eaten in college. Once I was full and the mess had been waved clean, he suggested a walk to aid in digestion.

"You don't *digest*," I pointed out.

"Yeah, but there's something I want to show you."

My eyebrows rose. "Has someone been a busy boy?"

"Just come see," he replied, pulling me to my feet.

The night was beautiful, clear and cool enough to make a light jacket feel cozy, and I held Gaw's hand as he led me toward the woods. As soon as I noticed the fresh path through the trees, I began to laugh. "Oh, you *didn't!*"

He smiled. "Maybe…"

Though his natural radiance lit the way, my feet didn't need it, having walked this trail thousands of times. At the end, I found myself on the shore of our childhood lake, complete with a recreated boulder.

"Well?" Gaw asked as I paused to take it in.

"You're too much," I said, and kissed him. "This is great. The real version is still icy."

We climbed up the boulder and sat together by the gently lapping water as the stars popped out. While Faerie's stars had no real pattern to their movement—and, I suspected, were never the same twice—they made up for their chaos with numbers and brilliance.

"This is nice," I told Gaw as we lay back to stare at the heavens. "Honestly, the lack of mosquitoes may be my favorite part…"

My joke died with a gasp as the aurora burst forth, flaming ribbons and curtains of green, pink, blue, and violet fire that danced across the sky. I hadn't seen such activity since the last night of strong solar flares back in Alaska, and I'd *never* seen such colors with my naked eye, shades as vibrant as if camera images had been transposed into reality. "What…where did…"

"Do you like it?"

Flabbergasted, I turned my head and caught the twinkle in his eyes. "*How?*"

"My secret."

After a time, I sat up again and unkinked my back, and Gaw joined me. "I can't believe you did this," I told him. "It's gorgeous."

"It's no trouble," he replied. "If you want the aurora here every night for the rest of your life, Cici, I can make that happen."

"I mean, I don't have to have a light show *every* night," I said, snuggling against him, "but this is really something, babe."

As I watched the rippling lights, I felt Gaw reach for my hand, and I squeezed his in turn. "You know," he murmured, "I remember what you said last summer about the lake being a great place for a proposal."

"I remember that day, too."

He hesitated, then asked, "Since I can't exactly go over there anymore in any sort of physical form…could this be good enough?"

I sat up and turned to look at him, then tried to read his inscrutable impression. "Gawain, are you…"

"I love you, Cici. Will you have me?"

My heart raced, and I couldn't help but laugh as my eyes pricked. "You know how I'm going to answer that."

"True," he replied with a smile, "but I'd rather hear it from you."

For a few seconds, the best I could do was nod. "Yes," I finally said, sliding closer to embrace him. "*Yes.*"

A moment later, he whispered, "Hang on," then pulled back slightly. Curious, I watched as a ring appeared in his palm, a delicate golden band set with what I at first took to be a diamond. When he lifted it, however, the stone flashed with the colors of the aurora playing above us, and I kissed him again as he slid it onto my finger.

I love you, he repeated.

I love you, too, I replied, and paused to breathe. "Do you want to continue this back at the house? Might be more comfortable."

"Done." He slid down and caught me around the waist before my feet hit the pebbly shore. "And let me apologize in advance—the Three are going to be so *awkward* the next time we see them."

I smiled and pulled him toward me as I leaned against the boulder. "Tough."

As we held each other, I felt his flash of amusement and opened my eyes. "What?" Wordlessly, Gaw lifted my hand, and I realized my weird little corona had manifested. "Huh," I muttered. "That's different."

"I'm sure it'll turn off if you concentrate…"

"Probably," I agreed, and smiled at our comingled radiance. "Problem for tomorrow, yeah?"

"Oh, definitely." He offered me his arm and grinned. "Walk you home?"

Looking into his eyes, my heart full to bursting, I met his lips with mine. *You know I'm already there.*

AUTHOR'S WORD

Stories end, and they don't.

The tale has a beginning and a terminus, of course. At some point, the events seem to come to a conclusion, the speaker goes silent, and the author puts down her pen—or in my case, walks away from her computer, blinking like a moviegoer who's stepped into the warm brilliance of a summer afternoon and wonders what the heck just happened.

Ending a book is always a strange feeling for me. There's satisfaction and relief, certainly, but also a sense of melancholy. The first person to whom a writer tells her story is herself, after all. When the players exit, the stage goes dark, and the house lights come up, she can't help but be a little sad. The characters we write may not exist outside our heads, but they occupy massive swaths of mental real estate during the writing of their stories, and we miss them when they're gone.

I began writing *Stranger Magics* in late January 2013. In the six and a half years prior, I'd spent much of my writing time working on another series that still lives on my hard drive. That series began in graduate school and stayed with me through much of my twenties, including law school, with the final book coming in the three months before I had to buckle down and begin bar review.

If you've not experienced the joy of an American legal education, let me sum up the final act like this. During your three years of school, you pay a large sum of money to a review company for a heavy box of books, which arrives on your doorstep shortly before graduation. These books cover many of the topics that you allegedly learned during your first year, plus some you've possibly never seen before. Over the course of the summer, with your diploma still wet, you commit the contents of those books to memory in hopes of passing the expensive exam that will determine whether you can practice law.

Needless to say, I wrote nothing for fun that summer, nor in the first months of my job. In a new town, embarking on a new career, I put fiction on the back burner and tried to keep my head above water.

But if you love writing, the urge is like an itch. By the following January, alone in my apartment with my puppy, I decided to play with an idea that had been percolating for a while. Starting a new book after spending so long with another cast of characters was admittedly daunting, but I had a hint as to my narrator: Colin Leffee, a half-fae bookseller and part-time pest remover with a permanent spot at his local bar. At that point, Slim Matherson was just a taciturn bartender. Joey Bolin was an eager young priest about to find himself in far over his head. Nosy Eunice Cooper was still nothing more than a meddling busybody, and as for Moyna, I had hope for her reformation.

I wrote *Stranger Magics* over ten months, and then I took a step back. I'd planned that book as a standalone novel, a palate cleanser from the series that had come before. As I considered the ending, however, I decided that it wasn't over. Meggy and Colin had so far to go. Moyna couldn't stay bound forever. Joey had set off to find himself. Besides, with Colin still feeling out the throne and Toula taking on a new job, I couldn't just leave the story unfinished.

It took me a little over thirteen months to write *The Faerie King*. By the time I dropped the last period, what was supposed to have been a heartwarming conclusion—Moyna making up with her parents—was in tatters. She wouldn't *do* that, which left me in an odd position. The happy ending of *Stranger Magics* was nothing more than a deceptive cadence, and I couldn't end the series on a total downer note.

Enter *Witch-Blood*, which I wrote at a relative sprint over two and a half months. I hadn't anticipated switching narrators, but Aiden needed a moment in the spotlight. Naturally, this led to *Blood Magic*...and suddenly, the contained world of that first book had overflowed its banks and spilled into territory I'd never expected to explore. I'd written Badger Parsons as a minor character in *Blood Magic*, a detective who'd wandered onto the scene in sensible clothing to investigate a homicide. Suddenly, she had the microphone and a whole new crew. *Fringe Benefits* and *Dreams and Nightmares* covered eight months in 2016.

Following two books with Badger and the Fringe, I knew that the next narrator was Ros Bolin. In 2017, I launched into *The Stolen Child* and *Lady of the Realm*, then segued straight into *Birthright*, Maria Corelli's story, and *Heir of Afallon*, Kitty Connolly's first outing.

But something was missing. Between *Dreams and Nightmares* and *The Stolen Child* was nearly a decade of unexplored silence. Writing *Unraveled* with multiple narrators allowed me to tell stories with voices that had been waiting but never quite warranted a full book.

Next up, and in a return to the timeline, was *Exiles of Conota*. Back in the early days of *Stranger Magics*, the Gray Lands had been an undefined space, rather like the border area on an old map marked "Here There Be Monsters." Hope Lozano gave me an unexpected guide to that realm.

Speaking of unexpected, Eadwig's arrival came as a surprise to me. When Toula first got her hands on Simon Magus's diary in *Stranger Magics*, its author hadn't sprung forth fully formed. Not until Grivam's chat with Badger in *Dreams and Nightmares* did I really consider Ed's background, and by *Shadow of the Magus*, he was ready to make amends. (Incidentally, *Shadow of the Magus* was the original title of *Dreams and Nightmares*. I'm glad I held it in reserve.)

By the time I finished that book, I knew I had two to go. I mapped out what would become *Crown and Chain* and *Realm and Reign*, and while I spent much of the next year working on other projects, I let them stew in the back of my mind. *Crown and Chain* was definitely the easier of the two to write—as with *Unraveled*, I gave play to multiple narrators whose stories I wanted to tell as part of the larger whole. I picked up with *Realm and Reign* two weeks after I finished the first draft of its predecessor, but it took me about a month longer to write it, even with a considerable script waiting for me. I'd had glimpses of Cici, Gaw, and the rest of the gang, but I didn't *know* them yet, and making the acquaintance of any character takes time.

I finished the first draft of *Realm and Reign* two days after Thanksgiving 2020, sitting in my childhood bedroom with my laptop on a folding table and my eight-year-old dog napping at my feet. After seven years, ten months, and one day...frankly, I didn't know how to feel. The characters who'd been living with me, whispering to me, and telling me their secrets had finally fallen silent.

Stories end, and they don't. My part in this is finished; I've said all I need to say. This story exists now outside my head, which is simultaneously marvelous and terrifying. It lives on without me, a dream reduced to words and *shared*.

And that, dear reader, is the strangest magic of all.

Ash Fitzsimmons
December 31, 2021

ACKNOWLEDGEMENTS

Thank you. For your time, your trust, your comments—*thank you*. It's been a privilege.

My thanks go to the Novel Chicks for their support. I couldn't ask for a finer beta reader than Adam Domby, who so generously made these books better.

And yes, here's to you, Mom and Dad.

ABOUT THE AUTHOR

When not writing fiction, Ash Fitzsimmons is an appellate attorney and an unrepentant car singer.

Find her online:
www.ashfitzsimmons.com

www.ingramcontent.com/pod-product-compliance
Lightning Source LLC
Chambersburg PA
CBHW020627020726
47494CB00001B/76